THORNS FOR DARREN

Sacred Tears

TIFFANY GRANT

Cover and interior designed by: Emilie Haney, eahcreative.com

Edited by: Denica McCall

Hardback: 979-8-9877973-3-4

Paperback: 979-8-9877973-4-1

Ebook: 979-8-9877973-5-8

For the ones who cannot see the good within them.
The past doesn't have to disqualify you for a better tomorrow.
You are worth fighting for.

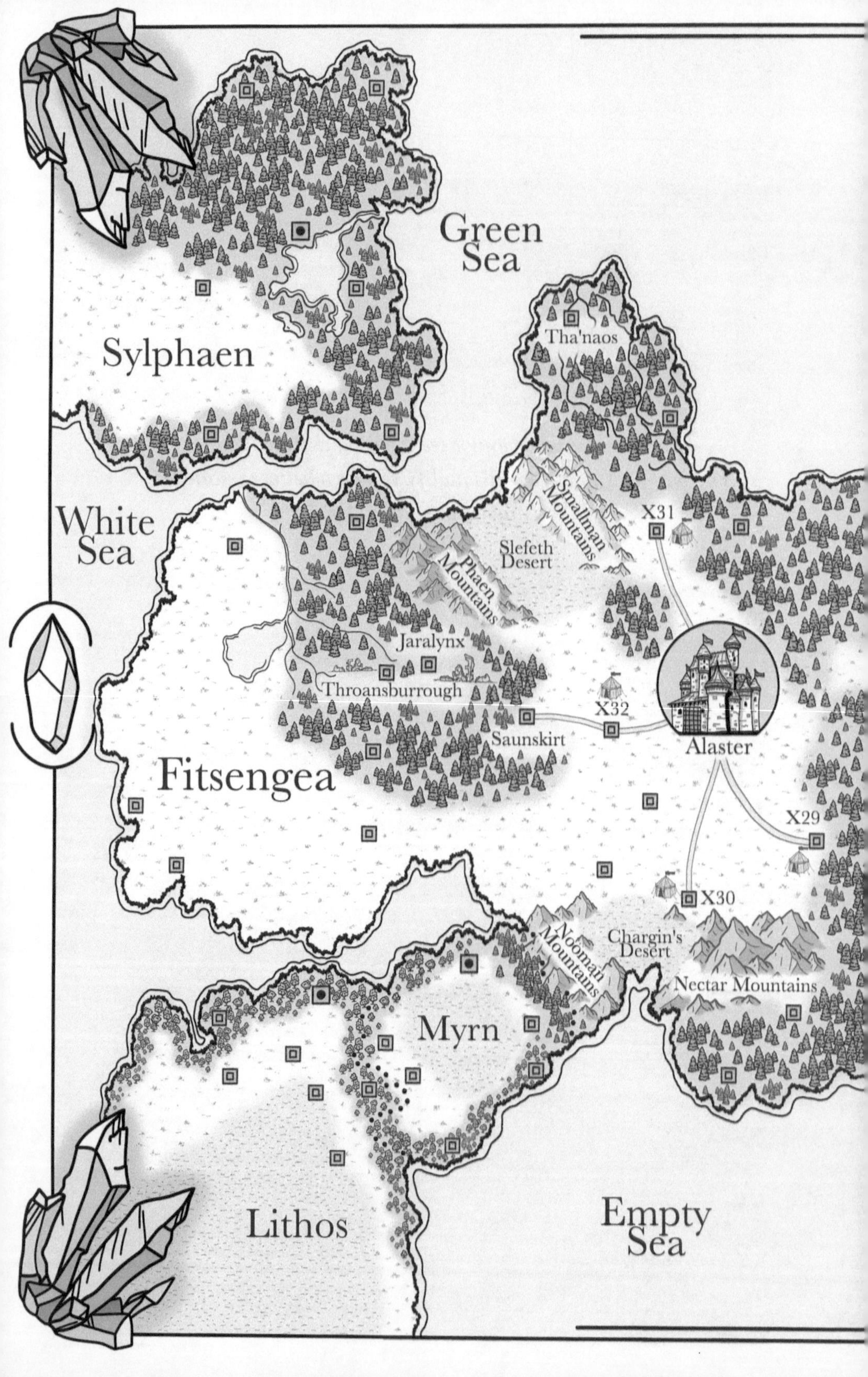

Green Sea
Sylphaen
White Sea
Tha'naos
Smallman Mountains
Slefeth Desert
Phaen Mountains
X31
Jaralynx
Throansburrough
X32
Alaster
Saunskirt
Fitsengea
X29
X30
Chargin's Desert
Noonan Mountains
Nectar Mountains
Myrn
Lithos
Empty Sea

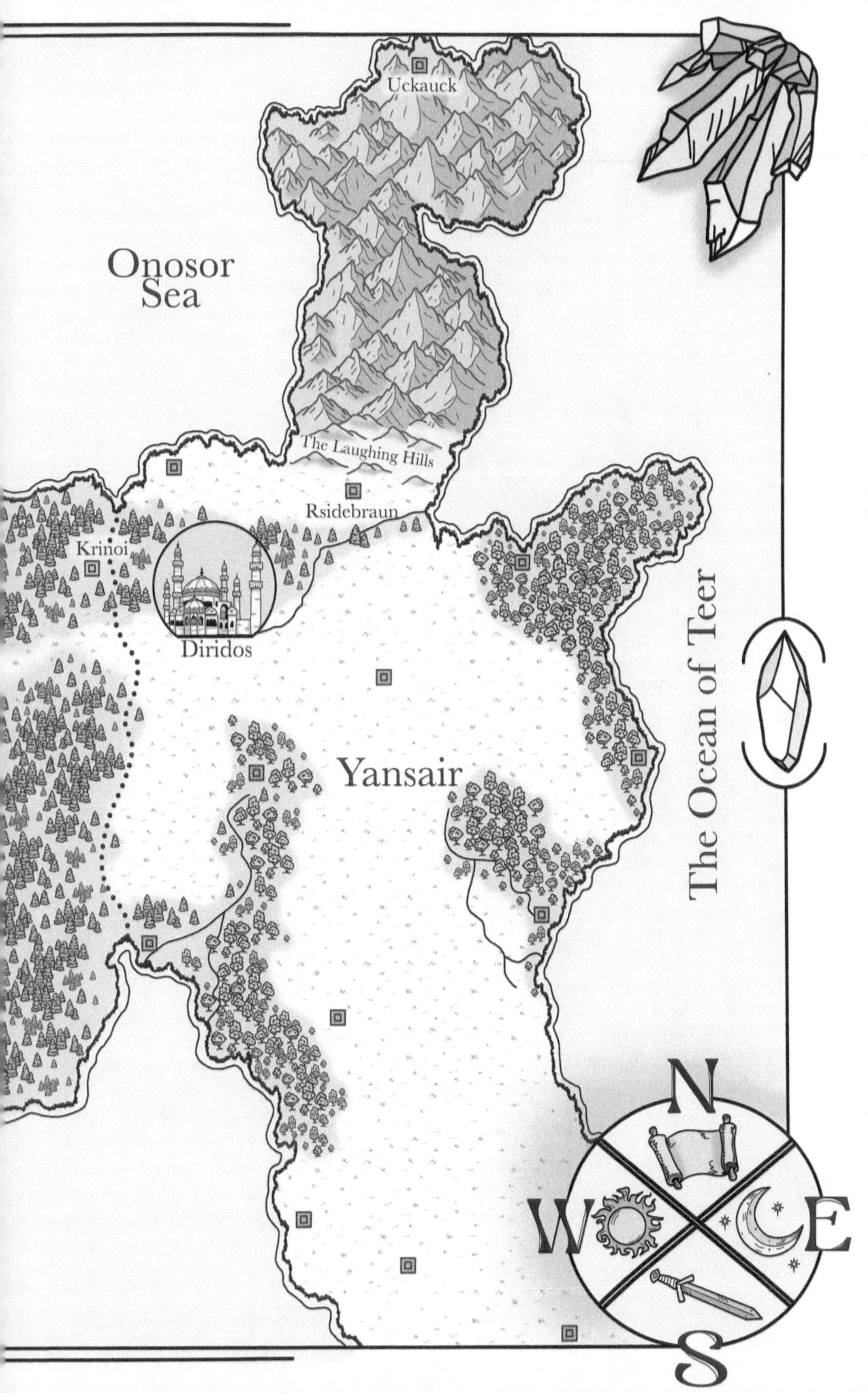

Onosor Sea
Uckauck
The Laughing Hills
Rsidebraun
Krinoi
Diridos
Yansair
The Ocean of Teer
N
W
E
S

Chapter One

"*D*arren!"

The terror in Iris's voice beat harshly through Darren's mind. *She needs you! Wake up! You have to help her!* The hounding panic jolted him upright, making him cry out Iris's name. Dizziness slammed through his head and dropped him back to the ground.

"Whoa. Hey, hold on there, mister. Not too quickly now. You're still in pretty rough shape."

The light coming through the tent flaps burned Darren's eyes, forcing them shut. The throbbing in his head intensified. A few moments passed before he was able to formulate thoughts into words.

"Where . . . am I?" Darren peeked an eye open just enough to see the young boy seated next to him.

The child appeared no more than ten. He wore an earthy-green tunic, slightly too large for his form, and sat on a cloth pallet near the head of Darren's bed. The boy grinned widely, crinkling the freckles across the bridge of his nose.

"Don't worry, you're safe now," the boy said. "You and your other buddies were rescued from that crash. It's a miracle any of you survived really! Well that one guy who was all cut up from the glass had a close call for sure, but he should make it just fine now. At least that's what my mama says. She's a healer, you know. She's been the one helping all of you. I try to do my best to help her. That's why I'm here right now, because she told me to look after you and—"

"Kale. What are you doing?"

The boy whipped his head around with a start. "I'm doing what you told me to do."

A woman who looked very much like Kale stepped the rest of the way into the tent. "I told you to watch over him, and that as soon as he woke up you were to come fetch me!"

Kale pouted. "I couldn't just leave him. He asked me a question. And besides, you're here now. He hasn't been awake for long."

"Which is exactly why he wouldn't want to have to put up with your rambling. Fetch me some fresh water. I'll take over from here."

Kale slumped his shoulders and stood reluctantly. As he plodded by, the woman sighed and reached out to stop him. With a smile, she thanked the child for watching over her patients. Kale lifted his head a bit higher as he exited the tent.

The woman turned to Darren with a soft chuckle and knelt beside him. She wore the faded blue dress typical of many of the working-class women in Fitsengea. Chosen for practicality and not to draw attention.

"You'll have to excuse my son. He's just a little overexcited by the whole ordeal. Now, how are we feeling this morning?"

Darren, his eyes finally adjusted to the light, focused on the woman leaning over him. She might have been the same age as his sister Marguerite. Her reddish-blonde hair was pulled back into a tight bun on top of her head, and her sharp, serious cheekbones and jawline battled with the easy cheeriness in her gray eyes.

"Terrible." Darren gave a weak smile.

The woman laughed. "Well, at least you're honest! That will make my job easier."

"Where am I?"

"You're quite a ways from the X32 checkpoint. All of the residents had to evacuate, so you're at one of our hideouts in the woods."

"Hideouts?"

"Yes, we had to flee the checkpoint about four days ago when it was attacked. Those fighters were the ones who dug that trench through the transport road. Checkpoint master Aiden will be more than willing to explain further later, but for now it is best to rest."

"How long have I been out?" Darren queried, noticing his clothes had been exchanged for a tan shirt and trousers. Judging by the fraying fabric, it was clear the outfit had once belonged to another.

"Nearly a day."

Darren's heart fell into his stomach. "A day! We've lost so much time!"

The woman spoke in a calming tone. "Don't worry, you will be able to get up soon, especially now that you're conscious enough to chew on some Mantriok leaves. The majority of your injuries weren't severe."

She reached into a pack tied around her waist and produced two Mantriok leaves. "Have you ever chewed one before?"

Darren nodded.

"I guess that means I can't fib to you about the flavor, then." She smiled at him and placed the leaves in his hand.

Darren popped the leaves into his mouth, fighting his reflex to gag as he chewed. Forcing down the putrid bitterness, he swallowed multiple times to get the taste out of his mouth. The leafy mash had an immediate effect on his headache as it traveled down his throat. Gingerly, Darren pulled himself up into a seated position.

"Good. You're progressing quite well." She grinned.

"Thank you for all your help, Healer . . .?"

"Markson. Healer Rachel Markson." She filled in his pause. "And what do you go by, sir?"

"Darren."

"Pleasure to meet you, Darren. I'm sorry it isn't under better circumstances."

As Rachel spoke, movement at the tent's door flap stole Darren's attention. In came Kale carrying a canteen of water. He promptly passed it off to his mother, and she handed it to Darren. Removing the cap, Darren gulped down the cool liquid, grateful to have something to wash away the Mantriok taste still trapped in his mouth. The fog over his mind steadily declined the longer he sat upright.

"Healer Markson, can you take me to see the others I traveled with?"

Rachel looked him up and down for a second. "I suppose it would be all right, but I don't know if they're awake yet, so I—"

"Oh! Almost forgot to tell ya!" Kale broke in. "Sam told me to tell you some of those other guys are up now."

Rachel winced and counted in a few slow breaths. "Kale, you should have told me that first."

"Sorry." Kale grimaced.

"It's all right, just try to not be so easily distracted, okay?" Rachel smiled, her previous signs of frustration disappearing. "Looks like you're in luck, Darren. I'll take you to your friends as long as you promise to not push yourself too much."

Darren responded with a determined nod. "I'll do my best."

Rachel wrapped her hands around Darren's arm, helping him rise from the ground. Every muscle screamed in protest, but Darren could still feel the Mantriok actively working to loosen the tension. Without those leaves, he doubted he could move after a crash like that.

The phantom sounds of Iris's screams pervaded his thoughts. What had happened to her? He was barely conscious after the crash. Maybe one of the others had a better idea. The twisting of his gut and racing of his heart screamed for him to run after her, but he didn't know *where* she was taken. *Taken. . . That's right, someone took her . . . But* who? The fighters who attacked X32? What would *they* want with Iris? Unless . . . unless it was *them.* Darren shoved down the frightening possibility. For that to be true, it would mean that army had used the transport system. It was the only way they could have attacked barely even a day after their own group left the checkpoint.

Lord Valomeer never would have allowed that. It would have been obvious who they were since Iris had *just* finished warning Valomeer about them. But if he *had* allowed them passage on the transport, then that could only mean . . . Ice shot through Darren's veins. *Valomeer didn't make an arrangement with those monsters, did he?* Perhaps they overtook Saunskirt and simply stole the transports? No, that was impossible. The time span was too short. There was no way the Saunskirt guard wouldn't have put up a fierce fight. Even a tiny skirmish would throw off the timeframe. This whole notion implicated Valomeer in treason, a threat against the Crown. . . . *Surely he wouldn't be so stupid as to . . .*

Darren's memory flared to life. Those men he had seen on the day they left Saunskirt. The ones who walked so uniformly up to Valomeer's gates, the ones he only glanced at while getting on the carriage. *They couldn't have been—*

"Hi, Sam. I've come to check up on my other patients." Rachel's voice broke through Darren's thoughts.

Though adrenaline bubbled through his body, Darren forced his attention on the present. Rachel spoke to a man that he would have assumed to be his age or younger if it weren't for the wrinkles around the man's eyes and the graying at his temples. Sam stood a head taller than Darren and had leathery, sun-worn skin and the muscle tone of a well-trained soldier.

"Good," Sam responded with an irritated look. "I don't think I can take much more of that man's whining! Maybe you can see about giving him something to make him sleep again?"

"After all he's been through, I think he has a little right to complain."

"He passed a little a *long* time ago."

Rachel shook her head and chuckled. "Any sound is a good sound, in my opinion. It lets me know they're on the road to recovery. Speaking of"—she turned to indicate Darren—"notice who I have with me?"

"Well, looky here!" Sam spoke with a growing smile. "Up and about already! Now *that's* a man for ya!" He stepped forward and held out his hand. "Samuel Lemkins."

Darren reached out and shook his calloused hand. "Darren."

"Darren, eh? Well, I suppose you're anxious to look in on your comrades? I'll not keep you, but there is much we need to talk about once you're done in there."

Nodding, Darren walked past Sam to enter the tent. "I look forward to it."

Bryant's moans greeted Darren as soon as he entered. "Doesn't anybody realize how much pain I'm in?" the man said. "I know you must have *something* to take the edge off! Or at least let me lie on a *real* bed. My back is killing me. Where's your healer? I want to see him! I demand to see him! It's not right to treat an injured man like this!"

"Would you shut up!" Grayson groaned from the far side of the room.

"My back, my back! I swear it's broken! Why won't anyone tend to me? Healer! *Healer!*"

Darren rolled his eyes and shook his head. No wonder Sam wanted to drug him. Strolling over to Bryant's side, Darren leaned over and gave Bryant a small smack across the back of his head, stunning him for a second. Bryant jolted upright, cursing and raising his fist toward Darren. "Why you little!"

Darren crossed his arms over his chest and smirked. "Sure are agile for a man near death."

Bryant froze in place. Slowly, he lowered his arm, faced forward, and lay back down on his mat, mouth set firmly into a frown.

"Marquis Turner! Is that you?" Grayson called out.

Darren turned around and smiled at Grayson. "Yes, it's me." He walked over to the soldier and kneeled at his side. "How are you feeling, Grayson?"

Grayson did his best to peer open his eyes and smile back, "I'll live."

Darren patted him on the shoulder. Grayson had bruises all over his body, the worst of which was the giant X across his chest, probably caused by the safety straps from the transport. The force of the crash likely gave Darren a matching design. But thanks to the Mantriok leaves, only a faint tenderness lingered around his midsection. Even though Grayson's bruising wasn't any great cause for concern, the sight of his bound head sent a shudder through Darren. Blood, now dried, had seeped through the cloth, explaining why Grayson had been out for so long. Bryant, on the other hand . . . *Milking things as always.*

"What about you, sir? Are *you* all right?"

Darren smiled. It was just like an Alastrian soldier to worry about the well-being of their superior. "Faring better than the hard done by Bryant, at least."

Grayson released an annoyed sigh. "In that case, you should be in perfect health. I swear, if I could, I'd *give* him something to complain about."

Darren chuckled. He could sympathize with him on that.

"Your Grace . . . the others, are they . . ."

"I am told they'll be fine, but I haven't seen them myself yet."

"Who told you?"

"The healer who's been watching over us." Darren craned his neck to see where she was.

He spotted Rachel kneeling on the opposite side of Bryant. She spoke softly to him, taking care as she looked him over. Since Darren's earlier physical rebuke, Bryant had adopted a more somber attitude.

"That the healer?" Grayson asked, following Darren's gaze.

"Yes, her name is Rachel Markson. She's the head healer in X32."

"X32? We're in X32?"

"No, we're currently . . . Well, I don't know much, really, but I'll find out soon enough."

"Sir, umm . . . what do you know of the lady? Is Lady Iris . . . well?"

Darren's face and heart grew cold. "I don't know."

Grayson let out a moan. "I was hoping that was just a part of my dream!"

"Did you see her being taken?" Darren asked.

"No, but I heard bits of her struggle. I . . . really wasn't able to focus for long."

Darren battled to swallow back his disappointment. He'd hoped Grayson could offer some pertinent information. Anything that might lead him to Iris. Perhaps the other three knew something. Or maybe the X32 residents had seen something?

"Hello, how are you feeling today, sir?" Rachel said, addressing Grayson. She leaned over him, inspecting his bandages and the rest of his wounds.

"Never better." Grayson grinned.

"Well, if that's the case, I'd hate to see you on a bad day."

Grayson's chuckle cut short as he winced and sucked in a breath through his teeth while Rachel changed the dressings on his head.

"Try to keep still, please. I'm sorry, but this is going to be tender for quite some time."

"Understood." Grayson replied.

"You're a braver man than me." Darren patted his shoulder again. "Healer Markson, how might I gain an audience with the person in charge?"

"Sam's just outside. Ask him," she said, her tone suddenly harsh.

Where had *that* come from? Had he done something to offend her?

"*Your Grace*, it would be best that you meet with the others as soon as possible. You may look in on the rest of those you traveled with later," Rachel instructed him.

Darren cringed inwardly. She had overheard Grayson address him with his full title. Of course she was able to put two and two together—Darren, Marquis Turner, Grayson calling him "Your Grace." Darren nodded at Rachel and moved to stand.

"Oh, and do be sure to be straight with them about who you are. Finding it out from a third party will not induce a kind reaction."

Darren nodded grimly and made his way out of the tent. If the discovery of his identity could make the woman *that* cold, he shuddered at the thought of how the rest would react. He had gotten too used to Iris. Darren smirked bitterly. *How could you forget so quickly? You're a hated man, Mr. Turner.*

Stepping outside the tent, Darren scanned his surroundings. The camp sat in a small clearing, encircled by one of the few wooded zones on the outskirts of X32's territory. About thirty large tents were set up, and each had room for a number of inhabitants. Sharp tension clouded the air around the campsite. Even the few children wandering about didn't seem eager to play.

Darren's eyes finally settled upon Sam, who stood just a few feet away. Sam kept his attention on a man who looked like one of the original soldiers from the checkpoint. Darren sighed and prepared himself for the ensuing hatred. *Whatever it takes. Iris needs you!* He gritted his teeth in determination. Making his way over, he caught the tail end of their discussion.

"Trey was pretty sure from what we found, but he brought back one of their discarded weapons to show the checkpoint master, just to be certain. Surely he would recognize the emblem."

A frown appeared on Sam's face as he listened to the report. Wrapping an arm around his chest, he allowed his chin to rest upon his other hand.

"What are they up to?" Darren murmured.

Darren was tempted to keep listening in, but being caught eavesdropping could cause far more problems. Clearing his throat, he announced his presence. Sam gave Darren a slight nod before looking back to the other man.

"Well done, Grant. I'll report your findings to the checkpoint master. Go get some rest before your next watch."

Grant offered a stiff nod and left, making his way to the other side of the campsite. Sam watched him go for a minute before turning his full attention to Darren.

"You saw to your friends?"

Darren nodded. "Well, two of them anyway. Healer Markson impressed upon me that I should meet with you and whoever is in charge around here before I see the others."

Sam narrowed his eyes. "Oh? That doesn't sound like Rachel."

Darren gave a slight bow. "Forgive me, sir, but I have not been entirely upfront with you."

Sam tilted his head and smirked, raising an eyebrow.

Darren ignored the expression and continued, "My full title is the Marquis Darren Alexander Turner."

Sam stared at Darren blankly. Recognition slowly percolated in the man's eyes. An uncertain anxiousness creased Sam's brow. Before Sam could connect the dots, Darren jumped at the chance to continue his story.

"I have been ordered by King Zaerin to return to Saunskirt in order to bring the Woman of Prophecy back to the Lord Valomeer. Before our business with the lord could be completed, the transport crashed. The crash, I'm told, was caused by the same people who attacked X32."

"Wait, wait a minute! Are you telling me you are *the* Darren Turner? The Marquis Turner, nephew to the king?"

"I am."

"So then . . . that makes you an *enemy* of the king." Sam took a step back, disgust dripping from his face. "Why would the king ask for *your* help? Why should I trust your word?"

Darren sighed. "If I wasn't trustworthy, I wouldn't have told you who I was and what I'm trying to do, would I?"

"I don't buy it." Sam brought his fingers to his mouth and let out a sharp whistle.

Out of nowhere, four men with swords rushed toward them and surrounded Darren. Darren kept his gaze on Sam, unflinching as the blades pointed at him.

"Quinton, go check on Rachel," Sam ordered, holding Darren's stare.

As one of the men rushed back to the tent, Darren fought the urge to shout something about wasted time. The last thing he needed was to antagonize the already strained nerves of these people. Their caution was valid considering their current circumstances. Being one of the main passageways between Alaster and Saunskirt, it only made sense that X32 residents would have heard all sorts of evil rumors about him. He would just have to suffer through this until he found some way of proving himself.

"Everything's all right in here, sir!" Quinton shouted back to Sam.

"Right." Sam studied Darren's eyes for a minute. "Gentlemen, escort this man to the checkpoint master. He'll know what to do."

The guards moved forward; their swords pressed up against Darren from behind. On the upside, this was probably the fastest way for him to gain an audience with the man in charge. Darren had never paid much attention to the political make up of X32, but it made sense that they deemed their checkpoint master the leader, because nearly everything would have to go through him anyway.

Darren followed the not-so-gentle prodding of his escorts through the campgrounds. Their little procession drew curious stares from most of the X32 refugees. *Would they technically be considered refugees, though?* "Refugee" was typically a term reserved for war, and this wasn't exactly a war. Yet he had the sinking sensation that this was barely the start. What was he thinking? Hadn't it already begun with the destruction of Throansburrough and Jaralynx? Darren glanced over a small group of children who stood huddled together and looking up at him with a mixture of fear and wonder. These children were alive because of Iris. The thought struck him so suddenly that he stopped.

"Forward," Sam barked from behind.

Darren picked up his pace. That was right—Iris *had* saved them. She had warned the checkpoint master about the possible attack. She had told them to flee. She'd used her authority as a fake messenger of the Diviner's party to express an urgency that would have put X32 on high alert as soon as they'd left. His heart beat hard in his chest. She should be here to see this. If only he could let her know about the difference she had made. If she could see the lives her rash action saved, maybe some of the sadness in her eyes would disappear.

The soldiers led Darren through some trees. Leaving the campgrounds behind, they continued into the more secluded area of the dry woods, following a twisted, nearly invisible path. The terrain soon became barer and rockier. They must not be far from the Smallman Mountains. The trail's incline increased slowly as they walked, and soon they were climbing up a good-sized hill near the foot of the mountains to their right. A broad view of the forest was visible to their left.

Darren noted the lack of evidence for a refugee camp. They clearly worked hard to keep themselves hidden.

In front of them stood a dead end, where a rockslide had created an impassable wall. They came to a stop in front of a particularly thick patch of Brenberry bushes. Two soldiers walked single file around the bushes, moving aside some shrubbery as well. Darren was amazed to find that the cleverly placed shrubs had hidden a very narrow path up through the mountains. He never would have found it by himself.

The soldiers quickly directed Darren forward, not allowing him the luxury of admiring their well-concealed pathway. The trail weaved in and out of the mountains. It didn't take long before they came to the mouth of a large cave, a single lookout standing at its entrance. Upon their approach, Sam stepped forward and made a motion with his hand. Two men emerged from the perimeter of the cave with arrows trained at Darren's head. Exactly what did they think he was capable of? *Apparently, the rumors about me are much worse than I thought. But I guess I should be flattered by my assumed abilities.*

Walking farther into the cave, Darren noticed the torches placed at intervals to light their way. They didn't have to walk far before they encountered another group of people. Three older men—one rather portly and two more slender—and one aging redheaded woman all watched as another young woman with curly blonde hair worked diligently on some odd contraption.

"Sir Checkpoint Master," Sam called out once within hearing distance, "Samuel Lemkins requesting an immediate audience."

The heavyset man standing in the middle of the group turned his gaze toward Sam. The checkpoint master wore a more disheveled form of his official uniform. Upon seeing Darren surrounded by the others, he raised an eyebrow. Darren recognized him as the man who'd greeted him and the others just a few days back, but his former pomp had all but vanished. The man who stood before him now exuded deep exhaustion. Which made sense considering he had a lot riding on his shoulders, probably more than he had ever bargained for.

"Who is our guest, Mr. Lemkins?" the checkpoint master asked.

"The banished marquis, Darren Alexander Turner," Sam answered.

"*The* Marquis Turner?" One of the elderly men beside the checkpoint master gasped.

His graying hair was slicked back high atop his head, and his features were quite angular and petite. All except for a large nose that kept a small pair of glasses in place. The man held onto the rim of his spectacles, appearing to study Darren's features in an attempt to verify the announcement.

"What is the traitor doing here?" the redheaded woman spat.

The woman was dressed in an outfit that mirrored the transport master's formal wear, though it too was dirty and tattered from time spent out in the wilderness.

"Technically he was neither banished nor officially deemed a traitor, Madaline." The third man corrected the woman softly.

While possibly the same age as the others, this man still maintained his dark black hair, though it was thinning in the middle and made him appear as if he had a very high brow.

Madaline shot him an annoyed look as the checkpoint master reprimanded him. "That's enough, Braethus. Mr. Lemkins, please continue with your report."

Sam nodded. "Marquis Turner was one of the men my crew discovered at the wreckage of the transport two days back. He has only recently gained consciousness. We await orders as to what to do with him."

"Put him under watch back at the campgrounds. I'll see to him later. We're busy with more pressing matters right now." He waved them aside and started to turn back to the woman working on the ground.

Panic surged through Darren's veins. He couldn't chance wasting that much time.

"Wait, no! Sir, please, I *have* to speak with you," Darren called out, trying to step forward.

Four swords pressing against his flesh halted his advancement.

Darren gave up moving, but that didn't mean he had to give up speaking.

"Hear me out! I beg you! It's a matter of life and death."

Sam spun toward Darren. "Enough! Take him out of here, men!"

"Whose life, exactly?"

Everyone in the cave paused at the checkpoint master's words. Darren swallowed before continuing, barely daring to hope that this would work. But right now he didn't have the option of only hoping. They *had* to help him. "Specifically, Iris Straton, but quite possibly everyone here."

"And how is one woman's fate tied to the rest of ours?"

Darren contemplated what he should reveal. *To hell with it! Holding back now will only hurt her.*

"She has been discovered to be the Woman of Prophecy who will save all Fitsengea from a foreign enemy. I, along with the other men on that transport, had been ordained by King Zaerin as her protector, but she was stolen away after our transport crashed. I need your help to find her."

"Aiden dear, you can't trust the word of a traitor," Madaline hissed into the checkpoint master's ear.

So she's his wife?

"Bah, there's proof enough for you right there, Aiden!" the man with the spectacles said. "He claims the king sent him. The man's a liar. The king would *never* use the likes of him even if this so-called prophecy woman existed."

"Woman of Prophecy," Braethus corrected.

"Oh, get off it, Braethus!"

"Just trying to keep the facts straight, Henry."

"Enough! All of you. I have neither the time nor the energy to waste on this. Marquis Turner, you weave an interesting tale, but do you have any way to verify such outrageous claims?" Aiden stared at Darren.

Darren's throat went dry. "I . . ."

The cave grew silent while everyone waited for him to come up with something. *Did* he have anything? The papers! That was right—back on the transport there were papers from his uncle for Valomeer. They would have the royal seal on them. Surely *that* would convince them. But how would they ever find them in such a mess? It would take far too much time.

"I have proof, but it's back on the transport."

"Fine, I'll send some of my men with you to go find it."

"No, that will take too long. Every moment wasted is a moment that takes them farther away."

"There may be a title attached to your name, sir, but it no longer holds any weight, not here. You *will* watch how you address me." Aiden's icy glare bore down on Darren.

Darren gritted his teeth. "All due respect, *sir* checkpoint master, but this goes *beyond* court etiquette."

"Well, either you take the time to find these so-called papers of yours, or you head back to my camp as a prisoner to await further questioning."

"But there's no time!"

"Umm . . . excuse me, sir Checkpoint Master . . ." The soft voice came from the woman kneeling on the ground. "But if I may? I believe I have a faster way to find out the truth."

"Yes, Tess?"

Tess stood, dusted off her pants, and indicated to the contraption behind her. "Ask the king yourself."

Chapter Two

Darren looked at the device anxiously. Stone lights lined the rock base carved out of a telltale white stone of the Smallman Mountains. What appeared to be a copper substance had been hammered into two thin sheets and stood opposite each other, fixed into grooves carved into the stone. Between the sheets and on top of the stone sat various colored crystals.

"Now, this won't be as clear as it normally is, because I had to do a lot of improvising, but the sound quality should be just as strong," Tess explained.

Her voice held a sort of rolling accent that hinted to the brutish tone of the seafaring people from Sylphaen.

"But what exactly *is* it, Tess?" Madaline asked.

"It is called a Rayl. It's a communication device that projects both picture and sound," Tess answered as she removed a few small tools from the underside pockets of her brown vest and rearranged the vest over her long-sleeved red shirt.

"And you mean to say the king has one?" Aiden spoke up while taking a few tentative steps toward it.

"Yes, sir checkpoint master. My people in Sylphaen had presented it as a gift to your king nearly a year ago. Just to warn you, technically no one other than our Grand Senate is supposed to know the frequency for King Zaerin's Rayl. Using it without proper protocol can lead to a year's imprisonment. We may come across some difficulty with the initial connection."

Darren looked up at Tess with a developing sense of admiration. *This woman sure is risking a lot for people who aren't even her own.*

Aiden walked over to the woman and clapped a hand on her shoulder. "When you told me you knew of a way to contact the king, I never expected something as advanced as this."

"Assuming that it works," Henry scoffed.

Tess moved as if not hearing the comment—which was possible considering how focused she was—then connected a few more items before finally leaning over the crystals in the center. After moving her finger down the length of each one in a specified pattern, she stood and removed a crystal hanging on some twine around her neck. Everyone watched intently as she whispered something and then blew on it, making it hum a soft purple color. She stuck it into a small slot on the stone and stepped back.

Every muscle in Darren's body tensed as he held his breath. Everyone focused on the machine while a melodic hum rose up from within. Even the men who guarded Darren lowered their swords a little. The copper-like panels vibrated while the crystals at the center glowed—first a slight purple and then a strong white light as the luminescence of the stone lights was also strengthened. The humming of the device grew so that it echoed off the cave walls.

"Does it do anything other than glow and make noise?" Henry shouted while clamping his hands over his ears.

Everyone ignored him, as their attention was transfixed on the Rayl. Slowly, an image formed in the center of the light above the crystals. Lights continued to refract off the panels before combining to form a picture about five feet tall. Darren strained his eyes, trying to make out the image before him. Was it a room? He could swear he saw some walls. Looking more closely, Darren realized he recognized the room.

That's my uncle's private study! It works. I can't believe it! This thing really works! Oh, Uncle, for once in your life, be where I need you to be and come answer this thing! Darren studied the image impatiently, practically willing his uncle to appear. *Come on, old man, where are you?*

"So, what happens if no one answers?"

"Quiet, Braethus! I think I can see something." Aiden's voice was raised in anticipation.

Every person in the cave leaned forward as one, searching for whatever it was that Aiden saw. Gasps echoed off the rocks as a figure appeared in the center of the picture.

"How did you gain access to this frequency?" a voice boomed from the Rayl as the figure came into focus.

No one seemed capable of a response save Tess, who immediately stepped forward and kneeled before the image. "Forgive this terrible breach in decorum, King Zaerin, but there is urgent news that must be reported, and we knew of no other way to contact you sooner."

The man in the image raised a cautious eyebrow. "Who *are* you, girl, and where are you reporting from?"

Finally able to collect himself, Aiden came in and kneeled next to Tess. "She is a traveling inventor from Sylphaen, Your Highness, and we are reporting from a little ways outside the X32 checkpoint."

"Checkpoint Master Aiden Valerus? What is the meaning of all this?" Zaerin narrowed his eyes as he scanned the crowd.

"X32 has been attacked, and the transport road connecting it to Alaster has been destroyed. Thanks to the wise warning of the Diviners, many people were able to escape unharmed, but we have still suffered much and fear that these attackers, whoever they are, plan on striking elsewhere."

"And what? Do you think my nephew has something to do with this?"

Aiden balked. He cast a glance at Darren, who was having a hard time fighting back a smug expression.

"Well, I-I . . . no—"

"Where is she?"

"Wh-who, Your Majesty?"

"The girl, the woman he was traveling with! The woman he was *supposed* to be protecting." His steely gaze held on Darren for a moment before returning to Aiden.

"She-uh-we-um-I-uh."

"Out with it!"

Oh come on now! This man is clearly scared out of his wits. Blasting him like this is only going to serve to fluster him! You always were miserable with diplomacy when dealing with those you felt beneath you.

"She was taken!" Darren called out above Aiden's stuttering.

"She was . . . *what?*"

"Our transport crashed because the road was sabotaged. After—" Darren stopped and looked at the swords in his face. "Do you mind? I think you can all see I was telling the truth now."

The men wavered then looked to Sam for instruction. With a frown, he nodded, and each of his men sheathed their blades. Darren took the opportunity to push past them and stand next to Aiden and Tess.

"After the crash, some men came into the wreckage and kidnapped Ir-the Woman of Prophecy."

"*What?* How could you let this happen? I knew I shouldn't have allowed you to be in charge. Do you at least know *who* did it?"

Darren shook his head bitterly.

"Pardon me, Your Majesty, but if I may?" Sam spoke up from behind Darren.

"Speak only if you have something pertinent to this discussion. Otherwise, keep out!"

Sam bowed then continued, "We may have a clue as to who is behind all of this. While on patrol, one of my men came across a discarded enemy weapon." He motioned to someone behind him. "On it is a foreign insignia." A soldier stepped forward and passed along a broken sword to Sam. "Surely His Highness will be able to recognize this design?"

Sam walked up to the image of the king and held the blade high for him to see. Embossed on the hilt of the sword was a bronze symbol crudely resembling an eye.

"That's a Yansairen blade!" Tess blurted.

Darren felt his heart plummet.

"Are you certain?" Zaerin looked at Tess, his eyes grave.

Her expression became chillingly serious. "My people have been at war with the Yansairens for three years now. I know their mark when I see it."

"How did they know she was there?" Zaerin roared at no one in particular.

"I hate to jump to accusations, Uncle," Darren answered, remembering once again his time in Saunskirt, "but I fear there may be some foul play from the Lord Valomeer."

"James? What in the lands conjured up that insanity!"

"Just listen! How else could the Yansairens have arrived by transport but by his approval? He was the only person who could have told them where we were, *and* he was able to ensure our return by placing that thing on her chest!"

"You have some valid points. But it is still hard to accept."

"Perhaps, in the meantime, would it not be best to limit knowledge of our current vulnerability in order to protect the people of X32 from any possible conspirators?" Tess suggested in an even voice.

Zaerin hesitated and drew his head back slightly as he scrutinized Tess. "Yes . . . that would be best . . ." Turning to Aiden, he continued, "I will dispatch some of my men as well as supplies to aid your people immediately. You will need to give me precise measurements of a safe distance for my transport to arrive. The Master of the Transports, Flynn, will handle the rest. *But* your priority right now is to aid my incompetent nephew in rescuing the Woman of Prophecy. *All* other matters are to be stalled until you can find a way to return her safely. Do you understand?"

"Y-yes, Your Majesty."

"Is there anything else you need to report?"

"No, Your Majesty."

"Good. Darren, bring her back." With his final command, the Rayl shut off and the image vanished.

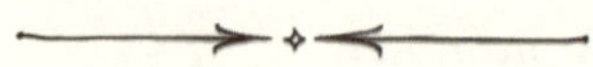

"Run, Iris! Go now!"

Iris moved fearful eyes around the scene before her. The world was engulfed in flames. She couldn't move, for her body no longer belonged to her. To her right lay a town watchman, his throat slit by their attackers.

"I said *move!*"

A strong hand clamped down on Iris's wrist and yanked her from her spot. Her panicked mind took a minute to register that they were moving forward. Iris She looked at her brother-in-law as he dragged her through the streets. Having been separated by the last explosion, it had taken her brother-in-law's return to snap her out of her shock. They ran between the houses,the soldiers close on their heels.

Dan held onto Iris through every twist and turn. Thanks to his quick thinking, they soon left their pursuers behind. She could tell by the strength of his grip that he was angry with her, and why shouldn't he be? She had caused him to be separated from his family. She wanted to apologize, but he wouldn't have been able to hear her above the sounds of battle. Suddenly, a hand jutted through a nearby window and latched onto Iris's hair.

Iris screamed as a man tried to pull her through. Dan whirled around and struck the man in the face, forcing the soldier to release his hold. As soon as she was free, Iris and Dan bolted from the area. Bounding around the next corner, Dan came to a screeching halt as he almost bowled over Julie. Upon seeing her husband, Julie threw her arms around Dan and kissed him. Iris saw Lori and Jacob were with her. Lori clung to her mother's skirt while Jacob, being slightly smooshed in between his parents' embrace, clutched Julie's neck. Dan scooped Lori into his arms. Julie ran with Jacob, and Iris followed behind as they searched for Julie's and Iris's parents.

A cry to their left caught their attention. They had been spotted. As they began to go right, the sight of the last of the town guard being slaughtered stopped them. Buildings went up in flames in front of and behind them.

They were trapped.

"There!" Julie cried. Iris followed her line of sight to a narrow alleyway that would take them to another part of town.

Dan passed Lori off to Iris before she made her way through. "Lori, it's too narrow for Daddy to carry you," he said. I need you to run in front of your aunt. Can you do that, sweetie?"

Lori nodded and followed her mommy and Jacob through the alley. Iris stepped in behind her, Dan going last. The kids could get through all right, but Iris and the others had to inch their way along with their backs pressed up against one of the sides. The fire from the surrounding buildings began to reach the wall facing Iris. A cry at her side stole her attention from the flames. Dan was doing his best to fight off a few of the soldiers following them.

"*Dan!*" Julie screeched.

"Don't stop!" he roared back.

Iris swiveled her head, looking between the two. She wanted to help, but she couldn't reach around Dan to do anything. While a soldier tried to drag Dan out of the passage, Iris grabbed onto his arm to pull him back. The building in front of them groaned as flames began licking down the sides. Dan shook Iris off him and shoved her down the alley.

"Go!" he yelled, looking past her to her sister. "*Go!*"

With that he was yanked away, Julie screeched "no!" and tried to reach him. At that moment the building started collapsing onto the other wall, forcing Julie to run out with Jacob. Iris pushed Lori forward, and they sped to the other side. Iris barely made it out before burning wood closed the gap.

"*Dan! No! Dan!*"

Iris looked up at her sister shrieking for her husband, unable to comprehend what had just happened. Dan was gone? Another screech from behind nearly stopped her heart. Iris clenched her eyes shut and screamed to the heavens. *"Holy Father!"*

Iris bolted upright into the waking world. Her whole body shook at the memory of her dream. No, the memory of the nightmare her life had now become. Fear consumed her. She tried to curl into a ball on the floor but was reminded that her hands were loosely chained to the wall. That was right—she was a prisoner. In a dungeon. All alone. And even worse, she was in Yansair.

Iris dropped her head and cried. Between her tears, she noted that she still wore the white and silver dress from Alaster—or at least what had once resembled the noble dress. Her outfit was now so torn and covered with dirt, it was nearly impossible to distinguish what its original form had been. She couldn't tell how many days had passed or even what hour it was. Iris's reddish-brown hair fell in tangled disarray around her shoulders, several strands hanging in front of her face. Her stomach groaned. The last time she had eaten was back on the transport. The pain in her heart tightened her throat. Even if she had food, she wouldn't be able to get it down. The thought of the transport brought a new wave of grief. She had killed them. Kyle, Jason, Bryant, Grayson, and . . . Darren. Killed by the crash or finished off by her kidnappers. And it was all her fault. Those men destroyed the transport road to capture her. They attacked X32 to capture her. Yansairens slaughtered Throansburrough and Jaralynx, to capture her.

"I'm sorry . . . I'm so sorry," Iris whispered between sobs.

Maybe things would be better this way, now that she was here. With her death, perhaps lives would be saved? No one else would be forced to sacrifice themselves for her. And why should they? What was her life worth, after all? Not this. She didn't deserve their sacrifice. How could one person's life *ever* be worth the cost of thousands of innocents? And yet . . . what right did she have to die *now*? Could she dare to dishonor their memory by giving up now?

Who was she kidding? Only a handful of them had any true

connection to her. All the others hadn't died on her behalf. She was just trying to make herself feel better, and she knew it. She needed a reason for all of this, a reason for the Holy Father to bring this about. Or *did* He bring it all about? There wasn't anything the Holy Father didn't know, didn't see coming, so why, for all that was good and pure, did He *let* it happen? Iris stared at the floor as tears rolled down her face. Again, she found herself not wanting to talk to the Holy Father, and yet she knew she had to.

Why am I here, Holy Father? Why is this all happening? I know . . . I know there is no sense in asking You why. You rarely, if ever, tell people why You do things. Have You ever explained Yourself to me? But I need it, Holy Father. I need You to give me something! I want to give up . . . Please, please take me away from this. I can't do this. I'm not worthy to be chosen by You. My heart can't take it. What can I do here anyway? They're going to kill me, Holy Father . . . And I don't know if I care anymore. Holy Beloved . . . oh, Holy Beloved . . . please . . . it hurts too much to try. My arms ache from these chains, my body is bruised from the crash, but my soul . . . my soul is dying! Am I being dramatic? Maybe, but how could I not be? I didn't ask for this! Why am I here? . . . No . . . I gave my all to You, years ago. I surrendered the rights of my life to Your will, but . . . if You love me, how could You let this happen?

Pain flooded Iris's spirit, halting her ability to think. She gritted her teeth, trying to fight her despair as her heart pounded within her chest. Tears fell heavy enough to leave a tiny pool on the rough stone floor. She longed for that moment back in the house of Peter, the Church official, when the Holy Father had finally spoken to her, refreshed her, given her hope. What hope did she have now?

"H-help me . . . Holy Father, *please!*"

What do I do?

"Live."

The word was spoken as clearly as if someone stood beside her and said it into her ear. Iris gasped and raised her head, half expecting to see a person standing before her. But no one was there. *Live? I'm just supposed to live? I'll admit, my thoughts have only been of embracing death at the hands of the Yansairens, but . . . live? That's it? That's all I have to do? But why? Why nothing else? Please, Holy Father, I need to know more. I need something to hold onto.*

"Set your heart on life. I will take care of you."

Iris threw her gaze around the room, shocked to hear the voice of the Holy Father once again. She had read the Sacred Texts ever since she was little. She knew all the stories of the chosen who conversed with the Holy Father, and the Holy Father actually spoke back in some way or another. But *never* had she experienced it. She knew the Holy Father still spoke to people, but not to her. She had assumed her meeting with Him back in Alaster was a one-time thing. Maybe she really was this Woman of Prophecy? The hope fluttering weakly in her heart surprised her. She wasn't supposed to die right now? *But what do I have to live for?*

"Live for me."

Iris looked up at the ceiling. *Live for You. . .* More questions tried to take over her spirit. Doubts came hard, fears of what her captors would do to her, considering the fact that Valomeer's badge was still attached to her chest. How *could* she live? Her trust in the Holy Father was shaken. She heard Him. He had even held her, but it wasn't like there hadn't been other times He had allowed atrocities to take place against His children. *Know my plans for you. . . .* The Sacred Text entered her mind as if the Holy Father had dropped it in Himself. Maybe He did? *Plans for prosperity, not harm. Plans of hope and a future.*

"I remain the same, Iris. This promise is for you."

Warmth flooded her heart and dried her eyes as the weight of peace crushed the weight of despair.

"Live for Me."

The tumbling of a lock being opened echoed off the prison walls. Iris turned her head to see the wooden door of her cell slowly creaking open. Light streamed in around a male figure, and Iris squinted at the sudden brightness. A young man walked stiffly down the three steps to the dungeon floor, followed by two other soldiers. Each man was dressed in leather armor overtop their shirts and around their torsos, shoulders, and forearms. This presented some protection, but she knew it was more to allow for swift movement. Iris looked up at their faces as they stopped a few feet away from her As she watched them, she detected an odd presence. They were obviously strong soldiers used to fighting, but the expressions on their faces weren't the same as the bloody fighters she had seen that night. *Are they . . . afraid of me?* As if to answer her question one of the Yansairens took a few hesitant steps forward and, with shaky hands, undid the shackles around her wrists. Once she was released, he took a hasty step back.

"Get up."

They are *afraid of me! At least these men are. They* are *rather young soldiers. I wonder if they're much older than eighteen?* Iris slowly struggled to her feet, every inch of her body stiff from pain. The stabbing ache shooting through her side told her she might have cracked or bruised a rib in the transport crash. Iris clenched her teeth as she forced herself to walk up and out of her cell. The tunnels they wove through were made of roughly cut stone. Iris didn't remember going underground, but then again, she had barely been conscious when they carried her down here. The soldiers who captured her had forced her to drink some concoction that left her incoherent for days, or at least what felt like days. How much time had actually passed?

Rounding the next corner, they came upon a stone staircase. The gray-black color of the steps seemed eerily alive. Everything here felt alive. Not the comforting kind of life, but the sinking, terror-in-the-pit-of-your-stomach kind of life. Each step, each hall, even the torches on the walls all possessed a foreboding presence. Perhaps it was her fear of the situation. Perhaps it was that weird eye-looking symbol etched onto everything. Whatever it was, it sent Iris's spirit into panic. Even her physical pain could not tear her mind away from her awareness of evil. That's what it was—the only word to describe it. Something here had immersed the whole area with evil. Iris hoped in vain that this overwhelming presence would begin to dissipate as they left the dungeons. Instead, the pressure of this evil spirit only seemed to grow as they advanced. She could physically feel the weight of it on her heart, pulling her down, making it hard to breathe. *Holy Father, help me.*

The pressure seemed to siphon off of Iris as she cried out. She should have expected the Father's aid, especially with the conversation in her cell. The Holy Father had made Himself spectacularly known in the last couple of days. He didn't even expect much from her at this point. Just "live." But the doubts were arrogantly persistent. In her current circumstances, just surviving could be the hardest thing she would ever accomplish.

Sunlight attacked her eyes as they stepped through a metal door. Iris tried to take a minute to let them adjust to the drastic change, but her guards refused to hesitate. Momentarily blind, she stumbled along as best as she could. Through squinting, she could see that she had been led up to a polished black-granite hallway. The sun streamed into this long corridor through the number of short, wide windows lining the tops of the high walls. On the ceiling were painted images of a great and bloody battle. At its center, dramatically posed, stood a giant, powerful creature. The body was that of a strong and healthy man, easily cable of crushing all opponents, while the head had at least four faces, one to look in each of the cardinal directions.

It seemed that some of the faces were vicious animals, but the one that looked down directly at her shook her the most. It had the face of a young, perfectly handsome man. But the spirit within his painted eyes hinted at something so hideous that Iris dreaded the image would somehow come to life. In the spot on its chest, where a heart should be, remained a hole in the shape of their favored eye symbol.

Sweat began to form upon Iris's brow. The hallway was unbearably hot. It had been warm in the dungeon, but the heat continued to increase the higher they rose. Iris's stomach felt weak, her ribs protested at each step, and fear and heat intermixed to sap her bones of all strength. But the eyes of that painting disturbed her the most. They stole her attention and terrified her heart. *Please, Holy Father, protect me! Save me from this place.*

A woman's scream snapped Iris's attention to a spot a few feet in front of her, where an old woman stood wearing a gold-and-red dress. She was covered in gold bangles, earrings, necklaces, rings, and even a gold-chain head scarf. She screamed out in rage and gestured wildly toward Iris. Iris's guards froze once more and then fell to the ground, bowing to the woman with their faces on the floor. The woman continued to scream incoherently, apparently enraged by the very sight of Iris. Iris didn't know what to do. She knew that she shouldn't bow to this woman, but she didn't know how to react to her screeching.

"Her eyes!" The woman finally managed to shout. "Cover her eyes!"

The woman continued to shout about Iris's eyes until another woman, whom Iris assumed to be her attendant, came bolting from the side holding a cloth hood.

Running up to her, the woman clutched her arm and jerked her down. Iris swore her ribs snapped at the sudden movement, but her cry of pain was muffled by the hood thrust over her head. The material was thick and stifling, impossible to see through. Iris remained still, partly because it hurt too much to move and partly because she didn't know what they would do to her if she didn't.

"You fools! How dare you desecrate this holy place with unclean eyes!" came the angry shouting of the infuriated woman. "Bring her to the judgment room, where you too will await your sentence for this treachery!"

Two battle-worn hands grasped her arms and began to yank her forward, catching her off guard and causing her feet to tangle beneath her. As they dragged her along, her heart beat hard in her chest, the cloth and her panic making it hard to breathe. What was this "judgment room"? Why did they have to cover her head? Surely they were leading her to her death, to the executioner's block.

What other logical conclusion was there? Why would they go to such an extent to capture her if not to put her to death? She was confused as to why they hadn't done it sooner. Perhaps they were planning on torturing her first? Why else go through all this trouble? A slow, metallic clicking noise echoed all around her. Iris assumed she was being dragged through the enormous doors she'd seen at the end of the hall. Outraged shouting flooded the corridors. The sound of such an angry crowd was terrifying. *Please, Holy Father, help me. I need Your strength! I need You!*

Her panic slowly subsided. The reassurance that she was the Holy Father's and the Holy Father's alone came to her mind and penetrated her heart. *It's okay. I don't know why, but it is. Holy Father, help me stand for You.* A small smile tugged at the corner of her mouth as she recalled the Sacred Texts where Followers faced their deaths with defiant joy, declaring His goodness to the end. That was true peace, true strength, a complete understanding of how not to worry about anything. Iris wished she had that capability, but for now she would simply cling to whatever reassurance fluttered through her heart.

Her guards roughly carried her up some steps. The cries around them intensified as they reached level ground again. She was dragged forward over the smooth, hard surface. Slowly, the chaotic screams around her melded into a savage chant.

"Kill her! . . . Kill her! . . . Kill her! . . ."

The Holy Father said I was to live. Remember that, Iris! Remember! Iris forced her breathing to slow. *Relax. The Holy Father is in control. I'll be okay . . . somehow. The Great Deceiver prowls about like a Reed Stalker, but he is toothless! He has no power over me, over the Holy Father. You told me to live, Father, so* help *me live!* As Iris prayed, the uproar around her seemed muted, as if the crowd could only muster a unified whisper rather than their previous death cry. The more she prayed, the less she heard them. It was almost like she wasn't even there.

Iris didn't hear the crazed woman from before coming up next to her to begin her speech until she stood right beside her. The woman had to raise her voice in order to compete with the zealous crowd.

"My children! My children! Quiet your just cries. Allow now your Great Mother to speak!" The woman spoke with arms stretched out to the thousands of spectators.

Her cry reverberated through them all as her presence commanded their attention and their silence.

"Look, look I say!" she cried dramatically. "The creature of destruction is here. She has entered our most sacred of places! But look again I say! She comes not as the great force we feared, for the Eye has seen. And the Eye has delivered the monster into our hands. Her blood is ours to take!" The woman bowed low. "Oh king of this great land, our foe has been brought to us. Her blood will flow on our thirsty land and finally, the dust will be quenched. Favor upon you, King, for now we will be strong, now we will defeat those heathens to the west. Hail the Eye! Hail our gods! Hail to the king!"

The crowd viciously echoed each of the woman's hails, pumping fists into the air to emphasize each one. At the center of the massive amphitheater sat an ornate throne and awning, elevated slightly higher than the stage and positioned straight across from it. King Thaylos rose from his throne and stepped to the edge of his platform so he could be better seen and heard. He stood silent for a minute as he looked down at Iris.

At last, his voice rumbled forth. "Heal her, break her, then spill her blood! This is the highest of death rituals the Eye demands! In one week's time, we will regain our former glory and rid ourselves of our last threat and then, my people, the end of Fitsengea! Thus is my judgment. Hail the Eye!" King Thaylos roared and threw his own fist into the air.

The crowd and the woman answered the hail with screams of approval. Beneath her hood, Iris wore a gentle smile. For the moment, her heart was at ease. *Let them scream. Let them plan my end. He told me to live. And no man can defeat my Father.*

Chapter Three

A loud *thwack* rang through the tent as Darren punted a nearby crate. Those stupid, self-righteous jackals! They were ordered to cooperate with him. Why the *hell* was he stuck in this tent?

"Marquis Turner? Are you . . . all right?"

Darren turned from his huff to see Jason standing at the opening of the tent. Darren's anger stuttered at the sight of Jason in good health. He let out a short sigh before responding. "Jason, how are you? You look okay."

Jason gave a quick bow. "I am quite well, sir. I was one of the first to awaken. No major damage done. I have been attending to Kyle. He . . . he wasn't quite as lucky as the rest of us . . ."

Healer Markson had mentioned one of them had been badly injured. The slight twinge he felt in his heart at the news surprised Darren, but he quickly dismissed it as sympathy for Jason. The man was obviously taxed by his concern for Kyle.

"He . . . he is related to you, isn't he?"

"Yes, Your Grace, Kyle is a second cousin of mine."

Darren paused, not really sure how to proceed. It seemed a bit odd to him that Jason would be so worried about a relative that he hadn't seen for so many years.

"Has the healer offered any more news about his condition?"

"She says that time will tell, but Kyle is a stubborn man. He won't give up easily, and neither will I."

"You . . . you and Kyle . . . um—never mind, sir. I'm sure it's none of my business." Jason fidgeted uneasily and looked at his feet.

"We *were* friends. You needn't worry about the rest. But, Jason?"

Jason snapped his head back up and stood at attention. "Yes, Your Grace?"

Darren sighed. "See I don't get that."

"S-sir?"

Darren plopped down on a crate he hadn't kicked in his earlier fit. After raking a hand through his hair, he let it fall to his side while keeping his eyes fixed on his feet. "Why do you do that, Jason? Why do you keep acting like . . . like I'm royalty?"

"Be . . . cause you . . . are?" Jason fumbled.

Daren laughed bitterly. "I was once, and I suppose I *technically* still am, but . . . Jason, I have been shunned by all Fitsengea for what I've done. No one accepts me as anything but a traitor now. Any other soldier would prefer I'd be thrown away in Alaster's dungeons rather than accompany me on a quest, even one sanctioned by my uncle. I suspect your training would force you to treat me with begrudging respect, at least. But you . . . you've gone to the other side of that. You and Grayson both act as if there is not even a spot on my record."

Jason listened attentively to Darren as he spoke. Taking a moment to think, he set his mouth into a serious line.

"Permission to speak freely, Your Grace?"

Darren let out a small snort and shook his head. *He's still doing it!* "By all means."

What did they do? Train away his ability for free thought?

"Your Grace, I don't think you're being fair. True, the majority may not trust you and some even hate you, but to say *all* is blowing it out of proportion. Grayson and I are no fools, sir. We have been taught well the military history of Alaster, and we know what you and my cousin have been charged with. But it's clear the king himself doubts the depth of your sentencing. Very little of what you were charged with was ever verified, and you yourself were never banished from the capital. From what I gather, you left because of the shame Kyle brought on your name by escaping during the trial. Each night after training with the guard, I would return home and talk about the scandal with my father. He is an extremely wise man, Marquis Turner. He warned me there were always two sides to every story and that to accept one without hearing the other was ignorant. He swore to me that something was off with what the people were being told. He felt in his spirit that there was an 'air of deceit to it all.' But the most important thing my father told me was that we were all children of the Holy Father. That it was never our place to judge another man's heart. To attempt that would be to claim we were gods ourselves."

"By that logic, what need is there for laws if no man can be judged?"

Jason shook his head. "I still believe in the righteousness of the law. But law is upheld by flawed men. Though I am too lowly in rank to speak in depth on such a matter. What I *do* know is I am not a judge—it is not my place to curse or condemn. Only the Holy Father can rightly judge the heart of man. I am called instead to love, to respect authority, to forgive, and let go."

Darren scrunched his brow and shook his head. "Are you sure you follow the same god as my uncle?"

"The Holy Father is infallible; His people are not. Making mistakes and wrong choices is in our character, but the Holy Father still loves us. What people may claim about Him may differ, the way in which they choose to interpret or not interpret the Sacred Texts may differ, but the character of the Holy Father remains the same. He is just, righteous, holy. His truth is the only truth, and only He can convict a man's heart. I trust and know that He will work all things to the good and for His glory."

Darren studied Jason's face as the man spoke. So much life danced in his eyes when he talked about his "Holy Father" that Darren didn't know how to process it. Jason was entirely loyal to his king and his country, and yet he was entirely loyal to his faith as well. Could he not see that under his uncle's rule, those loyalties could not coexist? And yet Jason hadn't reprimanded him for his snide remark about his uncle. Though maybe he didn't simply because he saw Darren as his superior. Still, Darren had the impression that wasn't it.

Jason shifted nervously and cleared his throat. "I-uh-apologize, Your Grace. I didn't mean to get preachy on you." He laughed awkwardly "The men in my unit are always teasing me about that. I am sorry if I overstepped my bounds." He gave a sincere bow.

Darren half smiled and leaned back on his crate, resting on his arms to maintain his balance. "You know, it has been quite some time since I've been mixed in with a world of protocol. To be honest, I never really liked it for the short time that I was. When I say don't worry about it, I mean it. Right now, talking like this, you can drop the formalities. Who is your general back in Alaster?"

"General Lance Richards."

"Lance! He made it to general already? Hah, he always said he would. Anyway, that's even better. Just pretend like I'm your general. Knowing how he was when training others, I'm sure he practices the right balance of respect and friendliness."

"Yes, sir." Jason smiled proudly.

"Thanks."

"For what?"

"Talking to you helped me calm down a bit."

"About the lady Iris . . . I heard some of the X32 soldiers talking as they passed by the tent Kyle is in. . . . They said something about Yansairens at the checkpoint?"

"They found a blade with the country's emblem."

"Why would Yansair attack a random checkpoint in Fitsengea?"

"How much of Iris's circumstances were you briefed on?"

"The lady Iris is the savior of our land against an unverified enemy, and I was to protect her at all costs, and—" Jason cut himself off, his face falling and shoulders sagging. "I failed."

Darren walked over to Jason and placed a reassuring hand on his shoulder. He thought about saying it wasn't the boy's fault, but he knew those words would sound empty. All he could do to encourage Jason was show him that he still needed his help.

"We'll get her back. I swear it."

Jason looked up at Darren, determination shining in his eyes, and nodded stiffly. Outside light poured into the tent as a figure pushed back the entrance flap and stepped in. Darren squinted. A slender woman with shoulder-length, curly blonde hair stood awkwardly before them.

"Marquis Turner, wasn't it?" she questioned as she played with her fingers.

Darren stepped forward, smiling gently. "You're the woman who created the Rayl."

A smile peeked through as she nodded.

"What can I do for you . . .?"

"Tess."

"Right, what can I do for you, Tess?"

"Your Grace, I have been asked to fetch you."

"Fetch me? Is it the transport master? Have they found something already?"

"No, Your Grace. I don't know who this man is. He approached me in the woods and asked for you by name. He refused to give his own for fear of being caught. I don't really know, but he seemed anxious."

Jason and Darren exchanged a look. "Did he say anything else?"

"He told me to tell you that if you came, he would help you get her back. . . . I'm assuming he means the Woman of Prophecy mentioned in the cave?"

Darren's stomach lept into his throat.

"Why didn't you go to the transport master with this information?" Jason interjected.

"To be honest, I don't know how dedicated the transport master is to helping you."

"Why are *you* so dedicated?"

Her expression was suddenly deadly as her accent lost its softness. "If I can help Fitsengea wake up and realize what Yansair really is, then that's all the motivation I need!"

Darren cringed inwardly, making a note to be careful around this woman. He stepped forward, eager to get back on topic. Any lead to finding Iris was worth following, no matter how suspicious a form it took.

"How do we find this man?"

Tess reverted to her previous soft demeanor. She began walking toward the mouth of the tent. "I will take you to him right now. He gave me instructions as to how to reach him."

"Wait," Jason called, halting Darren and Tess. "What about the soldiers set to guard you, Your Grace? It was hard enough for me to convince them to let me come see you. How will we convince them to let you go wandering through the woods?"

Tess smiled sweetly "I'll take care of it."

As they stepped outside, the two soldiers across the way tensed, watching their movements. Tess motioned for Darren and Jason to wait as she approached them. After a few moments of conversing, one of the men nodded. Tess turned back to Darren and Jason, indicating with her head for them to follow as she walked toward the woods. Darren and Jason fell in step behind her. Apparently, Tess held more clout with these people than Darren had given her credit for.

The trio attracted the uneasy gaze of nearly every person they passed while entering the forest. Darren's mind began to race as he pondered who exactly lay ahead of them. Past experiences screamed at him that this was some sort of trap. He was going to a secluded area to meet a man he knew nothing about. Doubly suspicious how he was anxious to keep his identity unknown. On top of that, this foreign woman he had met only hours prior was leading him. At least he had Jason at his side. That had to count for something, right?

Jason seemed reliable enough, but Darren really had no idea how the boy would handle himself in a dangerous situation. *The boy? Remember, Darren, he's only five years younger than you. But still, I've not known many twenty-year-olds capable of keeping their wits about them. Here's hoping Jason is an exception.* It struck Darren as comical how quickly he had aligned himself with Jason. Was he really so desperate for even the semblance of home that he'd been won by the words of a devout Alastrian soldier? Jason seemed sincere enough, but then again, Minister Teason had spoken with the same ease and conviction right after committing murder and treason. Only a man's actions mattered—they alone held the truth of his heart.

Shoes crunched through leaves fallen prematurely from the current dry spell, the only sound amidst the trio's silence. The thickness of the trees gave Darren a better inkling of how far away they actually were from the X32 checkpoint. All dense forest had been removed miles back to prevent any of nature's tampering along the transport roads. While these woods were still quite thick, Darren couldn't help but notice the prolonged drought was taking its toll. One errant campfire spark, with just the right amount of wind, would decimate this whole forest in mere hours.

From his tutelage as a boy, he recalled that these woods were coveted hunting grounds for fur traders, as the priceless Askgans called this land home. An Askgan pelt was softer than the finest silk sold in Myrn, with twice the warmth of typical wool. Thinking of that expensive material Darren's mind flashed back to the nights on the transport from Saunskirt.

Iris had loved the feel of the Askgan blanket under her fingers. She looked so sweet, yet fragile under the heftiness of the pelt. A small smile escaped from the corner of his mouth as he remembered their conversations under the stars. Fear surged through him at the thought of her seated in some cold, dark dungeon all alone. *She's tougher than she seems.* He tried to soothe himself. *After all she had been through . . . still she kept going, she's a fighter!* Ducking under a low-hanging branch as they rounded a bend on Tess's invisible path, Darren bit back a laugh, recalling how he and Iris first met. Oh yes, Iris was a fighter. Still, no one could fight forever. *Just hold on, Iris. I promise you, I'm coming!*

"We've been walking a good ways now," Jason said, breaking the silence. "Are you sure where you're going, or if we even *should* be going?"

Tess nodded and indicated a ring on her left forefinger. "Northeast is the direction he gave. We've only got twenty more paces to go."

Darren looked at her ring and noticed that it was actually a very small compass.

He raised an eyebrow at Jason, who mirrored his own growing disbelief. "Didn't you say, Tess, back at the camp—"

"*Way* back." Jason coughed under his breath.

"—that you had just been approached by this man? Shouldn't we have already crossed paths?"

"Why demand we come so far if he knows how urgent this is?" Jason added.

Tess stopped walking and looked at them. "He dashed off as soon as he spoke. Told me to meet him out here with you and then was gone."

"And you didn't find any of that questionable?" Darren asked in disbelief.

Tess merely shrugged while Jason and Darren stared at her. *She can't be serious!*

Tess turned around and started walking once more, calling over her shoulder, "Well, you gentlemen are out here of your own accord. If it seemed like such a bad idea, then why come along? Honestly, no one else seems to be doing anything about it, so what choice do we have?"

Jason and Darren eyed each other once more, both grim faced. Darren let out a sigh and continued following after Tess. Jason soon stepped in afterward, but not before muttering something about being the foolish soldier who got a marquis killed. They continued on in wary silence as their vigilance grew. Tess kept counting paces, strictly following her miniature compass.

"Three . . . two . . . and . . . one." Tess stopped and looked up. "This is it."

Darren let his gaze slowly scan the space before them. The three of them now stood at the edge of a large clearing in the woods. But he could see nothing in the expanse—no camp, no animals, and worse—no mysterious, information-bearing stranger.

"Oh!" Tess gasped, making Jason and Darren flinch. Tess's skin flushed in anger "Why, those good-for-nothing, robbing wretches!" Jutting her chin out in indignation, she began to strut out from the tree line.

Jason shot out his hand and grabbed her arm, jerking her back to them. "What are you doing? This is clearly a trap!" he hissed.

Tess turned to him, "Those murderous brutes ain't got but two brain cells to rub together! They have no right stealing his genius and using it for gods know what."

"What?" Jason whispered hoarsely.

Tess shook her arm out of his grasp. "They ain't got no right!" She spun to Darren, fire blazing in her eyes. "And they ain't going to keep it, either!"

Before offering an explanation, Tess took off into the clearing. Darren tried to go after her until Jason stepped in front of him.

"I'm sorry, sir, but it's just not wise. I—" Jason was cut off mid-thought by the hissing sound of an airlock opening.

Tess now stood halfway through the clearing, watching as what appeared to be a large door opened like a descending drawbridge. What the door was attached to, Darren couldn't see. It somehow floated in thin air, slowly tipping its way to the ground.

"Holy Father, You have got to be kidding me." Jason gaped and took a half step forward.

As the device continued, Darren finally caught on. "No . . . but . . . *how?*"

Lowering to the forest floor had not been a floating door but the gangway to a Yansairen airship. The vessel was made out of a reflective material that made it appear invisible from a distance. As Tess drew nearer, Darren caught sight of her reflection on its surface. His studies during his time under his uncle taught him of Yansair's attempt to build flying machines. His tutors had presented him with detailed drawings and designs. This thing was obviously theirs. But never had he thought the design would be successful . . . *and* made with the ability to camouflage itself.

As the vessel finally leveled with the ground, Darren caught sight of a tall male figure making his way casually down the gangway. The man, who appeared to be in his mid-thirties, held a hand to his eyes to look around. When the man's gaze settled on Tess, he lifted his head in recognition and made his way over, his long legs quickly closing the gap between them.

"Come on," Darren commanded Jason as he stepped out into the opening.

Jason followed, silently obedient, though Darren caught him flexing his hand by his side. He set his mouth into a grim line. Darren knew that gesture, and he too ached for some kind of weapon in his hand, anything to help them be better prepared. Tess held her ground in the center, arms crossed over her chest with her fingers tapping impatiently against her own skin. Meeting together at the same time, the three men exchanged furtive glances. The firm lines of the stranger's face, along with his short-cropped dark-brown hair and sparkling gray eyes, cast a faint recollection in Darren's mind. Did he know this man?

Clearing his throat gruffly the possible stranger spoke, eyes fixed on Darren. "Marquis Darren Turner, I am glad you came. You may not recall who I am, but we have met before. My name is Fredrick Maythan, lieutenant to Lord James Valomeer of Saunskirt."

Darren nodded as the memory surfaced. "Yes. We met you while boarding the transport from Saunskirt."

Suspicion quickly stole Darren's brief flash of calm. So Saunskirt *was* involved, as he had reluctantly deduced. Narrowing his eyes, Darren studied Fredrick for any signs of deception. "Tell me, why is the lieutenant of Lord Valomeer all the way out here, alone, with a Yansairen airship?"

"That is, if you truly *are* alone," Jason muttered, watching their surroundings.

Fredrick barely had the chance to open his mouth before Tess cut him off, blurting, "So who stole it? Who stole my grandpap's invention?" She jabbed her finger angrily into his shoulder. "Was it you people from Saunskirt? Your people have always been underhanded in trade relations! Or is that why you joined with Yansair? Gaining from their barbarian ways?"

Fredrick closed his mouth and tilted his head. "You already know of Saunskirt's treachery?"

Darren took a half step forward. "It's true? Valomeer has sold out his own nation?"

Darren cursed Valomeer's name as the betrayal hit him. Nodding, Fredrick's countenance turned into a mixture of grief and rage. He lifted his hands in an involuntary gesture of sincerity.

"I know I have no right to request your trust or belief," Fredrick said, "but I am doing what I can now to help the Woman of Prophecy. Which is what led me here to you."

Lifting his chin and narrowing his eyes, Jason spoke out, "How did you find us? How did you even know Marquis Turner was not only out here but attempting to help the Woman of Prophecy? If you not only knew the Lord Valomeer's intentions but were opposed to them, why have you not notified or warned anyone else? How do we know where *your* loyalties lie?"

"And why are you traveling in a Yansairen vessel?" Tess added.

Shifting his glance between Tess and Jason, Fredrick finally settled his increasingly intense gaze on Darren. "Your Grace, you and your comrades have every right to doubt and are wise to question me, but we haven't the time. I will explain further when we can afford the delay. We will save the Woman of Prophecy, I swear to you. But first, I need *your* help to save the children of Throansburrough and Jaralynx. I've done what I can to protect them, but I need others in order to successfully free them."

"Wait!" Darren balked, holding up a hand to interject as his heart raced with fearful hope. "The children are alive? Iris wasn't the only survivor?" Dashing his arm out, he grabbed Fredrick by the collar. "Where are they?"

Fredrick met Darren's eyes with steely determination. "They're being held at the abandoned X32 checkpoint, and if we don't rescue them soon, they *will* be sacrificed."

Chapter Four

The cold, stone, altar-like table sent icy shivers down Iris's back, which were worsened by the sweat rolling off her body from the room's growing heat. The pit of burning coals at the far corner perpetuated the room's uncomfortable hot air. Her arms and shoulders ached, being held for far too long stretched out above her head. Iris's long hair was matted by sweat in a tangled mess beneath her arms, with a number of errant strands clinging to her face. Her wrists were roughly bound together by an abrasive rope tied to a metal ring on the top side of the table, and her feet were pulled together and bound at the opposite end. Searing bursts of pain shot through Iris's torso as if she were being ripped in half. The pain was even worse around her injured ribs.

Exactly how I'm supposed to heal like this is beyond me! Iris gritted her teeth and took tentative breaths so as not to exacerbate her torment. Had she not known the edict passed by Yansair's king, she would have resigned herself to believing that she was about to become another tragic sacrifice to their All Seeing Eye. Still, their exact purpose for having her in this position right now she couldn't and didn't want to fathom. She had an inkling it had something to do with Valomeer's "death badge" on her chest, since she'd heard a lot of panicked whispering when they'd studied it and her other injuries.

Live, Iris, live. No matter what, you must live. Clenching her eyes shut, Iris prayed. *Honestly, Holy Father, if You hadn't personally commanded me to live, I would be begging for death right now. All these tormenting unknowns concerning the future are too much. I can't help but wonder if I really am Your chosen Woman of Prophecy. Am I really who You wanted for this, or did I just get this by default because I was the only one left standing? Holy Father, I know You hear me.*

Iris opened her eyes and looked at nothing in particular above her. "I know You hear me!" she whispered sharply through her pain. "You spoke to me before. Please, please come back. The-the peace You gave me on the stage, bring it back . . . please!" Tears welled up in Iris's eyes and escaped out the corners.

Pathetic, pitiful chosen one *you've turned out to be!* Iris mentally berated herself. *How fast I fall into despair! He spoke. You* heard *Him! Your whole life you longed to know His audible voice.*

"But Holy Father, my soul thirsts for more. Call me greedy—I know I am—but how else do You expect me to survive this?"

A tremble rippled through her body as more tears fell. The emptiness in her heart grew with the passing silence. And yet stubbornness sealed itself within her. She promised the Holy Father that she would live, and *never* would she go back on her word to Him. No matter what had happened to her in the past, she had never once turned her back on Him. She may have drawn back in her pursuit of Him, but never could she completely let go.

"Not even these Yansairen demons will tear me from You!" she spat out in bitter determination.

"My children."

The gentle rebuke stilled Iris's heart and mind. Her muscles tensed, bracing against an answer she didn't really want to hear.

"Y-your children?"

"Demons are here. They torment, kill, and steal. They

are spirits. But those people, they are my children. Call them as such. For as I love you, I love them."

Disgust swept over Iris's face "How can You love them? After all they've done?"

The words had no sooner slipped through her lips than Iris's heart flooded with guilt. She knew better. Had she not preached to Kyle, to Darren, to all the others about forgiving her family's murderers? Still, the thought of the Holy Father loving the people of Yansair as deeply as He loved her was both confusing and infuriating.

"***Iris, can you earn my love?***"

"I . . . uh . . . no."

"***Does anyone earn my love?***"

"No . . ." Iris spoke meekly, settling her eyes to the side.

"***My love, real love, is freely and sacrificially given. Whether my children love me back or not.***"

An invisible, cool touch gently wiped away the tears from both sides of Iris's face. Her heart quickened with love and longing for more of Him. *Forgive me?* Iris pleaded in her thoughts, unable to voice the words aloud.

Always. The Holy Father responded back clearly in her thoughts. Iris could sense His smile and kindness blanketing her mind. Taking as deep a breath as she could, she summoned every ounce of courage she possessed. She closed her eyes and focused on the memory of the Holy Father's loving touch on her cheek.

"How . . . What do You want me to do here, Holy Father? What . . ." She let out a sigh. "What do You want me to do . . . for Your Yansairen children?"

Strength wrapped itself around her as the Holy Father spoke with heart-melting tenderness and pained longing. "***Love them. Show them My love.***"

The Holy Father's longing for His lost children made Iris's own heart ache. He mourned for their souls, how could she not answer His plea? Heavy tears rolled from her eyes as a new desperation sprang to life within her. *But Holy Father, can it be done? Can Yansair be saved?*

A door creaked in the distance as a small burst of fresh air displaced the old, heated fog of the room. The sound of shuffling feet rattled off the stone, slightly muted by the decades of dirt and dust on the floor. Iris attempted to lift her head to see who her visitors were but was only able to crane her neck so far.

"There she is," rasped the voice of one of her guards. "Now get that thing off her chest!" the man commanded as he shoved an elderly gentleman to the side of the table.

Though tanned from time she could only assume spent working the fields, Iris noticed that this man's skin tone was quite different from the other Yansairens she'd seen up to this point. His was more reddish-brown instead of the pinkish undertone of the guard who stood behind him now. The man's white beard and hair stood in stark contrast to the rest of his body. Perhaps it was his hair falling in such disarray, surrounding various crinkles around his eyes and mouth that gave him the kindly air. But the dark-brown eyes that studied her also seemed to hold a note of compassion. Looking deeper into his eyes, Iris was almost shocked to see that the man's stare began to glisten. It felt like ages since she had seen such innocent vulnerability. Could she dare hope to find an ally in this man?

Licking dry lips and swallowing around his own emotions, the elderly man broke the awkwardness with a soft smile. "Hello, dear one. I am sorry we were not able to meet under better circumstances. Tell me, what is your name?"

Iris eyed him cautiously. *After all, this* could *still be some sort of ruse, whatever* that *might serve them.*

"I am Iris."

The old man opened his mouth to speak once more but was cut off by the impatient growl of the guard behind him. "Enough stalling, Hethers! This isn't a social visit. Fix her up and be done with it!"

Hethers stifled an annoyed sigh and spoke through a forced smile. "My apologies, sir, but a Saunskirt badge is not so easy to maneuver, and seeing as who lies before me is a young lady and not some wild beast, it would make the task much easier if I explained to Miss Iris what needs to happen next." Hethers turned his head as he continued to berate the soldier in a measured tone. "But by all means, lad, please feel free to rush it along. If you survive the lightning arcs from interfering with the badge too hastily, then you'll have to take the news to your witch woman that you caused the premature death of her grand sacrifice, forever dooming all of Yansair."

The severity of his voice made Iris quiver on the inside. The soldier coughed and muttered something about waiting outside. As the man exited and shut the door behind him, the air in the room stirred.

Hethers turned from the door and closed his eyes. "Patience, dear boy. Patience."

He exhaled and stood with his eyes closed for a moment. Iris watched as a smile crept up the corners of his mouth. *Who is this guy, Holy Father? And why does the name Hethers sound familiar to me? Can I trust this man? Should I trust him?* Flicking his eyes open, Hethers gave Iris a big grandfatherly smile and walked over to the end of the table where her hands were bound.

"Forgive me, dear Iris. I will only be able to undo the ropes for a short while. As frightened of you as they all are, they would surely put an end to both of us if they saw you unrestrained. Silly, really."

The tension on Iris's arms slackened, allowing her to lower her bound wrists to her chest. Hethers walked to the other end and freed her feet as well. He made his way to stand alongside her and gently helped her into a sitting position. Iris winced in pain at the movement but was distracted by the surprising strength this old man possessed.

Hethers clucked his tongue once Iris had been righted. "Shame. Normally we could get you healed up in no time. Though He does know best, doesn't He?" He smiled and patted her shoulder fondly. "Yes, my dear. You truly are something."

Iris gaped at him. "Who *are* you?"

"Name's Andrew. I'm the crazy old man the Holy Father sent to give you a bit of a hand."

Words flooded through Iris's mind, lighting up her memory. She let out a gasp "A.H. . . . *You're* A.H.? You're-you're Alaster's historian! It was *you*! *You* wrote the prophecy?"

Hethers chuckled. "Well, no, *I* didn't write the prophecy. I just reported it."

Iris shook her head, a little dazed. "Yes . . . that's right. I didn't mean . . . Why are you here? *How* did you get here?"

"Well," Hethers sighed, "once I couldn't convince King Zaerin how wrong Minister Teason was, I was imprisoned on charges of slander and conspiracy. After a short time, I caught wind of an assassination plot against me. With the help of the Holy Father and His children, I was able to escape both my death and my imprisonment. I gave up hope of anyone taking me seriously in Fitsengea, so I decided to try my luck in Yansair. I had hoped . . . that perhaps I could change their misguided thinking . . . their hateful ways. I fear instead I was only used to fuel the fire."

Terrible pain washed over Hethers's countenance, and his voice shook with remorse as he clasped Iris's hands in his own large, leathery fingers. "F-forgive me please, dear one. I am *so* sorry I failed you and your people. I would give *anything* to change what happened to you." Tears slipped out of his eyes. "The pain you've felt . . . the pain you still have yet to face . . . Holy Father never wanted this, you *must* know that!"

Tears brimming in her own eyes, Iris raised Hethers's hands to her lips and kissed them. "You were the only voice who fought for us. What is there to forgive?"

Iris's heart ached for the guilt this man had carried with him all this time. *But really what else could he have done?* By King Zaerin's own admission, Hethers had tried to fight, but he'd fallen from grace for opposing the king's favorites.

Hethers straightened as if a physical weight had been lifted off of him. He moved his right hand to pat Iris's and then let her hands go. He sucked in a deep breath and nodded, clearly resolving some hidden matter in his own mind. Iris watched him thoughtfully, still amazed she'd been led to none other than Andrew Hethers.

"So . . . what now?" Iris asked, raising both eyebrows.

"Now we ask for help from our Holy Wisdom as to how to get this badge off of you before it's too late." Grinning with a mixture of sympathy and guilt, Hethers pointed to the frayed and dingy collar of Iris's dress. "If you'll forgive me, my dear. I'm afraid we'll have to pull down the neckline a bit to get a better look. I swear I intend no impropriety."

She offered an understanding smile and nodded. Hethers gently pulled the fabric down a handspan and a half, revealing the gold-painted metal badge. The metal triangle had one curved side and two concave. The top point angled toward her shoulder, the center toward her left arm, and the final arced down. Between the bottom and midpoint rested a small teardrop-shaped crystal. Directly across the triangle, along the longest line, sat another crystal of the same shape and size. Inlaid in the center of the triangle was a third crystal, this one in a perfect spherical shape. Each small crystal was opaque white in the center and practically translucent around its perimeter. Hethers released a sigh, lowered his hand, and straightened.

Iris grimaced. "Bad news?"

Concern etched on his face, Hethers nodded. "I'm afraid so, my dear." He pointed to the badge. "I fear our time's much more limited than I'd hoped. The three crystals of Valomeer's golden badge have a three-pronged purpose. It is their reaction to the Smallman Mountain ore dust painted over the device which secures it to the victim's skin. These are the main reactors for the badge. They start off as a creamy, thick white color. Over time, the ore dust draws out a chemical from these crystals which will eventually charge up the device until it becomes critical, releasing a heart-stopping shock to the wearer. And thirdly, due to the discoloration of the crystals, it acts as an indicator to reveal how much time is left."

The blood drained from her face, and her body bobbled slightly as her balance suddenly vanished. She didn't want to ask, but she *had* to know. "How much time is left?"

"Just under four days. And only by the aid of our Holy Wisdom will I be able to stop it."

"But . . ." Iris fought to control her thoughts. "But I thought that's why you're here. Don't you know how to take this off?"

Hethers shook his head sadly. "I was pulled in here by reputation alone. The people of Diridos know me as the great Fiesian historian and therefore assume I have knowledge on all such things."

Iris blinked. "Diridos?"

"Oh yes, I'm sorry, my dear. Of course you wouldn't have been told where you are, aside from gathering what you could for yourself. Yes, this is Diridos, the capital of the Yansair kingdom. We are located about a week's ride from the boarder of Fitsengea."

Iris shook her head, confused. "But then how could I still have almost four days left? By all accounts, I should be dead already. Factoring in the travel time from X32 . . ."

"And you would be, had they not flown you here."

"Flown? Yansairens know how to fly?"

Hethers nodded. "They've been developing it for the past twenty years."

Iris sat dumbfounded for a second before she was able to respond. She let her eyes drop to her chest, remembering her limited time. "And you're sure there's nothing you can do?"

"My sweet girl, I would if I could. While I know much of nearly all the cities and villages of Fitsengea, the problem resides in the crystals. They are not ours. They are a well-guarded, secret substance from the northern country of Sylphaen."

Iris lifted her eyes. "Do you really think our Holy Wisdom will show you how to help me in time?"

Hethers clasped her hands in his. "We can only pray He does."

Holy Father, didn't You command me to live? So please, would You show us how to stop this?

Silence and emptiness met Iris's plea. She sucked in a quick breath through her nose as a terrifying revelation dawned on her. *He told me to live . . . but He never said for how long.*

The water pouches sloshed at Liam's side as he did his best to appear nonchalant while making his way to the cages. *Keep your eyes straight, determined yet casual. Don't draw attention to yourself.* This was his third trip back here on the same day. He might have been able to pass off the first two as orders, but even these soldiers knew suspicious behavior when they saw it. Yansairen soldiers never pitied their enemies. Any soldier who did was considered weak, and weakness sent one back as a slave. This was worse, though, for these prisoners were more than enemies—they were sacrificial offerings. To interfere with war offerings meant instant death to the offender, as well as any other males in their family line.

The Great Mother of Yansair had long deemed this a necessary precaution, because such vile, heathen ways were bound to be inherited traits. Or so the witch liked to claim. Liam knew the real reason, though. With the men out of the way, the women were left defenseless. Young girls of age would be forced into "preparatory battle duties" while older and younger ones would join the slave ranks. Liam's stomach churned at the thought of his oldest sisters being violated so. It was enough to make him want to turn back, but after all the professor had done for them, after all he had shown them, Liam knew this was right.

Besides, he had made sure to warn Sabene and Marcelle before he'd left. They knew what to do to protect themselves and their younger siblings if he failed here. *But you won't fail. You can't,* Liam commanded himself. He may only be sixteen years old, but he was the man of their home, and his brothers and sisters needed him.

The water thumped against Liam's legs once more, shifting his thoughts as the cages came into view. *These guys here need me right now.* Sweat glistened off his brow, making his curly dusty-blond hair stick to his head. This land wasn't as hot as Diridos, but it had a different kind of heat. The years of drought had left Diridos—and all of Yansair—with a dry heat. Liam had lived most of his life only knowing this sort of warmth. The drought had clearly been making its way into Fiesian lands as well, but the dampness in the air here remained, making every little bit of heat cling to one's body.

Sweeping his eyes left and right and doing his best to gauge the area unobtrusively, Liam took an arching path to the back side of the cages. Narrow black iron rods about seven feet high were planted firmly into the ground with barely enough room for a hand to fit through. The rods made two separate large circles. Inside both sat thirty children, all boys and all very tightly packed. The boys sat scrunched together, clearing at least two feet from the rim of the iron bars. Standing a few feet away from the rods, Liam gave a sharp whistle for the first circle.

At the sound, a thirteen-year-old boy stood up within the center of the large cluster. He glanced around before releasing two whistles of his own. Around the outer rim of boys, two more stood. Liam guessed they were both probably ten years old. The boys looked Liam in the eye and nodded. Liam responded in kind and untied two leather water pouches from underneath his oversized tunic. Grabbing one firmly in his right hand, he flung it over the top of the iron rods. Holding his breath as it flew, he watched it soar and then land squarely in the outstretched hands of one of the boys. The other children sitting closest to them released a collective sigh. As they exchanged relieved smiles, Liam nodded and made his way over to the next circle cage.

Two boys stood near the edge, and Liam tossed over the next water pouch. This time he waited as the boys produced two empty water skins and did their best to fling them back over to him. One cleared the cage with ease and plopped onto the dusty ground by Liam's feet. Liam picked it up and tucked it into the back of his pants underneath the tunic. The second one went up but lacked the same forceful throw as the first. Liam grimaced as the pouch skimmed the tops of the rods. The bag sizzled on impact then burnt to ash. The dust from what had once been a water skin flittered down forlornly. A few of the boys groaned but were quickly hushed by the others. The one who had made the failed throw looked near to tears. Liam gave him a kind look and did his best to silently convey to him that all was still well. The young boy took a deep breath and straightened his shoulders. Liam smiled and nodded.

Inside, he fumed at the rods. If only he could locate that negating rod! He knew he should have discovered it by now. Time was running out. If he couldn't grab it from wherever guardsman Ridin had stashed it, he could cause their whole plan to fall apart. These kids needed him. And worse, Fred was counting on him. If Fred came through before he was ready, Liam didn't even want to imagine the gruesome consequences.

Liam took a different path back into the main campgrounds. Guardsman Ridin's tent was at the center of the demolished X32 checkpoint. Weaving his way in an untraceable pattern, Liam finally arrived at Ridin's tent. He glanced up at the sky to take note of the position of the sun, just like Fred had taught him. Time was running out.

"Now or never," Liam whispered to himself and took a deep breath.

Peeking into the tent, he noted it was empty. Checking that no one was around, he swiftly ducked inside. *All right, Holy Father, now show me. Where did that slob Ridin hide it?*

Chapter Five

Fredrick, Jason, and Darren remained crouched behind the few errant boulders scattered across the land. Even though it was dark, they still preferred to utilize any extra cover afforded to them. Fredrick kept his eyeglass trained toward the pocket of bonfires glowing roughly two hundred feet in front of them. Glancing over his shoulder, Darren noted the eerily hidden flying vessel behind him. Tess had attempted to explain how this effect was achieved, but the complexity had been a bit too much for him to grasp. What he caught was that these machines nearly vanished when still, due to the outer metals' chameleon-like qualities, somehow achieved through a mixture of electricity and chemical compounds. It also retained a fairly silent flight capability. Under any other circumstances, Darren would have found this device remarkable. But knowing such a stealthy power was controlled by their enemies quickly uprooted the initial awe. *At least for tonight, it is our ally.*

"They're in position," Jason whispered as he looked up from the small communication crystal in his hand.

The crystal had been a dull, colorless rock only moments before but now glowed in a faint green hue. Tess had handed Jason a few of these special stones before parting from them at their initial meeting place. After listening to Fredrick's plea for aid, verifying his claims, and hearing his plan, Tess took it upon herself to speed back to the camp and enlist the help of others. The sight of the purple glow from Jason's crystal moments before proved her successful. Tess instructed Jason about the meanings behind each signal color. Purple meant aid was on its way, blue meant denial, green meant everything was ready, and red meant something had gone wrong.

Darren recalled being surprised, not at how Jason had stopped and prayed to his Holy Father that the red wouldn't appear, but at the fact that Fredrick had joined in. Apparently, Fredrick was also a Follower, alluding to some highly respected mentor of his who had directed him toward the very path they now stared down.

Darren looked at Fredrick. He knew he should harbor greater distrust toward a man willing to turn against his leaders in Saunskirt. It was rare for someone who had turned once to not turn again if a better offer appeared. Still, it made sense for Fredrick to be willing to stand against Valomeer if his original loyalties were rooted with Darren's uncle and the rest of Fitsengea. He knew it didn't matter if Fredrick would betray them later or not. What mattered was the fact that children from Throansburrough and Jaralynx were alive. Friends and family members of Iris may have survived. But if they didn't succeed tonight according to Fredrick's plan, these souls would be gone forever. Fredrick had told them he had a man on the inside at the soldiers' camp who would release the captives on his end, making it their job to take them the rest of the way to safety.

Several pops and explosions in the distance broke through the night's silence, and bursts of light penetrated the dark sky. Darren found himself transfixed by the show. He had heard of these "Night Lights" but had never seen them for himself. Shaking his head, Darren snapped back to attention as Fredrick straightened and began to make his way toward the remnants of the X32 checkpoint. Jason and Darren quietly followed while Darren kept his left hand on the sword Fredrick had lent him to prevent it from making any jostling noises.

A smile crept across his face as the thunder from the Night Lights continued. What a stroke of luck it was to have a Sylphaenian inventor like Tess on their side! Even better was the fact that she'd been able to salvage enough of her supplies to provide this brilliant distraction. *This sort of chance is enough to make a man wonder if someone is looking out for him.* Darren mused but quickly dismissed the notion.

Silently, the three men sped closer and closer to the bonfires. The cleared lands that made the transport roads possible allowed for a pitfall-free approach to the abandoned checkpoint—an invaluable route on such a dark night. But it also meant if things turned sideways, they had absolutely no cover to aid them in a hasty retreat. The heavy clouds created a moonless night. That had to serve as their cloak, because waiting for a more solid plan to form wasn't an option. According to Fredrick, the Yansairen soldiers stationed there would begin their ritual sacrifices in the morning. Everyone had been in agreement that no child's life could be considered expendable. They *had* to free them all tonight.

Coming within range of their target, Darren and the others slowed their approach. The sounds of the Night Lights continued to echo around them. Darren's eyes finally caught sight of what appeared to be two large, circular cages. Fredrick stopped abruptly, holding out his hand to signal the others to halt. After a second hurried motion, they all dropped to the ground.

Something was wrong.

Darren wanted to ask what it was, but with tension rippling like heat waves off of Fredrick, he knew they couldn't afford any noise right now. Jason lay in the dirt to Fredrick's left, Darren to his right, all three motionless and practically holding their breaths. Moving only his eyes, Darren caught sight of the problem—guards were patrolling the cages. There weren't supposed to be any guards. A sickening thought crossed Darren's mind. The very Night Lights that had made way for them to get this close had likely put the rest of the camp on high alert.

They had hoped the diversion would cause the Yansairens to be more flustered, but they'd made the grave mistake of misjudging their enemy. Darren's hand squeezed tighter around his sword. He looked over to Fredrick and Jason and gave them a stiff nod, which the other two reciprocated. All three men slowly advanced toward the soldiers. They were committed. They had to find a way to dispatch the guards and then make it to the captives. One mistake, one loud noise, and it would be three of them against at least a couple hundred men, if not more.

It's what she would have done.

Darren's heart beat faster as he thought of Iris. She would have never turned back, so neither would he. Darren would never be able to look Iris in the eye again if he didn't get these children out of here—*all* of them. Only a few more feet to go. Darren and his companions paused, quietly removing their weapons from their sheaths. They had to be quick, for every second counted. His swordplay skills were rusty, but Darren willed his muscles to remember. Closer and closer they crawled.

Adrenaline coursed through Darren's veins. It was now or never. He slowly drew himself up off the ground, making sure to stay low but freeing his body for the final run. He hoped with all his might there were only two guards. Darren took one final breath. *Boom!* A burst of fiery light erupted close to the center of the X32 checkpoint. The blast caused the guards to jump and spin toward the giant flame engulfing the sky. Darren quickly ducked down as he saw a figure running toward the two guards.

"Hurry! To the water! All men to put out the flames before they reach the full reserve!" The man barked the order in a ferocious tone, causing the guards to speed off to carry out his command.

As soon as the soldiers were out of sight, Darren, Jason, and Fredrick rushed the cages. The chaos from the inferno created enough noise that, coupled with the continued burst of Night Lights, they no longer had to fear being overheard. A mixture of hope and anguish struck Darren's heart as he approached the bars. Roughly thirty small, terrified souls sat huddled tightly together. They regarded him with wide, pleading eyes.

"Oh, Holy Father . . ." Jason whispered mournfully.

He stepped toward the iron rods and gently reached out a hand. The children stiffened and Fredrick shot his hand out and jerked Jason back.

"Don't!" Fredrick whispered.

Jason wrenched his arm from Fredrick. "The rods, they haven't been deactivated!" Fredrick explained. "One touch and you'll be killed instantly. If they were safe, the gate rods would be retracted."

Jason cleared his throat while Fredrick turned his attention back to the cage and called out to the children in a gruff whisper. "Hey, *psst*, hey! The lad who brings you water—anyone seen him recently?"

The children inside shuffled uncomfortably. Darren stepped forward, making sure to keep clear of the bars. "It's all right. We've come to rescue you," he called out to them.

Jason kneeled before the cage to echo Darren's sentiment. "Holy Father brought us here for you. He hasn't forgotten you."

The compassion and conviction in Jason's voice resonated through even Darren.

"We're gonna get you out, but I need you all to help us," Fredrick added. "The one who's been helping you. When did you last see him?"

Uneasy fidgeting rippled through the group until one brave voice managed to squeak out, "About an hour before sunset."

Fredrick nodded before turning away from the bars to look back over the fiery chaos in X32. Darren stepped up next to him so he could be heard, but not overheard by the children. "What do we do now?" he said. "Is there any other way to get the cages to open?"

Fredrick frowned. "Given our current position, the only way is with that negator rod. And seeing that Liam isn't here already . . ." He glanced back over his shoulder toward the captives and took a determined breath. "I'm going in to find him."

Darren looked toward X32, which swarmed with activity. The rush to put out the flames provided enough distraction to allow them to stand by the cages, but there was no way Fredrick could go searching for someone in the middle of all those soldiers and not be caught.

"You'll stand out like a sore thumb," Darren argued. "You'll never make it."

"We have no other choice. Neither you nor Jason knows what Liam looks like. Even if you *did* find him, he wouldn't trust you enough to work with you. This fire has been a godsend, but the time and cover it's brought is running out. I'm going." Fredrick moved to leave, but Darren caught him by the arm.

"We lose you, we lose our way out of here. Only you know how to fly that thing."

Fredrick shook him off and stepped forward. "So what are you suggesting? That we leave these boys here to *die* to save our own skins?"

Darren bristled. "I would *never* say that. What I'm saying is we need to think this through! Jason, back me up here." Darren flicked his gaze to Jason, who was still kneeling on the ground next to the bars. "Jason!"

Jason rose quickly and came to Darren's side. "Sorry, sir. I was speaking with the Holy Father."

"We don't have time for that sort of stuff right now," Darren snapped. "Your attention would be better served in helping us figure out what to do next."

"I already told you what must be done," Fredrick growled

"And I told you that's *not* happening!" Darren growled back

Jason cleared his throat. "I'm sorry, Your Grace? But like I said, I was speaking with the Holy Father, and I think He's told me what we're supposed to do."

Darren bit back an annoyed laugh. "Oh really, now?"

Jason simply nodded. "I believe He said we're to wait."

"Wait?" Darren echoed, incredulous.

"Yes, wait. Just a little longer."

Fredrick looked Jason in the eye. "You're certain? How do you know it was Him?"

"Because my heart knows His voice, but please check with Him yourself. You did ask Him what to do next, didn't you?" Jason replied matter-of-factly.

Fredrick closed his mouth. He let out a sigh and shut his eyes as well. Darren looked between the two men, feeling certain this was madness. *Well, at least it stopped Fredrick for the time being.* Opening his eyes once more, Fredrick looked back at Jason and offered a resigned nod.

"I'm not really sensing any obvious direction from the Holy Father at this point, but just in case you *are* right, I am willing to wait a few moments longer. If nothing happens after that, then I *must* go in after Liam."

Jason smiled. "Thank you."

Darren started to offer his own opinion on the matter when out of the corner of his eye he spotted a figure making their way toward them. It was a Yansairen soldier, moving away from the commotion within X32. Darren immediately pulled out his sword and indicated the approaching danger to Jason and Fredrick. Jason drew his weapon and moved into a ready stance next to Darren, but Fredrick's hands flew to his eyeglass for a closer look.

"Liam!" Fredrick gasped as his eyeglass settled on the figure staggering toward them. Putting the eyeglass away as quickly as he had retrieved it, Fredrick motioned to the others to follow him. "He's wounded."

Darren and Jason took off after Fredrick, both still unwilling to sheathe their blades. Reaching Liam's side a moment later, Fredrick put an arm around the boy's waist and draped Liam's arm around his neck to help him the rest of the way. Seeing how badly the boy struggled to carry his own weight, Darren sheathed his weapon and took up position on his other side. A knot formed in Darren's stomach at the sight of the severe wound on Liam's right side. The knot worsened as he realized how young this boy must be.

"The rod . . ." Liam groaned. "Take it. Release them."

Noting the metal bar sticking out of the bloodied sash around his waist, Fredrick grabbed the rod, motioned for Jason to take his place at Liam's side, and sprinted the rest of the way to the cages.

"You . . . need to help him." Liam spoke through gritted teeth.

Darren eyed Jason over the top of Liam's head as they made their way after Fredrick.

"We will, Liam. We're almost there," Darren said, trying to keep his voice calm.

"Either of you soldiers?" Liam pushed out, too drained to lift his head anymore.

"Yes, my friend. Save your strength." Jason spoke kindly.

Fredrick had already run off toward the second cage, using the rod to unlock it. Small boys of varying ages exited the first prison, looking at Darren and Jason as they made their way over with Liam.

"Then you know . . ." Liam said, "I'm not going to make it. I'll only slow you down."

Ignoring Liam's self-sacrificial plea, Darren called out to Jason, "Take the ones who are already free back to the extraction point. We'll follow as fast as we can."

"Sir . . ." Jason tried to protest, clearly uncomfortable with abandoning Darren.

"That's an order, Jason."

Jason nodded. "Yes, sir."

Gingerly shifting Liam more onto Darren, Jason took off toward the crowd. In a few moments, he'd gathered a few of the older boys to help him with the smallest children. Darren and Liam made it over just as Jason finished his instructions.

"With me at all times, boys. Anyone falls, help them up! Anyone lags behind, carry them if you must." Jason adjusted a small boy in his own arms. "Have courage. The Holy Father is with us!"

Hearing the Holy Father's name appeared to bolster some of them, made them stand a little taller. Jason glanced at Darren, who had stopped to rest with Liam. When Darren gave him a stern nod, Jason reciprocated.

"Let's go!" Jason cried.

Holding the child in his arms, Jason took off. He kept a quick but measured pace so the other children wouldn't fall behind.

"Please, sir . . ." Liam spoke once more. "Tell Fred . . . my sisters . . ."

"Call me Darren. And that's enough. You are *not* going to die here, understand?"

Darren noticed the sounds of the Night Lights had come to a stop. *Tess must have run out.* He glanced over his shoulder to see that the inferno was dying down. *We're running out of time!* Darren turned, glimpsing Fredrick through the darkness. He could see that more of the children had filed out of their prison, but he wasn't quite sure where Fredrick was in the midst of them. The children had begun to make their way back toward Fredrick's flying machine. Darren shifted Liam's position to strengthen his grip and began making his way forward to meet up with the others en route. Noticing the boy's breathing becoming more shallow, Darren feared the worst.

"Hey, you still with me, Liam?"

"Y-yeah . . ."

"Good. Now I need you to keep fighting, you understand? Because I'm bringing you with me no matter what. The job's not done yet, kid." Darren knew Liam was exhausted, but he had to give him a reason to survive.

"I . . . blew up . . . the camp. . . . What more do you . . . want?"

Darren smiled. "That was you?"

"N-needed . . . a distraction. Couldn't get . . . the rod."

Liam's legs crumpled so that Darren held the boy's full weight. "Whoa—hold on. I gotcha."

Darren gripped Liam tighter and paused, switching the boy around to his back. He kneeled slightly to better position Liam, then rose once more. Darren was surprised by Liam's weight. He must have had more muscle mass than he gave him credit for.

"Is that how you got hurt? The fire, I mean?"

Darren kept his posture tipped forward as he moved, knowing Liam wouldn't have enough grip strength to keep from sliding off.

"Ridin . . . caught me with . . . rod . . . fought. My first . . . kill."

Even through the exhausted delirium, Darren could sense Liam's despair. Darren's heart went out to the boy—to be so young and to carry such a burden.

"Can . . . Holy Father forgive . . . that?" Liam questioned.

"You were just doing what had to be done. If you hadn't, all those kids ahead of us . . . Well, now they get a future. No one can blame you for what happened."

"It's not man's opinion . . . that I'm . . . worried about . . ."

How was he supposed to answer that? *I'm the last person to turn to for the theology of Followers.* Darren scoffed inwardly. The Holy Father he knew of from boyhood was uncaring and judgmental. The Holy Father he'd come to know as an adult was nothing more than a political tool twisted by officials like Teason to guilt people into submission and support. Personal experience had taught him that faith in the idea of the Holy Father left one with only oneself to depend on in the end. Just look at Iris. What good ever came of her faith? Family and home gone, she herself kidnapped by murderous foreigners because of some writings from Followers hundreds of years ago. Why even care about what the Holy Father thought? And yet . . . *When it's all said and done, I bet she* still *won't turn her back on her beliefs.* Even in the middle of sorrow, anger, and confusion, Darren could see that relentless glimmer of love in Iris's eyes when her Holy Father came up in conversation. *And then there's people like Jason. . . . Come on, kid. Couldn't you have saved this question for* him?

"Liam?" Darren sucked in a few tired breaths, grateful to see they were finally nearing Fredrick and the others who were cramming themselves into the flying machine.

"Mmm . . ." Liam gave a weak grunt, no longer capable of forming words.

"Yes, Liam. . . . I'm sure the Holy Father can forgive you."

Whether it was doctrinally true or not, Darren didn't care. But he felt like it was something Jason or Iris would have said. As Darren and Liam finally made it up the gangway, Jason was quick to meet them and help the unconscious boy off Darren's back. Liam's skin had turned an ashy gray. Exchanging grim looks, Darren and Jason proceeded to carry his limp form inside. The doorway closed behind them and Darren found himself immediately pressed up against about sixty small bodies. They had barely been able to cram everyone inside. Jason and Darren had just enough space to kneel and lay Liam on the metal floor.

"And we're off!" Fredrick called out from somewhere above.

The engines fired up with a gentle whir, and the floor beneath them shifted as they ascended. Darren stroked a hand through Liam's sweat-soaked curls, the boy's body cold to the touch. His eyes roamed over to Jason, who sat opposite them with his head bowed in prayer as he kept his hand on Liam's leg. The quiet shuffling from the sea of faces caused Darren to turn his head. A few of the boys joined Jason in prayer, kneeling beside him. A longing pricked at Darren's heart. It had been a long time since he had wanted something to believe in as much as he did now.

Chapter Six

Another frustrated sigh bounced dully off the stone around Iris. It was the middle of the night, and no matter how hard Iris tried, she couldn't sleep. Her ribs ached in every position she turned. Not that there were many positions she could attempt while chained to the wall. Though maybe it wasn't so bad that she couldn't sleep, because any time she had, she only relived those horrid nightmares. *Too bad Darren's not here. Maybe I'd finally get a good rest then?* Iris joked sourly to herself. The thought of Darren brought a new onslaught of misery. *Please, please, Holy Father. Let him and all the others be all right.*

"Will I ever get to see him again, Father?" Iris whispered aloud.

Not if I die here. . . . Holy Father, please draw Darren to You. Let him commit to You again. Iris chuckled to herself as she realized how selfish those strains of thought seemed together.

"And no, Holy Father, not just because I want to be able to see him again. One way or another . . . he . . . Holy Father, he needs You more than he realizes or can admit."

He's not really that different than me in that way, I guess. A sad sigh slipped from Iris's lips. *Holy Father . . . thank You. . . . Thank You for the time You gave me with sweet old Hethers. Please . . . protect him. He's got to be in just as much danger here as I am. Holy Father . . . will I get to see him again? I truly hope so.*

It was *so* nice for her to have a companion, just one friendly and compassionate face to look upon. Her heart was in dire need of a friend. And she wasn't sure what it was exactly, but she had sensed in her far-too-brief encounter with Hethers that she still had much to learn from him.

A door in the distance creaked open, allowing dim light to bleed in from the torches lining the connecting hallway. Hurried footsteps descended into the dungeon cell. The flames of a few handheld torches cast an array of confusing shadows as Iris attempted to peer through the darkness and understand what was happening. *What could they possibly want at such a late hour?* A young soldier with long, braided black hair stepped forward and undid Iris's chains.

"Get up," he barked.

Iris moved to stand. Her slow motions apparently frustrated the soldier, because he didn't wait long before yanking her up the rest of the way. Iris gasped, her ribs burning.

"If you're supposed to be letting me heal, stunts like that won't do you any favors!" Iris snapped, her irritation too much to hold back any longer.

The soldier appeared as if he had just been slapped. He let his hand drop from Iris's arm and muttered an almost inaudible apology. Iris bit down on the inside of her bottom lip, willing herself to not spew the venom she was thinking. Iris and her entourage fell into an uneasy silence as they began their slow procession out of her cell.

She fumed inwardly, still having a hard time grasping this concept of how He could love these kinds of people. *You know, Holy Father, Your children can be real jerks sometimes!* A chuckle rippled through her spirit, catching her off guard. She could feel the Holy Father laughing. The side of her mouth curled into a smile in spite of herself.

"But what a beautiful opportunity to present them with Grace."

His thoughts in hers struck her so that she let out the slightest gasp. He was right, of course. How easy it had been to preach to others the importance of showing love, compassion, and gentleness to your enemies when her greatest enemy at the time had been none other than the town gossip, Emily, or the schoolhouse bullies from her youth. If the Holy Father's teachings couldn't be applied in any circumstance, then His words held no life, no truth. Iris could sense it even as she wound along the dim corridors. She had a choice. She'd reached a turning point in her thinking. She could remain reactionary and focused on these wrongs done to her, or she could embrace this "beautiful opportunity" to walk in His grace and gentleness. Iris took a slow breath, letting her shoulders drop as she released it.

Truly wonderful words with, of course, the perfect sentiment. Sarcasm bubbled around her thoughts. *You're right, You're always right. But Holy Father, I can't do this. Not without You. I need Your eyes. Your heart. I don't see them like You do, and I don't know how to make myself. Honestly, I don't know if I want to.* Rage and torment swirled within her chest, intense and sudden. Throansburrough lay before her mind's eye, and the screams of death echoed in her ears. *Julie, Dan, Mom, Dad, Lori, Jacob. . . .* Sweet memories flitted through her mind. Gathering at Mr. and Mrs. Zisken's for weekend meals, quiet nights of stargazing after the Grand Harvest Fest, teaching the Sacred Texts to the youth in the field on the outskirts of town. Everything that made up her life, made up who she was, gone.

Every time she thought her heart had a chance to breathe, reality promptly splintered it again. Those once-sweet memories were now tainted with the smoke of a burning village. And yet . . . Even here, even with this chaotic battle around her heart, she sensed the gentle whisper of the Holy Father's love. She didn't understand it, but did she really have to? *You're all I have left.* A tingling pressure brushed against her forehead followed by the flash of the thought of the Holy Father releasing a protective kiss upon her. Once more, the peace that sustained her within the judgment room filled her.

Winding up and out of the dungeons, Iris followed her guards.

They moved from one hallway to the next, the décor improving as they went. She recognized the area. If she recalled correctly, this was the same place that had led them into that hot hall before entering the judgment room. Iris groaned inwardly. She didn't want to have to endure another long meeting of chanting and yelling from a vast crowd. *Surely they wouldn't get up in the middle of the night for this, would they?* Much to her relief, instead of continuing straight, Iris's company swiftly turned to the left. As they walked, they came upon a pair of doors promptly opened for them by some attendants. Stepping through, Iris was hit with a gust of warm night air. A small gasp escaped her as she looked at the bright moon set within a star-studded sky. They walked down a path of open stone archways, offering her glimpses of the city between each one. Ahead of them stood a massive, regal-looking structure, its provocative intimidation radiating like a cloud around it.

Ornately carved marble doors came into view ahead. The guards in front of them drew open the heavy slabs as they approached. This place was far more opulent than the chambers she had previously frequented. Torches and stone lights kept most of the night's shadows at bay. *What are stone lights doing all the way out here?*

Stepping through the doors, an atmosphere of strength and reverence seemed to emanate from every surface. They were moving toward a source of great power, but instead of trembling under it as she might have, Iris was too distracted by the joyful anticipation the Holy Father infused into her. *Only You could find joy in this.* Iris smirked at Him.

"A beautiful opportunity."

All right, all right. I give. Whatever You want, Holy Father, I'll do it. Just show me how. Show me the hidden things.

Passing through a final set of doors, Iris's company entered a giant stone chamber. Carvings of people worshipping their eye symbol covered the marble pillars along the walls. *Throne room.* The thought lighted through Iris's mind. Peering between her guards, she could see a man and a woman on a slightly elevated platform at the end of the room. Though dressed in pricey linens that bettered her loftiest formal wear, the wrinkles and general disheveled appearance suggested they were in their bedclothes. The man paced in front of his throne as he watched them approach. The woman stayed seated on her adjoining throne, seemingly lost in thought as her gaze remained fixed off to the side. Both had beautiful, glossy-black, though slightly askew, hair, which seemed to be a dominant trait of the inhabitants of Diridos. The woman looked to be not many years Iris's senior while the agitated man seemed within his mid-forties. *The king and queen of Yansair called for me in the middle of the night? Why?*

Why wait after a couple days of imprisonment to suddenly call her up for presentation? Why would they disrupt their own sleep? Stopping at a space of maybe ten feet from the bottom step of the stage, Iris's group took hold of her arms and forced her into a kneeling position alongside them. She fought back a smirk as she noted the higher level of gentleness they used this time. Apparently for once, her quick tongue had done her some good.

"Great and honorable King Thaylos, we present to you the enemy of Yansair as per your bidding," the lead soldier announced as he kept his face to the floor.

Eyebrows knitting together in slight annoyance, Iris kept her head up and allowed her eyes to study the king. *Enemy of Yansair? I've done nothing wrong. If he intends to question me, he is going to be severely disappointed by how little I know.* Thaylos snapped his fingers and waved a hand curtly in the air, signaling the soldiers to take a step back from Iris. Anger pulsed from his black eyes as he stopped pacing and fixed his stance in front of her. *Why is he so mad?*

"Do you not see that you are defeated?" Thaylos's baritone boomed across the chamber.

Iris peeked to the right and left in confusion. Did he call her here to gloat?

"You can send no others! There is no one left but you. You are alone and pathetic. Your people were easily erased, and it took little to capture you." Thaylos pointed a finger at Iris as his voice rose louder. "You *dared* to stand against Yansair, but you failed!"

An image flashed through Iris's mind, smothering her rising anger. King Thaylos stood before her but transformed into a boy no bigger than little Jacob. His clothes swallowed him, weighing heavy on his shoulders. Wisps of darkness fluttered around his eyes and ears. Following the vision Iris saw this four-year-old little boy surrounded by darkness, completely abandoned by anyone who should have been there to tend him. She kneeled before the child as he began to wail. Her heart shuddered at his cries. She knew what it felt like to be alone, how it felt to be abandoned. She longed to comfort him. Reaching out her hand, the shadows strengthened into a furious wind that entrapped him. Little Thaylos screamed for help from inside the wind, terror and agony enveloping his pleas.

Iris tried to push back the winds to make it to him, but as she touched them, some of the shadows latched onto her hands, morphing into thick, sticky, black ooze. It began to creep up her arm, bringing a chill deep into her bones. The cold grew so strong that it began to burn. *Get off me!* Iris screamed at the darkness in her vision. *You're not mine!* Flicking her arm, she flung the ooze off onto the ground. It evaporated back into the wisps once more and rejoined the whirlwind torturing little Thaylos. *What is this stuff?* Iris questioned the vision. The image melted away, replaced with the full-grown King Thaylos of Yansair. He still bellowed about his and his kingdom's superiority and their unconquerable might from atop the dais.

Only a breath of time had elapsed. Though the image had left, the emotions lingered. King Thaylos was a tortured and lost soul—so small and alone. Iris felt sympathetic tears brimming in her eyes. *How could I find pity for him? Why should I care about the darkness that haunts him?* A loving rebuke floated across her shoulders. Iris physically sensed the Holy Father before He even spoke. Instantly, she knew she was connecting to *His* heart for Thaylos. *It's not pity. You genuinely ache for his pain. Holy Father, what was that black gunk around him?*

"Fear."

"What are you afraid of?" Iris spoke out loud without realizing it.

Thaylos cut off mid-sentence. Only the nervous shifting from onlookers broke the weighty silence. *Oh. Oh no!* Iris watched the king as his eyes grew wide with shock and slowly narrowed with loathing anger. *Stupid, stupid, stupid!* Iris chided herself. How could she have let those words slip out? Many mistook fear for weakness, and she could tell by his reaction that Thaylos was one of those people.

"You dare to cast a spell on me, witch?" Thaylos's venom-coated words spit back at Iris.

Did he seriously just call me a witch? Iris's indignation overturned any intimidation that should have been there. She locked eyes with the man that had destroyed her world. "I simply asked you a question, King Thaylos," Iris retorted coolly as boldness bubbled up within her.

The haunting screams of her home surfaced in her thoughts once more, bringing with them an anger she had fought so long to keep at bay.

"Experience has taught me, *sir*, that those who feel the need to forcefully cast an image of indestructibility only do so to cover their fear. And so I ask, Your Highness, what are you afraid of? As you so *compassionately* put it, there are no others. No one else from my village to fulfill your presumed prophecy of destruction. And here I sit, in your throne room, a trophy to the "unyielding might of Yansair," soon to die. So why drag me out of my cell in the middle of the night? Solely because you feel compelled to proclaim your strength, *prove* to me that you've won? No, it was fear that dragged you from the comfort of *your* bed!"

"Nightmares."

The Holy Father's whisper briskly broke through Iris's tirade. *Nightmares?*

"Queen Aaralee."

"Nightmares have been plaguing your queen?" Iris asked, her voice softening as the revelation slowly pieced together in her mind. Iris switched her gaze to the young queen, who shifted nervously. "The Holy Father has been speaking to you, hasn't He?"

"So you admit it!" Thaylos exploded in fury. "You have cast spells against my wife, the queen of Yansair! I demand you remove them at once!"

"Ask her."

Iris nervously obeyed, ignoring the king entirely. "Queen Aaralee, the Holy Father has commanded you to do something. What is that?"

Aaralee's eyes grew two sizes as she finally looked at Iris. She glanced at her husband, clearly not wanting to share. *So she hasn't told him yet.* Iris mused in surprise.

"How dare you address her directly. I have had enough of your attacks and your arrogance!" King Thaylos stormed off the dais toward one of the guards standing at attention. Snatching at the soldier's sheath, Thaylos drew his sword and spun back to Iris. "I don't care what the Great Mother counsels. I'm ending this now!"

Iris's heart tripled its speed as the king strode toward her. Her muscles tensed and her eyes closed reflexively as Thaylos lifted the blade above his head. *Holy Father!*

"My king, wait!" Queen Aaralee cried out, leaping from her chair.

Thaylos stood frozen in place, eyeing Iris with deep hatred. Moving gingerly to stand behind him, the queen attempted to reason with her husband.

"My king, you must not break your decree." She lowered her voice to hinder listening ears, though Iris caught each word. "You cannot give the Great Mother something to use against you."

Thaylos kept his glare fixed on Iris as he listened to his wife. Slowly, he brought the sword back down to his side. Iris felt the urging of the Holy Father to speak once more. *Seriously? You want me to press him* now? *He almost just took my head off!* The tightening in her stomach refused to relent. *Ok, ok! Fine!* Iris took a deep breath and concentrated heavily on keeping her voice calm.

"I am no witch, Your Highness. Nor do I have any desire for the destruction of you or your people. It is our Creator, the Holy Father, who has been calling your queen."

"You keep mentioning this 'Holy Father.' He is the main deity of you Fiesians, is he not?" King Thaylos questioned, reclaiming a stoic demeanor.

"The Holy Father is the one true God of all humanity, not just Fiesians." Seeing the king bristle at her declaration, Iris quickly added, "He calls you, Queen Aaralee, because He loves you." Iris balanced her gaze between the king and queen. "He loves all the people of Yansair. Your dreams are warnings, not curses. If you'll listen to Him, He will save this kingdom."

Queen Aaralee knit her brows together and pressed her lips into a thin line. It was clear that something Iris said struck a chord in the queen, but Her Majesty remained reluctant to voice the thoughts spinning through her head.

King Thaylos lifted his head proudly. "We do not bow to foreign gods."

No? Well, you sure get frightened by prophecies from them! Iris bit back the retort. King Thaylos turned to walk back up to his throne, and the queen quickly followed. Once she was seated next to him, Thaylos began to speak as he stroked the thick, black curls of his long beard.

"I have had enough of this for tonight. Our Great Mother will commune with the All Powerful Eye once more and break off your dream curses. You'll see. Your 'Father' is no match for the All Powerful Eye."

"Deceiver."

The anger the Holy Father harbored toward the name caused Iris to tremble in fear. She knew the Holy Father hated the Great Deceiver for how he hurt His children, but she had never *felt* His wrath like this before.

"Tell him, My beloved."

Iris cleared her throat to gain everyone's attention. "You may try, King Thaylos, but the Holy Father says the dreams will not stop. In fact, they will spread through the entire court. You will not escape them even in the waking hours. In two days, you will move me out of my cell."

"*Out!* Take her out! Back to her cell! We will hear no more of this!" the king shouted, pounding his fist on the arm of his chair.

Guards swooped in and picked Iris up off the floor. Though the swift movement caused her pain, she was grateful, for her legs had fallen asleep from kneeling for so long. Holding her firmly upright, the soldiers whisked Iris back to the dungeon, her feet barely touching the ground the whole way. Locking her back into her irons, the Yansairen soldiers left her to the darkness.

Iris sat in stunned silence as the latch on the door clicked into place. Her head spun and her heart thrummed in her ears. Slowly, her sight readjusted to the minimal light. Tears of overwhelming and conflicting emotions began to trickle down her face. Iris leaned her head back and let the tears flow in the quiet. The cool surface of the wall was oddly soothing. Iris closed her eyes and attempted to process the night's events.

"What was that!" she cried out in frustration.

"No, really, Holy Father, what *was* that? Why, why do I keep getting dragged through so much junk?" Iris snapped her eyes open and directed her complaints to the black void above her.

"I know You said I have to go back. At least I *think* You said I have to go back. . . . But do I *have* to? I don't want to face those people again." Her body began to tremble in response to her frayed nerves.

Iris put her head in her hands as well as the chains would allow and took a few deep breaths, trying her best to stop her shaking. She felt so fragile, so unsure. She had pushed too far back there. She had been so certain of her declaration while she'd spoken it. The words had seemed to flow directly through His mouth into hers, and yet . . . they *still* felt like they'd were completely from her at the same time!

"Why won't You speak to me audibly *all* the time?" Iris half lamented, half accused.

The image of King Thaylos raising the sword above her head echoed in her thoughts.

"I could have died!" Iris shouted.

Anger rose like a wave but subsided as quickly as it came. Iris flopped her head back and let out a defeated sigh. "But I didn't . . . I *should* be dead by now, a thousand times over. And yet . . ."

Tears filled her eyes once more as a wave of self-doubt and sorrow resurfaced. Lips quivering, she finally forced out a fearful whisper. "Why me . . ." Unable to speak around the constricting in her throat, Iris turned inward.

Why me, Holy Father? Of all people, why spare me? I'm not cut out for this! You speak over and over of loving these people. I tell You I will, but again and again I revert to anger. I'm not strong enough. . . . I'm not good enough. . . . Julie would have been so much better. . . . My people, their memory deserves better than me. . . . Iris's shoulders shook with her soft cries. She was so sick of being broken. She didn't want to cry anymore. She fought to calm herself down and hold it in. Still, the tears fell. *I can't even do this right!* Iris sneered at herself. The chaos of her emotions annoyed her. Finally, she gave up and just let herself weep. *Will the ache, the exhaustion, ever end? Will I ever* not *be a fool?*

Iris wasn't sure how much time had passed when her tears finally dried up. She felt drained in every possible way.

"Please . . ." she prayed to the Father once more. "Please, let what I told the king be true. And for once? Please . . . let me sleep without the nightmares."

Chapter Seven

"Oy! Sleeping like that is bound to put a hump in your back," Tess called out as she kicked Darren's outstretched foot.

Darren jerked his head up at the rude awakening. Grimacing, he attempted to rub the stiffness from his neck. He had spent the rest of the night sitting outside of Healer Markson's surgical tent waiting for a report on the brave young Liam. The healer still hated him enough to not allow him inside, but he wasn't going to let anyone drag him back to his "holding tent." It was sometime after dawn when Healer Markson had finished with Liam. Only time would tell if he would be strong enough to pull through. By all rights, Liam should have died on the trip back. It was a miracle he had survived as long as he had.

"You look like death," Tess declared as she plopped down in the dirt next to Darren. "And you smell pretty close to it too." She wrinkled her nose.

Darren chuckled as he rubbed his face, trying to wake himself up. "You're probably right." His smile slackened as he studied Tess's body language. "Bad morning, Tess?"

"It's that two-bit, slimy son of an alley cat! I'd like to take my crystals and shove them in his eye!"

Son of an alley cat? Must be a Sylphaenian thing.

"I'm guessing you mean Aiden?" Darren suggested, knowing that Tess, Fredrick, and Jason had been called away shortly before he had fallen asleep.

They'd been called in to report on their venture to X32. Darren had assumed that they hadn't requested his presence because he was still considered untrustworthy. That was fine by him. He had far more important things to do than put up with their political posturing.

"That spineless fool lets his counselors walk all over him," Tess fumed. "They're actually angry about all those poor boys you saved. Too many mouths to feed, not enough people or resources to look after them, it was an 'unsanctioned rescue plan,' blah blah blah."

"Wait. Unsanctioned?" Darren raised an eyebrow, suppressing a grin.

Tess shrugged. "So I told some soldiers that their dear checkpoint master had 'ordered' them to help me set off some Night Lights. They didn't ask, and I didn't have time to explain. Aiden's too sensitive about chain of command. You needed something done, so I got it done."

Darren looked at Tess. "Thank you for that, Tess. You've risked a lot for people you don't know. I owe you a great debt."

Tess waved him off. "It was the right thing to do."

The conversation ebbed as Tess's attention lingered on the people moving about the camp. It was midmorning now, and there was plenty of activity. Though technically hidden in the woods, the dry climate would quickly turn this clearing into dusty ground under the increased and condensed foot traffic. Dust meant a constant upkeep in washing and cleaning. Darren wondered how long the supplies might hold out for these people. Support from his uncle would soon become critical. With the Yansairens holding the checkpoint, and more than likely on high alert, hunting parties would have to be limited and cautious to not give their positions away.

"Any word on the kid?" Tess broke through the silence, keeping her eyes on some soldiers to their right.

Darren sighed. "He's still alive . . . by some miracle. The healer left for a break around dawn. She'll probably be back to check on him soon."

"You haven't been in to see for yourself?" she asked, still looking away.

Darren pointed at the men Tess was watching. "I'm not really a free man in this place."

Tess met Darren's gaze with a snarl. "What do they think you're going to do? Kill a kid you helped save in the first place?"

Darren shrugged and rolled his eyes. "Maybe they think I'll steal some of the medical supplies? At least I'm allowed outside."

"Of all the stupid—" Tess growled. "I am done with this Fiesian mess!"

Bemused, Darren cocked his head and watched as Tess jumped up. She brushed the dirt off of her clothes and straightened the tunic under her vest.

"And where are you off to?" he said.

Putting her hands on her hips, she nodded toward Darren's watch-dogs. "To do some *persuading*."

Darren smirked. "Good luck."

Tess nodded stiffly. As Darren watched her march over to the soldiers, his eyes caught on a friendly, though exhausted, face belonging to a man making his way around a nearby tent. Seeing it was Jason walking toward him, Darren smiled. Jason carried one small boy and was shadowed by four older ones. One of the boys was Kale, Rachel Markson's son. Noticing that the other children were the ones they had saved last night, Darren quickly rose to greet them.

"Morning, Mr. Turner!" Kale shouted as he waved at him. He jogged ahead of the others to reach Darren first. "I brought the guys with me to check on their friend, Liam. My mama said they should be resting, but they told me how could they rest when they gotta check on their friend? I mean, it makes sense to me, I'd want to know if my friend was okay or not too. I remember this one time when my pal Stevie got a cut on his finger from skinning a squirrel we caught this one time. And anyway, I felt real bad for him because he had to sit out the next trade's day fair. My mama said it was more because of him not listening than the cut, but still. Did you know he helped save their lives? The boy in the tent, not Stevie, I mean."

Darren fought back laughter. "Yes, Kale, I know."

"Oh yah! Well of course you know. You helped too! Ya know, Mr. Turner, I know my mama says you're bad news and all that, but I figure if you worked so hard to help my new friends here, then you can't be all that bad, right?"

Darren pressed his lips together, suppressing another chuckle at Kale's well-meaning enthusiasm. He reminded Darren of his younger brother, Mikkel, when he was that age. Patting Kale on the shoulder, Darren grinned. "I appreciate that, Kale."

"Good morning, Your Grace." Jason smiled through his weariness as he and his group caught up with Kale.

"Morning, Jason. Seems like you've acquired quite an assembly." Darren nodded to each of the boys, who stood fidgeting nervously in front of him.

"Your Grace, allow me to introduce Destin, Pace, and Jodie." Jason indicated each with his free hand. "As Kale mentioned, they were quite eager to check on Liam. Apparently, our friend in there did much more than just release them. He was their lifeline for quite a while."

The three older boys stood a little taller as Jason spoke of their savior. *Come on, kid. You have to pull through. Last thing these boys need is another heartbreak.* The squirming of the younger child caught Darren's eye. It appeared as if he was trying to burrow even deeper into Jason.

"And who's this handsome fellow?" Darren smiled at the child, trying to convey that he was safe.

Jason let out a nervous cough and grinned sheepishly. "This little guy is Jacob. He's kind of gravitated to me since I picked him up last night."

"He sure did get to squawking when he thought Mr. Jason wasn't gonna take him with us," Kale offered.

Darren chuckled. "You're a smart one, Jacob. Jason here makes for a great friend."

Jason's lips rose into a half-smile, and little Jacob finally moved his head enough to peek out at Darren. Darren's heart broke to see so much terror still clinging to his helpless face. Sympathy soon turned to visceral anger. *Animals! How can these Yansairens even dare to call themselves men? Attacking children, intending to use them as* sacrifices. *I swear, I'm going to murder every single one of those sons-of-Myrn.*

"All right, guys! Let's get inside," Kale shouted. "You can help me check his wound, and maybe we can see if he can drink some water yet. Mama taught me a lot about wound care, and since she split up her helpers between the other camp, that means I get to do a lot more helping." Kale continued to chatter as he led Destin and Pace inside.

Jodie hung back a step, "U-um . . . Your Grace?" he forced out as he played with his fingers, unable to look Darren in the eye.

Darren could sense a mixture of shame and unworthiness emanating from Jodie as he inwardly debated whether to continue speaking. Darren knew those feelings all too well. He took a knee to move into Jodie's line of sight. "Jodie, son, you lads have seen more than I can imagine, and last night you all showed a kind of courage that men twice your age aspire to. As far as I'm concerned, we're brothers-in-arms now."

Jodie slowly lifted his head, his face flushed. His eyes still couldn't quite meet Darren's.

"Brothers don't need titles, Jodie," Darren continued. "Please, call me Darren. And you're always welcome to speak freely with me."

Angry tears welled up in Jodie's eyes as he finally connected with Darren. "I watched them do it, Mr. Darren. I saw them turn my family to ash! I saw-I saw them take Sigmund. I saw them wipe out Jaralynx." Hot tears fell heavily down his face. "I t-tried to get us out. To get help. But I failed. I got Marcus killed because I was *stupid!*"

Darren and Jason exchanged concerned expressions. Jodie clenched his fists, his tears mixing with snot as he continued to break down. "I couldn't stop them. I couldn't keep us together. Please, please, sir! You have to save the girls! You have to bring them back!"

Darren's heart skipped a beat. "Girls?"

"Th-they separated us, put them on a flying machine." Fierce determination smothered Jodie's sorrow. "Promise me you'll save them! Promise you and your men will bring them back."

Stunned and unsure of how else to respond, Darren gently grabbed hold of Jodie's shoulder and drew him into a firm hug. The grip caused Jodie to lose all restraint as he buried his face in Darren's chest and bellowed his sobs. Darren wrapped his arms around him tighter, tears welling up in his own eyes.

Choking past the lump in his throat, he responded, "I promise. Okay, Jodie? You hear me? I promise you, we'll get them back."

Yansair, I'm going to make sure you burn for the torment you've caused.

Darren maintained his hold on Jodie until the boy's sobs and shaking lessened. He nodded to Jason, letting him know he was okay to go inside the tent to check on how the other boys were doing. As Jodie quieted and began breathing in a normal rhythm again, Darren felt a gentle touch on his shoulder. Glancing out of the corner of his eye, he saw Tess leaning over them. She looked at Jodie compassionately.

"Hey, hun, how about you and me go grab some food for you and the fellas in there?" she asked, indicating the tent behind them with a nod. "I know you boys probably haven't had breakfast yet. Am I right?"

Jodie lifted his eyes to Tess. He took a step back from Darren, wiped his face on the edge of his shirt, and took a deep breath. "No, ma'am, we haven't."

"Well, that just won't do." Tess smiled. "Come along, now, and help me carry back some portions worthy of heroes like you," she said, reaching out her hand.

Jodie scrunched his face. "I'm no hero."

Tess shook her head. "Real heroes rarely see themselves as such. But, hun, I was listening to what you were telling the marquis here, and trust me, you're the real thing."

"How?" Jodie cried out.

"Come give me a hand and I'll prove it to you." Tess winked.

After chewing his lip for a moment, Jodie finally took Tess's hand. As the two began walking away, Tess called out over her shoulder. "Oh, and, Your Grace? Your watchmen say you're free to go in and see Liam now."

"Thank you, Tess," Darren called back.

Tess simply raised a hand as she and her little companion made their way toward the food storage. Darren smiled to himself as he watched them go. *That Tess sure is an interesting character.* Darren pushed off his knee as he rose stiffly from the ground. It wasn't until he was standing that he noticed the number of people whose attention had been drawn in by their little exchange. *Great. More scrutinizing eyes.* Thankful for the chance to escape the stares, Darren quickly ducked into the surgical tent, nearly bowling Kale over upon entering.

"There you are!" Kale cried in a hoarse whisper. "We were wondering what happened." Peeking around Darren, he asked, "Where's Jodie? He change his mind?"

Darren stooped a little so he could whisper and still be heard. "Jodie has gone to get some food for you guys. He'll be back soon."

"Aw, what a great guy," Kale beamed. "Well, he can join us when he gets here."

Grabbing Darren by the hand, Kale dragged him over to where the others were kneeling around Liam's cot. A tiny bit of pressure lifted from Darren's heart at the sight of Liam, for some of the color had returned to his skin. A tug from Kale's hand indicated to Darren that he should kneel alongside them. Once on the ground, Kale explained in his not-so-quiet whisper. "We're all gonna pray for him now. Mr. Jason told us when more of us pray together, it makes our words stronger."

"Something like that," Jason chuckled from the other side.

Darren noted how even little Jacob positioned himself like the others, though he made sure to keep himself joined at the hip with Jason.

"All right, guys." Jason began softly directing the group. "I want you to gently put your hands on Liam as we pray. Just like we did last night." Jason nodded to Pace and Destin, who reciprocated.

Everyone save Darren immediately and solemnly obeyed Jason's instructions. Darren hesitated, battling with himself. He didn't believe in the Holy Father, but he wasn't calloused enough to steal hope from the others that a divine intervention might take place. Still, it didn't seem right for him to join in. He felt like he might mess things up. Darren didn't get to contemplate for long as a small elbow prodded him in the side. Kale motioned with his head, indicating he expected Darren to follow suit.

"C'mon, we gotta help. For Liam," Kale whispered.

"I—" Darren swallowed his rebuttal as he caught the gazes of the rest, all waiting for him.

Giving in, Darren put his hand on Liam's arm. He glanced over at Jason, who passed along an understanding and apologetic smile.

"Now, while I'm praying out loud, I want you boys to be agreeing and calling on the Holy Father and Holy Beloved's name. If at any time you feel like He's given you something to share, please do."

Each boy nodded reverently and closed his eyes as Jason began.

"Holy Father, we praise You for Your goodness. We thank You for Your love and Your kindness. Your Sacred Texts teach us that where an assembly gathers in Your name, Your presence arrives. So we praise You for Your presence. We call on the name of the Holy Beloved. In Your name, we declare healing life flow through Liam now. Holy Wisdom, release Your power, and flow through us, please. We agree with the authority You have given us through the name of Holy Beloved, and we declare that Liam's body be restored."

Darren's eyes danced around the circle, watching as the children agreed with each word Jason spoke. He saw Jacob peek his eyes open a couple times to make sure he was mimicking Jason well enough. With each glance, he'd scoot even closer to Jason's side. Moving his gaze down to Liam, Darren stared at his motionless, young face. The only stirring came from the slow rise and fall of Liam's chest. *Maybe . . . maybe this will work?* Darren thought as he watched. *Maybe it* was *their prayers on the flight back that sustained Liam enough to survive the trip to camp? Maybe . . .* Darren fought back a scoff and shook his head. *Who am I kidding? Prayers didn't help Marriam. They didn't save Throansburrough . . . And no divine power protected Iris. If you were truly the good god they say you are, surely you would have done some-thing. Iris's torment proves you don't exist.*

Anger and sorrow tumbled together through Darren's heart. Why was he even in this tent? Shouldn't he be forcing Fredrick to take him on his vessel and find a way to get Iris back? What did he hope to accomplish here? Why did he feel so responsible for this young Yansairen soldier? *Because maybe I'm partly to blame. . . . This whole conflict with Yansair, if I hadn't run away, I might have been around to help convince Uncle to do something, to believe Professor! I should have exposed Teason when I had the chance.* Darren blinked a couple of times as an overwhelming wave of shame crashed in on him. *Cowards destroy kingdoms. . . . That's what you said, right, Professor?* Self-hatred doubled in size as he sat there listening to Jason passionately call out to his god.

Darren couldn't take it anymore. He couldn't just sit by and watch others pray. He needed to *do* something. *Coward no longer. It's time to act!* Darren lifted his hand and backed away from the group. Just as he turned around, he heard a slight gasp that made him stop. Looking back, he saw Pace staring wide-eyed at Liam.

"What is it, Pace?" Jason questioned.

"He-he moved!"

"What? No way!" Kale bounced up. "I don't see anything." He pouted, inspecting Liam.

"I'm not lying! He moved. His fingers flinched!" Pace retorted indignantly.

Everyone watched intently now. The tent grew deathly quiet. Sounds from outside began drifting in, while all those inside seemed to be holding their breath.

"Please, Holy Father," Jason whispered.

Another gasp sounded. This time, Darren could see the slightest movement of Liam's fingers on the left side. He watched in awe, sweeping his gaze up to Liam's face. Slowly, the boy's eyelids began to flutter. *There's no way . . .*

"It worked!" Kale whooped, jumping up and dancing around. "You were right, Mr. Jason! You were right! Praying worked!"

Darren froze in astonishment, watching as the boy who should have died last night slowly opened his eyes.

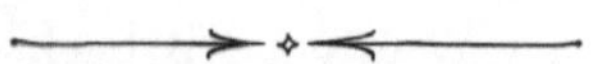

A soft breeze wafted through the open tent flap as the visitor stepped inside. The cool air was a welcome change from the growing heat of midday. Taking a deep breath, Kyle forced his eyes open and painfully shifted from his stomach to lie partially on his side to greet the newcomer. He couldn't help but let a half-smile slip when he saw it was Jason yet again.

"You really need to make more friends," he stated sarcastically.

Jason chuckled as he passed off a canteen of water and some bread to Kyle. "Oh, so are we finally friends now?"

Wincing as he lifted the water to his lips, Kyle forced down a few gulps. Following up with a few bites of the bread, he passed both items back to Jason, already exhausted from the effort. Resting his head again, he was finally able to smirk back at Jason. "Only a fool tells the man in charge of his food that they aren't friends."

Jason sat down on the vacant cot across from Kyle. Wearing that same annoying concern on his face, he studied his second cousin. "Pain any better today?"

Kyle let out a frustrated sigh. "Jason, stop using the kid gloves. This is the best I've been able to hold a conversation so far. Let's not waste what little strength I have on pity."

Jason shifted, clearly uncomfortable. "The healer said it was best to not stress you."

"You not wanting to stress me *is* what's stressing me," Kyle growled.

Jason scrunched his eyebrows and chewed the inside of his bottom lip for a second. "Well, you know about the wreck and where we are. . . . I don't think anyone's mentioned to you yet about Lady Iris's fate."

"What do you mean by her *fate*?" Kyle interjected, swiveling his head too quickly. Pain burst through him, forcing him back down.

"See? Healer Markson was right," Jason fretted.

"Boy, you better stop sidestepping the truth before I make you need that cot you're sitting on." Kyle's acid tone threatened.

"I'm only like seven years younger than you," Jason muttered to himself. "Fine, fine! What I meant by *fate* was that Lady Iris has been kidnapped by the Yansairens. We know for sure now that it is Yansair who has instigated all of this. Last night we rescued children who survived the massacres, and now we're preparing to sneak into Yansair to save Lady Iris. We plan to leave tonight."

Blinking a few times, Kyle fought to process through all the events and the emotions that now rolled inside of him. "Who do you mean by 'we'? And how exactly are you getting to Yansair?"

"Myself, Marquis Turner, and Mr. Fredrick Maythan. Fred has *acquired* one of Yansair's flying vessels, and we're going to use it as our cover."

Kyle stayed quiet for a minute. "Take Bryant too."

"I-I guess we could?" Jason cocked an eyebrow.

"Darren is an okay fighter, and I haven't seen you in action, but I assume you're fair enough, being an Alastrian soldier. Still, your age makes me suspicious of your experience. And I don't know this *Fred* guy." Kyle paused for a minute to catch his breath. "Bryant may be an idiot, but he's a brute and he has experience."

Jason pressed his lips together.

Kyle smirked at him. "You don't have to like a man for him to be useful."

"I don't believe the marquis would approve—"

"You can tell *Darren* that if he actually cares for Iris, he'll take all the help he can get!" Kyle snapped. With a devilish smile, he added, "And if that doesn't work, tell him it's my dying request."

Jason stared at him. "You're not dying."

Kyle closed his eyes, willing himself the ability to continue this conversation. He could feel his strength ebbing once again. His body hurt so much it made him nauseous. He feared losing the few bites of bread he'd been able to force down.

"Kyle? What are you not telling me?" Concern laced Jason's voice.

"Apparently there's an infection. Healer lady wasn't too hopeful."

"But . . . I thought . . . When I checked on you yesterday, she said waking up was a good sign."

"Prognosis changed this morning. Overheard her talking to herself."

"But . . ."

Kyle could hear the thoughts spinning in Jason's head.

"Surely an infection can't kill you?"

"Jason, she's run out of supplies, and she's stretched too thin," Kyle answered calmly.

Both men let silence settle in around them. Kyle didn't want to die, but he knew that when a healer held *that* expression on their face, it was time to get your affairs in order. Hearing Jason's cot creak, Kyle peeked open an eye to watch the man stand up. It honestly surprised him how heavily this news seemed to weigh on Jason.

"I . . . should probably go report in with Marquis Turner. You should get some more rest."

Kyle closed his eye again and gave Jason a wry smile. "Make sure to tell Darren the good news. He could probably use some cheering up."

Jason stopped in his tracks. "I've already witnessed one miracle today. I'm counting on Holy Father to make you the second, Kyle Druthers."

Darkness rapidly swallowed up Kyle's thoughts, and his breathing began to slow, but stubbornness demanded he have the last word. "You just make sure to get Iris back."

"Don't you worry. The Holy Father and I are quite the multi-taskers."

Chapter Eight

"What sort of a weak man cannot force his men to obey him?" King Thaylos bellowed from his private study.

Aaralee sat just outside the door on an elaborately embroidered love seat, her fingers mindlessly playing with the gauze embellishments of her deep-red gown. Ever since two of her attendants had come down with the prisoner's day terrors, the king had demanded they double their sessions with the Great Mother. And so she waited dutifully to accompany him to their next meeting. Though she did not intend to eavesdrop on her husband, his increased outbursts were becoming impossible to ignore. She knew he would likely share the outcome of this conversation with her anyway, but she preferred that he could do so on his own terms.

"I care not *how* you do it. Just get it done!"

Thaylos flung open the door, stormed out, and began pacing in front of the queen. Aaralee stood and softly closed the door behind him after glancing back into the room to see as the light from the Rayl cut off. Stilling her own thoughts, Aaralee adopted a gentle expression, hoping to somehow soothe the king's unrest. Remaining silent, she waited for him to address her first.

"By the Eye, I should know better than to trust heathens." Thaylos gesticulated to the sky. Stopping mid-stride, he looked to Aaralee and shook his finger. "The Great Mother warned me they were a foolish people."

Though it was also Caroline's *idea to align ourselves with those foolish people in the first place.* But Aaralee thought better of picking at the Great Mother's flaws and kept her stillness.

"That decrepit *creature* had the *nerve* to claim the badge wasn't an act of betrayal. He claims it would take at *least* three days to send word of the official removal process. If we didn't need access to the roads, I'd say we should not only cut ties with that dirty profiteer of his but have my men show him what it means to cross Yansair!" Finally taking a breath, Thaylos balled his fists against his hips and addressed his queen. "Is the Eye punishing me?"

Aaralee's eyebrows knit in concern. "My king, you were only thinking of your people. We agree that Saunskirt's claim of letting the prisoner meet with their king to ensure her identity was a ruse, a play for power. Intercepting the party and bringing her back here was the only way you could be certain her powers wouldn't grow, to ensure she'd be lost to her homeland forever. How could our All Powerful Eye fault you for any of that?"

Thaylos crossed his arms. "And our Great Mother had been *so* sure that Hethers would have the answers."

Hands folded in front of her, Aaralee felt distant from her husband. "The Eye sees all, my king. I am sure you will find a way," she encouraged softly.

Thaylos moved his hand to rest a knuckle against his upper lip, his sight escaping to some unseen horizon, calculating. "It *is* possible that Hethers is merely stalling for some reason."

Aaralee simply dipped her head in reserved agreement. She shamed herself for not being able to read her king more deeply. Five years of marriage and she still had so much to learn. Lowering her honey-brown eyes, she laid her hands gently upon her abdomen. *That isn't the only place you've failed your husband.* A wave of fresh sorrow surprised her, making her vision blur.

A strong forefinger and thumb raised her chin, causing a tear to escape down her cheek. Thaylos locked eyes with hers. He stroked her face softly with his thumb. Then, using his free hand, he grasped onto one of her small, delicate ones and raised it to his lips. Aaralee couldn't help but nuzzle into his touch as another small tear traced down her face. Lowering her hand and releasing her chin, Thaylos straightened once more, a stern cloud resting again on his features.

"Come, it is time for us to convene with our Great Mother."

"Yes, my king." Aaralee bobbed her head respectfully and followed a step behind her husband.

She was meant to support and encourage *him*, not the other way around. What a truly disappointing queen she was turning out to be.

The scraping of the metal latch being dragged across the solid wood door angrily echoed off the barren walls. *Either it's time for another health treatment, or it's time to eat,* Iris thought, peering through the shadows. It was difficult to tell how many hours had passed, let alone the time of day. She found herself looking forward to any opportunity to be freed from her chains. Shadows shaped like men appeared in the doorway, and one person was pushed hurriedly through. As soon as his foot hit the first step, the door slammed shut behind him. Iris perked up when she finally recognized her visitor.

"Mr. Hethers!" She smiled widely at her sole friend in Diridos. "To what do I owe this precious visit?"

Hethers chuckled as he patted the top of Iris's head. "Hello, my dear. Faring well, I hope?"

"As best as I can, I suppose?" Iris tried to force a lightness into her tone to mask the weight on her heart.

Moving in front of her, Hethers slowly sat on the ground. "Still fighting for optimism. Glad to hear that." Once situated, he looked back up at Iris, playfulness hinted in his tone "I'm told you've been quite busy, little one."

Iris tilted her head. "If by busy you mean trying to find a position that doesn't ache, then sure."

"Hah! You have no idea, do you?" Hethers bubbled with glee. "My dear girl, you have put the entire kingdom in an uproar."

Iris made a face. "How?"

"Ever since your late-night proclamation to the king, members of the royal court have been plagued with visions. They started last night and have begun to affect some during the day. Their Majesties are growing concerned, as it's interfering with the duties of the royal guards."

Iris gaped, stunned into silence.

Laughing, Hethers teased, "It appears that our Woman of Prophecy is surprised by her own power."

"No, I-it's just-I mean . . . Really? I was right? It *was* Him. But I-no. Wait, what power?"

Hethers threw his head back in uncontrolled laughter. Iris waited for him to quiet down, hoping he would help her make sense of all this.

"My dear girl, don't you see the beauty in this? How precious that our Holy Father chooses to partner with us! Our loving Holy Wisdom is moving through *you*, my dear. When you come into agreement with His will, such as you did making that declaration last night, you are able to walk more fully in your authority within the unseen realm!"

"My . . . authority?"

"Surely you know the Sacred Texts? For He has made us coheirs . . . ?"

Iris's eyes widened as she quoted the passage. "By His sacrifice, we are called sons and daughters, kings and queens of His court. For He has made us coheirs and co-laborers in the unseen realms." Iris paused, mulling over the implications. "But I . . . . Mr. Hethers, I doubted. I wasn't even sure if I was speaking the truth. And what's worse, I was angry at them. I was fed up with the king even though the Holy Father has told me again and again to love them as He does.

Why would He use me in such a miraculous way when I can't even obey Him?"

Hethers's eyes softened with empathy as he listened. She felt silly divulging her soul to another stranger. *Just like I did with Peter from the church council.* But too much pressure had built up inside of her. She had to let it out.

"And . . . And I'm sorry to be unloading this on you, but aside from partial conversations with the Holy Father, I haven't had much opportunity to connect with others down here." Iris grimaced.

Hethers shook his head. "It's quite all right. Please continue."

Tears stung the corners of her eyes as Iris fought for control over her emotions. "Why me? Why use me? Mr. Hethers, there were so many more wonderful and amazing people from my home, my own family! I *know* I'm not the best choice. Perhaps I was simply the last choice? But still, how can I do this? How do you love and save a people who murdered everyone you loved? And what do I know of royal courts or kingdom politics! If my declarations carry so much tangible power, how can I be certain I won't screw it up and misuse it? I could hurt innocent people. But also, if what you say about my authority is true, why has it only manifested now? I could have really used some of this a week ago. My goodness, none of this is even going to matter in a few days, because apparently my heart is going to be stopped by this stupid device put on me. Mind you, that was one of those times I could have used the Holy Father's intervention." Iris dropped her head in her hands, trying to breathe deeply and slow the pulsing of her heart. "I'm sorry . . . I just . . . I just don't understand," she whispered.

"Do you know how I came to be in this cell with you today, sweet Iris?" Hethers questioned gently.

She shook her head. "No."

Hethers's mouth tipped into a half-smile. "The king and queen of Yansair thought I might be able to convince you to lift this so-called curse. Do you know why?" Again she shook her head. "Neither do I," he chuckled. "What I *do* know is that the Holy Father, in His infinite wisdom and creativity, has used their fear to give us a way to encourage one another. Our true enemy, dear one, is the Great Deceiver and his dark minions. I am sure you know this. And while he fights for our death and destruction, our Holy Father will always find a way to divert his schemes to make way for *His* goodness. But do you know what has been one of the most successful schemes of the enemy?"

Iris peeked up at Hethers, her curiosity winning out over her brokenness.

"The grand lies that destroy our sense of identity, sealing away our access to our authority." Hethers shifted forward to clasp hold of one of Iris's hands. "Sweet Iris, every Follower has been granted access to move in the very sort of things you did last night, but so very few understand their true authority. The deeper we understand, the more we embrace who the Father says we are, the more opportunities we have to partner with Him to release His wonders."

"Have you . . . released His wonders before?" Iris furrowed her eyebrows as she studied him.

Hethers smiled. "Yes. Not to the same degree as you, but I have experienced the working of His miracles."

Iris frowned, chewing on the inside of her lip as her mind tried to dissect everything. She still didn't feel worthy.

"The Holy Father trusts you, Iris." Hethers spoke with loving sternness. "You have to choose whether you'll trust Him back. Whether you will believe what He sees in you."

"I . . ." Iris trailed off, letting her eyes fall.

She didn't know how to respond. She *wanted* to trust the Holy Father, trust His judgments, trust everything He told her. She knew she was supposed to trust Him, because she knew He was good. At least His Sacred Texts told her He was good. She wanted to believe He was trustworthy, but she just wasn't certain anymore. A slight squeeze from Hethers's hand brought her eyes back to him. His eyes glistened with understanding. "I wish I could make sense of this world for you, my dear."

Iris felt a prick of guilt at Hethers's concern. Here, this sweet old man was in just as horrible a place as her, yet he spent all his effort trying to comfort *her*. She hated the thought that she could be adding to his burdens by unloading her own. Squeezing Hethers's hand back, Iris forced a smile onto her face. *Enough self-pity for now.*

"Thank you, Mr. Hethers. You have been so kind to me. If it wasn't for you, I don't know how I would make it through. I wish there was something I could do to repay you."

"There is." He smiled back at her. "Don't give up!"

Iris let out a soft chuckle. "It's a deal."

The sound of the door bolt being dragged open intruded on their conversation. Both Iris and Hethers turned their heads to look as the cell opened.

"Time to go, old man," A soldier groused from the doorway.

Hethers slowly moved to his knees, pushing off the ground to stand. "Well, my dear, lovely to see you again. I am certain it won't be the last time." Giving her a wink and a smile, he turned to leave.

"Stay safe, sir. And until next time," Iris called out, echoing his hopefulness.

Alone in her prison once more, Iris released a long, slow breath. She craned her neck back to rest her head against the wall. Closing her eyes, she tried to will the heaviness in her heart away.

"Don't give up, Iris. You promised. Don't give up . . . don't give up . . ."

Whispers swirled through the night air, settling heavily upon Aaralee's ears. She couldn't make out what the voices were saying, but she could sense the depth of their hatred. Opening her eyes to peer through the inky blackness, she attempted to locate the source. Had someone dared to sneak into the royal bedchamber? Fearing an assassination attempt, Aaralee turned to awaken her husband. But instead of her hand meeting his sleeping form, it fell straight onto the feathery mattress. Where had her king gone? His place was cool to the touch, so he must have been missing for a while.

She was alone. The whispers grew in volume at the realization. She was in danger! She tried to call the guards outside for help, but a hand sprung from the darkness and clamped her mouth shut. A second hand attempted to grasp her throat. Aaralee grabbed at her attacker, fighting with all her might to throw them off. The assassin wrestled with Aaralee until they both fell from the bed. Once on the ground, Aaralee kicked herself away. Remembering that she had left her dagger sitting on the small table near the balcony, she thrust herself up and raced toward the weapon. Just as Aaralee was about to pick it up, the assassin dashed out their hand and took it from her. Aaralee and her attacker stood frozen on either end of the table.

"Who are you?" Aaralee demanded.

The figure chuckled as they twisted the knife over and over between their fingers. As her eyes adjusted to the bits of light filtering in from the balcony, the face of the assassin took form. Though the woman was seventy, her skin still maintained some of its youth. Her high cheekbones and air of importance exuded a regal presence. She had long silver hair with a braided section that framed the left side of her face and rested in front of her shoulder. On her forehead, painted in black, was their sacred symbol of the All Powerful Eye. Aaralee stared in horror at the Great Mother of Yansair.

"Caroline! What are you doing?"

A twist of disgust broke through Caroline's smirk at the mention of her true name. Slowly, she advanced toward Aaralee. With each step forward, Aaralee took one back, attempting to make her way to the door.

"Caroline, stop! I order you to stop! Guards!" Aaralee glanced over her shoulder, dismayed at the answering silence.

"You never did show me the respect I deserved," Caroline crooned.

Why was no one coming to help her?

"Caroline, where is Thaylos? What have you done?"

The gap between them was closing.

"I am your Great Mother, you impudent child! Stop speaking to me in such familiar terms."

Caroline raised the dagger above her head and lept through the air at Aaralee. Aaralee let out a scream when a burst of light appeared between them, knocking them both backward. Heart pounding, Aaralee watched as the light slowly dimmed and took the shape of a woman.

"You . . ." Aaralee whispered.

"No!" Caroline screamed from the other side, vanishing into the darkness.

Eyes widening in horror, Aaralee watched as the woman of light collapsed to the ground. Rushing over to the woman's side, she noticed that her own dagger had been plunged into the woman's heart.

"You-you saved me. . . . *Why?*" Tears fell from her eyes as she watched her savior die.

"Because . . . He loves you . . ."

The light and the woman disappeared in the next instant, leaving Aaralee alone in the dark once more.

"Protect My prophet, save the people."

With a scream, Aaralee jolted upright in her bed, sweat-soaked from yet another nightmare. Or was it a vision? She didn't know anymore. Taking a few deep breaths, Aaralee attempted to soothe her ragged nerves. Though exhausted, she dared not try to sleep again. Every time she did, she was assaulted by another message to "protect His prophet." Seeking distraction, Aaralee gazed around the bedchamber. Moonlight streamed in through the drawn-back curtains of the balcony. She recognized the silhouette of her husband leaning against the railing. Slipping her feet out from the covers, Aaralee crossed the cool stone floor. Her eyes rested on her husband's form as she paused behind him. Every muscle in Thaylos's back was tensed into knots, and his hands gripped the rail.

"Have you slept at all, my king?" Aaralee queried in concern.

"What's the point in trying?" he rumbled.

Moving to his side, Aaralee followed her husband's gaze across the moon-bathed kingdom. Far off in the distance, a large red glow pulsed as dark smoke swirled up into the night sky.

"Another raid?" Aaralee surmised watching the flames.

"It would seem that Hethers's followers have doubled their efforts since he turned himself in and news of that woman's imprisonment spread." Thaylos kept his steely glare fixed on the burning airship factory.

The king and queen of Yansair stood in silence under the night sky. They had been so sure that victory was in their grasp. The Great Mother had assured them that by attacking Fitsengea first, the All Powerful Eye would break the curse that held back the rains, making it possible to end their conflict with Sylphaen. All omens were for them. Even that one lord from Saunskirt had aligned his forces to their might, though he remained difficult to control. The Great Mother had promised a swift and easy victory. She was certain this would bring their salvation. She *still* advised the king not to give in. Aaralee didn't trust her, but she couldn't speak against her, for it would surely doom the king.

The memory of the woman of light from her dreams continued to thrum through Aaralee's thoughts. Over and over, that voice called to her, and even Thaylos was plagued with unwanted images. The Great Mother had tried for hours to cast them away to no avail. A longing awoke inside Aaralee that surprised her. *I need to speak with her.*

"My king?" she began tentatively.

"Hmm?" He grunted, only half paying attention.

"I request your permission to meet with that woman."

Thaylos turned his head to stare at Aaralee. "Are you out of your mind? The last time we spoke, that witch released a curse on the whole royal court!"

"Yes, my husband, I know. But—"

"Out of the question!" Thaylos cut in angrily, slicing his hand through the air.

"My king . . . *please.* I *know* you mean to protect me. I *know* my night terrors have weighed on you." She stepped toward him and placed a gentle hand on his arm. "It was *me* the dreams first came to. It was *me* her attention was drawn to when you confronted her."

Thaylos softened slightly at Aaralee's touch, allowing her to come in closer for an embrace. "You wish to speak to her alone, don't you?"

"Not without the guards, at least," she said, resting her head against his chest. "I will be cautious. But, my husband, what other choice do we have? If we wait any longer, people will go mad." Looking at the dying flames at the airship factory, she added, "How can your soldiers stop the traitors if they cannot rest?"

Thaylos stayed silent for a while before finally speaking. "And why do you think she will listen to you?"

"I don't know. I just have a feeling . . ."

"You and your *feelings*." He snorted. "One of these days, those feelings are going to be wrong."

Peeking her eyes up at Thaylos, her heart fluttered with hope. "Does this mean I have your permission?"

"Yes, my queen. Tomorrow when they bring that woman up for her treatments, you may go speak with her. I don't want you to have to wade through the filth of the dungeon, and there will be plenty of eyes to ensure your safety."

Resting her head against his chest, Aaralee smiled. "Thank you, my husband." She didn't know why this was so critical to her, but after seeing the prisoner as the woman of light in her dream, there were some things she just *had* to know.

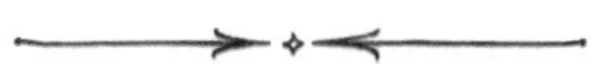

Darren scratched at the rough undershirt of the Saunskirt military uniform. He knew it was necessary to protect his skin from rubbing raw under the leather plating, but he could tell by the rough and thinning fabric that his garb had been passed along a few too many times. Frowning, he let out a soft sigh. Nerves. That was the real issue. They had crossed over into Yansairen lands, and shortly they would be touching down in Diridos. Somewhere in this godforsaken place was Iris. *Just keep fighting. I'm coming for you!*

"So how many throats do you plan on cutting?" Bryant broke through the tense silence.

Darren and Jason eyed each other before looking back at Bryant. "Not that kind of rescue," Darren answered.

"You know they deserve it," Bryant replied while sharpening one of his throwing knives. "After what they've done to our people, sounds like justice to me."

"The whole point is to *not* be noticed. We can't get Iris out if a whole army is after us."

Bryant leaned forward, a gleam in his eye. "But you want to, don't you?"

Darren looked away, unable to deny the hatred he felt, but they couldn't risk bodies piling up. Not only did they need to save Iris, but they needed to find all those young girls Jodie told him about. Bryant's bloodthirst disconcerted Darren. Again, he doubted if he made the right choice in letting him come. They needed the support, to be sure. Aiden had barely even let Fredrick take him and Jason out of the camp, a feat only made possible because of Aiden's fear of repercussions from Zaerin if they didn't get Iris back. Even so, there was no way Aiden would separate from any of his checkpoint guards. And Kyle *was* right. Bryant could be useful in a bind. While he didn't want to resort to fighting, only a fool wouldn't come prepared for it. Bryant had saved his neck a couple times throughout the years.

Kyle would have loved to rub Darren's face in this, knowing he had to admit Kyle was right. Would Kyle even be alive by the time they got back? A knot twisted in Darren's stomach at the thought. Ignoring it, he turned his focus to the landing of the airship.

Climbing down from the steering platform, Fredrick nodded to the others. "Everyone ready?"

All three nodded their agreement. Fredrick turned and released a lever that slowly lowered the gangway. Once it was completely open, Fredrick stepped out, Darren, Jason, and Bryant following close behind. Dry, warm air met them as they exited. Darren noted the dirt-covered ground as their feet kicked up small plumes of dust. Moonlight mixed with torches helped provide visibility for their surroundings. They had disembarked a bit outside the town, within a large compound that held a few other airships. Yansair didn't have many of these built yet, so they had very strict protocols for their usage. They currently kept the finished vessels separated from the building factory for protection. According to Fredrick, there was an underground movement in Yansair that didn't approve of their king's war with Sylphaen or their reliance on slavery. The addition of a conflict with Fitsengea really pushed them over the edge.

They began fighting back by finding ways to sabotage their military efforts, their most recent focus being the flying vessels. This explained the large amount of soldiers patrolling the grounds around them. Darren glanced at a few of the guards out of the corner of his eye as they made their way to the main gate. Each man they passed scrutinized their little group, but Darren made sure not to connect with their suspicious stares. He moved his hand to rest on the hilt of his sword while Jason shifted the pack on his shoulder as he walked beside him. They each carried one bag to help with their ruse.

Upon reaching the gate, they were greeted by one of the biggest men Darren had ever seen. He dwarfed even Bryant's height.

"Lieutenant Maythan, welcome back to Diridos," The giant voice rumbled in recognition.

Fredrick gave a curt nod. The soldier peered at Darren and the others as they stood at attention behind Fredrick. "New escort party?"

"Problem?" Fredrick replied.

The soldier shrugged. "Not at all. What business does Saunskirt have with us tonight?" With a flick of his hand, he quietly ordered another Yansairen to come and inspect each of the small packs.

"We're on retrieval duty this time."

The man raised an eyebrow. "Why come at this late hour?"

"We encountered some complications on the way," Fredrick answered. "Don't worry. We'll not bother your superiors tonight. We can see them in the morning."

The soldier shifted his gaze back to the airship they'd arrived in. "Complications?"

"Your airship is fine. Different sort of complications."

"All right then." He frowned. The second soldier completing his search nodded to his giant comrade. "I'll send report of your arrival. The general will call for you tomorrow. Be ready."

Fredrick nodded. "We'll be in the same tavern, as always."

The man raised his chin in agreement and signaled to his compatriots close by. The men ran to unlock and pull back the massive barrier that made up the entrance. Once opened just wide enough to step through, Fredrick led the way out. About twenty minutes later, they finally reached the residential area of Diridos. Fredrick wove them toward their destination, the Silky Tavern. As they entered, Darren scanned the gathering room. Very few souls were scattered around. *Not surprising at this hour. Only the most dedicated drunks would still be going at it.* Walking up to the counter in the center of the room, Fredrick waved to the portly woman looking through a ledger. The woman responded with a large, toothy grin.

"Why, is that my Freddy back again?"

"Evening, Mrs. Owling. Good to see you." Fredrick returned the smile.

"And you too, love! Oh, I see you have a new set of lads with you. Doing some more training, are we?"

Fredrick chuckled. "You might say that. So tell me, Mrs. Owling, my favorite innkeeper wouldn't have happened to keep my old spot open for me, would she?"

Mrs. Owling released a hearty laugh and reached across the counter to pinch Fredrick on the cheek. "Of course! Anything for my sweet Freddy!"

Darren bit back his own laugh.

"Sabene!" Mrs. Owling suddenly screeched. "Sabene!"

A young girl no more than fifteen appeared through a side door. "Yes, ma'am?" Her long dirty-blonde hair was loosely tied back with a simple ribbon. Curls fell every which way, fighting to be free from the ribbon's hold. Her appearance betrayed the heavy workload she carried.

"Sabene, hun, I need you to help these boys up to Freddy's usual place." She reached under the counter and passed a set of keys to Sabene. With her other hand, she grabbed an unlit candle, lit it with the one burning beside her ledger, and handed that over to Sabene as well. "Make sure they're good and comfortable, ya hear?"

Sabene dipped her head. "Yes, ma'am." Turning to her charges, she smiled meekly. "If you would follow me, please."

They made their way up a set of stairs along the left wall of the tavern. With very little light along the stairs or in the hallway, they had to make sure to stay close behind Sabene and her small candle. Unlocking the last room at the back, Sabene entered and used her candle to light a lamp hanging near the doorway. She lit a larger candle further in that was set in a stand on the small bedside table. Fredrick stepped to the side and allowed Darren, Jason, and Bryant to enter. Glancing once more down the darkened hall, Fredrick retreated inside and shut the door behind him.

Darren noticed two sets of bunks placed on either side of the room, and the bedside table with the candle was situated between them. The room itself was fairly small—just large enough for the bunks, the table, and two wooden chairs.

"Check the window," Fredrick ordered Jason.

One medium-sized window was latched shut with wooden shutters on the back wall of the room. Jason walked over to it, opened it, and stuck his head out. He came back in and signaled to Fredrick that all was well, but Jason continued to stand by the window to keep an eye out.

"Do we have any neighbors?" Fredrick asked Sabene, gesturing quietly to the opposite wall.

She shook her head. "Not many tenants right now, and no one next door. You are free to speak." She smiled at him and then blew out her candle, careful to keep the wax from dripping on the floor.

Free to speak? Is this young girl one of the contacts Fred mentioned before? Darren mused as Bryant pushed past them to pick his bed before the rest. *Some things never change.* Darren smirked.

"Sabene, I'd like to introduce you to Darren, Jason, and Bryant." Fredrick indicated each in turn.

"Gentlemen." She smiled at them politely.

"These men are Alastrians who will be aiding our movement."

Sabene curtsied. "Sirs, on behalf of the movement, we are honored by your compassion and your presence." Standing straight again, she looked at them with sad eyes. "It is not lost on me the terrible things our kingdom has done to your people, and though I know it cannot even begin to make up for it, I want to let you know I am truly sorry."

"Think nothing of it, sweet cheeks. Not like you did any of the killing." Bryant eyed her up and down.

Darren cut his eyes over to Bryant, giving him a warning look that made him turn away. Sabene blushed and fidgeted.

"Ms. Sabene," Darren said, "your sincerity means a great deal, and we recognize too that your people within this movement are risking a lot for strangers. It is *you* who has our gratitude." He bowed.

To be so young and carry so much. A sense of pride and respect expanded through his chest at the thought. Sabene nodded her thanks to Darren, then turned abruptly to Fredrick. "Please, is Liam well?"

Fredrick set his pack on the ground and sat down on the nearest bunk. Sighing, he directed Sabene to sit in a chair. "Your brother was severely wounded during the rescue of the children from the massacre." When Sabene let out a frightened gasp, Fredrick hurriedly continued. "He is on the mend. But I think it might be time for you and the rest of your siblings to retreat to the camps. Liam's absence from the troops will likely cause them to realize his involvement."

Sabene dropped her gaze and studied her fingers for a second. "I'll warn Marcelle to take everyone out by sunset tomorrow. That should give them the time they need to prepare."

Tilting his head, Fredrick eyed Sabene with a stern expression. "I said *all* of you."

Sabene squared her shoulders in defiance as her head shot back up.

"You don't know for sure they've found Liam out, right? Besides, it's not like the whole regiment knew we were his family."

"It's also not that hard to spot the physical similarities." Fredrick frowned.

"I don't care! There's still so much more I can do." She leaned forward and grasped Fredrick's hand. "Please! Fred, you know this is an important position. Soldiers come through here all the time. We can't lose this information line!"

"Bean . . ."

Sabene twisted her face into a pout and flipped her head to the side. Taking a deep breath, she turned back again. "Just a little longer, Fred. You still need me out here, and you know it. At least let me help you with whatever brought you this time."

Fredrick pressed his lips together. "Fine. But once this mission goes down, things are going to get a *lot* worse around here. I want you out before then, you understand?" Sabene nodded triumphantly. "All right, good. Now you better get back out there, Bean. Before Mrs. Owling starts to worry." Fredrick playfully bumped her arm with his fist.

Sabene's lips spread into a broad smile. Jumping up, she said goodnight to the rest, relit her candle, and hurried back to work.

"That's one tough kid," Darren remarked to Fredrick. "Think she'll be okay?"

Fredrick shook his head and sighed. "She better be. I'd never hear the end of it from Liam, otherwise."

"You seem pretty close with them," Jason added from his post by the window.

Fredrick smiled. "They've all become kind of like my adoptive family."

Smile fading, Fredrick unsheathed his sword. He stood and took calculated steps over to where Bryant was lazing on the other bottom bunk. "I see Sabene like a kid sister."

In a flash, he brought his sword within inches of Bryant's throat.

"What the heck, man!" Bryant cried.

"Like I said, she's a *sister* to me. And I swear to you, Bryant, if you ever speak to her like that again . . . if you so much as *look* at her wrong, I *will* turn you into a eunuch."

The assured iciness of Fred's tone seemed to zap Bryant's ability to reply. He stiffly bobbed his head.

"Good." Fredrick whisked the blade back and tucked it into its sheath once more.

Darren blinked a few times, trying to come to grips with Fredrick's sudden tonal shift. He couldn't say he blamed Fredrick, though. He probably would have had the same reaction if anyone had dared to do the same to his own sisters. A half-smile snuck across Darren's lips at seeing Bryant's face turn pale.

"All right then," Fredrick proclaimed in a cheery tone once more. "Let's get a short bit of rest. Sabene will finish work in a couple of hours. Once she's done, we can meet up and figure out what our next plan of action is."

Not wanting to waste time with undressing, each man simply removed their boots before climbing onto the thin bunk pallets. Lying on his back and resting his head on his hands, Darren stared at the ceiling from his position on top. *Soon, Iris, soon. We're coming, I promise.*

Chapter Nine

I ris winced as the comb was yanked through her wet hair. Attendants fussed all around her, racing to make her more presentable. Apparently, the queen was paying a visit to their little session today. While Iris appreciated finally getting to bathe and wear a plain new dress, she couldn't help but find the need to perfect herself to "honor the queen's presence" a bit ridiculous. *Might do her some good to get up close and personal with how nasty the dungeons are.* She hated to think what life might be like for their long-term prisoners. She knew she only got out as much as she did because they were attempting to speed up the healing process for her bruised ribs and discover a way to remove the badge. True, the oils they rubbed on her skin did seem to be helping her ribs a little, but she could do without the chanting to their Eye afterward. *At least I can retreat into my thoughts with You.* Iris grinned a little as she glanced up.

Another scream echoed down the hall. The servants around her paused their tasks, each glancing at Iris nervously. Iris sighed. *That's the sixth one in the past half hour.* It seemed the visions were getting worse, spreading beyond just the royal court. Not long before, one of the attendants in their room had been escorted out. *I know You have a purpose with all of this, but do they have to be so frightened? What are You showing them to incite such reactions?*

"Do you really want to know?"

Fear fluttered through Iris's heart. *Probably not. But . . .* She closed her eyes and focused on stilling the thrumming of her heart. *If . . . if the point comes where You need me to see . . . then yes, show me.* After her conversation with Hethers and her encounter in the throne room, Iris had decided to make more of an effort to leave herself open for the Holy Father to move. She knew herself better than to believe she'd get it right from here on out, but she had to try. It had surprised her that she was capable of feeling so much compassion for these people. She'd never been able to stomach seeing others in pain. Still, this ran deeper, and she suspected it was largely the Holy Father's doing.

Iris let her eyes roam around to watch the flurrying women. All appeared to be in their early twenties. Each was beautiful and dressed in expensive fabrics that fluttered smoothly with their movements. It was clear their outfits were meant to help keep them cool in the Diridos heat. These were not the typical caregivers Iris was accustomed to here. She wondered if they were handmaidens for the queen. Perhaps slaves? Each bore a small branding of the Eye symbol on their upper left arm. She had to admit she appreciated getting some distance from the ill-tempered guards who'd brought her up this morning. Iris glanced at the doorway to her side, feeling a twinge of guilt as she watched the men outside fight to maintain their alertness. *You would probably be in a bad mood too if you had to keep dealing with people reacting to those visions. Poor things undoubtedly get very little sleep.*

The crash of a metal bowl clanging on the floor startled Iris's attention back to the women. Iris winced again as the girl combing her hair yanked it through a little too hard.

"Téleaph! Watch what you're doing! You know what happens when you waste the oils!" the eldest of the group hissed as she quickly stooped down to rescue the precious aromatic liquid.

"F-forgive me . . ." Téleaph apologized, stepping back to make room as a few other girls swooped in to help clean up the mess.

Curious, Iris studied Téleaph for a minute. She seemed to be the youngest of the women, perhaps not even twenty yet. More curious was the difference in her appearance. Whereas the rest all had silky black hair pulled into a perfectly neat, thick braid, Téleaph's hair was a strawberry-blonde color. The beautiful waves were loosely pulled back and held in a gentle bun on the nape of her neck with a single, although large, hair pin. She must have been concerned that the piece wouldn't hold the style, because at least thirty times now, Iris had caught her feeling for it. Tears began to well up in Iris's eyes the longer she watched Téleaph's actions.

Why? Why does looking at her make me so *sad? And why can't I look away, Holy Father?* Closing her eyes and taking a calming breath, Iris forced her emotions back under control. The tugging of Iris's hair finally came to a stop as the girl got up from behind her and quickly stepped off to the side. Iris's wet hair sat in a tight, single braid, slightly cooling the center of her back. A pressing in Iris's heart drew her back to Téleaph once more as the young woman stepped near her. *What is it?*

"Warn her. Tell her that if she'll trust Me, I will save her sister."

What? Téleaph walked further out of the way of her disgruntled comrades, coming to stand nearer Iris. The urging intensified so greatly that before Iris knew what she was doing, she had thrust out her hand and grasped Téleaph by the arm. Stunned, Téleaph froze in place.

"Téleaph, please listen to me." As soon as Iris spoke, a flood of images and information came into her mind. "*Please*, the Holy Father urges you not to do this!"

Somehow the rest of the room remained oblivious as Téleaph took in Iris's warning with wide-eyed horror.

"Téleaph, *please*, the Holy Father loves you *and* your sister. He can and will save you both if you'll just trust Him. I know you think this is the only way, but it will only make things worse."

Finally coming to herself, Téleaph shook off Iris's hand. "I have no idea what you're talking about, you mad woman!"

"Téleaph-" A slap across her face cut Iris's plea short.

Everyone in the room turned to watch them now.

"No more talking! You will not spew your curses here."

Though she spoke forcefully, fear danced within Téleaph's eyes.

"Leave it to a Sylphaenian to bring trouble." One of the girls tsked in the corner.

"Téleaph! Come here!" the eldest woman commanded once more.

Backing away from Iris, Téleaph rushed over shamefacedly. Iris gently cupped her cheek, attempting to soothe the stinging. Tears battled to break free, but she fought against them. Sorrow over Téleaph's choice weighed heavily on Iris. The smallest amount of hope lingered that perhaps Téleaph wouldn't go through with it. The Holy Father's desperation for His daughter ached bitterly through Iris's own heart. Even though Téleaph may not know or accept Him, she was still His child and His heart longed for her, was broken over her. The more Iris tapped into the Holy Father's pain over this girl, the weaker her reservations became. Tears slipped down her face. Iris had to look away as she prayed. *Please,* please *protect her, Holy Father. Save her, somehow. Please!*

The sudden stiffening of the soldiers outside the door caught the corner of Iris's eye. Wiping away her tears, she turned to see Queen Aaralee approach the opening. She was an entrancing woman. Silky, soft raven locks were elaborately accentuated with a golden head chain that made it seem as if small stones of starlight dripped down her hair. Her soft, flowing blue dress added to her ethereal look. She didn't walk so much as float across the floor. The grace and elegance this queen possessed left Iris feeling deeply intimidated and embarrassingly unworthy. As Aaralee entered the room, all the women stopped their tasks and bowed low to the ground. Each kept their position as their queen stood in front of Iris.

Iris's insecurities began to melt away as she studied the expression on the queen's face. Making eye contact with Iris, nervousness and hesitation danced across Aaralee's features. *Is she . . . intimidated by* me? Iris blinked in disbelief. *What could I possibly carry that could sway a woman like her?*

"Me."

Oh . . . The presence of the Holy Father both calmed and terrified Iris in the same breath. *Please,* please *speak through me,* Iris prayed. She could sense all the questions, doubts, and fears swirling around Aaralee, and she had no clue how to assuage them. A moment of awkward silence passed between them as the queen stood staring at Iris.

"She is uncertain of how to address you."

Really? She could just call me by my name. I mean—oh. She doesn't know it. The realization struck her as almost comical. All this time spent here and the only person who asked her name had been Mr. Hethers. Apparently, either no one had caught him calling her by her name, or they were too frightened by any supposed spells she might cast to listen too closely.

"You're uncertain what to call me, aren't you, Your Highness?" Iris said kindly.

Aaralee blinked a few times before finding words. "It is not customary for Yansair to give much heed to its prisoners. You desire our destruction, so we have no need to know you on a personal level."

Iris studied Aaralee's eyes. "Have I been angered at the loss of those I love? Yes. I mourn for them daily. But greater is the call of the Holy Father's heart. Yansair is full of His precious children who are blind to the perfect love He has for them. I do not desire the destruction of *anyone,* because He does not. And whether you want to know me on a personal level or not is your choice. But, Queen Aaralee, *He* knows you and is calling to you. It is because of His love toward you that He has been visiting you in your dreams." Iris paused, trying to allow Aaralee space to respond.

The queen remained silent, but Iris could tell from the look in her eyes that Aaralee had not hardened her heart toward her or the words the Holy Father prompted her to say. Encouraged by her listening audience, Iris pressed in with a new piece of information the Holy Father whispered into her thoughts. "The dreams that warn you began the night I arrived, but that was not the first time you heard the Holy Father call to you, was it?"

Aaralee's face flushed, but she quickly composed herself. Iris found herself wishing she could possess that much control over her emotions.

"What is your name, prisoner?" the queen's voice rang out.

"I am Iris Straton, Your Majesty."

"Iris . . . I don't know what sort of magic you possess, but if your words are true and you wish us no harm, then I ask you to lift this curse of visions plaguing my people."

"What you see as a curse the Holy Father sees as a desperate plea to save His beloved."

"Will you or will you not end this?"

Iris waited on the prompting of the Holy Father before answering. "If you call on the name of the Holy Beloved, you and your people will be freed from these visions and dreams."

Revulsion danced in Aaralee's eyes. "The Holy Beloved?" Her tone practically spat back at Iris. "I thought you Fiesians followed only a single god."

"Those of us who believe, yes, it is one God who we follow."

"And yet you instruct me to call on another name." Aaralee turned up her nose.

Iris knew she walked a thin line. If she was to reach Yansair, she needed the heart of their queen. *Tread lightly, Iris*, she coached herself.

"I will more than happily answer whatever questions you may have, Your Majesty, if you truly desire to understand. But I know that right now you do not trust me. So all I can tell you is to call on the Holy Beloved for yourself and see what happens. If your All Powerful Eye truly is greater than my God, then what do you have to fear?"

"Prepare yourself."

Iris sucked in a sharp breath at the sudden warning.

"*Ahhhhh!*" One of the women attendants burst into piercing screams of terror. "No! No! No!" She threw her hands over her ears as if trying to block out some terrible sound.

"Guards!" Aaralee cried out.

Instantly, the men posted by the door were at her side awaiting her orders.

"Take her to the healing rooms with the others," the queen said. "See to it that she's kept there until her mind returns to her."

Sensing urgency from the Holy Father, Iris watched every movement closely. Téleaph's choice fast approached. Iris prayed for her to heed the Holy Father's warning. The soldiers helped the tormented attendant up from the ground, gently guiding her from the room. Only a few steps farther and the woman burst into another fit of hysterics. Flinging herself backward and out of the men's grasp, she crashed into a side table, sending numerous jars of priceless oils flying. While the guards attempted to recollect her, the other women quickly rushed in to save the costly liquids. Iris watched as Téleaph lagged behind. Slowly, the woman raised her hand to her hairpin and undid it, causing beautiful waves of hair to fall past her shoulders. Téleaph's eyes were riveted on the queen, who was enraptured by the current chaos. Iris watched in horror as Téleaph raised the dagger-like hairpin into the air.

"Don't!" Iris begged.

Flitting her eyes to Iris, Téleaph balked at the attention now being drawn to her. She flung herself at the queen with all her might.

"No!" Iris screamed as she lept from her perch, sending both Aaralee and Téleaph tumbling in opposite directions as she collided with them.

"My queen!" Fearful cries rang out as the crowd quickly caught on.

Iris lay on the ground, dazed from the force of the impact. *Did it work?* A surge of pain ripped through her body, the agony blurring her vision. Suddenly realizing how difficult it was to breathe, Iris moved a hand to inspect the source of her pain. Her limbs felt heavy, almost disconnected, and hard to control. Finally focusing, Iris glimpsed a golden object protruding from her left shoulder. *Téleaph's pin . . . She missed. . . .* Iris's thoughts rapidly deteriorated. She felt like she was underwater. *Can't move . . . Can't breathe . . . Why . . .* Vision darkening, Iris was only partially aware of the figure now leaning over her. All sound was muffled. A voice far away called to her. She strained to make out what they said.

"... did she ... Can you hear ... poisoned ... dying ..."

"Holy ... Beloved ..." Iris pushed out before her tongue lay dead in her mouth. Darkness swept in and Iris was gone.

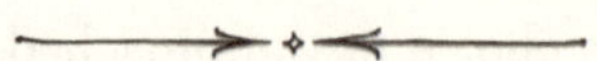

The dry dust of the road coated Darren's boots. He could feel the grittiness in his teeth. The capital of the kingdom had been the best fortified to withstand the drought's deadly effects, but given the appearance of their surroundings, it was easy to tell that even Diridos was beginning to wane. Weaving around the flurry of the market goers, Darren and Jason followed Sabene at a safe distance. The less connection they appeared to have with her, the safer things would be for Sabene.

Breaking off from the crowd to slip into a quiet side alley, Sabene disappeared into the shadows. After pausing to make sure no one else might have been watching her or them, Darren and Jason moved to follow. Weaving through a few more labyrinths of alleyways, they finally came to the quiet entrance of a bookbinding and repair shop. Not a soul traversed the area around them. Stepping inside, Darren caught sight of a leathery-skinned, middle-aged man seated on a stool behind the counter on the right. Making eye contact with whom Darren assumed to be the shopkeeper, the man tilted his head, pointing to the back room door. Darren dipped his chin and made his way through the door with Jason. On the other side, they were greeted by Sabene, who ushered them in the rest of the way.

"Marquis Turner, Sir Jason, I would like to introduce to you some of our esteemed leaders in the movement," Sabene stated respectfully as she swept her hand behind her to indicate the trio of people sitting at a medium-sized, circular table.

Darren blanched inwardly at the use of his title. Sabene would have picked up on it by overhearing his conversation with Jason earlier this morning. He needed to talk to Jason, *again*, about not using his title. At the very least, not around others. Darren caught the slightest flinching of the men and the woman at the table at his introduction. *Great . . . nothing like having rebels know you're an assumed traitor in your own nation. They're already going to be suspicious as is!* He could hope they didn't know the depth of the Fiesian scandals, but an underground movement couldn't afford to be uninformed. Yet another reason for him to be cross with Jason. This morning had already been punctuated by the fierce debate about who would accompany Fredrick with his reporting to the general. Initially, Darren had been eager to attend, thinking he'd have a better chance of picking up news of Iris's whereabouts. Jason had stubbornly refused to leave Darren's side, as he still felt it was his duty to protect his marquis with his life. Eventually, they agreed that Bryant would go with Fredrick, and Jason would accompany him to this clandestine meeting. Jason was wise enough to remain quiet after the decision was made.

"On the left is Mr. Oriel, in the center is Ms. Phineah, and on the right is Mr. Elias." Sabene continued with the introductions proudly.

It intrigued Darren to see that the leadership appeared to be such a diverse team. Oriel was clearly Yansairen with his pinkish-brown skin, full, curly black beard, and smooth, dark locks pulled back into a thick, rope-like braid, whereas Phineah had the perfectly flawless black skin and beautiful, large brown eyes typical of citizens of the Krine Islands. And finally, Elias looked to be yet another Sylphaenian with his fair skin, clean-shaven face, and sandy-blond hair. He hadn't realized how interconnected Sylphaen and Yansair had become through the years. Yansair had a nasty history of slavery. How many Sylphaenians had been stolen from their homes in the decades of unrest between these two countries? Darren recalled that this very issue was one of the main proponents that led to their war.

"We are honored to meet you, Your Grace. We welcome your aid to our movement." Phineah spoke with smooth eloquence. Smiling softly, she stretched her hand toward the unoccupied chairs around the table.

"Please, make yourselves comfortable. I am sure there will be much to discuss."

Phineah's voice instantly dispelled the tension hanging in the air. Darren noted the regal authority the woman exuded. Somehow, she reminded him of his late Aunt Valina. Valina had been the perfect queen. Compassionate, wise, and without pretense, with eyes that took command of a crowd. That was it. The depth he saw in Phineah's eyes mirrored what he had witnessed in Aunt Valina's so many years ago.

"It is a pleasure to know you." Darren nodded to each as he and Jason moved forward to sit down. "We recognize the risk you are taking in meeting with strangers, even if others you know may have vouched for us."

Phineah nodded while Oriel remained statuesque beside her. Glancing at Elias, Darren noted the Sylphaenian's clenched jaw and tightly crossed arms. *Looks like someone doesn't want to be friends.*

"It is true that we are more accustomed to working directly with Fredrick, but Sabene has informed us that he was called away early this morning to check in with Diridos' general." Phineah flitted her eyes over to the corner of the room where Sabene waited. "I do think it's time for you to get back, sweet Bean. We can't have Mrs. Owling catching wise to your prolonged absences."

Sabene nodded respectfully but cast an anxious look toward Darren and Jason.

"Don't worry." Phineah smiled. "We'll make sure Fredrick's charges return to him." Visibly relaxing, Sabene turned to leave. "Don't forget the parcels Oriel left for you behind the counter," Phineah reminded her.

Sabene smiled and quickly ducked back into the front of the shop. So much of Sabene's demeanor reminded Darren of Liam, brief as their interaction had been. It impressed him to think how much favor this young girl had seemed to garner with the leaders of this movement. *How many people make up their cause?* Darren wondered, but he knew it unlikely that they'd divulge such crucial information. *Still, it'd be nice to know what kind of support we can expect.*

"So why are you here?" Elias snapped as soon as Sabene closed the door behind her.

Phineah shifted in her seat, cutting in. "What sort of information are you gentlemen seeking? It seems a serious matter for Fredrick to be insistent that we three meet so soon."

Darren stilled the thrumming of his heart, swallowing back his hopefulness. "We know your movement came together to stop the destruction your king is unleashing in the name of conquest. We have a . . . friend we believe can help cripple King Thaylos's advances. King Thaylos, apparently aware of the danger our friend posed, sought to steal her away and succeeded. We've come to get her back."

Oriel glanced at Phineah out of the corner of his eye, and Phineah raised her eyebrows. Elias kept his chilling glare fixed on Darren.

"Any information you may have on the whereabouts or wellbeing of a newly acquired Fiesian captive within the king's court could greatly aid us in freeing her."

"Is that all?" Phineah asked in a calm tone.

Darren shook his head. "In the wake of King Thaylos's slaughter, many children have been stolen from their homes. We received a tip that a large group of young girls amongst those taken may have been brought here to the capital."

Phineah's features morphed into a mixture of sadness and anger. "They have likely been taken to the sorting grounds per Yansairen tradition. Hopefully the girls haven't been dispersed yet. We will get in touch with our people and let you know."

"I'm sorry, but," Jason inserted, "what are the sorting grounds?"

"It's where the officials divvy up the so-called spoils of battle," Elias growled. "Women and young children are filtered through to find out who will be assigned as slaves, who will receive training as future courtesans, and who will become sacrificial offerings. In other words, it's where the depraved play god."

Darren caught Jason clenching his fists until his knuckles went white. His own heart pounded angrily in his ears. Memories of Professor Hethers laying out the transgressions of their eastern neighbor resurfaced. The revelation of the sorting grounds had incited anger from many in the church and military councils. Yet again, Teason had opposed Hethers's stance of intervention and had eventually convinced those initially incensed that the Holy Father had not given Fitsengea His blessing to intervene. Darren ground his teeth as Teason's numerous manipulative speeches rang through his mind.

"How long does the . . . *sorting* process usually take?" Darren asked.

"Depends on the number of victims," Elias answered.

"We've been making some progress on tangling up some of their operations," Phineah added. "Holy Father willing, your girls haven't gone too far yet."

Jason perked up at the mention of his beloved God's name. *Interesting . . .* Darren studied Phineah a little more closely. Few, if any, of Krine's islanders followed any deity aside from their ancient ancestral worship. *What's your story, Phineah?*

A few soft knocks sounded on the door. The three leaders exchanged knowing looks before standing up from the table. Darren and Jason instantly followed their lead.

"Seems we'll have to cut this meeting short, gentlemen. Please forgive us." Phineah spoke calmly as she dipped her head, then met Darren's eyes. "We will be in touch, Your Grace. As soon as we hear anything definitive, we will let you know."

Darren and Jason shook hands with Phineah and Oriel and exited the shop. Scanning their surroundings, Darren caught a glimpse of a few Yansairen soldiers rounding the corner toward them. Jason fluidly turned to help block Darren from the view of the oncoming soldiers. Taking a few casual steps back, they both allowed the shadows of the neighboring buildings wash over them. Darren watched the soldiers for a minute, making sure they hadn't been spotted. The young men drew nearer to the shop they'd just left. Had they been discovered? Darren noted the stiffness and serious demeanor the soldiers carried.

"Patrol," Jason whispered at Darren's side.

Darren nodded in agreement. Those men were simply doing their rounds. *Time to go.* Almost as one mind, Darren and Jason turned down the alleyway behind them, managing to escape the notice of the patrol just in time. Another half hour later, they found themselves back in their room at the Silky Tavern. Frustration rumbled inside Darren as he sat in the wooden chair against the wall. Jason repositioned himself by his post at the window.

So little accomplished, and half the day was already gone. Yes, he knew things like this took time. Information wasn't easy to acquire, and mistakes came at a deadly price. But Darren couldn't help but feel that time was not in their favor. Who knew what sort of horrors King Thaylos might be unleashing on Iris? If she was still alive. No. He refused to let that thought land. Shifting in his seat, Darren's eyes rested on Jason, and a new sense of irritation sparked.

He needed to get it through this kid's head that he did not need to be babysat. But time was too short for him to attempt to break through Jason's stubborn view of duty. Normally, Darren would let such annoyances go, but seeing it prevent him from moving freely forced him into confrontation. They had to wait for Bryant and Fredrick's return anyway.

"Jason, we need to talk."

"Yes, Your Grace?" Jason turned to face him.

Darren inwardly cringed at the title. "Jason . . ." He took a breath, trying to maintain his calm. "We've talked about this. You have *got* to stop using that title."

Jason's shoulders drooped. "Sorry, sir. I-I know I messed up . . . earlier this morning. It's not safe to use your title around here. I know it could cost us our lives. I submit myself to whatever punishment you see fit."

Darren scrunched his brows and cocked his head. "I'm not going to punish you. I am not your keeper. Just like you shouldn't be mine."

"Sir?" Jason questioned taken aback.

"No more playing the watchdog, Jason. There's no need to protect me. I know how to take care of myself, trust me. No more forcing yourself to stay by my side. Understood?"

Jason shifted uncomfortably for a minute before finally responding. "I'm sorry, sir, but I have to respectfully disagree. While you know how to fend for yourself, I am duty bound to stand by your side."

Darren rolled his eyes. "No, you're not. The reason you are here is because my uncle placed you on watch over Iris, not me. Any duty to the Crown ends there."

"But . . . you are part of the Crown. You admit that you are King Zaerin's nephew, and as an Alastrian soldier, you know it is part of our oath to protect the royal line."

"I've been kicked out of that line," Darren scoffed with more bitterness than intended.

"Outside actions cannot erase identity."

Darren narrowed his eyes, annoyance shifting to anger. "My identity is of little importance."

Jason's eyes softened but his tone took on a surprising edge. "Just because you don't believe in your importance doesn't negate its reality."

Darren clenched his jaw as he stared Jason down. Jason knew Darren could easily order him to obey, and he would instantly acquiesce, but if Darren did that, he would be stepping right into the role he was trying to avoid. Where did the man get the nerve to say these things to him?

"Duty or not, Jason, I warn you. I came here to find Iris, and I will *not* let anything or anyone get in the way of that."

Jason closed his eyes for half a second, took a breath, and faced Darren once more. "Then I pledge myself to the fulfillment of that goal . . . if . . . you'll allow it? . . . sir."

Darren tilted his head as he unwound some of the emotion from his muscles. "I really don't understand you."

Jason grimaced and sighed. "I get that a lot."

Shaking his head, Darren leaned back and looked up at the ceiling. "All right, I give. Just . . . take it down a notch, would you?"

A smile of relief crept across Jason's face. "Yes, sir."

Keys jiggled in the lock, pulling their attention to the door. Fredrick and Bryant stepped in, both eerily quiet as they closed the door behind them. Seeing Bryant somber made Darren concerned. Standing up, he took a few strides in their direction. "What's wrong?"

"We got some news . . ." Fredrick began sadly. "It seems that our Miss Iris stopped an assassination attempt on the queen this morning. In the struggle . . . she was stabbed with a poisoned blade."

An overwhelmingly large hole opened up within Darren. "What are you saying."

Bryant locked eyes with Darren and swallowed. "Your girl . . . she's dying."

Chapter Ten

"But why did you bring her here?" Thaylos demanded as he paced the foyer.

"Because she saved my life," Aaralee answered in firm calmness.

"She is a prisoner! Enemy to all of Yansair!"

"Her being in the healing room beside our chamber has not erased any of that."

"But why *this* room?" He pointed emphatically at the door. "You could have, *should* have sent that woman to the healing rooms befitting her filth!"

Aaralee's eyes narrowed. "That *filth* is the *only* reason I'm standing before you now!" Breathing in deep to maintain her calm, Aaralee continued, "My king, this woman is dying a painful death because of *me*. She had more to gain by letting the assassin succeed, but she chose to sacrifice herself for her enemy. Approve of it or not, we are legally indebted to her. Short as her time may be."

"And how are we to know this isn't some sort of ruse? If she truly was affected by that poison, then why hasn't her curse lifted? Our people are *still* being tormented."

"My king, we are no strangers to death. You know as well as I do what it looks like. This is no trick. And as to the curse . . ."

Aaralee hesitated. But seeing Thaylos growing impatient, she pressed on. "I don't think she's in as much control as the Great Mother led us to believe."

Thaylos stopped dead in his tracks, his countenance taking on a dark shadow. "Careful, my queen. You know how dangerous it is to speak against our Great Mother."

Aaralee cast her eyes down submissively. "Yes, my husband. Forgive me."

Softening at his wife's repentance, Thaylos took a step toward her and gently grasped her shoulder. "You are forgiven. I know you have been put through so much these past days, so it's only natural to become confused."

Aaralee bit back her retort. She wasn't *confused*. But she knew she couldn't counter the king's statement without angering him further. His temper was so short these past few months prior to the prisoner's arrival, and it had only gotten worse within the last week. Swallowing her own frustration, Aaralee gently touched Thaylos's hand resting on her shoulder. She allowed concern to echo between her eyes and her voice as she pled with him once more.

"My husband, I do not request that we place any trust in the prisoner. I agree it is wise that we stay on guard even at this time. But the Law of Honor is quite clear on how we are to respond to a sacrificial act for the rulers of Yansair. We can't allow the detractors any more fodder to bring you down. You know how highly the people respect the Law of Honor."

Thaylos let out a sigh and moved his hand from Aaralee's shoulder to tenderly grasp her hands in his own. "Ever my wise counsel. Yes, forefathers of my past have been undone before for not respecting these laws. We will not fall into repeating their mistakes. Still, your tenderness concerns me, my queen. I cannot permit you to be alone with that woman."

Lifting his hands to kiss them, Aaralee smiled lightly "I wouldn't dream of it."

The door to the healing room opened, and a young healing apprentice stepped out. She quickly dropped to the floor to bow before her rulers.

"Your Highnesses, the healer invites you in now to see to the prisoner. She's been in and out of consciousness and is suffering greatly. She has been asking for our queen."

Thaylos tensed. "We will speak with her."

The apprentice nodded and moved to the side, allowing the king and queen to enter the room. Since all the curtains of the chamber had been let out, the only light remaining was the soft glow of the stone lights along the walls. On the tables along the sides sat various medicinal vials that the head healer had been attempting to concoct an antidote with. The far side of the room held a bundle of incense burning on the ritual altar, calling to their All Powerful Eye for aid. Thick, pungent smoke coated the room. Aaralee fought back the cough rising in her throat. She knew the incense was necessary to honor the Eye, but breathing in its sickly-sweet haze always irritated her lungs.

Moving to the far corner of the room, they came to the extravagant bed meant to hold Their Majesties in times of illness. Instead of the heavy down comforter usually present, an airy, light sheet was draped across a trembling form. The prisoner lay in the bed, sweat-soaked and struggling in pain. The woman's skin had worsened in color since Aaralee had seen the other soldiers carry her from their meeting place. Instead of ghostly pale, it now took on a greenish tint with some purpling here and there, along with far too many blisters and boils to count. The prisoner's body clearly had an aggressive reaction to the poison. She wouldn't last much longer. Aaralee could distinctly see nearly every vein. A shudder passed through her own body. *That could have been me.* Glancing at the bedside table, Aaralee's eyes caught on a strange metal object with two small crystals next to it. Not recognizing the tool, Aaralee turned to question the healer.

"Laurel, what is that for?"

Following the queen's line of sight, the old woman kept her head low as she answered, "That was the Saunskirt badge, Your Majesty. Apparently, the poison forced the badge off."

"Cruel bit of irony," Thaylos mused aloud as he stood transfixed at the end of the bed. "To be released of one painful death because another overtook you."

It surprised Aaralee to see the flash of concern spark through her husband's eyes. Was he actually feeling sympathy for this woman? Seeing him send a few discreet glances her way, Aaralee understood better. He too was feeling the weight of what could have been, of how close his own wife had been to lying in that bed.

Moving to stand at the side of the mattress, Aaralee bent for a closer look but still kept a safe distance. Even from here, she could sense the king tensing. Quieting her frustration over his irrational fear, Aaralee leaned in again toward the suffering soul before her. Why would anyone do something like this? Why sacrifice themselves for an enemy? She didn't understand.

The prisoner's eyes fluttered open weakly as a moment of awareness seemed to dawn on her. The woman turned her eyes to meet Aaralee's. Was that relief she saw on the prisoner's face? Her lips began to move, but the voice was too soft for Aaralee to understand. Knowing her husband could not handle her drawing any nearer, Aaralee turned back to the head healer for help.

"The prisoner is trying to say something. What is it, Laurel?"

Laurel dutifully came to her queen's side and bent her ear to just above the prisoner's lips. "She is saying she is glad to see you well, Your Highness. She has been worried about you. And she thanks you for the care you're now showing her. She says . . . it . . . pleases the Holy Father." Laurel stood once again so she wouldn't block the queen's view of the dying woman.

Thaylos grunted contemptuously at the mention of the Fiesian god, but Aaralee kept her gaze on the perplexing woman before her. The same question continued to pound within her until she couldn't help but let it out.

"Prisoner . . . I-Iris . . . you saved my life. Why?"

Laurel promptly leaned back over the prisoner to listen for the reply. An eternity seemed to pass as Aaralee waited. Finally, the old woman looked up at her queen in reluctance, clearly not comfortable to speak what she heard.

"She says, Your Majesty, because . . . *He* loves you . . ."

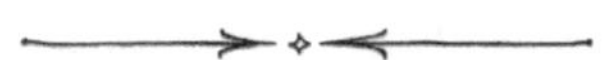

Hot sunlight broke through the darkness yet again as people worked to unload the much-needed supplies. Kyle winced each time the rays fell across his face. If he was going to die, couldn't he at least die in peace? Surely there was another medical tent they could use to store Healer Markson's supplies? They probably figured it would be empty of its occupant soon enough, so it made sense to get started now. Still, he longed for uninterrupted sleep. He just wanted to be left alone. If he had the strength to chase them off, he would have. Instead, his voice remained trapped within his broken body, barely able to rise much above a whisper. He could no longer roll to a different side without excruciating pain pulsing through the infected wounds on his back. He was trapped on his left side. Granted, having his arm go numb was a bit of a relief in comparison.

Another beam of light assaulted his eyes, forcing him to squeeze them shut. What he wouldn't give to face his head at the other end of the cot. But that task he couldn't accomplish without help, and he wasn't about to stoop so low as to ask anyone for a favor.

A tentative touch on his shoulder caused Kyle to pry one eye open. A beautiful woman with large, pale-blonde ringlets loosely resting above her shoulders leaned over him. She held up a canteen of water and smiled. *Her again!* Kyle groaned inwardly. *Just let me be, woman!* Her persistently stubborn visits to tend to him when he just wanted to be left alone in his misery grated on his last nerve. What did he have worth living for anyway?

"Hello, Mr. Sad Sack. Me again." Tess offered him a broad smile.

"Gotcha some fresh water. And wouldn't ya know that we finally got that supplies from Alaster?"

Annoyed, Kyle narrowed his eyes.

"Now, I won't be having any attitude from you this time, Mr. Sad Sack. I've got my boys with me, and you will be responding to their kindness in the way they deserve." Tess spoke in a playful tone edged with a serious warning.

Summoning what strength he could muster, Kyle turned his head slightly. Attached to Tess's hip was a small boy he guessed to be between two and four. A couple of older boys stood to either side of her. Kyle recognized one of them as the overly enthusiastic son of the healer. He didn't know where the rest came from nor why Tess felt it necessary to tote them along with her. Kale kneeled on the ground beside Kyle's cot so he was eye to eye with him. Concern etched tiny little furrows across the kid's face.

"Hey, Mr. Druthers." Kale spoke in a surprisingly soft tone. "You're really not looking so good, are ya? Don't worry, me and my pals are going to change that."

Kyle offered Kale a sad smile. The little guy had a good heart—that much he could give him. Tess squatted down on the ground next to Kale, shifting the smallest boy to rest on her knee. She looked at the child as she cooed to him.

"Okay, baby, I'm going to need both hands now to help Mr. Kyle here. Can you be the *best* helper ever and stand right next to me?" The child gave an almost imperceptible nod of agreement. "That's my amazing, big boy!" Tess smiled as she gave the child a tender kiss atop his head and set him down the rest of the way.

Scooching closer to Kyle, she gently lifted his head so he could drink from the canteen. Tess frowned when she saw his face contort in pain.

"So sorry, hun. I know it's miserable, but you have *got* to get more water down. I promised Jason I would keep you going at least until he got back, and I aim to have him a cousin to return to."

With considerable effort, Kyle finished off most of the water in the canteen. Lowering his head to rest it on the makeshift pillow, Tess took out a clean cloth and soaked it in the last of the water. She proceeded to wash the sweat from Kyle's face and neck.

"Now, my sweet boys here have been begging me to take them to every hurting body in camp so they can pray over them. I don't know if you heard or not, but apparently these lads carry a special kind of power with their god. Practically raised another young man from the dead. Isn't that right, Kale?"

"Yes, ma'am," Kale beamed. "And if the Holy Father can help Liam, I'm sure He'll help you too, Mr. Druthers. So, is it okay if we pray for you?"

Kyle tensed at the name of the Holy Father. He began to work up the strength to thank them for their kindness but admit he wasn't interested.

Leaning closer to Kyle as she continued to cool off his face and neck, Tess whispered in his ear. "Say yes to these precious babies, or so help me, I will make sure you regret every passing minute."

Angry but knowing better than to test her when he couldn't fight back, Kyle forced a weak smile onto his face and answered Kale in a hoarse voice. "Go for it, kid."

Kale's eyes lit up as he and the rest of his friends quickly gathered around him and placed their hands on his body. Each took turns petitioning their beloved creator. Kyle studied Tess as she watched "her boys" like a proud mother. He doubted any of them belonged to her. None of them carried a trace of her distinct Sylphaenian features. Could these be the surviving children from the massacre? He had overheard many whisperings from the X32 residents as they'd moved in and out of his tent. Amazing how freely people felt they could speak when standing in front of a man they knew was dying. It wasn't like he could give away their secrets.

A new heaviness seemed to press in all around Kyle as he waited for the children to stop praying. He could feel his consciousness beginning to slip away. He hated fading in and out like this. Fighting with all his might to stay present, Kyle let his eyes rove around to try and keep his mind active.

The sound of someone rushing in and nearly crashing into others on the way grabbed everyone's attention. It was enough of a distraction to reignite Kyle's thoughts. Unable to shift his head to identify the person, he could only assume the voice belonged to a young man. He sounded like one of the checkpoint guards who had come by before.

"Everyone up and out, *now*. We have to go."

Kyle recognized that tone. He'd used it many times to cover his own panic. *What happened?*

Tess scooped up the youngest boy as she stood. "What's going on?"

The guard tensed at seeing the children. "I'll explain on the way. No time for packing. Grab what you can and go. Follow the guards into the mountains."

Immediately, the other people in the tent latched back onto some of the crates they had set down and ran out of the tent as the guard held back the flap to let them pass. Once everyone except for the crew surrounding Kyle left, the guard put up a hand in front of Tess.

"Not everyone is going to be able to fit in our fortification in the mountainside," the guard said. "We have been instructed to send the children and the wounded on the transport back to Alaster."

"My mom?" Kale stepped up, fear lacing his voice.

"She's helping bring out the patients. You make your way to the transport, Kale, and I'm sure you'll run into her."

Kale nodded and turned back to Kyle's cot, promptly untying and retying the straps in a practiced manner.

"Kale, hun, what are you doing? You and your friends need to get going," Tess instructed.

"And we will, but if my mama is getting her patients out, I'm gonna help. This cot can be transformed into a carrier real easy. All you gotta do is move some of the straps off the brace on the sides and place them up here. Mama taught me. It'll be just a second."

The three other boys stepped in to help. Two held the fabric of the cot taunt to make sure Kyle wouldn't fall through as they changed the ties. Tess knelt with the boys, holding the fabric, and lent her hands to their task. Within a moment, they had detached the top from the brace and had the carrier and Kyle resting on the ground, ready to go.

Pointing to the long sides of the carrier, Kale instructed his friends. "Pace and Destin, you guys take that spot there. Jodie and I will get the other side. Ms. Tess and Mr. Anson, could you each grab the head and feet positions? Mama says Mr. Druthers needs lots of help, so we'll need to move him as smoothly as possible."

Everyone, save the guard, quickly took their places. Moving the small boy from her arms so he could cling onto her back, Tess called to the guard. "Come on, you heard the kid. Get in your spot. We have to hurry."

The guard jogged over and grasped at the feet. "All right, then, on my count. One, two, and lift! Now, move quickly."

They passed out of the tent and began briskly making their way through the campground. People ran around them, carrying what they could and trying to follow the directions the checkpoint guards gave as they passed by. The smell of smoke wafted through the air. As they ran, harsh popping sounds echoed from a great distance. Though drifting in and out of consciousness, Kyle was present enough to know what was happening. *Gunshots . . .* Someone, somewhere, was fighting.

"All right, spill, soldier boy!" Tess cried out over her shoulder. She faced out away from Kyle's head, keeping her end lifted from behind. "We're on our way now. What's going on.?"

"Those Yansairens discovered one of our camps. We think they were searching for the boys. Aiden has ordered everyone to retreat. We're not taking any chances of them finding the rest of us."

"So why are you here and not over there helping them fight?" Jodie challenged Anson.

"Soon as we get as many of you out as we can, the rest of the guard that can be spared will get to them," Anson answered calmly, deflecting the child's accusatory tone.

An anxious cloud settled over the group as they all rushed onward to the distant clearing where the transport was located. Many other children rushed alongside them, being led by either another guard or the children's mothers. But because of having to carry Kyle, their group lagged behind. Fifteen minutes in, Destin's and Pace's strength began to ebb.

"Tighten up, guys!" Jodie commanded them. "We can't let Mr. Druthers roll off!"

Stirring themselves up again, both nodded to Jodie and obeyed.

"You're doing a great job holding on, Jacob," Tess encouraged the small boy on her back. "Keep that grip strong, baby, and we'll make it through this."

A strange sense of shame washed over Kyle as he listened to their struggle. Who was he that these kids would put so much effort into helping him? If these boys knew, if Tess or this guard had any idea what sort of man he was . . . what things he had done . . . *You're wasting your time.* Kyle's mind soon went dark as he fell into another exhausted sleep.

Opening his eyes, Kyle noted the openness of the sky. *No trees . . .* They must be getting close to the transport road. Crossing this terrain was quite a risk while under attack in the middle of the day, because there was no cover. *What was Aiden thinking?* Kyle could feel by the sway of his carrier that the rate of their escape had slowed drastically. *They're tired . . . but they can't get lax now!* They needed to just leave him and go. Kyle tried with all his might to open his mouth and order them to drop him, but his body refused to cooperate. Why were his lips glued together like this? His mind worked but his body wouldn't obey.

"Okay, boys, I can see the transport in the distance," Anson declared. "You have all done a great job, but I need you to let Tess and I take care of this the rest of the way."

"No, I told you before I wasn't gonna stop till the job's done!" Kale protested.

"Kale, hun, you boys have been amazing, but we agreed that when we saw the transport, you would take Jacob and rush on ahead," Tess pressed lovingly.

Sounds like they had this discussion a couple of times while I was out.

"I know, but—"

"Mr. Anson!" Destin shouted as he looked back toward the tree line. "They found us!"

The team halted abruptly as Tess and Anson followed Destin's line of sight, where a handful of Yansairens emerged from the woods. Once they spotted the transport and the people moving toward it, the soldiers broke into a dead run in a desperate attempt to cut off their escape.

"Take Jacob and run, now!" Tess commanded.

Jodie reached up and took Jacob from Tess's back, and all four of the older kids sprinted for safety. The swaying of the carrier switched to a frantic jostling that sent surges of pain through Kyle's body. Anson and Tess panted heavily as they jogged along.

"Some of them are gaining!" Anson warned. "Think you'll be able to drag this guy the rest of the way?"

"If I have to. Why?"

"They get any closer and I'm gonna have to slow them down."

Tess snapped a look over her shoulder. "What? No! That's suicide!"

"Only option," Anson answered resolutely.

"*Aghhh!* All plagues on Yansair!" Tess screamed.

Ahead of them, the children successfully signaled to the small group of checkpoint guards waiting by the transport, alerting them to the imminent danger. Two moved to rush those nearby inside while the other three sprinted as hard as their legs could carry them toward the enemy. *Just leave me!* Kyle's mind screamed at them. Their lives weren't worth his.

"Ready!" Anson called to Tess.

They both paused abruptly as Anson set down his end, withdrew his sword from its scabbard, and spun back around to take on the closest advancing soldier. Tess squatted to lower her end and yanked Kyle's arm to drape him across her back. Kyle let out an involuntary yelp of pain at the harsh movement.

"Sorry, hun," Tess apologized. "Just hang on. We'll get you through this."

Gritting her teeth, Tess pushed up on her legs while hanging onto Kyle's arms. She pitched forward and put every ounce she had into getting him to safety. A few curses slipped through her lips as she dragged him.

The ringing clang of metal striking metal sounded behind them. Anger pumped through Kyle's veins. He was so useless. *Work!* He screamed at himself. *Work, body! Legs, move! She can't do this without you.* The checkpoint guards were closing in, but they were still too far out. *Useless prayers! Useless Holy Father! If You were worth anything, You'd show up now!*

"Ah!" Tess cried out as her legs buckled underneath her, causing them both to drop straight down.

"No! . . . No! . . . No!" Tess shouted at herself between huffs of breath. "Get up!" she commanded herself as she took another gasp of air, clenched her jaw, and rose on wobbly legs.

As she attempted to move one sluggish step forward, Kyle felt a warmth expand through his body. His muscles tensed instinctively, and his heart beat faster as he realized he could flex his toes. Summoning everything he had within him, he began to drag a leg forward.

"Kyle?" Tess said.

Pulling up the other leg, Kyle swayed upward, taking as much weight as he could off of Tess. He panted heavily as the heat swelled into an intense fire throughout his body. Tess took the chance to switch him from her back to lean on her side. Since he still wasn't completely able to hold himself up, Kyle allowed Tess to keep carrying him. The two moved in a staggered jaunt. Kyle's vision blurred in and out of focus as they forged on, but his feet kept going. The blood in his veins pounded in his ears as his head became overwhelmingly dizzy. Suddenly, another man joined up beside them, grasping Kyle on the right and shifting most of his weight to his own body. The man's two comrades continued to sprint past to reach Anson's side in time. Feeling as if something had burst within him, Kyle blacked out entirely.

The touch of cold metal on his skin brought him to once more. *We made it inside?* Kyle opened his eyes to Tess holding him on the floor of the transport, bracing him along the back wall. Others were positioned beside them who apparently hadn't had the time or space to strap in.

"Everyone, hang on!" a voice called out from somewhere as the doors began to close.

Harsh mechanical sounds hissed around them as the transport started up and then took off. Tess held Kyle firmly, keeping him from sliding around. Soon the calm, steady humming of the transport settled in. The quiet was broken by scattered sniffles and hushed wails. Kyle felt Tess trembling as she continued to cradle him.

"Oh, Anson . . ." she moaned softly.

Her mournful cry tore at Kyle's heart. Yet even more lives lost because of him. It wasn't right. . . . *I will* make things right, Kyle swore to himself as he faded into the darkness.

Chapter Eleven

A heavy cloud of incense soaked the room in an artificial haze, leaving a strange aftertaste in the mouths of anyone who walked inside. The Great Mother had become desperate for the revival of Yansair's most dangerous prisoner. Whispers echoed through the court halls that if the prisoner could not be saved in order to be "purely sacrificed" later, then the All Powerful Eye may never lift the curse of the drought from their lands. The Great Mother instructed the palace attendants to keep three times the normal amount of healing incense burning inside the prisoner's borrowed chamber, without pause. Since the amount of incense bundles brought up from the sacred hall had been woefully miscalculated, the servants were forced to put off their usual tasks to aid in its transportation.

People rushed in with their stacks, bringing a new level of chaos and confusion into the royal healing room. Many new faces came to fill the gaps made by those struck by the day terrors that continued to pervade the palace grounds. A group of new slave girls followed their etiquette trainer into the mess. Headmistress Yanira declared this stress a good opportunity to test the girls and see which ones could handle themselves with grace. After all, only the best royal courtesans knew how to flow naturally with elegance no matter their circumstance. It also didn't hurt to gain the favor of the Great Mother by jumping to fulfill her needs.

The stream of young, wide-eyed girls followed their leader into the heart of Yansair's whispers. Some split off to deliver the incense to the altar, while others were whisked to the side to receive a quick teaching from one of the associate healers. Pulled along with the healer group, Sara tried her best to fade into the background. The more unseen she could remain, the better off she would be. Fighting hard to not get separated from the other Throansburrough girls at the sorting grounds, she caught the eye of Headmistress Yanira. Recalling how the mistress and her lackeys had checked her skin and teeth for flaws made Sara shudder involuntarily. She couldn't afford to stand out. Sara hated the peering eyes, and she had already witnessed how toxically favorites were treated by the other girls. A tan-skinned man with a clean-shaven face dressed in the customary whites of the healing division strolled purposefully toward the group as they stood by a table strewn with medicinal concoctions.

"All right, ladies, listen up. I will *not* be repeating this. As you can see, I don't have room to be wasting any extra time on you lot," the young associate healer barked. "My name is Barth. You will call me Healer Barth. But you are *not* to call me at all unless you do something horribly, horribly stupid that might get someone killed. Understood?"

"Yes, Healer Barth," the group answered in unison.

"Good. Now, who of you here can tell me *why*, upon the Eye, courtesans need to know the healing arts?" Barth scanned each uncertain face until his eyes settled on a lanky brown-haired girl with almond eyes and pouty lips. "You, what's your name?"

"Ersmé," she answered softly.

"Ersmé, why do you need to know healing?"

Twirling a strand of hair around her finger, Ersmé paused for a second before answering. "Be-cause . . . it'll make us more . . . desirable?"

"Two points for Ersmé. You children will one day join the ranks of the lofty royal courtesans—that is, *if* you're deemed worthy of favor. The more skills you have to entertain or tend to your patrons, the more likely you can keep your position."

Moving as mechanically as he spoke, Barth brought forth a case of vials filled with varying liquids. Handing a vial to each girl, he continued.

"*But* if you lack the skill set, your pretty face won't keep you from being bumped down to the guards—ahem—*revelry* houses." Making eye contact with each of them, Barth released the first hint of genuine care as he warned, "Trust me, girls. You *don't* want to end up there."

A new terror settled over Sara as she studied the vial in her hands. Apparently, remaining unseen wasn't safe either. Eyes drifting to the windows covered by the heavy curtains, Sara's heart picked up its pace. There *had* to be a way to escape this nightmare. Jodie would never forgive her if she didn't try.

"I've handed each of you one of the basic medicinal treatments all healers start with. Do *not* open your vial until I instruct you to do so." Barth turned toward the mixing table and motioned for the girls to follow.

As the rest quickly obeyed, Sara noticed that Ersmé allowed herself to be pushed to the back. Sidling up next to Sara, Ersmé whispered into her ear. "That's the sixth time I've caught you studying the windows in the past half hour."

"W-what?" Sara whispered back, matching her tone.

"Come on, this is our best chance! No one is looking at us. Escape with me."

Looking around the room, Sara realized that Ersmé was right. Every person's attention was set on their task. None seemed to know the two of them even existed. But . . . could this girl be trusted? And even though they weren't currently being watched, it wasn't like they could walk out the doors without being noticed by *someone*. Or could they? So many people were coming and going. Maybe . . .

"Either come with me now, or get left behind," Ersmé whispered angrily as she placed her vial back on the table.

Sara pressed her lips together as her brow creased. Ersmé turned to leave. Taking a breath and setting down her own vial, Sara pursued the girl. Seeing that Ersmé made her way further into the chamber instead of toward the only door, Sara stepped up hurriedly behind her. "You have a plan?" she whispered.

Ersmé nodded as she kept her eyes watchful. "We'll hide until evening. Once it's dark, we'll escape using the windows."

"But we're at least three stories up," Sara countered as her steps faltered.

"We'll worry about that later. Now, let's go! We stand around talking and we'll start to draw attention."

Cautiously but swiftly, they made their way back to the far corner of the chamber. People whisked past them without a glance, as if they'd turned invisible. Realizing they were drawing closer to where this feared, magical prisoner was being kept, Sara's eyes widened in panic. Surely Ersmé couldn't intend for them to hide beside a woman who terrorized an entire nation? *Just go back. It's not too late to turn around. There has to be other ways to get out. Right? But . . . what if this is it?* Moving forward, Sara noted two soldiers standing guard in front of the alcove that housed the prisoner. Ersmé swiftly stepped out of their line of sight, pressing herself up against a column and using its shadow as cover. Sara matched her actions.

"How do we get around *them*?" Sara lamented.

"Beyttini. She's one of the girls near the incense altars. It's her job to come up with a distraction."

Sara shifted anxiously. "H-how long do you think—"

"*Fire!*" A terrified screech sounded from somewhere behind them.

Screams erupted as the scent in the air shifted from perfumed incense to the dark, smoky smell of burning fabric. The guards standing watch over the prisoner bolted from their posts to put out the flames before they spread too quickly. In the chaos, Ersmé and Sara grasped at their chance to dash over to the opulent bed and search for a hiding place. Sara fought the rising urge to look at the form beneath the bedsheet. Ersmé didn't give the woman a second glance, quickly ducking under the bed. Sara knew she should follow, but her feet stayed rooted in place. The draw to find out who this prisoner was grew stronger, and she was only briefly aware of another figure running up behind her. Beyttini came up beside Sara and paused until she noticed Ersmé beckoning to her from beneath the bed. Immediately, the delicate, toffee-skinned girl joined her compatriot in her hideaway.

"What are you doing?" Ersmé hissed at Sara. "Hide, or you'll give us away!"

Though she knew Ersmé was right, Sara just *had* to know. Slowly, with great fear, she lifted her eyes to follow the outline of the woman's form as she lay stone-like on the bed. When her gaze landed on her face, Sara was disturbed by the woman's discoloration and boil-covered skin. The ragged breathing and the color reminded her of when she'd visited her grandmother the day before she had passed. As Sara studied this prisoner's face, something began to stir within her. The woman didn't *look* dangerous. In fact, she somehow looked . . . familiar? As if Sara had seen her before. *I . . . know her. . . . No, that can't be. But . . .* Taking a step closer, Sara gasped and thrust her hands over her mouth as the realization grabbed her.

"Miss Iris!"

Tears welled up in Sara's eyes as she looked upon her favorite teacher of the Sacred Texts. Her heart twisted to see this precious reminder of home. "Oh, Miss Iris . . . what did they do to you?"

Sorrow streamed from her eyes as Sara stepped forward and grasped Iris's hand. Her voice quivered with each broken breath. "Please . . . please . . ." Sara's shoulders trembled as she fought back the moan caught in her throat. Leaning in close, she begged in a painful whisper, "Please . . . Miss Iris, please don't die." Tears dripped off her chin and splashed onto her discolored hand. "We need you. I need you. . . . Th-the girls need our help, a-and I can't do it. . . . I'm not big enough—strong enough. Please, Miss Iris, this can't be an accident! It just can't! These-these people fear you. You can stop this. They told me what you've done. You're what we've been praying for, I'm *sure* of it. At least . . . you just have to be. So please . . . wake up. Please."

Desperation swelled inside Sara. Something within told her this was her last hope. Feet lifting from the floor, she curled tightly against the woman's lifeless form. A wail overtook her as she buried her face into the sheet covering Iris's stomach.

"Please, Holy Beloved! Holy Beloved, *please*! Holy Beloved!"

All thoughts of hiding and escaping vanished. The need to cry out to the Holy Beloved consumed her. Ersmé and Beyttini gave up trying to silence her.

"Let the fool get herself caught!" Ersmé hissed. "I will *not* let her steal my chance!"

The approach of hurried footsteps drove Ersmé and Beyttini further under the bed. Gasps of horror and outrage ricocheted through the chamber.

"Get her off of there!" the head healer, Laurel, commanded.

Rushing to obey, a soldier grasped at the wailing Sara. "Augh!" he cried as he jerked his hand away and attempted to shake off the pain.

Eyes widening in confusion, the man stretched out his hand once more to lay hold of Sara, who continued to sob the name of the Holy Beloved, but he yanked it back with a shout of pain.

"What are you doing?" Laurel demanded. "Remove that child! She could harm the prisoner!"

The guard stared, mouth agape, at his hand. Turning it toward Laurel, everyone gasped as his skin swelled and blistered.

"Impossible . . ." Laurel's eyes widened in disbelief.

"Fool, you're simply becoming aware of your injuries from putting out the fire!" snapped the elder soldier. "Get out of the way!"

Shoving the younger man aside, he thrust his hand out. As he hovered just above Sara, his eyes grew large. Clenching his jaw, he pushed forward to remove the weeping child. The sickly, pervasive smell of burning flesh rose in the air as she grasped her wrist.

"Let go! You're destroying your hand!" Laurel commanded.

The younger soldier jumped in and wrenched the man away. The mangled mess of his hand turned even Laurel's seasoned stomach.

"Barth! Quick! Take this man to the healing rooms. Call on Adora. She might be able to save his hand if you move fast enough."

Running up to the man's side, Barth grasped him around the waist as the soldier's knees buckled beneath him. Sweat poured down his colorless face as he bit back cries of anguish. Another young healing apprentice balanced out the other side, helping Barth whisk the ailing soldier to Adora.

"And what of you?" Laurel asked the remaining soldier.

Shaking off his shock, the soldier straightened, regaining composure. "I will stay until others can release me of my post."

Laurel pursed her lips. "Very well. We'll do some temporary care for your hand here until your replacements come. And as for the child . . ." Laurel's words trailed off as she studied the scene.

Sweat soaked through the young girl's clothes, plastering the fabric to her skin. Tears streamed down her face, dampening the sheets lying across the prisoner's stomach. Waves of heat rippled through the air above them. As the child's lamenting persisted, the prisoner's breathing grew deep and slow, as if she was sleeping soundly.

"Madame Healer!" cried a panicked attendant. "The boils! Look!"

Laurel gasped as she witnessed a boil sink down into the prisoner's skin and fade until only a delicately smooth complexion remained. One after the other, the sores closed up or vanished entirely. Frantic rustling burst from beneath the bed as Beyttini clawed her way out, gasping for cool air.

"What is going on here?" Laurel demanded as the attendant grasped hold of the wilting Beyttini.

The child's long, dark hair clung to her dripping body. Pushing the hair from her glazed eyes, Laurel assessed the hideaway. Beyttini's skin was hot to the touch and she appeared moments from unconsciousness.

"Child, tell me, what have you girls done?" Laurel grasped Beyttini's face between her hands, attempting to make the young girl focus on her. "Do you know how this is happening?"

"Er-Ersmé . . ." Beyttini pushed out "Help her." Weakly, she pointed beneath the bed before completely collapsing in the attendant's arms.

The soldier rushed to lift the bed skirt and kneeled on the floor to investigate. Splayed out on the ground was Ersmé's inanimate body. Dropping onto his side, the soldier reached his uninjured hand in and clamped onto a limp arm, swiftly pulling Ersmé from the suffocating heat radiating off the bed. He dragged her a few steps back and rested her body on the stone floor. The female healing apprentice, Fairen, rushed forward, inspecting the sweat-drenched child's vitals.

"Her pulse has slowed, but she's alive," Fairen reported to Laurel.

"Seems these two have succumbed to heat stroke." Laurel pursed her lips while studying both unconscious forms. "You'll need to reduce their temperatures immediately. Fairen, you and Danes see to these two quickly, and watch them closely. We don't know what role they've played in this phenomenon."

Fairen nodded as two more attendants stepped in to aid her and Danes. Keeping her eyes fixed on the prisoner and the still-wailing girl, Laurel frowned and spoke to the young soldier. "We clearly don't understand what sort of power is at work here, but whatever it is, the danger is serious. Until we can better discern the source, no one should approach the prisoner or the girl. My healers are stretched thin as it is. We can't afford to add to the patient load."

"Yes, Madame Healer." The soldier nodded as a palace attendant nearing middle age applied a salve to his burnt hand.

Laurel turned around with a sigh, seeing a gathering crowd of onlookers. The young courtesans-in-training huddled together by the table of medicine. "All right, which of you knows where your Mistress Yanira has gone?"

Wide eyes darted around. Finally, a petite girl with tawny beige skin squeaked, "I-I think sh-she's gone to-to, um, fetch more guards." She kept her pure-black eyes fixed to the floor as she spoke.

"I knew it was a mistake bringing training courtesans into this. Why I ever let Yanira talk me into her hairbrained ideas, I'll never know! Fires, magic, and now a gaggle of useless, terrified children. The

Eye knows I have enough to combat already," Laurel vented to no one in particular.

"Madame Healer," the woman tending the guard's hand interjected, "I can see to these girls until Mistress Yanira returns, if you wish?"

"Forgive me, but what was your name again?"

"Kamile, Madame Healer."

Narrowing her eyes as she studied the woman for a second, recognition buzzed in her mind. This woman was one of the Great Mother's closest attendants.

Laurel nodded. "It'll have to do. Take these children back to their quarters. Remain with them until Mistress Yanira returns."

"Yes, Madame Healer." Kamile dipped her head as she rose to usher the young girls from the healing chamber.

As they left, Laurel refocused on the bed. How could she ever explain this to the king and queen? The Great Mother was going to be livid knowing an impure not only disrupted the Eye's healing rituals but that whatever was taking place was far more effective. The rate at which the prisoner's skin had healed and color had returned to her face was impossible. What sort of sorcery was Throansburrough's prophet capable of? What exactly had they brought upon Diridos?

Chapter Twelve

A soft red-and-yellow light undulated across Darren's face, accentuating the deep, angry furrows of his brow. The bonfire's flames twisted about in tandem with the passionate cries of worship from the warriors who danced in the dark. Fists clenched so tight they ached, Darren flitted his boiling glare between Phineah and Jason as they whirled and sang at opposite ends of the fire circle. The tempos of the drums and other instruments ran fast and lively, matching the furious intensity of the people spinning and trumpeting their songs of praise to their Holy Father. What sort of sick and twisted lot had he aligned himself with? Not an ounce of the recent news they received deserved such an outpouring of worship to a deity who clearly wasn't doing them any favors.

The children stolen from Fitsengea had already been largely dispersed throughout the sorting grounds. In the streets, the Diridos guards boasted of a successful attack on those "annoying X32 inhabitants." Apparently, yet another traitorous source within the walls of Alaster was giving away the residents' position—an unnerving notion of how far the betrayal reached. And then, there was Iris.

Darren swallowed hard and stalked away from the secret gathering.

Escaping the fire's light, he happily welcomed the somber blue-white of the moon. He wasn't foolish enough to wander far, but he needed enough distance so the music could drift away with the wind. The heat of the day had finally begun to lift. Darren inhaled a slow, calming breath, willing the pinprick of tears in his eyes to dissipate. His mind bounced over the last two weeks. *Only two weeks passed, and nothing will be the same again.*

Uncle Zaerin would surely declare war out of hubris, but would the other lords back him? Valomeer may just be the beginning. Uncle Zaerin never was good at making friends. For all her brilliance and clout, Alaster was not as mighty as she seemed. She would not last long without her allies, and treachery from within would speed that along. War was coming, and Fitsengea might not survive. Anxiety and anger wrestled for dominance over Darren's heart.

"Iris . . ." his voice trembled. "I'm so sorry . . ."

Squeezing his eyes shut and gritting his teeth, anger won out. *My family line brought this upon us, and I'm too pathetic to stop it. How many lives must the Turner reign destroy?* The knot in his stomach grew as the muscles along his back and shoulders tensed. *You* have *to save those girls.* Darren's thoughts darted around, desperate to find a problem he could solve. Anything to lessen the darkness their kingdom helped to create. Throansburrough would live on through its children. *She* would live on.

Had he really given up on Iris? Was he so quick to turn from a fight? He started pacing involuntarily as a new wave of self-loathing swathed around him. The soft thud of feet casually working their way through the trees froze Darren in place. Scanning the darkness, he saw a figure approaching.

"Darren?" the figure questioned as he drew near. "Everything all right?"

Recognizing Fredrick's voice, Darren uncoiled his shoulders. "You about gave me a heart attack."

Fredrick smirked as he stepped into the moonlight. "Sorry about that, but *you* were the one who decided to traipse through the dark alone."

"I needed some air," Darren replied shortly, hoping to be finished with this conversation.

"You needed *air*." Fredrick scoffed and cocked an eyebrow. "You do realize you're outside, right?"

Darren pushed a breath out through his nose, letting his focus drift up to the moon. Fredrick stood silently, watching him, only the soft rhythm of their breathing breaking through. He turned his face into the moonlight and crossed his arms over his chest. Fredrick's calm and stoic presence beside Darren thrummed agitation through his blood.

"If you have something to say, spit it out." Darren's calm tone thinly masked his annoyance.

Fredrick smirked and glanced at him out of the corner of his eye. "Do you *want* to talk?"

Darren grunted. His eyes blurred in and out of focus on the shadowy forms of the trees. They stood tall and nearly leafless. Diridos was running dry, a land limping along.

"Are the reports of Yansair's drought as bad as we've been told?" Darren asked in spite of himself.

"Worse." Fredrick sighed. "They've succumbed to mining cave systems for underground rivers. The capital here has had some luck, causing quite the exodus of people to Diridos."

"But their technological advances and trading power has kept them prosperous enough to survive."

"It's waning, though. Yansair has grown desperate."

"Desperation is dangerous."

"Perhaps . . . but a desperate people with unshakeable hope and stubborn faith, now *that's* something to be feared."

Darren's eyes narrowed as his lips curled into a slight sneer. "How can you people remain so cocky at a time like this?"

Fredrick turned to him and raised an eyebrow. "Cocky? Is *that* what you think is going on here?"

"I wouldn't label that raucousness back there as particularly mournful," Darren shot back.

"No, I suppose you wouldn't," Fredrick answered thoughtfully. "Do you think it's time we all give up, then?"

Darren snapped his head to Fredrick. "Of course not! I'm saying you should all learn to read a situation and know how to handle it with the solemnity it warrants!"

Fredrick held his gaze with gentle eyes. "Mourning is the process of grief you undergo when it's time to let go of something, when a dream is gone, when it's all over. *This* isn't over, Darren." His kind eyes sparkled with hope in the evening's blue-white glow. "What you saw back there was certainly not mourning, but it wasn't necessarily celebration either. It was our determined intercession, our desperate cry to our Holy Father to choose to believe in His goodness and that He will come through, our promise to keep fighting beyond our breaking inside and pour out our lives for what is right. It was our taunt to the Great Deceiver of this world that even his greatest darkness will not cause us to falter. Darren . . . did you not see the tears that fell from their eyes as they danced and sang?" Pain spread through his features as he continued. "Do you really count us so heartless? You have *no* idea the *years* of torment these people have undergone. Don't for one second underestimate them as being flippant. Too much has been sacrificed for that."

The calm ferocity of his words slashed through Darren's anger, and shame spread around his heart. He was so arrogant and single-minded, he'd forgotten what was happening here hadn't started with Iris. It hadn't even started with Fitsengea. His world may revolve around his homeland, but the rest of the world only occasionally collided with his own.

Darren winced and sighed. "Sorry, Fred. I lost sight of the scope of all this."

Pressing his lips into a thin line, Fredrick replied with a twitch of a nod and turned his gaze up to the moon. Both men embraced the silence as it settled in around them. A slight breeze whispered through the trees, stirring dried leaves from their branches and pulling them lazily to the ground.

"Fred, how long has Valomeer been partnering with Yansair?"

Fredrick stiffened beside him. "They've been secret trading partners for years. Maybe even decades. Saunskirt has profited greatly from the Sylphaen and Yansair war. But this outright treachery? Those talks began about five years ago."

"Five years ago . . ."

"Yes, after it was clear King Zaerin no longer had an heir. Lord Valomeer believed it was only a matter of time that the Turner reign would come to an end."

An intense pain squeezed Darren's heart. "Marriam's death ushered in all of this?"

He suddenly wanted to retch. Spitting to rid the taste of bile rising into his mouth, Darren braced himself against a nearby tree.

Fredrick offered Darren a knowing look. "Princess Marriam's murder opened up the talks for a new sort of an alliance, and slowly, over the years, Lord Valomeer began to indoctrinate his military force to approve, promoting the most agreeable and weeding out those still loyal to the Crown."

I did this. I caused all of this. Darren's heart pounded in his ears. There was so, *so* much blood on his hands. A curse fell from his mouth. *Iris . . . It's all my fault.*

"I started all of this," Darren finally managed to voice. His legs gave out and he fell to his knees. "Throansburrough, Jaralynx, now X32 . . ."

"Did you kill her, Darren?" Fredrick asked.

Darren whipped his head up. "No!" Fury rattled his bones, then drained as intensely as it came. "But . . . I should have stopped it." His head dropped again as he squeezed his eyes shut and clenched his fists.

Fredrick walked over and dropped to one knee beside Darren. "An excuse that a vengeful opportunist like Valomeer was aching to jump at." He placed a hand on Darren's shoulder. "Lord Valomeer and King Zaerin have been at odds with each other for as long as I can remember. Darren, don't be so eager to claim responsibility for the deeds of wicked men. With or without your scandal, Valomeer's betrayal would have taken place."

Footfalls pounded up from behind them, causing both men to look up. Jason sprinted to Darren's side, hand grasping the pommel of his sheathed sword. "Your Grace, are you all right?" His wide eyes scanned Darren.

Fredrick slowly tilted his head up to Jason with a look of incredulity. "At ease, soldier. It's been a bit of a tough day for all of us."

Jason kept his stare fixed on Darren. Taking a few deep breaths, Darren willed his heart back to a normal rhythm. His annoyance rose when he glanced up at Jason.

"You have *got* to relax," Darren growled.

A flush spread across Jason's face as he faltered back a half step. "I-I'm sorry, sir. It's just, when I saw you were missing, and then you collapsing to the ground from far off . . ." Jason quickly shifted to standing at attention. "My poor judgment is to blame, sir." Dipping his head, remorse danced through his voice. "I hope you can forgive me for failing yet again, sir."

Darren cocked an eyebrow. "We've been through this before. Why not try taking Fred's advice. At ease, Jason."

"Sit with us for a minute, kid." Fredrick patted the ground next to him, grunting as he shifted into a more comfortable position. "Enough warring for tonight. Stillness is just as important."

Jason paused, looking to Darren for permission. Darren moved from his knees to sit fully on the ground and then lifted his chin a little, encouraging Jason to join. His shoulders releasing some of their stiffness, Jason relinquished and sat to Darren's right. All of their gazes wandered off to the distance. Something about the presence of his silent companions placed a balm on Darren's heart. He could breathe again. But there was a darkness lurking just out of reach, edging in around him. Fredrick's words stabbed at his thoughts. Valomeer made it possible for Yansair to begin their terror, but *he* had made it possible for Valomeer to betray them. Vengeful opportunist or not, the fact remained that Darren was at fault for affording him the opportunity.

An image of Iris appeared before his mind's eye. Her face twisted in anguish and disgust as she learned the truth. He imagined her hatred. Worse, he could see the tears in her eyes. His thoughts flooded to the torment she endured, now with a new, filthy layer procured by his own hands. She didn't deserve this.

"She's going to be okay." Jason spoke at last.

Fredrick and Darren turned their heads as one, waiting for him to continue.

"Lady Iris, I mean. I felt it when I was dancing. This *peace* settled over me." When Jason's focus rose to Darren, an almost otherworldly confidence shone from him. "Sir, I know you don't trust the Holy Father, and I know I don't seem that seasoned, but . . . I have faith in the prophecy from the Sacred Texts, faith in Lady Iris. What the Holy Father has spoken *will* come to pass. We can't give up just yet."

Muscles tightened in Darren's jaw as he bit back a reply. Jason's stubborn hope grated against his nerves. *I was that stupid once.* Pulling his gaze away, Darren studied his fingers as he spoke. "Careful, Jason. Hope has a nasty way of dropping you into some impossibly deep pits."

"It can also bring you back out again, when rooted in the right place," Fredrick interjected. "If you hold on long enough."

"I should make sure Bryant isn't getting into trouble," Darren offered disconnectedly, ignoring the comment as he shifted his weight and rose from the ground.

Fredrick grunted. "You're probably right." He stood once more and stretched. "Back into the fray we go."

A smirk pressed at the corners of Darren's mouth as Jason and Fredrick quietly walked back with him. Aggravating or not, their persistence was somehow admirable. As they neared the worship gathering, he noticed that the earlier fervor of the drums was now a slow, steady thrum. Sporadic dancers continued a gentle sway as the majority rested, seated in the dirt around the dimming fire. A few feet from the group, Darren locked onto the agitated pacing of Bryant. Noting their approach, Bryant hastily strode in their direction.

"You!" Bryant said in a low, rough voice while pointing at Fredrick. "What's going on with your people?"

Fredrick cocked an eyebrow.

"That little power trio. They ducked off quickly after some sort of messenger popped up. If something's up, I want to know."

Darren and Jason exchanged glances as Fredrick studied the distance. A little ways off, the forms of four figures conferring in the woods could just be made out.

"Wait here." Fredrick gestured with his hands, eyes narrowing, then swiftly jogged over to the meeting.

"Sir?" Jason whispered to Darren.

"I don't like this," Bryant grumbled.

"Just hold on," Darren advised, keeping his eyes trained on Fredrick's retreating form. "These guys still don't trust us. We could cause trouble if we go charging in. Fred's got this."

Jason nodded dutifully but glanced at Bryant. "How long have they been over there?"

Bryant crossed his arms tightly over his chest. "'Bout the same time you ran after old weak-kneed here." He tilted his head toward Darren, who rolled his eyes. "Thought better about following. I'm not the kind of guy who puts others at ease, so to speak. Been watching, though, making sure they don't run too far. These fanatical types can never be trusted."

Ignoring Bryant's griping, Darren studied the distance. Fredrick wasn't the most animated man, making it nearly impossible to gauge the situation by his reactions. After about a minute, Darren caught sight of Fredrick waving them over.

"That's our cue." Darren nodded and took off at a light jog, with Jason and Bryant following close behind.

Reaching the gathering, Darren noted a young boy no more than twelve among them. His jet-black hair was tied back in the traditional braid, slicked down from drying sweat. His face appeared flushed from running, though his breathing had steadied. Oriel stood to Phineah's right, ever the silent statue, and Elias to her left, immediately glaring at Darren's approach.

"Your Grace." Phineah dipped her head. Ethereal moonlight reflected in her eyes and cast a radiant glow across her smooth skin. "We've just received some promising information. We may have a way of tracking down the children."

Darren half stepped forward. "How?"

"Some eyes inside the palace came across sorting grounds sale records. There was a ledger written up specifically for the daughters of Throansburrough and Jaralynx."

A breath of hope caught in Darren's throat. "How do we get our hands on those papers?"

Phineah hesitated, flicking her eyes to her comrades and back. "We'll have to acquire them ourselves. Our point of contact in the palace is too precious to risk."

"So it's a break-in, then." Bryant smirked and cracked his knuckles.

"You find risking lives amusing?" Elias accused, narrowing his eyes at Bryant.

Bryant shrugged. "Only if you do it right."

Elias threw an angry look at Darren, clearly blaming him for bringing such a creature along. Darren suppressed the urge to outwardly cringe.

"Definitely not putting them at ease," Jason muttered under his breath, barely within Darren's hearing.

Fredrick broke through the rising hostility. "Oriel has volunteered himself to help get you in and out. He's the best chance for blending in, being a native."

Phineah nodded. "Though Yansair is no stranger to foreigners due to slave trading, around palace grounds they still draw suspicious eyes. Especially if caught unaccompanied."

"Wait," Darren interjected, turning his eyes back to Fredrick. "Fred said *you*. Does that mean you're not joining us?"

Fredrick pressed his lips into a thin line. "I'm afraid so. I had to buy us more time for sticking around Diridos without raising alarm. I was able to convince one of the major lieutenants that he desired to have another detailed meeting with me."

A fresh rise of nerves surprised Darren. He hadn't noticed till now how important Fredrick's presence had become to his sense of security. Worse was Oriel's gruff stoicism, making him almost impossible to read. *We didn't come all this way for comfort.* Whatever the cost, they *had* to help those young girls.

"Right, then. What do we need to do?"

"Return back to your inn and get some sleep. Oriel will arrive early to gather you. Make sure to dress in your Saunskirt gear," Phineah calmly instructed before turning to address the young boy. "Piéter, the papers, please."

Reaching into a satchel at his side, Piéter first unwrapped a small rock bound up in a piece of cloth and quickly polished it. *No. That's not a rock. That's a stone light!* Darren's eyes widened as the little orb began glowing, allowing Piéter to search through his satchel for the correct set of papers.

Jason turned his head away from the others and whispered to Darren. "Since when did Yansair have access to stone lights?"

"Thank you," Phineah spoke at last as she took the proffered parchments from the boy and handed them off to Darren. "We were fortunate to obtain an old set of supply orders from one of Saunskirt's regiments. They are innocuous enough to require little inspection, but they offer a steady alibi for your presence on palace grounds."

Glancing over the documents, Darren's mind remained fixated on the stone light. Alaster proudly guarded that technology; it was practically *the* symbol of the capital. Saunskirt wouldn't have access to trading them unless granted by the royal council, and with Valomeer's and Zaerin's well-known hatred for each other, any sort of agreement was unlikely. It was rare for even typical Alastrians lucky enough to obtain one to part with them. They'd equate it as giving up their identity. So how in all the lands did this young messenger boy from Diridos so casually possess it? For a nation the Royal Church council deemed too unholy for any association, Fitsengea seemed more and more entwined with Yansair.

Phineah released Piéter to return to his masters. The boy nodded and used his stone light to guide his way as he raced through the darkness. Unsettled by mounting implications, Darren refocused on the conversation.

Phineah seemed to study Darren's expression as she concluded her instructions. "It will be best if we all part ways for the evening. Any plan executed on lack of sleep only promises ruin."

Darren stiffly nodded and shook Phineah's hand. "Thank you, for everything. We'd be lost without you. Those girls would be lost without you. Everything you're risking in this, just . . . thank you."

Phineah firmly returned the handshake, eyes glistening. "May the Holy Father be with you tomorrow. Sleep well, Your Grace."

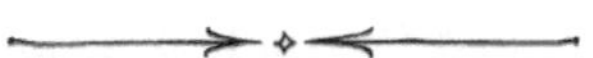

Warmth spiraled slowly through Iris's body, igniting her nerves with lingering tingles. She pulled cool, refreshing air deep into her lungs. Her mind lazily awoke, processing and assessing what she could hear and feel. Stubborn effort was required to peel her eyelids open. The pupils of her violet-blue eyes dilated in search of light, and Iris blinked a few times to force them to focus. Slivers of daylight escaped through the curtains of the silent chamber, pushing back just enough darkness to allow for clarity.

Iris skimmed her surroundings. At first, she mistook the lilting haze for her bleary, sleep-filled eyes. After blinking a few times, she realized smoke hung in the air. A pungent, sweet smell accosted her nostrils. *Well, I suppose it's better than the dungeons.* A new revelation caught her off guard. *The pain has stopped.* Relief encouraged further investigation.

Iris clenched and unclenched her fists, then wiggled her toes. *I can move again!* Drawing a hand across the sheet and up to her line of sight, she marveled at its healthy, smooth tones. *How?* Raising the silk sheet covering her, Iris inspected the rest of her body. *No boils or blistering anywhere! What happened? Surely I didn't dream all that up?*

Pushing herself into a sitting position, a surge of pain shot through her left shoulder. She sucked in a breath and winced, immediately halting her motions. Noting the bandaging, memories reignited. *Okay, so not a dream. At least the stabbing part, that is.* Iris smirked to herself. *Wait!* Eyes growing wide, she tentatively pressed her right hand to her chest. *The badge. It's gone!*

A slight stirring off to her right forced Iris's attention to the bed. Someone was sleeping next to her. *What in the lands?* The figure lay curled in a small, tight ball with their back a hand's width away from Iris's side. Too curious to allow her weakness or injury to get in the way, Iris gingerly wormed her way upright. She sucked in a breath, still unable to see the face, and braced herself as searing pain radiated across her shoulder while she leaned over the body.

Small fingers rested just in front of a nose, and a mess of long, walnut-brown hair obscured most of the face. *A little girl? What would possess them to allow a child to snuggle next to the so-called scourge of Yansair? Who is she?* Iris chewed on the corner of her lip. She could move the girl's hair for a better look, but that was too invasive for an unknown child. *Should I wake her?* Her own trembling limbs interrupted her dilemma and forced Iris to lie down once more. Clearly, she was weaker than she'd thought. Gazing at the ceiling, her eyelids began to droop. Blinking a few times she quickly lost the battle, succumbing to heavy slumber. As time slipped away, soft footsteps and hushed voices crept into Iris's senses.

"Perhaps, Your Highness. But we cannot know for sure."

"I feel no unnatural levels of warmth," Yansair's queen stated resolutely.

"I—yes, Your Majesty." Laurel sighed.

"And as you can see, the prisoner and child have not reacted to our approach." Queen Aaralee's voice grew more distinct in Iris's ears.

"Yes, Your Majesty." Laurel paused. "Your Highness, is . . . King Thaylos—"

"He is detained with our Great Mother and need not be disturbed," Aaralee cut in.

"Yes, Your Majesty."

A sense of knowing percolated through Iris's mind. *She's taking quite the risk to come see me.* Slowly, Iris opened her eyes again. Queen Aaralee stood at the side of the bed, her brow furrowed and lips pressed firmly together, intently surveying the figures on the bed. Honey-brown eyes connected with Iris's. Iris's lips rose into a frail smile.

"I am so pleased to see you well, Your Highness," Iris rasped.

Good grief. Was that my voice? The last time she sounded that pitiful was when Lori had so kindly shared that dreadful chest cold nearly a year ago.

Keeping her gaze locked with Iris's, Aaralee instructed Laurel, "Fetch some water for the prisoner, please."

Laurel promptly shuffled over to a nearby table to procure a wooden cup. Returning to the right side of the bed, Laurel passed it off to Iris's outstretched hand.

"Thank you." Iris smiled gratefully, slowly working herself into a viable drinking position.

Though matching the warmth of the room, the liquid brought instant refreshment. It washed away the incense and smoke taste from her mouth. Swallowing the last drop, Iris passed the cup back to the watchful Laurel.

"How is your throat now?" Aaralee asked.

Clearing it briefly, Iris reconnected with the queen. "Better. Thank you, Your Highness." *Probably could do with a few more glasses, but best not to press too soon.*

"Good." Aaralee nodded curtly, her eyes scrutinizing the whole of Iris's body. "Tell me, prisoner, was this all a ruse to get into my good graces?"

Iris blanched. "I'm sorry, what?"

"Did you bewitch one of my maidens against me, then use the chance to feign heroic sacrifice and eventual miraculous recovery all to trick us into submitting to whatever demands you hold?" Aaralee's features were flat, except for the fire dancing behind her eyes.

Iris's mind emptied briefly at the audacity of the accusation. Mouth hanging open, she blinked multiple times, fighting to regain her senses. Slowly, she drew her lips together, biting on the inside of her mouth as her face scrunched in deep anger. The queen's idiocy scathed against her fragile nerves.

"You honestly believe *I* did *all* of this as a convoluted manipulation tactic?" Iris finally managed, barely holding back a snarl.

Aaralee tipped her chin up, looking at Iris down her nose. "Well. Was it?"

Iris narrowed her eyes in turn. "Does it even matter what I say now? If this is truly what you believe, there is nothing I could say or do to prove otherwise. If you have made up your mind against me, any truth I speak will be attributed to this ridiculous witchcraft fantasy you all hold so dear."

"So you deny it, then?" Aaralee maintained her infuriatingly calm demeanor.

The thought flared up that perhaps Iris should curb her tongue better, but she was done caring. "Of course I do. But let me remind you, Your Highness, that it was *you* who went after a peaceful people *unprovoked*! It was *you* who slaughtered innocents wholly unaware of the existence of your *prophecies*. It was *you* who chased me down, dragged me into your kingdom, and made me your prisoner. It was *you* who had the dreams before I was anywhere *near* you! It was *you* who called to meet with me. It was *you* who condemned me to a cruel death! And yet, it was *you* who was spared from a vicious assassination attempt, whereas *I* endured every excruciating ounce on your behalf. But sure, why not? Clearly, *all* of this has come together *just* the way *I* wanted it to. Tormented and utterly alone, boy am I glad my efforts have paid off!" The sarcasm dripped so thickly at the end the tone was almost tangible.

As the rush of indignation drained away, Iris's body forced her to recline once more. Perhaps she should stop now? The way she dared to address the queen in this moment was suicidal. But what did she have left to lose? They were going to kill her anyway. Might as well get in her shots now. Since keeping her eyes open seemed to only steal her strength faster, Iris kept them shut for a moment as she pressed on.

"Tell me, Your Majesty, if I really am as powerful as you all believe, then why"—her voice hitched with emotion, surprising even her—"why was I not able to save them?" Opening her eyes, she met the queen's steady gaze. "Why would my people be caught so unaware? Why would I remain helpless to protect them? Honestly"—Iris chuckled bitterly as she continued her confession—"the *only* reason I am this *Woman of Prophecy* is because I am the only one left. I wasn't *chosen*, I am what you got stuck with, what *I* got stuck with." Flicking her focus to the ceiling, she finished softly, "This goes far beyond me, or even you. We're in far less control than any of us are comfortable admitting."

Laurel snorted with disgust. "I'm sorry, Your Highness, but I cannot hold my tongue any longer!" Planting her hands on her hips, she awaited the nod of approval from her queen before continuing. "The prisoner bemoans being the *only survivor* of her people, and yet it is clear she summoned to herself a child from Throansburrough to drain the child's life for her own! Do not be fooled by this ploy for sympathy. It is all an act, I am sure of it."

A child of Throansburrough! Iris's eyes went wide as her heart pounded.

"They're alive? How-how many?" Iris trilled in tentative excitement, not truly pausing to listen.

She had to know who rested beside her. Sitting up far too quickly, a searing pain exploded in her shoulder, sending white dots shooting through her vision. She cried out in anguish and instinctively cradled her shoulder.

"Easy. Or you'll tear the stitching," Laurel admonished, instantly embracing her Head Healer role once more.

Iris blinked back tears and hissed in a breath through clenched teeth. Releasing it, she drew herself higher and moved to wake the child next to her.

"Prisoner, you must lie back down! You'll reopen the wound! Your Majesty, I—"

Queen Aaralee calmly lifted a hand to silence the old woman. Obediently, Laurel stopped and bowed her head. Aaralee kept her eyes fixed on Iris as she leaned over the child, timidly stroking the girl's hair. The girl finally stirred. When her bleary eyes connected with Iris, a lazy smile spread across her face. "Miss Iris, are you feeling better?"

Iris's vision blurred as tears escaped. Her throat constricted as her hand pushed the hair from the girl's face. Swallowing around her emotion, she nodded. "Yes, Sara, *much* better." Iris vainly attempted to wipe away her tears as they raced down her cheeks.

"Good." Sara yawned and then turned her head away, immediately falling back asleep.

"So it's true, you *do* know this child," Queen Aaralee stated coolly.

Iris's lip quivered as she kept a sob in check, her hand dutifully running through Sara's hair. *She's alive! That means others survived too. Is it even possible?* Iris took in a couple shaky breaths as her attention remained on this embodiment of hope. *But why drag them all the way out here? What do I do* now, *Holy Father? How can I* possibly *help them?*

"Yes," Iris breathed at last. "I know her."

An odd warmth began to flow from her wound. Dizziness blanketed her mind, and she tried to shake it away. Iris trained her focus back on the queen. "*Please*, Your Majesty, *are* there others?"

Queen Aaralee's form began to dance within her vision.

"That's enough now, prisoner," Aaralee rebutted in calm firm.

Iris's limbs trembled. "*Please* . . . tell me—" Her body crumpled as her strength vanished.

Aaralee reached out to keep Iris from collapsing on the child. Her head lolled against the queen's chest.

"My family . . . please . . ." Iris mumbled, eyes closed.

"Laurel. Bandages, quick. She's bleeding."

"I *told* her she'd pop a stitch!" Laurel fretted.

Chapter Thirteen

"And I'm telling *you* these boys don't leave my side!" Tess stomped her right foot, hands on her hips.

The Alastrian soldier, Amos Deleon, squirmed under her fiery glare. Clearing his throat, he tried again. "Miss Tess, you don't seem to grasp the gravity of my words. I have orders to bring you to the palace straightaway."

"And I'm sayin' the palace has plenty of room for a few more!" Tess cried. "I gave my word, to one of *your* people no less, that I'd watch out for this man." Tess cried, sharply pointing to Kyle, who lay on a makeshift pallet on the platform of the transport station.

Sunlight floated down between the arches as the last of the early morning shifted into noon. The wounded had been placed side by side along the ground, awaiting their turn with the Alastrian healers. Rachel Markson was already among them, Kale shadowing close behind. Even members of the Royal Church of Alaster had arrived, offering prayer and counsel. The refugees who were well, though shaken, huddled off to the sides, uncertain of where to go. Soldiers patrolled to and fro, conversing with the members of the X32 guard who had made it onto the vessel and attempted to quell the chaos. The surviving boys of the massacres listed like a tiny, frightened army behind Tess. Closest to her sat Jodie, Destin, and Pace. Little Jacob remained attached to Tess's left leg, hiding from the guard and investigating him at the same time.

"These sweet loves here have been through enough upheaval." Tess swung an arm out, indicating all of her boys. "*Your* leadership did *nothing* to protect them when needed most! So excuse me if I can't trust them to the likes of you. *Someone's* gotta be their advocate. So either you can stuff your orders, or you can find a way to accommodate me *and* my charges!"

Amos clenched his jaw. "Miss Tess, orders are not the same as a request. Either you come willingly with me now, or you force me to take more drastic measures."

Tess squared her shoulders. "I'd like to see you try."

Amos stepped forward, accepting Tess's challenge as a hail from the distance cut him off.

"Amos! Is that you, Amos?" Grayson called out cheerfully as a fellow Alastrian soldier helped him hobble over with a walking stick as a makeshift crutch. "Thanks, Cedrick. I should be good from here." Grayson smiled at his helper, who warily acquiesced. Leaning more heavily on the crutch, Grayson focused on Amos and Tess. "Should have known they'd trust a standup soldier such as yourself to take charge of this insanity."

A bit of Amos's rigidity melted away as he studied the bandaging on Grayson's head. "Grayson, sir, what happened to you? Are you sure you should be walking about?"

Grayson cocked an eyebrow and leaned in a little closer to Tess. "Do I really look that bad?"

Tess smirked, eyeing him up and down. "Depends. What does normal look like for you?"

"Comforting," Grayson teased back. "Don't worry, my friend," he said to Amos. "I'll be fine in no time. We both know General Lance will make sure of that."

Amos chuckled. "If you can walk, you can patrol, right?"

Grayson smiled. "Exactly. Now excuse my intruding, but I don't think any of us could help but overhear the growing row between the two of you?"

Tess crossed her arms. "And what of it?"

Grayson maintained his cheery disposition. "I was just wondering, Amos, are you able to divulge who gave you the orders in the first place?"

Standing straighter, Amos gave a curt nod. "Was the Minister Teason, sir."

"I noticed others of the church council present. Is it possible the high minister is nearby as well?"

"A-actually, yes, sir, he is. He's just through the gate, waiting in his carriage."

"Perfect!" Grayson beamed. "Surely our high minister was simply unaware of the responsibilities Miss Tess carries. I'm certain if we just did better to inform him of the circumstances, we could all find an arrangement to our liking."

Amos faltered momentarily, glancing between the genial Grayson and the challenging Tess. "I . . . I suppose so. As long as the lady agrees to not slip off somewhere before I return."

"Slip off?" Tess laughed. "Hun, where exactly do you think I could go with all these lads unseen?"

Amos scrutinized her a second longer before Grayson chimed in. "It's all right, friend. I'll keep my eye on her. On my honor as a soldier, we'll all be here once you get back."

Amos nodded formally then about-faced to reconvene with High Minister Teason. Tess eyed Grayson suspiciously as his brother-in-arms faded from sight. Sweat trickled from Grayson's brow as he leaned more heavily on his crutch.

"All right, spill. What are you up to, soldier man?" Tess demanded as she stooped to lift Jacob to her hip.

Grayson turned his head in the direction of the resting Kyle. "You said you made a promise to watch over this man, correct? The only Alastrian soldier who'd even ask such a favor would *have* to have been

Jason, meaning we're connected in this whole thing now. Whatever *this* is." He chuckled sadly.

"*Who* are you?" Tess's eyes narrowed.

Grayson turned back to Tess with a soft smile on his face, though defeat clouded his eyes. "Jason and I were set to protect the Woman of Prophecy under Marquis Turner. I can only surmise that you are the Sylphaenian inventor who helped Jason and the marquis save these boys from the Yansairens?"

Tess nodded as her free hand fiddled with a crystal tied to a thin leather strip around her neck. "So, you're the other soldier, the one too wounded to join in?"

Grayson grimaced and sighed. "Look, Jason could never have foreseen us ending up back in Alaster like this. Do you know the type of man his cousin is?"

Tess tipped her chin up. "Wanted criminal or not, I gave my word and I *will* keep it."

Grayson held her eyes. "There's only so much I can do to protect you."

"I don't recall asking for it." Tess readjusted Jacob on her hip and wiped a smudge of dirt from the boy's cheek with her thumb.

Grayson studied the child in her arms sadly. "No, but you can't care for all these boys alone. I honor the heart and spitfire you carry, miss, but *no* one lasts long alone. And as you said, these lads have been through enough already."

Tess sighed as she pushed Jacob's bangs out of his eyes. Jacob leaned into Tess in response, his head resting on her chest.

"I can do my best to speak on your behalf," Grayson offered gently. "If nothing else, the high minister should help us bring the boys' plight to the king's attention. Between His Majesty and the Royal Church, the children should be well tended. As for Kyle?" Grayson sighed. "I can't make any promises. One way or another, the man has to pay for his crimes."

Tess's mouth twisted as she studied Jason's cousin on the stone floor, warm rays of light dancing over his form. "Crime or no, there *must* be a cousin for Jason to return to. I gave him my word, and if I can't keep it, it'll lose all its value."

"Then may the favor of the Holy Father rest upon you, Miss Tess." Grayson dipped his head.

The bustling sounds of the transport station crept in around their conversation, leaving them to await Amos's answer in silence. Some of the children began growing restless, so Tess enlisted the help of a few of the X32 guards to play some games with them. Grayson joined in by sitting with a small group and used some pebbles as a substitute for his favorite marble game as a child. Kale rejoined his buddies, chatting away and leading a couple others around to comfort and pray for the wounded. As Kyle stirred, he soon found himself surrounded by a gathering of compassionate little hearts. The noise level continued to grow as some of the Alastrian soldiers joined in on an impromptu footrace with the older boys. Having free reign to laugh and play with other children and adults finally began to bring light back into their eyes.

Engrossed with watching their games, Tess hadn't noticed Amos walking up until he was almost right upon them. Lagging a few calculated steps behind was an austere elderly man with a snow-white beard resting upon his proud chest. Gray eyebrows framed deep cobalt eyes, and thin lips held in a tight line were almost entirely hidden by his facial hair. The old man's wrinkles expanded from his brow to high atop his bald head. The deep royal blue of his ostentatious vestment was accented by golden chains that kept a pure-white cloak in place.

Upon recognizing his presence, both the X32 and the Alastrian guard halted their activities and stood at attention. The rest of the crowd stooped to the ground respectfully, save for the children who didn't know better. Grayson pulled himself up from the ground so he too could stand at attention. Tess held herself tall and rigid as both men approached.

"Presenting our holy high minister, Teason Faysal," Amos trumpeted to the crowd.

Teason nodded his acceptance as he drew nearer to Tess. Visible sadness washed over his countenance as he took in the scene before him.

Raising his hands into the air, he addressed the gathering. "Faithful children of Fitsengea, when word of your horrific tragedies reached us, our hearts broke for you. These frightening and uncertain times may cause you to feel you are alone in this world. As the high minister, I hope to assuage those fears and declare you are neither alone nor forgotten! We of the Royal Church pledge to offer our homes and our hearts to you." Pausing, he sighed heavily then raised his voice in greater passion. "We may not yet understand the Holy Father's purpose in this, but I can say with certainty, His goodness will shine through in the end. Stay strong in your faith and let us show our enemies that the hearts of the Fiesian people are not so easily destroyed! May the glory of the Followers be the glory of the Father!"

A thunderous "amen" rippled through the crowd. Teason lowered his hands and nodded, releasing the people back to their duties. Tess maintained her stonelike stance, arms crossed with fingers drumming upon herself in open aggravation. Meeting her eyes, Teason dipped his head.

"Madame, I am informed that our people owe you a great debt of thanks for your ingenious methods of not only opening the line of communication for the X32 people but also making a way to rescue these precious young souls." Teason rested a wrinkled hand gently on the top of Jodie's head, who stood with his friends as a human wall blocking out Kyle.

"Giving aid to people in need is what anyone with half a heart would do." Tess narrowed her eyes, unmoved by Teason's gracious words.

Teason smiled gently. "You clearly sell yourself short, my child. And so, it is my desire to do whatever I can to repay you for your heroic actions."

Tess kept her silence. Teason's eyes softened as he glanced over at Grayson, who kept his posture as upright as possible while leaning on his crutch.

"You, young man, were guard over our Woman of Prophecy?"

"Yes, High Minister."

Teason nodded solemnly. "And it was you who requested my presence here now?"

"Y-yes, High Minister."

"You have a peacemaker's heart, my boy." Teason grinned.

Grayson lowered his head in respect.

As merriment overtook his features, Teason addressed Tess and Grayson as one. "Such beautiful spirits are a rare find indeed. I know your concern lies with your duties, but please be at rest and know that my goals align with yours. For that reason, I have taken it upon myself to bring forth wagons to carry not only you but all in your charge with me to the palace. It is my desire to host a banquet of remembrance in honor of the shining jewels of faith and purity that Throansburrough and Jaralynx have been."

A murmur broke out amongst the massacre survivors.

"We are greatly humbled by your generosity, High Minister." Grayson bowed as deeply as he could manage.

"It is far more blessed to give than it is to receive," Teason chuckled. "Well then, my children? Shall we make our way to the palace?" he cried out boisterously to the group.

A number of the boys joyously echoed their assent and scampered off after Amos, who led the way. Tess kept her place, causing Jodie, Destin, Pace, and little Jacob to hold their ground as well.

"These lads aren't my only charges." Tess spoke with thinly veiled terseness.

"Indeed." Teason sighed with sudden gravity. "Young Amos informs me that you have somehow inherited the care of one Kyle Druthers." Teason's eyes scanned to Kyle, who had yet again drifted off. "The poor, lost soul." Teason tsked, shaking his head, concern etched on his face as he turned back to Tess. "Fear not, my child. Even the law isn't so heartless as to abuse a broken man."

"And I'm just supposed to take your word for it?"

A smirk pulled at the corner of his mouth. "Just as you gave your own?"

Tess sneered. "Sylphaen knows all too well the value of an Alastrian word."

"Knowing that we caused distrust amongst our allies has greatly distressed us of the Royal Church, but our first allegiance *must* be to our Holy Father."

Tess stepped forward as Grayson cut in. "Miss Tess!"

Tess clenched her teeth and fists, holding her ground but keeping her silence. Teason calmly looked over Tess's head and called to a nearby elderly church council member who was in the middle of tending to a patient.

"Peter? Once you've finished your time here, please have your helper-guards transport Mr. Druthers to the palace grounds infirmary. Once he is settled, send me word immediately."

Peter visually verified Kyle's location, nodded his agreement, and returned to his current task. Teason smiled his thanks before speaking gently to Tess once more.

"My dear, I fear there is nothing I can do right now to convince you that we only have your best interests at heart. Still, will you not accompany me with the rest of these innocent ones to a much-needed time of stability and merriment? If we hurry, I'm sure we can catch them."

Her eyes softening upon the remaining boys, Tess let out a sigh as she waved them on. "All right lads, go with the others now." As the children timidly progressed forward, Tess hissed a final remark before joining. "I *will* be checking on Mr. Druthers' arrival to the infirmary."

"I'm certain you will." Teason grinned. "Young Grayson, are you joining us?"

"Yes, High Minister."

"Wonderful! Now, my girl, do be a dear and lend a hand to our recovering peacemaker."

Tess acquiesced but not before throwing a final, hot glare at the high minister. As the whole crowd dispersed, the gentle Peter kneeled beside Kyle. Peter's lips pressed into a grim line, eyes casting a pleading look to the sky. A sad sigh escaped his lips. "Please, Holy Father, come."

———>·<———

Sweat dripped from Darren's brow, threatening to roll into his eyes. The weight of the crates in his arms exacerbated his discomfort from the rising heat. The noon sun blazed proudly in the sky as they made their second of four loading trips. Hoisting his stack atop the mound by the cart, Darren locked eyes with Oriel, who brought out a small barrel of black powder. Darren squinted into the contrasting darkness of the armory's opening as he mopped his sweat with the short sleeve of his under tunic. Moments later, both Jason and Bryant appeared with their own stacks. Dropping the items with a grunt, Bryant claimed a nearby crate as a chair.

"I knew Lord Valomeer had a thing for weapons trade," Jason said quietly. "But knowing this shipment alone barely scratches the surface bodes poorly for us."

"If we're lucky, maybe the arrogant lout will end up blowing himself up." Bryant jerked his head toward the small stack of black powder barrels.

Jason frowned. "It's likely Lord Valomeer is trying to figure out how to replicate it himself. Also not good for us."

"Even if he does figure it out," Darren offered as he leaned against the cart, "it's an unwieldy weapon at best. Not even Yansair has a full grasp on it yet. Still . . ."

Darren's train of thought cut off as Oriel passed him an empty waterskin. "Let's go."

Looking at Bryant and Jason, who both stiffened, Darren exhaled and clasped the waterskin tighter. "All right. Jason, Bryant, stay vigilant."

Bryant grunted, and Jason held Darren's gaze for a second before giving a stiff nod. Oriel and Darren moved toward the palace that lay just behind the armory. The plan was to get to the records room as quickly as possible. Both Darren and Oriel carried empty waterskins to cover their ruse of refilling at one of the wells as they completed the order for Valomeer. Bryant and Jason would stay behind, slowly continuing to pack the cart to silence any suspicion. Oriel knew enough of the royal layout to recall an interior well had been dug deep down to the hidden underground river that flowed somewhere nearby. Only in recent years did the palace risk creating a possible access point into the noble grounds. They could either risk secret entry or risk losing connection to pure water. With a land as dry as this one, water was worth dying for. It also meant an increase in security.

A tight ball of pressure pulled at Darren's insides with each guard grouping they passed. The challenge was to remain acutely aware without being obvious. These men knew to watch for the skittish, and it was imperative Oriel and Darren became invisible. Skylights and windows strategically placed produced a much-needed cross breeze, keeping the air fresh and cooling Darren's damp skin. The brilliance of the sun kept the wall torches unlit. Darren's skin prickled as he yet again noted a number of stone light features ensconced between each torch.

Who of the council has gotten into bed with Yansair? Stop it. You're jumping to conclusions. Maybe the veins of the stone light ore stretch into Yansair as well? Darren gritted his teeth and tightened his grip on the waterskin. *Wishful thinking. Is Uncle unaware of the depths of this treachery?* A sour remembrance slithered through his mind. The better question: Would Zaerin even *do* something about it if he was? *Focus on the here and now!* Darren berated himself as he exhaled through his nostrils.

Rounding a few more bends in the hall, they quickly approached their point of divergence. From here on out, it would be obvious they were no longer just collecting water. Staying close to Oriel and the Saunskirt gear would help stave off most questioning, but any who were truly curious would be able to unravel their story. As one, both men tucked away their waterskins behind their leather chest plates.

Few, if any, servants scurried about along these more centralized passageways. Even the guards began to thin out. *Strange.* Small hairs on Darren's arms and neck stood on end. Flexing his fingers, he willed his hand to stay relaxed by the customary blade at his side. How trustworthy were these contacts who could lead them right to where they needed without ever meeting up with them? Darren's eyes darted over the empty rooms they passed. Their target was fast approaching. The sickly-sweet smell of incense crept in around them, thickening with each step.

A deep, terrorized cry pierced the air, stopping Oriel and Darren dead in their tracks. The man's torturous howls persisted, ricocheting up from the last turn they needed to take. Feet slapped heavily against the stone floors behind them. Swiveling his head back, Darren caught sight of two Yansairen guards running at full speed.

"Move!" The man in the lead barked.

Oriel and Darren had just enough time to throw themselves to the side as the soldiers barreled past. Oriel tilted his head, and they too picked up their pace to investigate. Reaching the corner, they watched as the guards struggled to lift their screaming and writhing compatriot from the floor.

"Accursed Fiesian witch!" one of the soldiers groused. "When will she leave us be? I'm *telling* you, proximity to her is what makes it worse."

"Shut up and lift!"

Hooking the panicked man as best as they could under both his arms, they staggered past Oriel and Darren, far too engrossed in their task to be bothered by others. Darren and Oriel strode around the corner and straight into the record room. The room was a fairly small enclosure covered in categorized cubby holes of varying parchments along the walls and shelves for the larger bound tomes down the center. Finding the room unoccupied, Darren kept watch by the door as Oriel began to search. Darren left a crack in the door just big enough to see out. Eyes fixed on the hall, his heart thudded in his chest.

"Oriel, is the 'Fiesian witch' who I think it is?" Darren kept his voice low as he glanced in Oriel's direction.

"Not now," Oriel grunted, fixated on skimming through the labels on the shelves.

Darren tightened his fists. "He said she was nearby."

"Focus, Your Grace," Oriel growled as he sped to another section.

Darren felt his face flush as he clenched his jaw. "Why do you refuse to answer?"

The rustle of pages was the only reply until a ripping sound reached his ears. Within seconds, Oriel appeared with papers in his hands. "Got them. Now let's go."

As Oriel approached, Darren spun toward him and thrust him up against the wall adjacent to the door. He pinned Oriel by holding his right forearm against the man's throat. Darren's face came within inches of his, his rage thinly suppressed. "It *is* Iris," Darren's voice rattled. "The Woman of Prophecy is here, quite possibly down the hall, and you were going to have us leave without a word!"

Stern eyes held Darren's. "She wasn't the mission."

"You *knew* she was here."

"Our information was unreliable at best."

"Well now it's verified, and we're getting her out."

Oriel slowly brought the papers into view. "One woman instead of the lives of a hundred children? If you attempt this, you will be caught and they will be lost forever."

Darren shoved himself away from Oriel but kept an accusatory finger trained on him. "This wasn't your call. You should have told me, told us! We could have gotten her *and* the records, had we known."

Oriel smoothed his beard and stepped away from the wall. "Knowing *where* she is doesn't verify she is in a state where she can be moved. When we find out if she is healing as we hoped, then we can free her."

Darren cursed under his breath. Oriel was right. There was no way for them to escape with Iris right now. They had no cover, no plan, no exit strategy, and no necessary support. If he went tearing after her now, they'd all be killed.

"You better pray to your god we're not too late," he growled venomously.

Oriel gave no reply, simply offered the pages to Darren. Snatching them, Darren glanced at the writing. A list of ages, physical descriptors, locations, and prices were neatly and coldly organized. Numbered like cattle, stripped of names and identity. A weight tightened around Darren's chest and throat, making it hard to swallow. *You hold her heart in your hands.* These children were her home, something to come back to.

Thoughtfully folding the pages, Darren tucked them into his under tunic beneath the chest plate. Oriel stoically nodded and Darren turned back to the door. Before he could grasp the handle, it flung open. A razor-sharp sword extended through, stopping just short of Darren's throat. Following the vicious metal up to the hand wielding it, Darren locked eyes with a man with deep, dark skin and full lips. His black hair and beard were shortly cropped. Darren could have sworn Krine Islanders never traveled this far east. And yet one not only stood before him but wore the armor of a Yansairen soldier.

"Out," the man barked.

Darren and Oriel moved cautiously, raising their hands in compliance. Stepping into the hall, they were greeted by five Yansairen guards, all with weapons drawn.

"What is the meaning of this?" Oriel demanded as the guards clamped cuffs on their wrists and removed their weapons.

"Silence, traitor!" the first soldier spat back.

The entourage swept Darren and Oriel back down the halls and out of the main palace grounds. As they traversed an open, stone, arched path toward another complex, Darren caught sight of an additional cluster of soldiers taking the same path just ahead of them. Two heads bobbing in the center of the group grabbed his attention. Stomach dropping, Darren grimaced as he placed the taller, messy-haired one as Bryant. The shorter, slim framed one had to be Jason. This did not bode well. Winding through the next building, they soon came upon a series of steps that spiraled down into what he assumed to be their dungeons. Darren kept all his senses on high alert, counting the turns and calculating the distance back to the door outside. Escape would be their only option. There was no one else to come save them, and far too many lives depended on their survival. Maybe there was still a chance to feign innocence? Surely Fredrick could kick up a fuss on the pretense of them being Saunskirt soldiers. *But who tipped them off?* They called Oriel a traitor. This was more than simply being discovered in the records room.

The guards shoved Darren and Oriel through a doorway. Darren locked eyes with Jason as the soldiers chained his hands above his head against the wall. A mixture of relief and crest fallen battled across Jason's features. He winced as the shackles tightened. Two men wrestled Bryant into position next to Jason. As Bryant snarled and snapped at them, Darren noted the blood sprayed across his leather breastplate. Once both hands were secure, one man took his sword pommel and hammered it into Bryant's side, doubling him over.

"Hey!" Darren challenged, stepping toward his attacker as they readied a second blow.

The guard behind him grabbed a handful of Darren's hair and yanked his head back. Darren clenched his jaw. The guards dragged Oriel and Darren to their companions along the wall and swiftly clasped them into irons. Without a word, the soldiers left the room, whisking the heavy door shut with a reverberating thud.

"How'd they know?" Bryant's low growl broke the silence. "Who ratted on us?"

"Stop," Darren ordered coldly.

"They're probably listening," Jason filled in.

Eyes flicking to the blood on Bryant's borrowed uniform, Darren frowned. "Are you injured?"

A malicious, toothy grin spread across Bryant's face. "What do *you* think?"

"So much for feigning innocence." Darren sighed and leaned his head back against the cool stone. Taking a breath, Darren closed his eyes. "How many, Bryant?"

"Two," he cooed. "Could have been more if the kid had the stomach for it."

"And exactly what good would that have done?" Jason countered. "It wasn't a matter of stomach, but of wisdom. Your *instinct* to cut first may have cost us everything!"

Bryant shrugged and used his shoulder to scratch an itch on his chin. "Why else bring me along, then?"

Darren angled his head to the right. "Oriel, anything we should prepare for?"

Oriel's jaw worked for a minute as the muscles in his neck strained. He glanced at the door and then back to Darren. "Torture. If we're lucky, they'll bore of that quickly."

"Great," Darren breathed.

"Pray their Great Mother doesn't get a hold of us, but if she does, guard your heart or she *will* control it."

"And exactly how do you *guard your heart?*" Bryant scoffed.

Turning to answer, Oriel was interrupted by the heavy click of a key turning over a metal lock. The rusty hinges creaked loudly as the solid oak door pulled open. The broad back of a Yansairen soldier appeared as the man stepped backward into the cell. He stood slightly stooped from the weight he dragged. Peering around him as best he could, Darren studied the soldier's bundle. Fabric was torn and covered in dark-brown dirt and some wet, deep red stained patches. *Dried and fresh blood?* The package was long and cumbersome, its shape perplexing. Awkwardly, the soldier pulled through, muttering under his breath in protest.

The limp body of a brutalized and bound man came into full view as the soldier shuffled in front of them. Dropping the body to the ground, Darren winced as the man's head bounced harshly on the floor. The soldier straightened, stretching his back. Looking to his audience, he offered a wink and a wicked smile before stepping away. The immobile figure had dark hair, wet from a gash alongside his head. His left eye swollen shut, and his bottom lip puffed up under a thick coat of blood. His clothing lay in tatters, each tear framed with blood stains.

Darren's eyes widened as his insides flipped. Oriel stiffened beside him.

"Fred!" Darren strained against his chains.

Bryant sucked in a breath and cursed. "Is he dead?"

"No." Jason leaned in, straining his eyes. "He's breathing, thank the Father."

Darren pulled against his restraints, desperate to get closer. Beside him he could hear Oriel beginning a hushed, fervent prayer.

"Fredrick, can you hear me?" Darren tried again.

The slightest stirring caused everyone to hold their breath. An unintelligible sound croaked through Fredrick's lips, and the muscles in Darren's shoulders unwound. *He's conscious—that's* something.

"Good afternoon, gentlemen," a commanding feminine voice lilted from the doorway.

A slender, small-statured woman in a ruby-red and gold chiffon dress strode into the room. The gauzy embellishments fluttered entreatingly with each step. Her bare arms swaying in rhythm betrayed her fading youth through folded skin running down to frail fingers. Smooth silver hair flowed freely down her back, except for a small braid that rested in front of her left shoulder and framed her face. The deep wrinkles across her pinkish-brown skin were particularly accentuated along the black eye symbol painted on her forehead. Eyes so dark that they appeared without pupils slowly scrutinized each of the men fastened to the wall. Stopping in front of Darren, the woman's red-painted lips curled into a malicious grin.

"Oh yes, we've been expecting you."

Chapter Fourteen

The Great Mother of Yansair stood proudly in front of her newest victims, her three closest attendants behind her awaiting orders. Beckoning silently with the twirl of her bony fingers, one woman in particular stepped forward. Oriel sucked in a sharp breath and stood straighter at the sight of her.

"Which one, Kamile?" the Great Mother ordered.

Kamile hesitated, unable to raise her eyes from the floor. Quietly, she lifted a finger to single out Oriel. She dropped her hand quickly and took a step back.

"Thank you, Kamile." The Great Mother smiled ruefully. She shifted in front of Oriel, and her wicked grin grew wider. "So, *you* were the contact. I wonder, though. How much do you know?"

Oriel kept his body rigid and his eyes fixed on a point beyond his interrogator. The Great Mother chuckled then turned her gaze upon Darren. Her eyes bore through Darren, and his breath caught in his throat in surprise. A literal heaviness pressed on his chest and shoulders, making him take a staggered step back into the wall. The rough stone helped to keep his knees from buckling. A piercing pressure encircled Darren's head, making him lock his jaw. His heart hammered through his chest as he fought to breathe.

"Did you search them, Tomik?" The Great Mother queried, keeping her drilling stare on Darren.

The soldier who'd first ordered Darren out of the records room shifted uncomfortably in the doorway. "We-we made certain to remove their weapons, Great Mother."

Eyes flicking over the uniforms her prisoners still wore, the Great Mother frowned. "So no, then. You disappoint me, Tomik."

Tomik lowered his head. "Yes, Great Mother."

Threatening smile returning, she stepped closer to Darren. "You're hiding something."

His gut churned within as bile rose in his throat. The old woman's nearness caused a visceral nausea to roll through him. Tearing his eyes away, Darren finally gulped fresh air. The Great Mother stepped back, folding her arms calmly in front of her.

"Tomik, remove his armor and the under tunic."

"Dirty old hag," Bryant taunted.

The woman arched an eyebrow. "Patience, licentious one. We will talk in a moment."

A low growl rumbled in Bryant's throat. Tomik unsheathed his dagger and made quick work of cutting away the fastening ties, then used the same blade to slit the worn fabric so it fell from Darren's shoulders. As the tunic slid down, the empty waterskin tumbled out. The sorting ground records fluttered to the ground. Tomik stooped to retrieve the papers and passed them off to the Great Mother. Turning them over in her hands, a bemused chuckle trilled out. She refolded them and held the papers between two bony fingers to angle them behind her.

"Kamile, be a dear and return these to their home."

"Yes, Great Mother." Kamile dipped low and retrieved the documents before exiting the room.

Thrusting out her hand, the Great Mother clutched Darren's face, forcing his eyes to hers. Darren's heart leapt in shock, for the strength of her grip was unnatural.

"What is it about you that intrigues me so?" Her tone danced with eerie mirth. "The All Seeing Eye has fixed his gaze on you, boy. Who are you? Tell me your name."

A haze pervaded Darren's thoughts, rapidly dulling his senses. He fought to keep his silence; a small warning cried out in muffled words. He could feel a forceful loosening on his tongue.

"Hey! You nasty witch, you promised me a turn." Bryant's rough voice shattered through.

Darren clamped his mouth shut again. The Great Mother cried out in disgust and spun toward Bryant. "Impudent filth! Know your place." Her voice rattled in anger. "You want my attention? You will regret your outburst." Snapping her fingers, one of the other female attendants stepped forward. "Prepare the Elixir."

With a trembling curtsey, the woman rushed off with the other attendant.

Tomik stepped up beside the Great Mother. "Great Mother, I mean no disrespect, but . . . will this not complicate questioning?"

"On the contrary, Tomik. This will speed things along nicely. Now, please complete a proper search of our prisoners. I will return when the Elixir is ready."

She pivoted away and sauntered gracefully out of the room.

> ◇ <

Within Alaster's palace grounds stood a medium-sized stone building. Detached from the other structures but still close by, it provided just enough room for a decent herbal garden along its perimeter. The tall cutouts in the walls offered great ventilation and plenty of sunlight for the building's large one-room interior. Two wide, dark wooden doors made up the entrance. A small crowd huddled together on the few steps leading up to it, awaiting an answer from the woman standing before the entrance.

"Miss, I am so sorry, but we just cannot allow so many children to go back with you." The young Alastrian healer frowned with empathy. "I *know* you truly mean well, but the medicinal quarters just don't have the space for this many visitors."

Tess sighed heavily and resituated Jacob on her hip. She glanced back at the ten other boys who had decided to follow her around. "How many *can* you let in?"

The woman's brow furrowed. "Including yourself, three."

"Only three!" Tess moaned.

The healer fidgeted, rubbing her left arm. "Yes, miss. These are the main quarters on palace grounds. With the addition of X32 patients, we're already overcrowded. With too many people, we can't properly care for our charges."

Tess groaned. She was not in the mood to be forced to march most of her boys back to the guard's dining hall. The hall was the only area spacious enough to house all the children as well as a number of X32 residents, but it was not a good permanent solution for the growing restlessness of the young boys. While chewing her bottom lip as she mulled over her options, one of the doors behind the young healer swayed open. A handsome man of about thirty appeared in its opening, his thick chestnut hair bouncing along with his cheery gait. He laughed freely with a younger man walking with a crutch. The injured man caught sight of Tess and waved.

"Miss Tess! What brings you and these fine gentlemen to the medicinal quarters?" Grayson's genuine smile lit up his whole face.

Tess responded with a sad smirk. "Well, me and my boys had planned on making some rounds to check on our people inside, but it seems I overestimated how many could tag along. So now we'll be heading back to the dining hall."

A ripple of soft groans and sighs sounded behind her, making Tess grimace.

"Pardon me, my lady," Grayson's friend spoke up. "But if I may be permitted, I'm certain my men and I could easily provide a solution?"

Shifting Jacob to her opposite hip to rest her arm, Tess studied the affable gentleman. "And you are?"

"Forgive my indecorum." Grayson bowed his head. "This is the admirable General Lance Richards. It is to his regiment I report."

Lance chuckled. "You're far too gracious, Grayson." Dipping his head respectfully, Lance smiled at Tess. "It is an honor to make your acquaintance, my lady."

Tess nodded in turn. "And what exactly do you have in mind, General?"

"Please, call me Lance. Grayson here tells me that you've acquired a small battalion of fine young men full of fire. I fear my own men have gotten a little too comfortable as of late. What do you say, lads? Do you think you could help whip my boys back into shape?"

The children murmured hopefully behind Tess. A grin rose at the corners of her mouth. "Ah, so it's to be combat training, then, is it?" Laughing softly, she shrugged. "Fine by me as long as they're willing. And you, if I receive *any* negative reports of the ongoing fights between your people and these kind souls"—a sinister glint flashed across Tess's eyes—"there is no battalion in all of Alaster that could protect you."

The muscles in Lance's face tightened as a light shone from his eyes. "My lady, you have my word that no harm shall come to them."

"Right then. Everyone joining the general in his games raise your hand," Tess called out.

Each boy present eagerly thrust his arm into the air. Tess looked down at Jacob, who still clung to her, and jostled him gently. "And what about you, hun? Do you want to leave too?"

Keeping his head on her chest, Jacob gave the slightest nod with eyes fixed on Lance's welcoming smile. Tess sighed as she handed Jacob off to one of the older boys. Lance grinned and bowed his head once more to Tess.

Clapping his hands together boisterously he proclaimed, "All right then, men. Onward to glory!"

With the rallying cry and pumping his fist in the air the collection of children quickly mimicked their new leader and fell in step. Tess chuckled as she turned back to the healer. "Seems like it'll be just one visitor after all."

"Yes, miss, but if any of the children decide later on they want to come through, they are fully welcome. Just in smaller quantities." She smiled.

"Shall I escort you, Miss Tess?" Grayson offered, gesturing to the open doorway behind him.

"Actually, I need to check on two people. Could you direct me first to Kyle?"

Grayson bobbed his head as he turned into the hall while Tess followed close behind. "And the second?"

Tess's eyes wandered around the expansive hall. Over a hundred small wood-framed beds sat in two rows, making up the perimeter of the room. Nearly every one was occupied.

"Liam. Jodie, and his companions were eager to know how he was getting on."

A grandfatherly man covered in wrinkles and lacking any hair sat on the side of his bed mimicking the facial contortions of the little girl with frizzy red hair in the bed opposite him. Tess giggled at the dire competition of who would laugh first. A woman holding a tray filled with sweet-smelling porridge whisked around Grayson, unloading a bowl onto each stand next to the beds. Following behind, a teenage boy lugged a heavy pail of water, splashing bits here and there as he fought to match the woman's arduous pace. At every bedside, he unhooked the ladle attached to the bucket and sloshed a scoopful into the waiting wooden cups. Tess winced as a man stitched up a wounded leg while the patient bit down on a thick strap of leather. His knuckles turned white as he gripped the sides of the thin mattress. Tess clasped onto the crystal tied around her neck and shuddered.

Bringing her focus back to Grayson, she studied him more closely. Though still using the crutch to steady himself, he already moved around better than earlier that morning. Whatever medicine they treated him with must have been potent for this sort of turnaround.

Looking ahead, Tess noticed two uniformed soldiers standing at attention at the foot of a bed. The bed's occupant lay on his side with his back facing them. Fresh, bright-white bandages wrapped around his entire torso. The stations next to him were empty. Clearly, this patient was not to have any unapproved contact with others.

Tess's cheeriness gave way to a frown. "That's Kyle over there, isn't it?"

A slight sigh escaped Grayson "Yes, Miss Tess."

Tess tightened her grip around the crystal as she gritted her teeth. "Do they guard him for his own safety, or for the nobles'?"

"A bit of both." Grayson paused suddenly, bringing them both to a stop. "You may have acquired some sympathy for Mr. Druthers on Jason's behalf, but make no mistake, my lady. Mr. Druthers is not a pitiable victim. He has been convicted of treason and murder. Do not let sympathy rob you of wisdom."

Tess cocked an eyebrow. "Hmm, but wasn't your precious marquis tried for the same crimes?"

"Well-I—" Grayson fumbled.

Tess shrugged. "Convictions don't always guarantee guilt, now do they?" She smirked and patted Grayson on the shoulder. "Don't worry, soldier. This isn't my first dance. I'll keep both eyes open, okay?"

Grayson frowned and started walking again. "Yes, Miss Tess."

When they reached the guards, Grayson saluted. He was able to convince the men to give Tess and Kyle some space. As Grayson conversed with his fellow soldiers, Tess moved to the side of Kyle's bed where he could see her.

"Hey there, Mr. Sad Sack," she cooed playfully. "These Alastrian healers treating you all right?"

Kyle let out a long sigh and peeked one eye open. "Hello, Tess."

Plopping down onto the bed next to his, Tess crossed her arms and pouted. "You *do* realize I'm the one who kept you out of a cell, right?"

A smirk fought at the corners of Kyle's mouth. "Yah, I heard about your little tantrum."

Tess bristled. "Careful, such generous praise is liable to give me a big head."

Kyle opened both eyes as his features softened. "Sorry . . . I . . . Thank you, Tess."

Uncrossing her arms, Tess fiddled with her crystal. "You're welcome. But you avoided my question. How are you feeling?"

Kyle watched her fingers as they mindlessly twirled the necklace, light refracting off the crystal every now and then when it hit just right. "Still weaker than is acceptable, but the staff seems hopeful again."

Tess rested her hands in her lap. "You're far more talkative than before. Jason will be pleased."

Kyle laughed and winced. "That has to be the first time anyone has been grateful to hear me talk more."

Tess smiled gently, though her eyebrows remained drawn in concern. Silence invaded the space between them. Tess flicked her eyes between the guards and Grayson and Kyle. Kyle studied her face.

"Seems wrong, doesn't it?"

"Hm?" Tess cocked an eyebrow.

"Caring for a man just to dispose of him in a prison later. That's what you're thinking, aren't you?"

Tess twisted her lips as her hand went back to her crystal. "Depends, though, if you *are* the man they say you are."

Kyle raised an eyebrow. "You doubt the sovereignty of the king's council and their *entirely* impartial system to decree only the most righteous verdicts?"

Tess smirked but stayed quiet.

Tipping up his chin, Kyle indicated Tess's necklace. "That's a betrothal crystal, isn't it?"

A wistful look flitted across Tess's face as her hand paused over the special token. "You know my culture?"

"It's an exquisite piece. And the man who wears its match?"

Tess's cheeks bloomed into a soft pink as giddiness danced in her eyes "Callum."

A sad smile crept across Kyle's face. "My congratulations to you. May you two be reunited soon."

Tess crooked her head to the side "Now don't tell me you were getting sweet on me, Mr. Sad Sack."

Kyle's tone sobered. "No, just remembering something I've lost."

Tess shifted awkwardly and then stood. "Well, sir, you better keep yourself on the mend. We gotta give Jason some good news to return to. Sorry I can't stay longer, but I still have other people to see before I make it back for Minister Teason's banquet."

Kyle's face darkened. "Watch yourself around that man, Tess. He's not to be trusted."

Smiling wryly, Tess turned to leave. "Funny. They say the same thing about you."

Thrusting out a hand, Kyle feebly grasped the edge of Tess's tunic, making her stop. Sweat broke out across Kyle's brow. He grimaced, and his hand trembled, but his grip persisted. "This isn't a game. I *know* you have no reason to believe me, but he's dangerous, Tess, and if he's fixed his sights on you, then trouble is headed your way. Don't get caught alone with him, you hear me?"

Tess removed Kyle's hand from her tunic and rested it back on the bed. "All right, hun, I promise."

Giving Kyle's shoulder a motherly pat, Tess waved Grayson down so they could leave. Moving further into the building, Grayson led Tess to a curly blond-haired teenager who carried on a conversation with the water boy from earlier. A sense of relief washed over Tess to see Liam sitting up of his own accord. Finally, some good news to bring back to her boys.

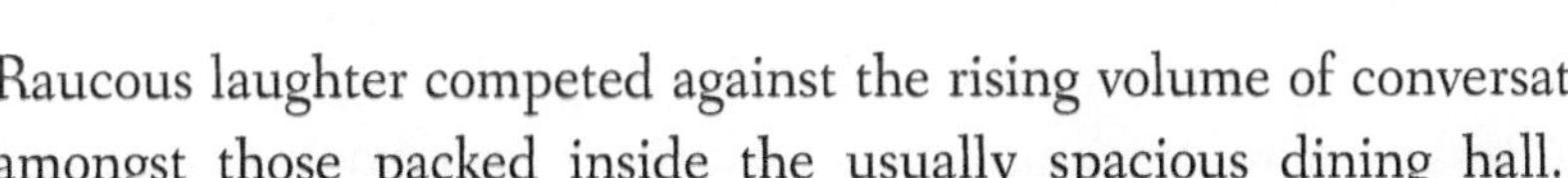

Raucous laughter competed against the rising volume of conversations amongst those packed inside the usually spacious dining hall. An alluring bounty of food had been laid generously across the multiple long tables inside. Though unable to personally attend the feast, High Minister Teason had made sure no expense was spared on behalf of his guests. General Lance's regiment sat interspersed with the boys of Throansburrough and Jaralynx. Tess struggled for elbow space, as she'd been tightly sandwiched between Jodie and Kale. On the other side of the table sat the youthful general himself. Their section of the long table was currently enraptured with one of the general's harrowing tales about protecting nobles as they'd campaigned through the land of Myrn in his younger years. Even Kale fell speechless in the presence of the charismatic, yet somehow humble, Lance.

"But did you die?" Kale blurted.

Lance pressed his lips together tightly, swallowing his laughter. Tess choked on her water.

"Come on, Kale, really? He's sitting right there!" Jodie rolled his eyes.

Kale crossed his arms and lifted his chin. "So? Maybe he was brought back to life afterward."

"You can't be serious!"

"I can too!" Kale challenged. "The Sacred Texts have several stories where just that happened!"

When Lance laughed, the deep, comforting sound rumbled in Tess's own chest. "You have to give it to him there, Jodie. Though—sorry to spoil it for you, my friend—my story isn't quite as glorious as the resurrection tales."

Kale deflated slightly, and Jodie's eyebrows knitted together at his friend's distress. "That's okay, Kale. Remember what your mama said? Liam's recovery practically *was* one of those stories."

Kale perked up, a toothy grin shoving away his earlier embarrassment. "Oh yah! Sorry for interrupting you, Mr. Lance. Please tell us the rest of your story."

Tess bumped Jodie with her elbow. As he looked up at her quizzically, Tess gave him an approving wink. Jodie glanced over at Kale and then back to Tess. With a pleased grin, he shoveled another spoonful of stew into his mouth and refocused on Lance. A tap on her shoulder caused Tess to crane her neck to look behind her. A young boy, who appeared to be no more than ten years old and who was dressed in a nondescript white robe, stood patiently behind her. Bowing his head, he folded his hands together. The sleeves of his robe practically swallowed them whole.

"Pardon me, but are you Miss Tess of Sylphaen?"

Intrigued, Tess turned around fully to face him. "I am. How can I help you?"

Head still bowed with eyes to the floor, the boy spoke with practiced precision. "High Minister Teason, who sadly could not attend the feast, has personally requested an audience with you. The matter is urgent, and he asks that you come at once."

The hairs on the back of Tess's neck stood on end. "All-all right. Allow me to collect myself, and I'll be with you momentarily." Turning from the acolyte, Tess addressed the group. "Sorry, gents. Seems I've been summoned."

Lance stopped mid-story, eyes darting between the acolyte and Tess. "I see." A shadow flitted across his eyes. "I'll see to it that one of my men accompanies you along the way."

"That will be unnecessary, General Lance." The acolyte stepped forward. "Our high minister has already arranged for one of your men to join us—Mr. Grayson Solis."

As if on cue, Grayson appeared behind the general, his own summoning acolyte close behind. No longer requiring the use of his crutch, Grayson was able to bow properly before addressing his superior. "General Lance, I have been called on by the high minister. Requesting permission to oblige."

The general's scrutinizing eyes lingered on the first boy for a minute. A pleasant disposition quickly washed away the look. "Of course, Grayson. We are always honored to give our time to High Minister Teason. It appears your friend, Lady Tess, will be joining you. I request that you keep an eye out for her, soldier."

Grayson dipped his head. "Yes, sir."

Tess released a nervous breath. Rising from the long bench, she found her sleeping pallet and retrieved her leather vest. She never liked to be too far from her tools tucked inside the pockets. Once she rejoined Grayson and the acolytes, they made their way out of the noisy dining hall and into the stillness of the night air. The brilliance of the moon rendered the various stone light lamps almost obsolete. Pivoting toward the center of the palace grounds, Tess and Grayson were led to the Royal Church. The building lay only a breath away from the back entrance to the throne room. The smooth silver stone that made up the façade of the place of worship glistened brilliantly in the moonlight. Tess swore that tiny gemstones must have been inlaid with the stone to get it to sparkle so.

Intricate stone-carved artwork depicting tales from their Sacred Texts framed the dark oak doors. One small piece blazed a luscious ruby red amongst the silver carvings. Stopping to investigate, Tess noted it was red crystal. She noticed etchings of faceless humans kneeling in awe around the heart-shaped stone. The image soon bled into another scene portraying the same figures in great sorrow as the life around them withered. Tracing the carvings with her eyes, she saw a holy being directing to a path of paradise. Some humans sought to rescue the others by sharing this path, but the others refused to follow, choosing to worship the crystal rather than embrace life and freedom.

"I know this story," Tess spoke softly. Grayson stood beside her as she studied the work. "This is your creation story, isn't it?"

"Part of it." Grayson nodded. "This depicts when the Great Deceiver won over the hearts of the Father's children by tempting them with the Heart Stone. The creature of darkness had promised it would turn men into gods."

"Oh, that's right. And that act of self-worship brought forth the eternal divide between man and your Holy Father."

"Praise the Father for the Grand Rescue, though."

"Grand Rescue . . ." Tess drummed a finger on her lip for a second. "Oh! That's where your Holy Beloved comes in."

A smile crept across Grayson's face. "You have much more knowledge about our Sacred Texts than I would have expected a Sylphaenian inventor to possess."

Tess shrugged. "My friend Philestra back home is a Follower from the land of Jarice. She says your Father sent her to Sylphaen to 'share His truth and love.' It can get hard to drown her out after a while." Tess rolled her eyes but knew her tone betrayed a sisterly fondness.

"A messenger from Jarice. Now that is intriguing." Grayson held his chin. "Would love to make her acquaintance, if I may."

"I don't see why not. I'm sure you'd have plenty of things to talk about."

One of the acolytes gently cleared their throat. "I am sorry, but our high minister *did* say it was urgent."

"Not urgent enough to come fetch us himself," Tess muttered under her breath. "Couldn't even make it to his own banquet."

"I'm sorry, did you say something?" Grayson asked as they stepped through the church doors.

Tess waved off his concern. "Just griping to myself—don't worry about it."

The foyer of the building held another set of doors that led directly into the sanctuary. But instead of entering, the boys turned to a side door on their right. Passing through, they entered a cozy, carpeted hallway that followed the length of the sanctuary. Large oil paintings of formidable-looking holy men hung on the walls, each accompanied with a name plate and their very own stone light feature to allow for a perpetual spotlight on them. The ones nearest the entry had a glow slightly dimmer than those further in. They had to be *very* old for the stone lights to have started losing their luster.

The usefulness of a stone light wasn't eternal, but once mined from its original vein, it could last through a few generations. Hence why they were often passed down Alastrian family lines. What Tess wouldn't give to get her hands on those elusive mineral veins. It was a common misconception, due to the name, that stone lights were just rocks mined from the Fitsengea mountains. Rather, they were minerals akin to the crystals that ran through Sylphaen. These similarities allowed for the two mineral types to be highly compatible in her experiments. But stone lights were nearly impossible to attain outside of Alaster. Perhaps when things calmed down again in these lands, she could arrange her meeting with whoever ran their trading system. If she kept her wits about her, she could start building connections within these walls.

When they approached the end of the hall, Tess tipped her head. Two somber Alastrian soldiers stood at attention on either side of the only door in the entire corridor. *Alastrian holy men need bodyguards?* Looking closer, Tess noted a slight difference in the uniform design from what Grayson wore.

"Your high minister has his own military force?" Tess whispered as they drew closer.

"Different regiment. These are under General William's command."

Tess raised her eyebrows but stayed silent. The acolytes walked between the men and opened the door. Grayson stepped to the side and gestured with his hand, allowing Tess to go first. Once they entered, the acolytes retreated from the room and closed the door behind them. The room was a dimly lit study. The dark-stained wood of the bookshelves and paneled walls almost blended in with the deep browns of the furniture. The rug on the floor was a dark forest green. A fireplace held a steady blaze, casting the room in warm tones of orange and yellow. Standing behind an overstuffed armchair, Minister Teason held a clear glass teacup and took a long draught. Lowering the cup, he grinned widely at his guests.

"Ah! Mr. Solis and Ms. Delengando, your prompt arrival is truly considerate. I sincerely apologize for not only being unable to attend the meal but for having to cut your time short."

Tess bristled. "I never gave you my last name."

"My dear girl, I am the main connection to the Creator of our universe. Would you not expect me to be well-informed? Now please, would you both join me?"

Teason waved his hand toward the other unoccupied armchairs.

Tess balled her hands into fists and followed Grayson. The minister turned to the side table next to his own chair and brought forth two more glass teacups. The piping-hot liquid inside was a beautiful rose pink color that seemed to sparkle whenever light passed through it. Tess studied the cup for a moment.

"The glass is from Myrn," Teason answered her quizzical look "The set was gifted to me by one of their artisans." Holding his own cup aloft, he turned it back and forth in the air. "Truly talented craftsmen in that nation—some of the most delicate and intricate glass-work I've ever come across."

Tess set her full cup down on the small table between her chair and Grayson's. "What was so urgent that you called us away from *your* feast in *our* honor?"

Grayson sputtered into his cup. Placing his down, he used the back of his hand to wipe his mouth. He shot Tess a warning look and quickly intervened. "Forgive us, High Minister. We know that for a request to be made by you it must carry great weight. Please, how can we be of assistance?"

Sadness swept across Teason's face as he looked upon Grayson. "Such a noble peacemaker you are, young Grayson, and so eager to serve. If only these were different times."

Grayson shifted uncomfortably in his seat. Tess crossed her arms and began tapping her foot.

"First, I need to verify some information before we can proceed with the issue at hand." Reaching into a hidden pocket within his vestment, Teason retrieved a small, curved cobbler's knife. Laying it in the palm of his hand, he presented it to Tess. "Does this happen to be yours, my dear?"

Tess leaned in closer. A series of uniformly spaced notches ran down the side of the worn leather handle, just like the ones she used for measurements on her own equipment. Eyes widening and then narrowing in concern, Tess's hands flew to her vest, investigating the various pockets. Her mouth dropped open slightly when she discovered an empty slot.

"How did you—"

Teason closed his hand around the blade and drew it back to himself. "As I suspected." He nodded gravely.

"I'll be having that back now, thank you," Tess demanded, hand outstretched.

Teason sighed. "If only it were that easy, my dear."

"Excuse me?"

"Grayson"—the minister ignored Tess's indignation—"would you help an old man stand? Eighty-two years takes a toll on one's bones."

Awkwardly shifting his focus between the high minister and Tess, Grayson rose to aid the leader of the Royal Church. He stepped in front of the minister and, taking his proffered left arm, gingerly lifted the old man up. Teason grunted from the motion.

"You will be remembered well." Teason spoke with a pained look then slashed Grayson's chest with the cobbler's knife in a violent arc.

Grayson touched his fingers to the blood on his tunic while his pleading eyes sought the minister's face for an explanation. With a stumbling step back, he looked at Tess, who sat in horrified silence. Grayson tried to speak, but no words would come. Tess lept from her chair and caught him as he fell.

"Guards, guards! Help! Come quickly!" Teason raved at the top of his lungs, tossing the knife to the floor.

Tess sunk to the ground, cradling the dying man in her arms. The door behind her burst open as the soldiers rushed in. Teason jutted out an accusatory finger. "Arrest her! She has slain this dear boy trying to get to me!"

Tess snapped back to attention, hatred burning in her eyes. "Poison? You dipped my blade in poison?" Hands clamped down on Tess's arms, ripping her away from Grayson. "No, wait. Stop! It was *him*! He attacked Grayson. He might have an antidote nearby." Tess kicked and screamed against the guards.

Teason rushed to Grayson's still form as the men dragged Tess away. He made a big show of beseeching the Holy Father on behalf of the poor boy's life.

"You have to believe me. I didn't do this!" Tess clawed at the door-frame as they pulled her through. "Please! Don't leave him alone with that monster. Grayson, Grayson, listen to me! Keep fighting it! Grayson!"

Tess's panicked screeches drifted down the hallway as she was whisked away.

Chapter Fifteen

The courtesans' chamber buzzed with concerned whispers and speculations. All the women huddled together along the far side of the room, none daring to even shuffle in the direction of the back corner. Lavish curtains, cushions, and other lounge furniture draped about the chamber. Though night had fallen, the room was still brightly lit by the combined efforts of stone lights and torches. A few skylights allowed for the moon's glow to pour in. Tendrils of flowery incense danced up to the ceiling, mixing with the savory smells of the tender meats recently cooked and served for dinner. Normally the courtesans were free to either dine in their quarters or feast alongside their favored nobles, but tonight they were to remain the reluctant watchdogs for their new guests.

As the women anxiously tittered, the main doors to the chamber opened. A woman in her forties slunk through and began to make her way toward the forbidden corner. One of the courtesans gasped and rushed to the woman's side, clasping onto her hand.

"Kamile, wait!"

Startled, Kamile froze. "What's the matter, Gwen?"

Gwen held fast to Kamile's hand. "You mustn't go back there, Kamile. *She's* there."

"She?" Kamile turned. "You don't mean the prisoner?" Gwen nodded. "The queen brought her *here?* Why?"

Gwen bit her bottom lip and shook her head. "We don't know, but it's not our place to question Her Majesty."

Kamile gazed at the others sitting tightly together along the wall. "Have none of you braved speaking with that woman?"

Gwen dropped Kamile's hand and took a step back. "Of course not! We don't want to be struck with the day terrors, or whatever sort of curse that witch can conjure."

Kamile furrowed her brow as she focused on where the woman lay. "I have to fetch some vials for the Great Mother."

"The Elixir?"

Kamile nodded.

"Why did you leave them in here?"

Kamile drooped a little. "I had them with me when escorting the courtesans-in-training back from the royal chambers yesterday. By the time Mistress Yanira had finally returned to relieve me, I had forgotten all about them."

"That's right!" Gwen gasped. "You were there for the burning."

Kamile pressed her lips into a thin line. "Surely I'll be fine as long as I don't get too close."

"May the Eye be upon you." Gwen relinquished and made her way back to her cushion.

Watching her friend retreat for a moment, Kamile took a deep breath and headed further in. Taking the three wide steps up to the elevated resting area, she fought to remember where exactly she had left her satchel of vials. Recalling the day of the burnings she dredged up the image of the section she had waited with the children. Closing her eyes briefly she groaned. In the corner sat a daybed where the prisoner and the strange Throansburrough child slept. Butting up against the wall and lying a few feet away on the floor was her satchel.

"Perfect," she muttered under her breath. "Please don't be awake, please don't be awake, *please*," she chanted quietly.

Tiptoeing in, she kept her gaze zeroed in on the bag. Her eyes darted between the bed and her prize. Stooping down, she grasped hold of its strap and draped it over her shoulder. She couldn't help but look again at the daybed when she stood once more. Violet-blue eyes connected with her own. Kamile froze, heart plummeting as her skin blanched. The prisoner studied her closely, grief soaking through her features.

"She was your sister, wasn't she?" the woman said.

A self-protective fire burned away her fear, giving her strength to glare back. A tear rolled down the prisoner's cheek, instantly diminishing the flame. Kamile held her tongue, perplexed as to what she should do, while the prisoner's bottom lip quivered.

"I pray you can forgive me for failing her. I tried to stop her. I didn't know what else to do when she wouldn't listen."

Finally able to uproot her feet from the floor, Kamile turned to leave. "You have the wrong person. I have no ties to you."

"Kamile," the woman called out, slamming her to a stop. "Téleaph wouldn't heed my warning, and disaster fell, but it would have been worse had I not intervened. At least, that is what I feel the Father saying. Please don't ignore me too. You know Him. You've felt His pull. So trust Him to save you! If you don't wait on the Father, you *will* die."

"There is no redemption for me," she said, then rushed from the platform and through the door.

Once in the hall, Kamile fell back against the wall and fought to slow her racing heart. The frailest voice whispered in her thoughts to go back. Looking over her shoulder, Kamile stared at the door leading back into the chamber. Gaze fixated on the handle, she drew her satchel close to her chest and hugged it. Eyes glistening, she wondered what salvation looked like. Clenching them shut she shook her head and pushed herself from the wall. The Great Mother was *not* the sort of woman one kept waiting.

Failure. The word ricocheted through Iris's thoughts as she woke. She'd failed to make the king and queen listen, she'd failed to stop Téleaph, and now she'd failed to rescue Kamile. *Please let the impressions be wrong!* Iris scrunched her eyes closed, willing it to be so. Still, the heaviness would not relent. Breathing out slowly, she brought her focus to her surroundings. Distractions would be her saving grace. The first rays of dawn pressed through the night's curtain, flitting in patches through the skylights. The rhythmic breathing of deep sleep rose and fell from the opposite end of the chamber. Wriggling her way up slowly to neither disturb her sleep-mate, Sara, nor stress the wound in her shoulder, Iris peered across the way. A smirk rose at the corner of her mouth. The elegant royal courtesans of Diridos lay in a heap of gauzy fabrics and sprawling limbs. Clumped so tightly together it was difficult to know where one person began and the next ended.

"What a terrifying creature I must be." Iris chuckled ruefully.

A slight stir of sheets brought Iris's focus to Sara. The young girl slumbered soundly, with only the gentlest of twitches. *Is it safe for her to sleep so long without waking for food or water?* Iris's brow knit together as her lips pressed into a frown. *Then again, who am I to talk? Goodness knows the last time I had something to eat, let alone drink.* She placed a hand on her stomach. *How is it I'm not hungry?* Flicking her eyes skyward, she chuckled. *That You too, huh?* The non-response brought a slight sigh from her lips. Why did His voice have to be so inconsistent?

A reflective surface in the distance briefly cast light across her face. Peering across the way, Iris noted a largely undisturbed spread of meats, cheeses, and unknown fruits strewn on a long table butting up against the far side of the room. One of the morning rays brushed across a serving tray at just the right angle. *I wonder if I could manage to get some food and water for Sara?* Determination roiled within her. *If I go slow enough, I'm sure I can make it. There's no way any of the courtesans will be brave enough to help out.*

Inhaling deeply, Iris balled her hands into fists and squeezed her eyes shut. She exhaled slowly and opened them. Gingerly, she pushed herself out from under the thin sheet. A fiery stab shot in starbursts through her shoulder, stealing her breath. Stopping for a half second to mentally prepare, Iris fought on. She pulled her legs over the side and flexed her toes, testing for strength. The balls of her feet came into contact with a smooth stone-tiled floor. Shifting forward, her feet soon lay against its refreshing coolness. Iris moved to stand but her knees gave way, forcing her to grasp the edge of the bed. Heart thrumming in her ears, tears stung at the corners of her eyes. Iris gritted her teeth, holding her shoulder as she drew in quivering breaths. *Walk.* She fiercely commanded her body. Righting herself once more, Iris used the bed as a crutch.

With one sluggish step after another, Iris soon stood a foot away from the bed. A tickle of sweat threaded down the back of her neck and formed in beads across her brow. Slowly releasing her breath, Iris zeroed her focus onto the serving table. She inched her way closer to the end of the platform. Her knees trembled as the sweat increased. Clenching her jaw so that it started to ache, Iris studied the path. *Just a little farther. You're almost there.*

Dizziness threatened to overwhelm her as darkness rimmed her vision. An unpleasant churning in her stomach added to the heaviness stuttering her progress. Toes cresting the edge of the short steps down, Iris's strength fled her body and she toppled forward. But a woman's body halted her descent. Strong yet elegant arms took hold of Iris, allowing her to rest against the woman for a second.

"Thank you," Iris managed, too weary to lift her head. "I need water and food for the child. Would you mind—"

An image crashed through Iris's mind like an intrusive daydream. She saw King Thaylos and Queen Aaralee. They stood in a hall, arguing in quiet but intense voices. She could see the vein throbbing in Thaylos's neck, the wide, panicked eyes. Aaralee stood, graceful and resolute. Her earthy-green chiffon dress fell in flowing pleats, shoulders poking through cutouts in the draped neckline. Their words reached Iris's ears.

"You said once she was better, even conscious, that she was to leave our healing chamber. Well, she's gone, isn't she?" Aaralee crossed her arms over her chest.

The scene blurred in and out of focus around the golden bangles on the queen's wrists.

"Are you *defying* me?" Thaylos rumbled.

The bangles morphed, coiling tighter around the queen's wrists. They seemed almost alive. The vision jumped in closer with only the Eye symbols on the jewelry standing sharp and clear. A hairline fracture splintered through the band.

"No, my king, I am trying to *save* you."

Iris blinked as the scene vanished just as quickly as it had come.

"Your stubbornness is what hinders your healing. Could you not have waited just a little longer?"

A breath caught in Iris's chest as she recognized the earthy-green dress. The clinking of bangles danced around her ears as the woman shifted Iris around, directing her back to her bed.

"We are not such savages as to refuse you water. If you persist so, you'll never recover," the queen gently rebuked.

Why is she being so kind? "Sorry." Iris smiled weakly.

Queen Aaralee helped Iris lie back on the bed, drawing the thin sheet over her. In the distance, a few of the women stirred. Hearing the soft rustling behind them, Aaralee spoke without turning. "Why have you not provided for these two?"

The air was sucked from the room.

"Were you not charged with watching over them? How is it, then, the prisoner was made to stumble her way for a mere cup of water?" Though no malice clung to her voice, its weight seemed to saturate the listeners.

"We-we have failed you, Your Majesty," a timid voice bemoaned.

"Then rectify the error."

"Yes, Your Majesty."

Footsteps shuffled across the polished stone floor, followed by muffled clangs of bronze tableware. Within a breath, two large cups of purified water and a tray filled with meat, cheese, and a selection of fruit appeared on the stand beside the daybed. Aaralee nodded her approval.

"Two of you shall remain behind, but the rest are dismissed for your normal duties."

The women weeded out the unlucky two to remain as the rest gratefully hurried off to their ever-so-pressing tasks. Courtesans Gwen and Rue quietly took their posts a few feet behind Her Majesty, who sat on a divan facing Iris on the daybed. Iris gently held the golden chalice between her hands. The metal slightly chilled her skin. Her fingertips traced the ornate etchings around its rim. When she brought the cup to her lips, the crisp wetness unleashed a repressed desperation in her body. Her dry mouth and throat greedily embraced every drop.

Placing her chalice back on the tray, Iris reached for the second one and started to wriggle her way toward Sara. Aaralee raised two fingers in the air and flicked them in Iris's direction. Rue stepped forward and gently retrieved the cup from Iris's hands, directing the prisoner to lie back down. Gwen stroked Sara's face with a motherly coo and pulled her upright, then scooched in behind her and allowed Sara to rest against her chest. As Sara's eyes fluttered open, Rue approached with the chalice.

"You need to drink, little one," Rue soothed, tipping the cup to Sara's lips.

Though she was bleary-eyed, Sara's body instinctively responded to the needed hydration. Iris sat transfixed by the scene. They were so kind, so tender. Could their compassion be genuine? Flicking a glance to the queen, who waited in silence, Iris knit her brows together.

"There's a good girl." Rue smiled as Sara drained the cup. "Would you like some more?"

An almost imperceptible nod bobbed from the child. Rue stood and fluttered off to the main table for a refill. Gwen kept the girl's wilting form sitting up against her side. Patting Sara's arm gently, Gwen kept her voice low and soothing. "Are you hungry, child?"

"Just thirsty," Sara feebly pushed out with half-open eyes.

Iris's pulse quickened as she chewed on the inner corners of her lips. Their care seemed honest and pure, and it left a sour taste in her mouth.

"Thank you, for your kindness toward her," Iris offered to Gwen and Rue as Rue returned with Sara's water.

When Sara finished the last drops in the chalice, Gwen gently rested the child's head on a pillow. Both women silently resumed their posts behind the queen. Aaralee sniffed, tipping her chin up haughtily.

"I told you, we are not savages, prisoner. We are more cultured than you Fiesians like to believe."

Iris's body stiffened. She counted a few breaths before she could trust her own response. "Your Highness, please don't perceive what I'm about to ask as a slight toward you. It is a question for clarity's sake."

The queen merely raised an eyebrow and waited for her to continue.

"To what degree is a Yansairen queen involved with the governing policies of her nation?"

Aaralee shifted her position, eyes narrowing. "What do you mean?"

"I'll admit, I'm woefully undereducated on the makeup of your land. I know for Fitsengea, while we have a king, he does not make all decisions on our laws alone. Both a royal council and church council partner in the process. Is Your Majesty also involved in such things?"

Aaralee's head tilted ever-so-slightly as her eyes looked Iris up and down. "You finally obtain an audience with me, and you desire a lesson in politics?"

Iris's lips curved up at the edges. "Forgive me, Your Highness, but wasn't it *you* who sought an audience with me?"

A flush of pink rushed to the queen's cheeks and her eyes widened. A surge of pride vibrated through Iris. She had ruffled the queen's feathers. Good.

"Your Majesty, you have said twice now that you are not savages here. You declare culture, sophistication. You boast of great power and invulnerability. You treat both me and my friend here with kindness. You took me into your own chambers to help save my life. All these words, and these few actions, they . . . they are at odds with a much darker side of your kingdom. And I'm not sure you even know it exists."

"What side would that be?" The queen spoke in disinterest.

A fire roiled inside Iris's stomach, the heat spreading to her extremities. But she kept her voice cool and resolute. "Do you even know the conditions in which you so civilly house your prisoners? Or how about the theft of young children from their homes to then thrust them into slavery? Is *this* your act of kindness? Perhaps an unprovoked slaughter of a weaker people is a symbol of culture and might? You gained no land, no prize, no physical reward in that attack. Your land is still dry, your war with Sylphaen rages, and now you've added a new enemy to the board. Does this not seem like darkness to you?"

"You Fiesians always twist things against us. We are not blood-thirsty savages. You rewrite stories to suit your arrogance, always thinking you're the only ones who know the true powers that keep our world. Yansairens fight with honor. My men set out to save their homes. And do you expect them to simply abandon the children left behind? Having them join our land is an act of mercy."

"Look at the child next to me. Your Highness. Really look."

Aaralee begrudgingly acquiesced. A rush of knowing pulsated through Iris's thoughts.

"Is it mercy to be stripped of your home, your people?" Iris challenged, "What of relational ties beyond our village? Thrown into a culture, a world, where she has not an ally but herself? From the trauma of seeing your soldiers kill her family to the trauma of being trained to *service* those same men. After all, she was placed, along with those other slave girls, under the control of your Mistress Yanira, was she not? And is she known to be a kind and fair woman?"

Iris cut her eyes to Rue and Gwen, who stuttered back a step, faces reflexively twisting in unspoken anguish at the memory of their master.

"I thought not." Iris's voice dipped down softly, brows knitting together as she studied the courtesans.

The sight of their queen eyeing them at the side drained the blood from their cheeks. Both quickly fixed their focus on the distance, silencing the emotions on their faces.

"I thought you were woefully undereducated on the makeup of our land," the queen said.

Not wanting to get sidetracked by *how* this knowledge had found her, Iris chose a misleading truth. "I am familiar with *some* aspects, Your Majesty."

The response appeased the queen momentarily.

"Your Highness, you did not answer my question," Iris braved. "Do you *truly* consider these things mercy?"

Aaralee shifted her eyes, her countenance tightly drawn. "We are not monsters." Her voice trembled as her honey-brown eyes connected with Iris's, moisture gathering at their rims.

"We are not your animalistic heathens, your ignorant, illegitimate barbarians. Your-your whores of the underworlds, as you and your nation declare." A deep red spread across the queen's face and down her neck, and her breath came more quickly. "We are *not* nothing!"

Air was sapped from Iris's lungs as understanding flew across her mind's eye. Generations of cruelty, mockery, and arrogance had been heaped upon their land. The haughty rejection of aid to a desperate people publicly denounced as unclean but privately taken to bed. Both in the figurative and literal senses. The thefts and dismissals of value. The conspiring to unravel their honor in the eyes of the world's court. Yansair may not be innocent, but neither was Fitsengea blameless.

"All of you Fiesians are the same," the queen spat out, her glare burning through Iris.

"I am a representative of my nation, but not all in my nation represent me. I am sorry for the ways my people have wronged you."

But that doesn't justify genocide! Iris longed to add, but her tongue remained captive. Apologies bookended with accusations, no matter how just, were only thinly veiled manipulations. Remorse needed room to breathe in order for it to be genuine. *Time for a different approach.*

"Your Majesty, why *have* you sought a meeting with a condemned woman such as me? Prior to the"—Iris stilled an involuntary shudder—"*incident*, I mean."

Aaralee's jaw tightened, her gaze flicking to the side almost imperceptibly. Almost. Iris kept her patience as silence crept in around them.

"You are dismissed," the queen commanded her attendants.

The terror-filled protest screaming from their eyes caused the queen's tone to grow harsher. "You *will* wait outside the door. The Eye will see to my wellbeing."

Rue and Gwen bowed deeply, keeping their gazes fixed to the floor. They whisked out of the room and closed the door behind them. Aaralee kept her gaze on Iris the whole time.

Aaralee stood. "You realize there is no hope for your survival."

Iris blinked a few times, head swimming.

"Self-sacrifice or not, your blood *will* be spilled to appease the Eye." Her voice was calm and matter-of-fact.

"Our Great Mother is certain the Eye intervened by sending this child." She waved her hand in Sara's direction. "He would not be robbed of his ritual."

Iris balled her hands into fists as the muscles across her neck and shoulders tightened. The nerve to attribute the Father's work to the Great Deceiver!

"Seeing that this child is tainted by your presence, the Great Mother will inevitably call for her *purification* as well."

Iris's eyes widened as her heart thrummed in her ears. "You can't—"

"Perhaps it would be wisest to round up all the Fiesian girls to cleanse our lands, just to be safe."

"Please," Iris breathed out, tears pricking at the corners of her eyes.

Had she so gravely misjudged this woman's heart?

"Of course, your curse will end as soon as you do. My people will just have to bear it until that time. We are made of stronger stuff here in Yansair than you Fiesians. It wouldn't have been so easy to wipe you out, otherwise."

Iris's mouth went dry, and an eerie numbness clawed into her fingertips, slowly threading its way up her arms. Aaralee began to pace back and forth casually. "And here we had been so terrified of you pitiful people. And for what?" Her eyes narrowed as she studied Iris, mouth twisted in a sneer. "A pathetic little woman claiming a lesser deity as her covering. You are nothing, prisoner, your god is nothing, and all you've sought to accomplish has failed. I'd laugh if it wasn't so sad."

The bangles on her arms clinked together as she dipped down to fiddle with her dress. Straightening once more, a golden, gem-encrusted dagger rested comfortably in her right hand. The blade had a snakelike wave to it. A black, inch-wide line ran down its center, and the metal glinted in the light. Iris stiffened, sucking in a sharp breath through her nose. What in the lands was going on? *Holy Father?* Her tongue lay heavy in her mouth, making it hard to swallow. Fingering the edge of the knife, Aaralee continued.

"Truly pitiful. And despite my better judgment, I do feel a sense of sorrow for your sad little self." Turning the blade around, Aaralee held out the golden handle toward Iris.

Iris blinked a few times, mouth slowly dropping open. Aaralee leaned in closer, lifted Iris's right hand and placed the blade within it.

"You wanted mercy, and so I grant it to you now. Let your suffering be no more." She hovered just above Iris. "Go on, do it." The whisper danced across her rueful smile, and her eyes glinted with malice.

Iris's fingers tightened slowly around the hilt. Aaralee lingered above her within perfect range. Was the queen trying to bait her into attacking? Iris cocked an eyebrow and smirked. Turning the blade toward herself, she extended the hilt back to the Yansairen ruler. "Thanks, but I'm good."

Aaralee straightened, retrieving the dagger. Tucking it back into its sheath, she returned to her seat and plopped down.

"Your Holy Father is annoyingly persistent." She pouted, crossing her arms in front of her chest.

Iris blinked rapidly, thoughts whirling. These dips and turns of conversation proved impossible to track. Aaralee stared at Iris for a minute, eyes narrowed, lips pressed together.

"You really don't know?" the queen asked.

"I'm sorry, Your Highness, but I'm not sure—"

"Why didn't you attack?"

"I—"

"You were given the *perfect* opportunity!"

"Do you . . . *want* to die?" Iris tilted her head.

"Of course not." Aaralee flicked her hand in the air at the absurdity. She leaned toward Iris, resting her forearms on her knees. "But we're sworn enemies. Why *wouldn't* you snatch that chance?"

"Sworn enemies?" Iris stifled a snort. "*You're* the ones who declared that, not me."

Aaralee bounced up into a standing position. Fingers drummed against her lips as she started pacing back and forth. *Holy Father, help me. I am so lost!* Iris's brow twisted as she watched the queen trapped in some sort of inner battle. Should she say something? With Her Majesty being *this* sporadic, she feared *any* sort of engagement. She had to think of the girls now.

Iris flicked a glance to Sara, who rested soundly. Her sharp tongue could be the end of them. It was no longer a matter of how *she* felt. Aaralee whipped around mid-pace, dress fluttering around her and bangles clinking down her arms. Hands on her hips, she jutted her chin into the air. "Say the name," she demanded.

"I-what-huh?" Iris fumbled.

"Ask your god, then speak it." Aaralee sighed and rolled her eyes.

Iris's pupils dilated, heart picking up speed. "Oh—okay . . ."

Slowly inhaling, Iris closed her eyes to focus. *Holy Father?* Eyes shooting open, Iris's mouth gaped. "A-Andrew Hethers?"

The queen gave a curt nod then spun away. Striding across the room to the door, she grasped the handle and flung it wide. Gwen and Rue squeaked, jumping back as one. Aaralee pinned her eyes to Rue.

"Collect Professor Hethers and bring him here at once."

Rue gave a hasty curtsey then flew down the hall. Iris stared, stomach churning. *Holy Father, what have I done?*

Chapter Sixteen

"Think he's dead?" Bryant's voice broke through the heaviness.

As best as Darren could tell, night had come and gone since the old lady had run off after her concoction. He doubted any of them had even slept, considering their chains didn't afford many opportunities for rest. Darren's eyes were almost as dry as his mouth, and the muscles in his shoulders burned from being held aloft. Numbness crept through his fingers from the lack of blood flow.

"I hope not," Darren answered at last.

Fredrick's body lay in the same position it had been tossed in yesterday.

"If not now, he probably will be soon enough." Bryant sighed.

Darren glared at Bryant. He would have kicked him if he was within reach.

"What? I'm not rooting for that. I'm just saying unless someone looks after him soon, he probably won't make it. Not with that head wound."

Darren's stomach churned and dropped. "Exactly how does saying *any* of that help Bryant?"

"Look, I had to put up with choir boy whispering sweet nothings to his little deity all night long. Maybe I was just desperate for a different sound?" Bryant growled.

"In other words, you missed the sound of your *own* voice." Darren rolled his eyes.

"Never sang in the choir," Jason chimed in. "And I've been praying for Fred. But that's not the real issue, is it?"

Bryant huffed out a breath. "Fine, I'm worried about him too."

"Since when did you start caring about others?" Darren replied flatly.

"I'm not an animal," Bryant snapped back.

Oriel snorted.

"I'm also not as dumb as you assume." Bryant raised his voice. "That dying man on the floor is the only one who knows how to fly their stupid contraptions. Getting out of *here*"—he rattled his chains for emphasis—"is of no use if we can't quickly get out of Diridos."

Darren gritted his teeth. "After all these years, I shouldn't be surprised, and yet you always seem to display a new layer of selfishness."

"Maybe, but for someone who so proudly totes that self-righteous badge, you sure did keep in step with me for most of that time."

"And maybe," Jason inserted, "we're all just scared. Scared for those we care about, for what's to come. Maybe we should remember who our *real* enemy is."

Heat rushed to Darren's face as his heart twisted in his chest. He hung his head and sighed. "Sorry. You're right. And Bryant, you *do* make a good point, even if your tact is crap."

"I know." Bryant shrugged. "But for what it's worth"—he paused for a few breaths—"I *do* hope he makes it, not just because of his skills."

Darren cocked his head, studying Bryant out of the corner of his eye as a short laugh escaped his lips. "Really?"

Bryant faced forward, gaze fixed to the far wall. "He fought for our people when everyone around him stood against him. He has my respect."

The smirk faded from Darren's lips as his focus drifted down to the painfully still figure. "Yeah . . ." he whispered.

Oriel cleared his throat. "The witch should be returning soon. There is little I can say to prepare us for what is to come. Stories warn that her greatest power is turning the wickedness of men's hearts against them. Her magic is strong. It will claim your soul if it is not already spoken for." He narrowed his eyes as his voice took on an edge. "Darren, Bryant, call on the Holy Father in this time or lose yourselves. Convert, don't convert, I care not. But cry out His name and maybe He will be merciful."

Bryant grunted. "He thinks this is the first time we've dealt with torture."

"Mere torture would be a blessing," Oriel countered in a flat voice.

Bryant rolled his eyes and snorted. "Magic."

The tumbler to the lock turned over with a weighty click. Keys rattled back out as the door creaked open and two Yansairen guards marched through, one resting his hand on the pommel of a sheathed blade, the other stiffly carrying a small rack of vials. The tubes contained a gel-like liquid that shimmered black with small red flecks, swirling with each slight jostle. Darren instinctively clamped down his jaw. If they expected them to take the Elixir peacefully, they were sorely mistaken.

The Great Mother glided in behind the men. She wore a flittering golden dress, her arms barely visible between her litany of elaborate bangles. Today, her silver hair was braided into a thick bun on the crown of her head save for that same small section she kept down and braided in front of her shoulder. Deep-red lipstick accentuated thinning lips, and her slate eyes instantly chilled the room. *Terrifying yet somehow alluring.* Darren's stomach knotted. She eyed Oriel but halted in front of Darren, lips curling up wickedly.

"Good morning, gentlemen. I trust you slept as well as you deserved." She chuckled, eyes riveted on Darren.

That same tightness coiled itself around Darren's chest, lungs compressing within him. The pressure rolled up to his head, lying against his temples. A sweat broke out across Darren's brow. He clenched his teeth and willed his expression to still as the Great Mother's thin fingers reached out and caressed his cheek.

"Oh, come now, why are you fighting so hard, boy? You're only making it worse for yourself," she cooed. "I've broken far greater men with ease. You *will* tell me all your little secrets."

Her fingers became a vise grip on his face. Her fingernails cut into his skin, drawing out small lines of blood. She shoved the inside of his cheeks in between his clamped teeth. The Great Mother's black eyes latched into Darren's, connecting beyond a gaze, somehow attaching to an unseen tether.

"Give me your name." Her voice held calm command yet echoed and rattled around in Darren's head.

Her words soon became like claws, a tearing hunt slashing through his thoughts, each wave burning as they tore through his defensive layers. Tears welled up in the corners of Darren's eyes, and sweat poured from his hairline. Veins rose on his neck and throbbed in his face. His vision hazed and a metallic taste filled his mouth as an anguished screech suffocated on frozen vocal cords. Darren's throat constricted so tight that airflow was minimal. The witch's words shredded his eardrums.

"Get off him, dirty hag!" Bryant roared, lunging against his chains.

The woman didn't blink. Instead, she thrust her free left hand against Darren's chest, banging the back of his head on the stone. He cried out in pain.

"Yield!" her volume raised "Your name!"

Darren felt his tongue loosen in his mouth; his jaw slowly pried open.

"Braet sin a' Beloved valin!" Jason's fierce shout erupted.

A cool breath ricocheted through Darren's bones, and his body went slack. The witch faltered, face flushed and nostrils flaring. Darren gulped air. Fighting the urge to retch, he spit out the blood from inside his cheeks. The Great Mother spun to the door and screeched.

"Tomik! Rod!"

Thrusting her hand in the air, she waited as Tomik strode through the opening and passed off an item wrapped in a snakeskin bag. Gingerly peeling it back, the woman revealed an ebony metal pole. Careful to not touch it with bare hands, she kept the item firmly in the grasp of the snakeskin binding. Her eyes widened beyond what was natural as her mouth screwed into a tight smile. She stalked toward Jason.

"You *dare* invoke your god in the pure tongue? In *my* lands?"

Jason met her wild eyes with a steady gaze. "I speak as He leads me."

Her eye twitched. "Do you heathens know of the sacred ambassador of the All Powerful Eye? The divinely powerful creature gifted to our lands?" She paused to look across the room, stopping on Oriel. "The traitor knows. Which means he also knows what *this* is." She held the rod aloft, making Oriel stiffen and suck in a breath. "Yes, the traitor does," she cooed softly.

Her demeanor settled back into her earlier chilling confidence. The Great Mother turned to Jason. "The beast is the Ash Viper, a serpent that dwells in the underwater caverns weaving beneath Diridos. A single bite will kill a full-grown man. What makes this divine being different from any other poisonous snake?" Her eyebrows rose and then dropped as she chuckled. "You see, the venom of an Ash Viper does not simply paralyze the heart. It turns the blood within your body to dust."

Her teeth flashed like fangs beneath her crimson lips. She glided the wand through the air, waving it closer to Jason. "The Eye blessed me with harnessing that power. This rod by itself will not destroy you. We would need more for that. But alone, it *will* maim you and teach you to never invoke the aid of another god in my presence *ever* again. You filth."

The Great Mother thrust her hand forward and jabbed the narrow end of the rod into Jason's right shoulder. Jason's head snapped backward, screaming out every drop of air from his lungs. His face and neck flashed red, veins popping up, muscles tensing all over. The blood vessels on his shoulder rose and darkened. Black ran down his right arm to the tips of his strained, outstretched fingers, and the muscles down his right arm pulsed, twisted, and danced in unnatural ways. Tears streamed from Jason's eyes. Snot ran from his nose. The black lines from the rod continued to spread, starting to arch their way up the side of his neck, across to his chest. The bloodcurdling screams pumped fire through Darren as his heart hammered in his chest.

"Parshtoc!" Bryant cursed, fighting his chains.

The witch stayed riveted on her agonized victim. Bryant inhaled hard through his nose, bent his head backward, worked his mouth for a second, then flung his body forward, launching a thick mucus-laden spit blob right onto the Great Mother's face. She flinched, removing the bar from Jason as she did. Jason's legs buckled as he wheezed for air between sobs. Their tormentor flicked the slime from her face with one hand. She strode over to Bryant and promptly backhanded him across the face.

Bryant's lower lip bled from the force, but his mouth curled into a monstrous smile. "That tickled." His chuckle rumbled out, slow and low.

Darren kept his facial expression in check. *You've got to stop antagonizing this woman! Making yourself the focus of her wrath won't save us, Bryant. It'll only kill you.* Yet a sense of pride thrummed through him, making Darren almost wish he had joined in.

"Give them the Elixir," the Great Mother commanded calmly, eyes flitting between them. "And if they don't cooperate, kill one of their compatriots, *slowly.*"

The soldiers moved swiftly, one uncorking a vial while the other wrenched open the captive's mouth. Shoving the tube between his teeth, Darren choked as the sludge glopped down his throat. For a split second, it tasted like honey, then slammed into a flavor of rotting flesh. It burned and itched the whole way down, churning his stomach even before its arrival. The soldier clamped a hand over Darren's face, ensuring nothing came back up. The burning surged through his stomach then shot to his extremities. His fingers and his toes flexed, and his skin felt as if something slithered all over him. Shadows danced before Darren's eyes, overlapping the figures in front of him, morphing and remolding them into hideous beasts.

His mind drifted from his body as numbness overtook him. The cell spun in unfamiliar colors until suddenly, his feet landed on solid ground. A deep red, ornately designed carpet cushioned his boots. Looking up, he could see that the inner walls of Alaster's castle surrounded him. *How?* Darren stepped forward, moving down the long passage. His fingers lifted to run across the gray stone, smooth and cool to the touch. Inhaling deeply, a heavy mustiness with a slight cut of lavender flooded his nose. *Marriam's fresh lavender, to brighten the air.*

His eyes froze on the sleeve of his outstretched arm. The ruched sleeves of a royal blue Askgan tunic with golden embellishments lay crisp and smooth on his body. Lifting the edges, he inspected the outer vest and trousers, which were equally elaborate. *What is going on?* Where was the dungeon? How was he back home? Is this what death looked like?

"Darren, there you are!"

His chest tightened, breath catching in his throat. Pivoting on his heel, tears crested his eyes. Before him stood a young woman. Her wavy brown hair was loosely pulled back from her sweet, round face. A rose-pink gown gracefully cascaded down her slim figure, its flowing bell-sleeves delicately patterned with embroidered roses. Freckles danced across the bridge of her tiny, upturned nose, and her eyes shone back at him, just a slightly lighter shade of green than his own.

"Marriam," he choked out.

He took a faltering step forward, hand reaching for hers. Marriam pulled back, her face souring. "You *promised* me, Darren."

"And I meant it. This was the last job. Kyle and I agreed we were through. He's set up now, Marriam! Surely Uncle will take his proposal seriously." Darren smiled gently and laid a hand on her shoulder. "Uncle welcomed *me* back in, didn't he? I'll convince him on Kyle's behalf—just give me time."

Marriam removed his hand from her shoulder. "And how exactly are stolen riches supposed to sway decades of decorum?"

The scene hazed and flickered. They no longer stood in the hall. Bookshelves surrounded them. Marriam was now dressed in a deep plum velvet gown. She flipped through a book on the navigation of the White Sea. Darren hesitated a few steps back, a torn piece of paper crumpled in his fist. His heart thrummed in his ears and his throat went dry. *Turn around!* Darren screamed at himself. If he could just change this moment. He would find another way to save the others. *Turn around!* His feet strode forward, his body deaf to his pleas.

"Marriam." *Stop talking, don't involve her. This is where you failed her.* "We have a problem."

He was bound within himself, doomed to act it out all over again. His cousin turned to him, her eyes red and puffy. He caught the line of dried tears on her face. *You should have just comforted her.* She swiped a hand across her face quickly and pressed on a smile. "Yes, Darren?"

He held the note aloft, shaking it in the air. *You didn't come to her for help. You came to her because* you *were hurt.* His spirit vibrated within him, railing against a body refusing to obey. His voice sprung forth. "Your *love* is going to get himself *killed.*" He slapped the crumpled plan into her soft fingers.

Marriam's eyebrows stitched together, her mouth barely moving as she read the words. Blood drained from her cheeks as she quickly folded the page and drew it to herself. Eyes darting around the library, her lower lip quivered as her breathing quickened. She stepped close to Darren and whispered hoarsely, "Darren, this is *treason.*"

"I *know,*" Darren whispered back, scanning again for listening ears. "He's pissed because the king denied him your hand."

"And how does stealing the crown jewels fix that?"

"Better yet, *how* did he get this information?" Darren's eyes roved across Marriam's face. "Only the inner circle knows about those escape passages."

Marriam narrowed her eyes. She took the paper and shoved it back into his hand. A deep red flushed over her face as her nostrils flared. "I should slap you across the face for even insinuating." Her frozen tone cut through him.

Hotheaded dolt. She saved you from that world, and you dared to spit in her face like that?

"Darren, you *must* convince him to not go through with this." Her eyes glistened.

"Me? I've tried. He won't listen!"

"He won't even come near me after what happened. He probably thinks he's protecting me." She rolled her eyes, then sighed. "You're not wrong about this being inside information. It would never just slip into his hands like that. It *has* to be a trap. If they catch him in the act, you *know* he'll be executed on the spot! And anyone with him. The church and royal council count them as holy relics."

"And stepping foot inside the chamber unbidden forfeits a right to a trial. I know." Darren sighed.

"Promise me"—Marriam clasped onto his hand, determination dancing in her eyes—"Kyle will not step foot inside that hall."

Light and shadows pulsed around them. Now Kyle paced before him. They stood in his small room above the tavern.

"It's clearly a trap, Kyle." Darren fought to keep his voice low.

Kyle rolled his eyes and crossed his arms. "I know my sources. They've gotten me in and out of the palace before."

"This is different. You're not thinking clearly. Marriam—"

"*Don't* bring her into this," he warned.

Darren narrowed his eyes. "You're acting out against her father. *You* made her a part of this."

Kyle halted in place, slowly turning his head to Darren, a dark scowl contorting his features. "You spoke to her."

"She has a right to know!"

Kyle sprinted across the room and jerked Darren up by the collar, practically foaming at the mouth. "Do you have *any* idea how much danger you put her in? Of course this is a trap! I don't care. That arrogant son-of-Myrn needs to be put in his place. But to tell Marriam? You forced her into making a choice she never should have had to make! And if she does what I know she'll probably do. . ." He shoved Darren away, forcing him to stumble against the wall. "They'll try her with conspiracy against the Crown!"

Darren coughed around the rawness of his throat "*Not* if you don't go through with it."

"It's too late for that. I won't abandon the others. I gave my *word* I'd see them through this."

"It's *never* too late to back out! And sometimes a word poorly given *shouldn't* be kept."

"Turning my back on people isn't in my nature, unlike *some*."

Kyle's shadow shimmered and twisted, shifting into a new form. Into Darren's form. His replica glowered back at him. Its voice his own but *not*.

"Letting people down is your prime personality trait. Isn't it?"

Kyle stood frozen in place, stuck in the scene. The shadow stalked slowly toward Darren. "Pretty quick to save your own skin too, aren't you?"

The words vibrated in Darren's chest, turning his stomach.

"It's easy to paint yourself as savior when you only see the outside, but"—he thrust his hand into Darren's chest in a swish of smoke, sending spines of ice through him—"peel back the layers to see the true motivators, and a *very* different story comes to life."

The fist clenched around Darren's heart, making him gasp.

"You told yourself it was an act of sacrifice—running with Kyle and the others. But what was the *real* impetus? You stole from countless people not to save your family, but because you craved power—to be seen." Flashes of every pickpocket, every score, swam past Darren's sight. Images of how each theft rippled in impact, hurting people's lives. "You disappointed and dishonored your father, his namesake, every time you crept away from home to satiate your greed."

A figure stepped out of the shadows, instantly morphing into the wide-shouldered, towering figure of Alek Turner. His piercing eyes created a gnawing hole in Darren's gut. Tears trailed down his father's cheeks. Darren reached out to him, but his father turned his face away in disgust and vanished.

"You were finally getting what you wanted in the royal court."

The figure held its other hand out, and small images of people bowing and curtseying danced across the palm. Faint echoes of "Your Grace" arose from each person reverently lowering their heads to him. His shadow-self stepped back beside the frozen Kyle, gleaming white smile shining eerily beneath its dark countenance. Kyle reanimated, speaking as one with the shadow.

"Marriam deserved peace of mind at the very least, but you stole that from her."

The room spun, flipping Darren behind himself. Once more, he stood on palace grounds. The moon shone overhead, and a cloaked figure stood at his shoulder, facing away.

"You have a choice, young marquis," a haggard voice rasped. "Allow that vile temptation you call a friend to finally pay for his crimes. Be the first in your line to atone for the sins against the Holy Father's shining jewel, or . . ."

Darren shot out his hand and grasped the arm of the old man. "Death threats are unbecoming of a high minister, Teason."

"Mere consequences, boy." The lines of Teason's face sharpened under the moonlight. "Only blood can blot out blood. You can purify this land, or you can defend the infection."

"You're a sick, self-righteous monster. If *this* is what your Master demands, I renounce all ties to you and Him right now."

A reflection of Darren's shadow creature danced in Teason's eyes before the man blinked it away. Teason methodically removed Darren's hand from his arm. "You do this, boy, and you force my hand. I will not permit another Turner to desecrate this holy position."

Darren clenched his jaw, breathing deep before responding. "I have no tie to the throne, old man. You have your pious lady. Marriam will be your perfect holy relic to purify the lands."

"But *you* have her ear. The filth *you* associated with has already defiled her heart and weakened her mind. This is your chance to cleanse her of that influence once and for all."

Darren turned to face Teason head on. "You *dare* to speak about your future queen in such a manner?"

"Boy"—he practically spat the word in Darren's face—"my ultimate allegiance was never to mere mortals. The Powers *I* serve demand perfection! If the current line must end so that this land can be made right before Him, then so be it."

"This is treason!"

"So is defending Mr. Druthers and his little bandits. If you want our aspiring queen to fulfill her duties, then let those men die."

"I care not what comes of me in the end, but when my uncle hears of your threats against the princess—"

"The king has long turned a blind eye to your wicked ways. He was not ignorant of them. What reason have you ever given him to take your word above mine?"

"I'll make him see."

"And so you seal your family's fate."

The sky darkened as Teason vanished. Darren's breathing quickened, his thoughts screaming within him. He needed out. He had to get away.

"Darren?" The soft voice shattered through him.

His legs were numb and heavy. With great effort, he turned himself around. Iris stood before him in a solitary stream of light, but invisible hands held him away from her. Her face was so pale, her eyes red-rimmed and wide, her lips trembling as she reached out to him.

"Darren, please." Tears slid down her face.

His skin crawled all over, and his stomach turned inside out. Darren's head spun, draining his strength. A deep bitterness swelled inside his mouth, then his shadow emerged from his body and stalked toward Iris. Darren fought against his restraints, heart racing. The shadow demon thrust out its hand, clasping Iris's throat. Iris's fingers clawed at it, her eyes pleading with the beast. But it only clenched tighter.

"Why, Darren?" she choked out, looking into its eyes, her lips purpling.

Darren raged against his invisible captors. "No!"

His shadow form smirked at him, giving a final squeeze, and then wisped away. Iris crumpled to the ground. Fired burned in Darren's veins and swelled through his chest. Shouting as he ripped himself free, Darren scrambled to Iris's side. His fingers trembled just above her limp figure. Choking around the lump in his throat, Darren drew Iris up to him. Cradling her tenderly, her head lolled backwards. Her skin was so cold.

"Not her too, Darren."

Darren looked up to see Marriam leaning over them. Her skin held no color, and her eyes seemed hollow. "Is no one safe from you?"

A shudder rippled through his body. He wrapped his arms tighter around Iris, burying his face into her. The chill of Marriam's fingers stroking his head brought Darren's eyes up to her. She reached down and brushed his tears away. "You are a disease, Darren, destroying everything you touch. Why do you make us suffer so?"

Darren's chest grew tight, the pressure constricting his lungs. Marriam clutched Darren's chin and brought his eyes up to her vacant ones. "Do not doom this girl as you did me. It is not yet too late. These events have not come to pass." Her free hand ran through Iris's hair. "Set this world free. Let it no longer be shackled with your presence."

Iris turned to smoke and whisked out of Darren's grasp. The ground cracked and wrenched apart just inches from where he knelt. Marriam stood at the chasm's edge, hand outstretched to Darren. "Please, let me help end your torment," she said.

The ground beneath him was solid and firm. The breeze that swept across the chasm pushed the hair from his eyes and dried the tears on his face. *This is real. If you go, you will not return.* Somehow Darren knew that if he took Marriam's hand, he would actually be embracing death. Slowly, he rose to a standing position. Marriam was right. His life, his lineage, left a trail of brokenness in its wake. If ending things now offered even a glimmer of hope for Iris, for his people, then it must be done.

Darren kept his face forward, not daring to look down. He couldn't lose his nerve now. One methodical footstep after another, he reached the edge. Marriam's icy fingers linked into his. Gently, she pulled him to herself as she stepped off the rim. Darren's right foot followed, but a small tug on his left hand locked him in place.

Looking down, Darren saw a small boy, no more than six, pulling him back. Light reflected off his every surface, almost blinding against the void of the chasm in front of him. Peering past the light, he made out the child's features. Shaggy black hair hung in front of his face, obscuring his eyes. His clothes were thin and fraying, with a patch on the knee of his trousers and the elbow of his shirt. Warmth emanated from the boy, seeping through his hand and up into Darren's arm. A rush of fresh air poured into Darren's lungs as a pressure lifted from his shoulders.

"I want to go home," the child spoke at last, lifting his face up to Darren.

His hair shifted out of his face, showing green eyes with golden flecks staring back at Darren. This boy *was* him.

"Take me home."

Darren's mouth dropped open as he studied his past self. His heart wrung at the innocent desperation in those eyes.

"Please. He keeps asking, and I miss Him."

The hair on the back of Darren's neck stood on end as a gentle tingle ran down his spine. Cautiously craning his head over his shoulder, Darren was struck by the purest light he'd ever seen. His mouth went dry, and his eyes burned. His heart pulled toward the presence, aching to break free of its mortal cage to be enveloped by that light. A sharp pain raced up his right arm, snapping his head back to see his fingers were still entwined with the corpse-like Marriam. She hovered in the darkness, still trying to take him with her. The ice from her hand shot into his own, piercing his bones. But at his back, the light soothed and warmed, somehow exuding a sense of compassion toward him.

"Please, let's go home," his younger self begged once more.

Darren released his hold from Marriam, but her fingers curled around him tighter. She yanked against him with unnatural strength.

Darren tipped forward, starting to dip down into the chasm. His younger self held fast, but his grip began to give. They were going to lose this battle. *Not yet. It's not time!*

Darren looked back over his shoulder. "Help me!"

A rush of wind and light slammed into him. In an instant, Darren opened his eyes as he gasped for air. Kneeling over top of him was Tomik. The Great Mother paced in agitation at the side. Darren's head and chest throbbed, and every limb burned. He was back in the dungeon but for some reason lay on the ground. The rancid aftertaste of the Elixir swilled in his mouth, scratching and itching against his throat. A rattling chest cough escaped his lungs while he turned his head to the side and spit up a small glob that had been lodged in his throat. He continued coughing heavily for a few moments until Tomik placed a hand behind his neck and carefully sat him up. He produced a small wooden cup of water and brought it to Darren's lips. The water instantly soothed the irritation. Taking a second gulp, Darren swished it around his mouth then spat out the last traces of the Elixir.

"Well done, boy," the Great Mother cooed, brushing her fingers through his hair. "Thought we lost you for a moment, but you fought your way back."

Exhaustion swam through him, but Darren managed to move his head out from under her talons. She huffed at his response and straightened. "Still testy, I see." She sighed, but a grin soon crept across her face. "Though I suppose that is to be expected of a royal."

Darren's heart flipped in his chest. How much of his nightmare had she been able to see?

"Oh yes, you told me *everything*, my dear marquis. About Marriam, your uncle the king, and even about how you know our special prisoner. Miss Iris, was it?" She smiled broadly, crossing her arms over her chest. "I know everything, Darren Turner."

Chapter Seventeen

S ara snuggled closer to Iris. She looked up at her teacher's face. Weariness was etched all over Iris, but she kept her violet-blue eyes sharply fixed ahead. Iris kept a protective arm draped around Sara, her fingers gently and absent-mindedly tracing tiny circles on her shoulder. The motion soothed her a little, but it was hard to feel at peace with the queen staring them down across the way. Her Majesty's eyes flicked over to the newest visitor, an elderly man with tan skin and white hair. He stood in the gap between the daybed and the divan. His face was turned down, his hands crossed and clasped in front of him.

"Do you have any idea what you are asking of me?" the queen spoke at last. Her voice was stern, though Sara picked up on a hint of fragility.

"We didn't say anything," Iris challenged.

Sara kept her head laid against her teacher's side. She didn't know why, but just being able to feel the vibrations of Iris's voice blanketed her with a sense of security.

"You call me out in front of my king," the queen snipped back, "and you"—she shifted toward the old man—"You have been conspiring with my own people."

"A conversation does not equate to conspiracy, Your Highness." The old man dipped his head. "I shared ideas. Your people listened and have drawn their own conclusions. Just as I have asked the royal house to at least be willing to consider."

Queen Aaralee huffed and stood, sweeping herself behind the divan, arms crossed in front of her. Spinning back to them, she jutted out a finger at the old man, bangles clinking up and down her arm. "Quit downplaying your role!" She waved a hand at Iris. "Both of you! None of this *we just talked*, or *I'm just the last one*. It's ridiculous! You have flipped my world inside out. You don't get to shift blame for that."

Iris's fingers stilled on Sara's shoulder and tensed a little. Sara craned her head up, watching the muscles constrict on Iris's neck as her lips smashed into a thin line. Her teacher's nostrils flared as she drew in a slow breath. Sara remembered that look. It had never been directed at her before, and it wasn't often that Miss Iris got so flushed in the face. When *had* she last seen that look?

"Your stupid Holy Father won't give me a moment's peace. All those warnings, these visions! I can't recall the last time even before the *prophet's* arrival that I got a decent night's sleep."

"So sorry that *your* slaughter of our people has made things *so* disagreeable for you."

The queen's eyes blinked wide, pupils dilating then narrowing on Iris. *Colton.* That was the last time Sara had seen Miss Iris explode. Colton had just finished rubbing Jenny's face in the mud because she'd refused his request to court her. He may have only been sixteen, but he was already a head taller than Miss Iris then.

"Demanding I turn my back on centuries of tradition to bow to a foreign god is slightly more than *disagreeable*, prisoner."

"I encouraged you to simply call on the name of the Holy Beloved, to test Him out and find the truth for yourself. I made no demands of bowing."

Miss Iris had thrown her shoe at him back then, hit Colton square in the back of his head. He'd yelped all the way home like a whipped dog. When his pa had come charging out in Colton's defense, Miss Iris had stayed rooted in place. She didn't even blink at the heap of rotten words he'd thrown at her. Her fire from back then danced in her eyes now.

"You're stalling, Your Majesty." Iris's tone flirted between firm and gentle. "Why summon Mr. Hethers? Why leave yourself alone with those you've deemed so dangerous and disruptive? You have no court before you, so your pretense is unneeded. Speak with boldness—you are free to do so."

Sara's heart thrilled within her. For all Miss Iris's spunk and liveliness, never had her voice been so commanding or captivating. It was her, but it wasn't, as if a presence had entwined itself with her words. It soothed Sara. Pulling her eyes away from Iris, she watched the queen's poised façade melt away.

"Your Holy Father—Holy Beloved—whatever you call Him, has plagued me with visions. He told me to test you. I did not trust your self-sacrifice to be genuine, but I also could not deny the possibility. He has warned me of plots against my life, but I was unsure if I could believe Him. Endlessly He pursues! But how can you trust a stranger or His messengers? I-I challenged Him on this, and He told me to test you, prisoner."

"So, you risked your life by offering the dagger?"

The queen tilted her chin up. "I was never in any danger. You would have failed and then been easily dispatched. Either outcome was beneficial. Be done with you for good or finally get some answers."

"Finally *received* the answers already given, you mean," Iris muttered under her breath, just loud enough for Sara to catch.

"And the request of my presence, then, Your Highness?" Hethers interjected in a cautious tone.

"Your name came to my mind, though the sound of the thought was foreign to me. I assumed it must be from your god, and the prisoner verified it for me."

Thoughts have sounds? Sara raised her eyebrows. She'd never experienced sounds in her thoughts before. She tried to imagine what a thought might sound like.

"Now that you have your confirmations, how are you wanting to proceed?" Iris shifted slightly, then winced. She raised her hand to her wounded shoulder as she let out a slow breath through her nose. Sara studied her movements, eyebrows knitting together.

"I'm not converting, if that's what you're insinuating."

"Wouldn't dream of it." Iris half smirked.

The queen's eyes drifted off for a moment, her hands rubbing her forearms. Taking a deep breath, she spoke at last. "The truth, prisoner, Professor, is that your people are a danger to my own. Your god is far more protective of you than we anticipated. You being our destruction may have become a self-fulfilling prophecy." Her eyes remained riveted on Iris. "Either way, you cannot stay here. And your death will not set us free."

Sara sucked in her breath, hand grasping Iris's. If the queen sent Miss Iris away, she'd have no one to turn to. She'd have to go back to that wicked Mistress Yanira, and she just knew Beyttini and Ersmé had to hate her for messing up their escape plans. Miss Iris squeezed Sara's hand back. Her teacher would never abandon her, but the choice wasn't up to her.

"So send me away. Let me return to the capital before our nations dissolve into war. Release our children back to us as a goodwill gesture. Healing will take time, but we can stop things from getting *much*, much worse."

"I don't hold as much power as queen as you assume."

Iris shook her head. "Speak with your king. You hold more sway than you think."

"Your Majesty," Professor Hethers added, "You *have* to make yourself heard. All of our people depend on it."

A cloud descended over Queen Aaralee's features. She stood for a minute, fingering her bangles. Their clinking unnerved Sara, for they were so loud amidst the queen's silence. Panic surged through her veins, making her heart thrum in her ears, as tears welled up in her eyes. The queen was their only hope.

"Please," Sara's voice cracked through a restrained sob.

The queen's eyes shot to her.

"Please, I want to go home." A thick tear rolled down Sara's cheek. "Please, let me go home."

"Sara." Iris whispered the gentle warning in her ear and drew Sara closer.

Queen Aaralee's eyebrows drew together as her attention remained on Sara. For a brief moment, her left hand rested on her abdomen as her lips pressed together. Dropping her hands to her sides, the queen stood taller and lifted her chin. "Before I do anything for you, prisoner, first you will free my court from their torment."

"Gladly. All you have to do, as I said before, is to ask the Holy Beloved yourself."

Queen Aaralee nodded, opened her mouth to speak, then closed it again.

"Holy Beloved, would you please . . ." Iris offered.

The queen squared her shoulders. "Holy Beloved of the Fiesian people, spare us from these tortuous visions." Iris raised an eyebrow. "Please."

Miss Iris let out a breath while Sara held her own. The professor shifted in place. The queen held her hands out to her sides, eyes scanning the room. "Is that it? How do I know it worked?"

Sara looked up at her teacher, who sat very still with her eyes closed. Was it possible that the Holy Beloved didn't hear the queen? After all the bad things this place and these people had done, Sara found it hard to believe that He would be willing to do anything for them. Miss Iris gave a twitch of a nod and opened her eyes. "Check your healing rooms. You will find all their patients have been discharged."

"If I find it not so, we will be having a very different sort of conversation, prisoner. Now, as to the professor"—Queen Aaralee turned to the elderly man at last—"I am placing this child here in your care."

Sara sucked in a breath, fingers gripping tighter to Iris. Her teacher gave her shoulder a reassuring squeeze. The professor moved to speak, but the queen raised her hand, silencing him.

"She has become an unknowing target. Being the catalyst who cured the prisoner, it won't be long before it is said she has been defiled by communing with a foreign god. No matter if Caroline—the Great Mother—declares it to be the Eye's intervention, I know too well it is only for show. The child stands as a threat to her unchallenged authority."

Sara's heart thrummed, and her stomach clenched as it grew queasy. Her eyes widened while she held her breath, hoping the queen's plan would guarantee her safety.

"Begging your pardon, Your Highness," the old professor spoke softly, "but how would the little one be any safer with me?"

"By becoming your personal attendant. My king has been intrigued enough by your skill with words. She will aid you in the restoring of our oldest histories. Removing the child from the prisoner's side will remove her from the line of sight long enough to hopefully allow you to take her with you."

"Take her?"

The queen nodded and looked at Iris. "Pray to your god, prisoner, for it is time I attempt to make escape possible for all three of you."

Steam rose in small tendrils, lifting the subtle, sweet scent of the seadrop flower into the air. The rustling of parchments across the table stilled as Thaylos watched Aaralee pour a second cup of his favorite tea. A small smile displaced his previous frown before vanishing again. Aaralee gently opened a small jar on her tray and scooped a little spoonful from inside. The perfect gold of the honey almost glowed in the sunlight streaming through the skylight. Stirring it into the tea until it was perfectly melted, she took out the spoon and set it back on the tray.

A queen had no need to serve another, but it had always given Aaralee a small joy to perform these kinds of tasks for her king, and it usually helped to put him in a better mood. Aaralee paused when she heard the harsh scribbling of his pen across the pages before him. Would this be enough? Better she test it first. Moving to his side, she gently placed the crystal teacup by his hand. She stood and turned to walk to the door.

"Stay," the king softly called out.

Aaralee stopped.

"I could use a presence such as yours right now."

Aaralee's lips lifted into a soft smile. Her heart still fluttered whenever her king called for her, but a pang of guilt knotted her stomach. Manipulating his emotions so he would receive her requests more favorably did not sit well with her. Yet she knew no other way to bring him into such a difficult conversation. Aaralee returned to the king's side, standing just a few paces behind his chair. The scribbling of Thaylos's pen yet again banished the silence.

"The healing rooms are empty," he stated without looking up from his documents. "What do you make of it?"

"My king?"

"Have you . . . *sensed* anything? Can this sudden shift be trusted? Is the prisoner having mercy on us because you cared for her?" His voice was calm, almost disinterested.

Aaralee knew better. He was worried, and she couldn't blame him. This was not how she wanted to broach this subject. She'd have to tell him she'd called on the Beloved's name. She had betrayed the Eye, betrayed her king. But she couldn't lie. The prisoner had kept her end of the bargain so far. If that woman truly spoke truth, then for the salvation of her people, she had to get the prisoner out of here. Thaylos's pen halted.

"Why do you keep your silence, my queen?"

Aaralee's throat tightened. She forced a deep breath past her constricted lungs. "Have I served you well as your queen?"

Thaylos swiveled his head to meet her, his eyes burning with rage. "Who dared to cause you to question this? Tell me their name!"

Heat spread across Aaralee's face. "N-no one, my king."

The king's eyes widened at her stammer. His features softened as he turned back around. Fingers reaching for his teacup, he traced its rim tenderly.

"Aaralee . . ."—hearing her name sent tingles shooting down her spine—"when Her first Majesty, Linleigh, passed, I swore I was a cursed man. Queen and heir lost in a moment, a war passed down from my father, the growing plague invading my land. The Great Mother tried to better advise me, but in my gut, I knew. I was a cursed and forsaken king."

A quiver slipped through Thaylos's voice, stilling Aaralee's heart. She stepped toward him involuntarily, her hand hovering just above his shoulder. Thinking better of it, she withdrew her hand and clasped it to herself. She couldn't draw attention to her husband's weakness. Even though she comforted him, he'd feel shamed by her.

"It is my curse and my curse alone that has hidden life from your womb. *My* curse that turns Yansair to dust. But you, my queen"—Thaylos pushed his chair back and stood to face Aaralee—"You are my cure. I knew it the day of your presentation to me. The darkness my existence has wrought is far-reaching. But in you, I found my hope again. Aaralee, *you* are the hope of our people." He reached out his hand and gently squeezed hers. "You are the queen who will heal this land. Why do you think I desire your presence at court? Yes, you have served me well, but you have also saved me."

Aaralee let her mouth drop open slightly as her pulse thrummed in her ears. A sob tightened her throat, and tears threatened at the corners of her eyes. She could not, would not, manipulate this man. Whatever punishment may befall her, so be it. Her king deserved her full honesty.

"I spoke with the prisoner and called out to her god as she requested."

Thaylos's face fell, hand dropping away from hers.

"She promised if I asked their Beloved to release the curse, he would. And he has, my king!" Aaralee rushed ahead, hoping he'd hear her.

Jaw setting into a harsh line, Thaylos took a step back. "You abandoned the Eye to call on other gods?"

Aaralee's brow knit together, and panic swirled in her chest. "I merely spoke to him, my king. There was no conversion, no transaction. I had to try something! Never would I do something frivolously. My judgment has served you well, has it not? It has not failed us before."

He turned away from her and paced to the opposite side of the table. "There is a first time for everything."

Tears burned in her eyes. "Please." Her voice quivered around the constriction in her throat. "Please hear me out, my king. If I am your savior, your curse breaker, then let me save you. We must let that woman go."

Thaylos spun to face her, his cheeks a deep red and his eyes wide and wild. "Let. Her. Go?" Every word was clipped out in a cold fury. "Are you so poisoned against me? Has your love dried up for our people just as your—" He began to point to her womb but froze.

His eyes watered as he watched the tears slip down his wife's face. She clasped her hands over her mouth as she fought to contain herself. Her face held no color, and her shoulders shook ever so slightly. The king's hand went limp at his side, and he turned away once more. Aaralee swallowed hard around stifled sobs.

"I would never conspire to hurt you, my king," Her voice strained above a whisper. "I l-love you. I-I would die for our people." Tears rolled heavy down her cheeks as small hiccups bubbled to the surface. "Please, *please* look at me." She took a stuttering step toward him but stopped herself.

Her whole body trembled as a bone-rattling chill seeped into her. Her eyes scanned her husband for any sign of movement, but he stood resolute with tense shoulders and fists clutched at his sides. He was fading from her; she could almost see him disappearing. Her heart beat so hard in her chest that it burned.

"I knew . . ." She breathed deep and steadied herself. "I knew the risks of what I did. And if you must disown me and sacrifice me to the Eye in order to keep his favor, then so be it." The king inclined his head ever-so-slightly in her direction. "But know this, my king. I would do this a thousand times over if it meant saving our kingdom, saving *you*."

A weighty silence cloaked the room. Barely even their breaths could be registered. A heavy thudding upon the study door shattered through the tension.

"Enter," King Thaylos bellowed.

With a grand flourish, the door swung open and in swooped the Great Mother, dress billowing around her. She swept herself in front of Thaylos and greeted him with a slight bow. Her eyes beamed with mischief and her painted smile sent an unnerving shiver down Aaralee's spine.

"Your Majesty, we have been blessed with great favor from the Eye."

Thaylos waited for her to continue.

"We have not only captured members of the rebellion but have discovered that Marquis Turner, nephew to the king of Fitsengea, is with them."

Aaralee's heart lept into her throat as an unexplained uneasiness thickened around her.

"What good is a banished royal to me?"

"Have a little creativity, Your Highness. Banished or not, he is still a bargaining chip, and who knows what sort of information the Eye and I could pry from him. He may yet prove a vital tool in the upcoming conflict."

The king raised a hand to comb his fingers through his beard. Lowering his hand again, he turned so he could look at his queen. "I have another idea."

Dizziness washed over Aaralee. She had to remind herself to breathe.

"Feed him false information to take back to his king. The kind that will divide attention and resources. A false surrender, if you must, but make it so he thinks he and his spies discovered it. Make it so he suspects nothing."

The Great Mother nodded, eyes narrowing in thought. "Very wise, my king. Only one problem may arise. The marquis, being banished, as you said, will not likely have the trust of his king to cause him to fall for such information."

Thaylos turned his attention to the queen, looking into her eyes. "You will release the Woman of Prophecy to accompany his return. She will corroborate his message."

"Please do not think me impudent, Your Highness, but that witch will easily use her powers to see through any such ruse," the Great Mother said.

Thaylos turned back to the old woman. "Then threaten her. We still hold the children of her home. If she wants them returned to her, she will help ensure our victory."

A slight gasp escaped Aaralee, causing the Great Mother to focus on her with a raised eyebrow. Aaralee immediately dropped her eyes and pressed her lips together. The Great Mother lingered on her for a moment before shifting back to the king. Thaylos's eyes remained locked on his bride, but the harsh lines in his face had softened. Wearing a sour expression, the Great Mother pierced the king with her gaze. Clearing her throat, she drew Thaylos's attention back to her and plastered on a motherly smile. "Brilliant as ever, my king. Leave everything to me. It will be done."

Thaylos nodded as the old woman sashayed out of the study. Watching the door close behind her, Thaylos stepped quietly back to his chair and seated himself at the table. He retrieved his quill and fell back into scribbling on his documents. Aaralee's tongue felt plastered to the roof of her mouth. Her ears buzzed and her fingers grew cold. Her conversation with the prisoner about mercy soured her thoughts. Her king would use children as pawns in his war? Surely it was just an empty threat. Wasn't it?

"You are free to go."

The emotionless voice of her king snapped her back to the present. His frigidity threatened to reawaken her tears. Not trusting her voice to speak, Aaralee merely curtsied and left the king's study.

"I don't think you've really thought this through is all," Kale whispered hoarsely over Jodie's shoulder.

"Shh!" Jodie hissed back as he leaned further around the corner of the infirmary's outside wall.

Jodie's eyes stayed fixed on the guards loitering near the front door.

"How do you even know it's Mr. Druthers we need to talk to?"

Jodie sighed and ducked back into the shadows of the wall, pulling Kale with him. "Look, I *don't* know, okay?"

"But—"

"But he's the best chance we got. You've heard how the adults talk. He and the minister are sworn enemies. If anyone will have dirt on the old guy, it'll be him."

Kale's face twisted as if he'd smelled day-old fish. "May not be smart to refer to the high minister as the 'old guy.' The Holy Father might make your thumbs fall off or something."

Jodie rolled his eyes. "He's not gonna rot my thumbs, Kale. If the minister is the liar we think he is, then if anything, I think the Holy Father is on our side with all of this."

Kale pursed his lips and studied his own thumbs for a second. "I suppose you're right." His shoulders drooped. "Boy would Mama kill me if she knew."

Jodie fought back a growl. "No one is making you do this, you know."

Kale shook his head and straightened, puffing out his chest. "Not true. My honor is making me. Justice must stand at the end of the day, or all that is good will fall with it." His eyes connected with Jodie's. An intense fire burned inside them but was soon replaced with kindness. "You of all people know what that looks like."

Jodie's heart writhed. His throat tightened and his gut clenched. At that moment, he was struck with the fact that Kale had lost his home too, and quite possibly people he loved. No one knew the aftermath of the Yansairen attack on the camps. Whatever they'd been using to communicate with was no longer getting through. Jodie's previous frustrations melted from his shoulders. Not trusting the strength of his voice, he merely answered Kale's sincerity with a determined nod. The boys turned their focus back to studying the narrow ventilation gaps cut higher in the stone.

Jodie pointed. "Those look just wide enough for you."

Kale held his chin between his thumb and index finger. "You might be right. At the very least, it'd let me get a better look inside." He dropped his hand and looked back to Jodie. "I'll have to stand on your shoulders, though."

Jodie nodded. "Just make sure not to wiggle about, okay?"

"Statues *wish* they were as sturdy as me." Kale beamed a toothy grin and puffed up his chest.

Jodie dropped down on one knee and laced his fingers together. Kale placed his foot between Jodie's palms and launched himself up with the other. The ease with which the boy clambered up to his position gave Jodie a slight shock. *This kid may be one of the few boys near his age who could challenge his own climbing skills.*

"Sugar rats!" Kale cried out after a minute. "My head's too wide. Can't get in this way."

"Can you at least see anything?" Jodie asked, pressing his own back against the side of the building to keep himself from wobbling.

"Uh . . . y-yeah. Yes, I can. Looks like it's real busy inside. Mostly people from the checkpoint."

"Okay, what about Mr. Druthers? Can you see *him?*"

"I don't–oh wait! There he is. Way back in the far corner. And it looks like they got a couple guards around him." Kale let out a heavy sigh. "There's no way we'd get in without being seen."

Jodie chewed on his bottom lip for a second then grunted as he readjusted his grip on Kale's ankles. "Maybe being seen isn't the issue. Adults ignore kids all the time. We just need them to not take notice."

"That's it!" Kale bobbed excitedly, causing Jodie to stagger.

"Statues don't bounce, Kale!" he hissed.

"Sorry, let me down. I know what to do."

As Jodie guided his climb back down, Kale plopped happily on his feet in front of him. Jodie panted, bracing against his knees to catch his breath.

"All right, what is it?" Jodie asked after a minute of watching Kale practically vibrate out of his skin.

"I made friends with the kid who brings patients water."

"Of course you did." Jodie smirked.

Kale would make friends with a tree if he were so inclined, and before the sun had set, the whole forest would have joined him. Jodie just didn't have the energy to be that personable all the time.

"I'm betting I can convince him to let me swap places with him."

"Won't those other healers notice?"

Kale pursed his lips. "Doubt it. You told me yourself they're crazy swamped. If we both go in, they'll likely just be happy for the extra hands and leave it at that."

Jodie nodded. "Not like we have any other choice. So how are you gonna find this kid?"

Kale's proud grin took up half his face. "Stay here." He spun on his heel and took off before Jodie could respond.

After about an hour of drawing stick figures in the dirt, Jodie heard the light crunch of small feet jogging toward him. His eyes followed the sound until the lanky, bouncing form of Kale popped into the shade. In place of his usual oversized green tunic now hung an equally oversized, well-worn beige version. In the upper left corner, stitched with fraying golden thread, was a shield-shaped emblem. Kale handed an identical tunic over to Jodie, which afforded him a closer look at the stitching. The shield was segmented into four sections—a sun in the top left, a scroll to the right, a sword beneath the sun, and a moon with stars beneath the scroll. Jodie traced his fingers thoughtfully over their lines before finally turning to Kale.

"So, good news is that my pal got us in," Kale said with a hesitant smile.

Jodie stood and pulled the healer's tunic over his head.

"Bad news is"—Kale sighed—"we're on cleanup duty."

Jodie paused, almost afraid to ask. "What *sort* of cleanup?"
Kale winced as the color in his skin faded slightly. "Bedpans."

Chapter Eighteen

Seething anger bubbled within Kyle's veins. Each passing moment only intensified the fury, but he was still a prisoner of his own body. His teeth ground together as he pried his right hand out from under his side. As he rebelled against his own pathetic weakness, his breathing quickened. If he hadn't been such a miserable excuse for a man, maybe his arm wouldn't have gotten trapped beneath him and gone numb. Maybe if he had been smart enough to not allow that last healer redressing his wounds to lay him directly on it, he wouldn't be in this place right now. Kyle felt a deep furrow carve into his brow. Stupidity was his persistent flaw, wasn't it?

He had been dumb enough to get on that transport that carried Iris and the others back to Saunskirt. He should have known better than to touch anything tainted by the king's maneuverings. A prick of guilt whispered through him. He tried to shove it down, but the twinge only grew, twisting through his gut and his chest.

Kyle sighed. He couldn't keep hiding behind misplaced anger. It wasn't the weakness in his limbs or the searing pain down his back that was the problem. In fact, he preferred the moments when the pain flared because it cut off the incessant flow of thoughts. When a body can't move, the mind makes up for it with its own wandering. The airy trill of Iris's laughter danced as a phantom sound past his ears. Tess's crinkled nose in response to his sarcasm flitted through his mind. Kyle's taste buds languished for the warm ale from his and Bryant's favorite joint back in Tha'naos. His heart shuddered, recalling the light in Jason's eyes as he'd described the memory of them searching for skipping stones as young children. Kyle squeezed his eyes shut, hoping to wash their faces away.

Instead of darkness, his mind's eye was thrust into a face with light freckles, a small, upturned nose, velvet-soft lips, and glistening light-green eyes. Breath swept out of his lungs and his eyes snapped back open. Kyle fought to still his inner trembling. Would she ever stop haunting him?

"How can so much devastation stem from just one place? Such a piteous creature."

A roar thrummed in Kyle's ears as his heart battered against his chest. Deep heat rose within him, causing sweat to break out across his brow. Darkness rimmed Kyle's sight. Adrenaline burst through his veins and the wisdom to not react faded fast.

"High Minister, are you sure it's safe for you to—" The protest from one of Kyle's guards cut short as a long shadow fell across Kyle's face.

"Fear not, my son, for darkness has no power over bearers of light. This being can do nothing to me—the poor, lost soul." High Minister Teason Faysal stood a handsbreadth away from Kyle's face.

That decrepit monster was getting a kick out of towering over his helpless body. Despite his better judgment, Kyle ground his teeth with a viselike grip, sucked in a breath, and held it as he forced his right arm back under his body. Fire burning in his eyes and veins throbbing down his neck, Kyle leveraged himself into a reclining position.

"Ever full of defiance, Mr. Druthers," Teason sighed, shaking his head.

"Time sure hasn't been kind to you." Kyle eyed the man up and down. "But hey, at least each year brings the outside closer to matching what's on the inside." His sneer shifted into a wicked grin as he caught a flush rise across the minister's drooping cheeks.

Teason turned his eyes to his vestments and smoothed them down in a play of disinterest. "Such a lost and self-destructive soul you are."

"Get to the point, old man. What do you want?"

Teason loosed a drawn-out sigh. "This world is not of my own making, Mr. Druthers. The Holy Father moves in ways that contradict our finite minds. Hate me if you wish, but I am bound as a vessel to His divine will."

"You are enslaved to your pride. Your arrogance is the lifeblood to your delusions."

"Deflection, pure and simple, boy. *Your* pride robbed Fitsengea of a most righteous queen." Teason's calm demeanor cracked a little. "Why couldn't you have just let her be?"

"*Parshtoc!* Don't you *dare* bring her up. Everything you are is an insult to her memory."

"The feeling is mutual." Teason raised an eyebrow. "And yet, I wish to offer you a chance at redemption."

Kyle narrowed his eyes. His initial burst of adrenaline was wearing down. The muscles in his body trembled as he fought to stay upright.

"Our tragic Lady Tess has gotten herself into some terrible trouble."

Kyle held back another curse. News of Grayson's death had trickled down to him between the whispers of the healers and guards. How much blood was on those leathery fingers?

"But instead of allowing this dear soul to simply be cast aside for her heathenistic ways, the graciousness of the Holy Father revealed a better path to me. A way for two rebellious children to be saved."

Teason's pontificating created a foul taste inside Kyle's throat and mouth. The show this *creature* put on for everyone else around him made Kyle wish for the strength to get in one good swing.

"I offer you this divine chance to partner with our merciful Creator and help reform this deceived woman."

Kyle blinked a few times, processing the absurdity, then let out a short laugh. "You that hard up for new acolytes, Teason?"

Teason's thin lips curved into a deep-set frown. Wrinkles quickly embraced the folds, heightening his hatred and disapproval. The lines were a familiar resting place for his skin. "You mock the wisdom of the Holy Father?"

"I mock the power-hungry coffin-dodger before me."

The high minister swooped down so that he was eye to eye with Kyle. He was so close that Kyle could feel the heat of the old man's breath buffeting across his face. The minister's voice dipped into a low growl. "Listen here, you waste of space. Either you help me control that woman, or you'll be first in line for the gallows in three days."

Kyle held the man's glare. "Why would she listen to me?"

"Because you have a common enemy—*me*."

Fire danced in Kyle's eyes as the minister waited for his reply. Feeling the strength in his muscles about to diminish entirely, Kyle snatched his chance and spit straight into the high minister's face. Teason reeled backward as Kyle flopped back down onto his bed. The guards shouted as one rushed over to the minister's side and the other backhanded Kyle across the face. The warmth of fresh blood trickled from Kyle's lip, but he was too busy laughing to care. The guard reared back for another strike but was stopped by a shout from the high minister.

"Do not be tainted by his wickedness, my dear child. Leave him be."

The guard lowered his hand and dipped his head in shame. Teason took a cloth offered to him by the other guard and wiped his face. "Stealing moves from your old friend, Mr. Kennies, I see. A foolish decision indeed."

Kyle cut his laugh short, and his tone went frigid. "If I was taking cues from Bryant, there would be a blade sticking out of your chest right now. Pass me a knife and I'll be *happy* to demonstrate."

Teason shook his head and tsked. "Over and over, the Holy Father tries to show you mercy, and you stubbornly choose death. His judgment is upon you, boy. The will of the Holy Father cannot be undone."

A malicious chuckle bubbled up from Kyle as he watched the high minister turn to leave. "Sure thing, old man. Whatever you say."

Maybe he should have played along and allowed Teason to think he'd turned him. Yet Kyle knew there was no hiding his hatred for that man. Live or die, he no longer cared for himself. But one thing he *was* set on: Teason would die before he did.

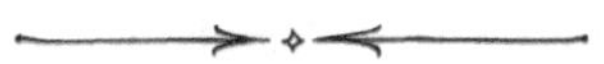

Jodie and Kale briskly made their way out of the large healing hall and ducked back into the shadowed alley beside the building. No one seemed to notice them slipping away. Jodie leaned against the smooth stone wall and let out a heavy sigh. "All that work, and for nothing!"

Kale's shoulders slumped. "There really is no getting close to Mr. Druthers now, is there? Not after he tried to attack the high minister like that."

Jodie leaned his head back and studied the clear blue sky above him. "Well, I wouldn't say *attacked*, necessarily. It was just some spit, after all." He crossed his arms over his chest and studied the dirt on his shoes. "It definitely didn't call for that one guard trying to beat an injured man."

Kale started pulling off the oversized servant garb. "At least the high minister stepped in to stop that guy."

Jodie kicked at a rock in the dirt, frustration boiling inside him. "I guess. I still don't trust that old coot."

A slight squeak of discomfort sounded from Kale, bringing Jodie's eyes back to him. A shadow was etched into the furrows of Kale's brow as his mouth drew into a tighter line. Jodie tilted his head, wondering at the boy's sudden change in demeanor. "Something you want to say?"

Kale blinked his eyes back into focus. "Oh, I, uh. Sorry." He winced and started to pick at the dirt under his fingernails. "It's just that"—he loosed a pent-up sigh—"What if the high minister *is* in the Holy Father's will?"

Heat swelled in Jodie's chest. "What do you mean?"

"Just that maybe the high minister knows something we don't. Like, how could you spend your whole life connected to the Holy Father like that and then get anything wrong? He's like a direct line or something to the Holy Father, isn't he? Maybe, I dunno, maybe—"

"Maybe Miss Tess is a cold-blooded killer?" Jodie blurted, heat flushing through his whole body. "Maybe the Holy Father *wanted* your home overrun by those monsters? Maybe I was *supposed* to watch my big brother be struck down as he tried to keep me from being dragged away? Maybe I was *supposed* to fail at saving the others and lead Marcus to his bloody death? Is that what you're saying, Kale?"

Kale took a shuffling step back. "No, I didn't mean—" His voice dropped off as his eyes started to glisten.

Hot tears built up in the corners of Jodie's own eyes. "If the high minister is so close to the Father and hears from Him like we've been told, that means he knew all this was coming." Jodie gestured wildly into the air. "He would have *known* about those murdering creatures, and he did *nothing* to stop it from happening. And do you know what that means, Kale?" Jodie stomped closer so that he was almost nose to nose with Kale. "That means the Holy Father *wanted* it all to happen. That it was *in His will* for villages to burn, for my friends to be stolen from me. *His will* to let His devout people be ripped apart again and again. And if that's true, then—" Jodie's voice cracked as his body trembled, and a few errant tears traced down his face. Jodie looked down and clenched his fists, unable to give voice to his thoughts.

"What's going on over here?" a male voice sounded a few footsteps away.

Jodie's heart skipped a beat, instantly flushing away all other emotions. Turning to the voice, his muscles uncoiled when he recognized the kind features of General Lance.

"You boys know better than to wander around the palace grounds by yourselves."

Kale sniffled and stepped between Jodie and the general. "It's my fault, sir. I got bored and wandered off. Jodie just arrived to tell me to come back with him."

Lance' studied them both for a moment. "That so?"

Jodie stared at the back of Kale's head as the boy bobbed his affirmation. Queasiness twisted through his middle. He didn't know if he would have covered for Kale like that if he had just received the same tongue-lashing. He hadn't said' anything necessarily cruel about Kale, but he also hadn't tempered his anger. A thick, cold weight spread across his shoulders, forcing his feet forward.

"No, sir," Jodie spoke up "Don't let him take the blame, please. I was trying to find out the truth about Miss Tess."

"We *both* were." Kale stepped in again.

A slight smile pressed at the edges of Jodie's mouth. Kale was determined to not let his friend suffer alone. A slow sigh leaked out from the general's mouth as his eyes immediately softened. Lance dropped down to one knee to meet the boys at eye level. "Look, I get it, lads. Lady Tess means a lot to you, but—"

"We know she's innocent," Jodie cut in.

"And we gotta do something to help her," Kale added.

Deep grief flashed across the general's face, surprising Jodie and stealing the words from his mouth. In that moment, Jodie finally noticed the redness that rimmed the man's weary eyes.

"Sir," Kale said more gently, "Mr. Grayson trusted her, didn't he? She'd never do anything to hurt him. She risked everything to save my friends. She helped my people when the Yansairens first came. She had no reason to attack the high minister. It just doesn't make any sense."

General Lance took a deep breath. "I know."

Jodie widened his eyes as he took a step forward. "You do? Then why—"

Lance held up a hand, stopping Jodie. "Please. I need you two to let this be, for your own sakes."

Jodie and Kale exchanged uncomfortable glances. Lance leaned in closer with a sharpness in his eyes that mesmerized Jodie.

"Upon my honor, the lady will not be abandoned." The young general moved back and stood upright once more, his normal cheeriness returning to his eyes. "Still, she would not spare me if something happened to any of you. So once again, just let this be."

A chill ran down Jodie's spine as pride swelled in his chest. How could anyone refuse orders from a man like him? Glancing at Kale out the corner of his eye, he noticed his friend stood a little taller.

"Yes, sir," they both agreed.

The general escorted them back to the dining hall, keeping them engaged in lighthearted conversation along the way. Little embers of hope vibrated to life in Jodie's chest. If General Lance was truly for them, then maybe they'd be okay. A part of him couldn't shake his caution, though. He'd wait as requested, but not for very long.

>—<

Fiery reds comingled with brilliant hues of pinks, oranges, and the slightest hints of purple in the clear evening sky over Diridos. Kamile watched the sun dip out of view. It was setting far quicker than she was ready for. Closing her eyes, she took a slow, deep breath. She held it until a burning ache stabbed through her lungs. In a whoosh, she let it all out again. Despite her attempt, the knot in her gut did not disband. Instead, it grew, now crushing her chest. Working the muscles in her jaw, she opened her eyes. With hands rolled into tight little balls, she turned her back to the skyline.

Though it took only moments to reach the door that led down into the dungeons, every step seemed to steal her strength. The fleeting thought of turning back taunted her resolve. Kamile struck it down as quickly as it had appeared. Pretending tomorrow wouldn't come would not stop its arrival. The torches lining the steps conjured cruel memories from her past. Nekane's fate was supposed to be the last—it was why she had aligned herself with darkness.

Pain pulsed through her body, forcing Kamile to halt her descent and catch her breath. Trembling overtook her, sweeping away her control over her own legs. Shooting out a hand, Kamile caught herself against the earthen wall. She leaned forward, allowing her forehead to rest against the cool, smooth surface. Memories of Nekane's face floated through her mind. She saw him as the precocious toddler with chubby cheeks and fluffy arms. He had broken *so* many of mother's plates and collectibles by the time he was six. Then came the obnoxious teen years. He so badly wanted to be the man of the house, but her ten years on him left Kamile to run the family after Mother died in childbirth and Father never returned.

Breathing deeply, Kamile pushed herself away from the wall and continued her trek down. Visions of the past continued their assault with every move forward. Before she realized it, she stood in front of two tall, broad-shouldered guards. Their hands clenched the hilts of their sheathed blades as their eyes burned through her.

"State your business," the one on the right barked.

Kamile swallowed, hoping her voice wouldn't betray the thrumming of her heart. "Our Great Mother has permitted me the rite of farewells."

The soldier to the left leaned over to his compatriot and whispered, "She's the Great Mother's right hand. She's good to go."

The first guard eyed her for a moment longer before finally relenting. "All right, go on. But keep it brief."

Kamile nodded, queasiness swirling within her stomach. The man on the left turned around and unlocked the door behind them. Stepping to the side, he allowed Kamile to enter then shut and locked the door behind her. Kamile dug into the hidden pocket within her dress and pulled out a small, rough shard of a stone light. It gave off just enough of a glow that she could make her way around the cell. Along the opposite wall sat a rickety wooden bed frame devoid of any bedding, with only a few slats of wood across the center to keep the person reclining there above the ground. The small figure raised her head just high enough for the stone light's glow to fall across her eyes. Kamile reminded herself to breathe.

"This wasn't supposed to happen again. I fought *so* hard to keep you safe," Kamile spoke at last.

"Kami," her baby sister's voice croaked, a smile growing across her face.

Kamile stumbled forward, falling to her knees beside the bed frame. Her shoulders trembled as tears fell. "Why, Téleaph? Why? It was *my* job to care for us! You should have spoken with me first. Why didn't you come talk to me?"

Téleaph tilted her head. "And who did *you* speak with before you made *your* contract with the witch? With whom did you consult before avenging Nekane and taking Queen Linleigh's life? You sold your soul for revenge. I did it to save you from *her*."

Kamile raised shaky hands and cupped Téleaph's face, using her thumbs to stroke away the tears that escaped from her sister's eyes. "But you were free."

Téleaph rested a hand over one of Kamile's, snuggling closer into her touch. "A slave in a palace is still a slave, Kami. When sunrise comes, *then* I will finally know freedom."

Grief twisted around anger. She wanted to shout at her sister for being so dumb, yet nothing came out but weeping. Kamile drew herself closer and buried her face into Téleaph's torso.

"I'm so sorry I failed you, Kami." Téleaph curled around her big sister. "This was supposed to cancel your debt to the Great Mother. You sacrificed *so* much for us. I just wanted someone to finally do the same for you. I missed my chance, and now the queen still lives." Téleaph gripped the folds of Kamile's clothes. "But now there's no one left to save but yourself." Téleaph peeled her sister off herself so she could look Kamile in the eye. "There's no reason to submit to her any longer. *Please*, at last, be selfish and escape her claws."

Kamile choked back a sob. She wanted to tell Téleaph the truth—that she was too far gone. From the things she had done under the Great Mother, there was no redemption. She would never escape that woman. Instead, Kamile nodded stiffly. This would be her final gift to her sister, a lie of hope. She wouldn't be permitted to witness the execution as per Yansairen law. Traitors to the Crown deserved no notoriety. They were to die, forgotten by the world. She couldn't be a source of strength in that place, but at least she could send Téleaph off with the belief she'd inadvertently bought her sister's freedom. A thought twisted through Kamile's heart that forced her to pull her sister back into a desperate embrace. Apparently, their family was never meant to know freedom while still alive.

———> ◆ <———

"Why do you think they didn't just finish him off? Why allow us to tend to him now?"

The strain in Jason's voice sent an ache through Darren's heart. He forced his focus to the bowl of water on the ground before him. Dipping the torn fabric in and swirling it around, a dark-brown cloud mixed with hints of red appeared. It wouldn't take long before this water was useless. Squeezing out the excess, he leaned back over Fred, dabbing away both dirt and dried blood from his wounds. Thankfully, the man had finally regained consciousness earlier that morning, but he was still weak, prone to slipping back out again. A small bead of sweat ran down Darren's bare back, catching the smallest hint of air circulation and sending a shiver down his spine. A few inset stone lights high out of reach cast just enough of a glow so that all within could move about without injury.

"Why move us all to another cell, for that matter?" Jason winced. "They had the perfect torture set up for questioning."

"Maybe they got everything they needed out of us," Darren answered, keeping his eyes on his task. "I know they did from me." He paused, hand hovering in the air as haunting images from the Elixir flashed through his mind.

Silence hovered between them for a moment before Jason spoke. "No one blames you, Your Grace. It was out of your control."

Darren continued cleaning Fred's wounds. "Vetting the people we worked with and the sources we followed was in my control, though. I failed us by letting my fear rule my judgment."

"The responsibility rested on my people's shoulders. Taking blame for our betrayal just leaves you doubting your leadership skills. It doesn't fix anything," Oriel offered as he leaned against the wall beside them and slid down to the stone floor.

"You didn't betray us, Oriel," Jason tried to encourage.

Oriel pressed his lips into a tight frown and fixed his eyes forward. Silence built up around them once more before Jason broke it.

"Any change with Bryant?"

Oriel shook his head. Darren looked over to the other side of the room, where Bryant sat in a wide-eyed, catatonic state. He breathed but rarely blinked. Terror trembled in his eyes, but no matter how hard they tried, they couldn't snap him out of it. He hadn't moved or spoken since the day of the Elixir. Hollowness gnawed at Darren's insides. Bryant was a pig who had done many despicable things in his past, most of which Darren knew little to no details of. He always distanced himself from the man, and yet, seeing Bryant trapped in torment like this, all Darren could think of was the many times Bryant had saved his life over the years. Knowing what the Elixir had done to him and how close he'd come to being lost to it halted all the old, disparaging thoughts.

"So why *do* you think they didn't just kill us all off?" Oriel pondered.

Darren sighed and sat back on his haunches. "We're bargaining chips now."

"You, I get. You're part of a royal line. And perhaps they hope to use me to either negotiate with or oust the resistance. But the kid and the other two?"

"For one, I'm twenty years old," Jason interjected. "But that other part? Maybe they plan to use us against you?"

"For your sake, I hope not." Darren met the soldier's eyes.

"It's all right, Your Grace. I've made peace with being expendable." Jason smiled sadly.

Darren clutched the rag in his hand as a lump formed in his throat. His eyes drifted over to Jason's right arm. It lay mangled and useless beside him. Darren could tell by the twisting of Jason's face every few moments that his pain had not stopped since yesterday. The sweat pouring from Jason's brow and the tensed muscles along the left side of his neck concerned Darren.

"Jason, you should take some time to rest," Darren said. "Oriel and I can keep watch over the others."

Jason shifted forward as if to say something but halted abruptly, his face pinching as he took a second to regain his breath. Features relaxing again, he smiled weakly then leaned his head back against the wall and closed his eyes. Darren felt his brow wrinkle, and the lump in his throat thickened. It unnerved him that Jason couldn't even fight him on the matter. His gaze drifted over to Oriel, whose eyes stayed fixed on Jason.

Darren switched back to Fredrick. The lieutenant of Saunskirt rested deeply. At least he had no fever. Plus, all bleeding had stopped. There was no way to be certain about possible internal injuries, but the peaceful look on Fred's face gave Darren a sliver of hope.

"We're in pretty deep, aren't we, Oriel?" Darren said softly.

"Afraid so."

"Any hope of escape?"

"If someone on the outside can scrounge up a miracle, maybe." Oriel turned to face Darren. "But if it's up to us, I don't think so."

"Acquiring miracles has never been my strong suit." Darren dropped his eyes to his hands.

The conversation drifted away, neither of them finding a desire to press on. Oriel was right. Barring an outside miracle, there was no escape for them. Especially not with three out of five being so severely crippled. Grief shifted to anger. The daughters of Jaralynx and Throansburrough left abandoned, and Iris just out of reach. This couldn't be the end, not when they'd come so far. Darren gripped the fabric of his pant leg. His mind swept back to a few weeks ago when he'd first met Iris. He raised a hand to the side of his head, a pained smile growing on his lips. She never had explained why she had clobbered him with that stick. *Something about mistaken identity, wasn't it?* He shook his head, recalling her faceplant in the dirt. His indignation had vanished in that moment. It was clear the woman was unwell. The moment he'd looked into her eyes, a yearning to embrace her, to protect her, had flared to life. The intensity of it frightened him, so he did his best to shove it down and forget it.

She's going to be all right. Jason's words from the night of the bonfire floated through his mind. Darren let his eyes lilt over to where Jason rested fretfully. He had tried so hard to not put any faith or hope into that declaration. Focusing on the mission before had helped, but now watching the sweat pouring from Jason's brow and his labored breathing, Darren saw the cruel truth. He *had* been clinging onto those words. His desperate anchor to a world in which he *hadn't* failed Iris, and she *wasn't* left dying alone in a stranger's land. He should know better by now than to believe that anything he associated with could exist without pain.

Why *had* he stepped back from that ledge in the Elixir world? Because a child form of him longed for home? He had no home, *deserved* no home. Marriam's ghost was right. What was there left to hope for?

Small metal hinges creaked from the direction of the dungeon door, halting Darren's thoughts. Swiveling his head around, he watched as a small wooden slat flipped open to reveal a guard's eyes.

"Against the wall. Door's opening," came a muffled voice.

Darren exchanged a glance with Oriel. Oriel stiffened but flattened his back against the stone. Reluctantly, Darren left Fred's side and sat beside Oriel. Keys twisted in the lock until the tumblers within clicked into place. The old metal screamed its protest as the thick wooden door swung inward. In stepped their old torture pal, Tomik, unfurling a small piece of parchment and using the light behind him to read.

"As per the Eye's code, Yansair's great King Thaylos has opened discourse with the heathen King Zaerin of Fitsengea regarding the spies illegally sent into the palace. Before moving forward with negotiations, a sign of well-being from the heathen king's nephew has been requested."

A sour taste swirled through Darren's mouth. *What a pompous show.*

"Marquis Turner will draft a letter proving his good health, which will be written in the presence of a Fiesian witness to verify no coercion took place in the writing."

A young girl of about eleven years stepped out from behind Tomik, carrying an armful of parchments and writing tools. Darren raised his eyebrows as he watched the child step further into the dungeon. Surely this was not the witness they referred to? His uncle would never tolerate such an obvious mockery to his throne. Another figure followed after the girl, an elderly man with dark skin and bright-white hair. Watching the gentleman shuffle forward, Darren let out a gasp through his constricting throat.

"You are provided two hours to draft a proper reply, which will then be reviewed before it is presented to the heathen King Zaerin. Do not abuse this courtesy," Tomik concluded, brusquely rolling up his parchment.

Stepping back through the door, it was swiftly shut and locked behind him. Darren only half registered Tomik's departure as he pushed himself up from the floor. Tears brimmed in his eyes. He had to swallow a few times before he could finally choke out a word.

"Professor?"

A brilliant, wrinkled grin met him. "Little Turner, it has been so long."

Chapter Nineteen

Darren took a stuttering step forward as the strength in his muscles waned. He halted in place, incapable of pushing on. Andrew Hethers swooped in to fill the gap. The ferocity in the old professor's grip surprised him and somehow soothed Darren's raw nerves, as if anchoring him back to the ground. A shuddering exhale rattled from his chest. Darren lifted his shaky hands and clasped onto his lost mentor's back. Thickness coated his throat, and he fought a losing battle to clear it.

"My dear little marquis, how in all the lands did you end up here?"

Darren closed his eyes and breathed in deeply, swallowing back obstinate tears before answering. "A long list of really bad decisions."

The professor took a step back but held onto Darren's forearms. His eyes shone up at him. "Though dark the journey, your arrival here may be more fortuitous than you assumed."

Eyes glancing to the side, the professor let out a gasp before Darren could counter the man's optimism. "Oriel! By the Father! You're in here too?"

Darren stepped out of the way to allow his mentor a better look. Oriel scrambled to his feet and bowed stiffly at the waist. "Forgive me,

Professor. Through a misjudgment of character, I unwittingly led these men into a trap."

Hethers opened his mouth to reply but stopped short as his focus flicked downward. "Oh, my dear Beloved. Don't tell me that poor soul is our valiant Mr. Maythan?"

Oriel stood straight and followed his gaze. "Yes, Professor."

Hethers whisked over to the unconscious form and knelt over him. A weighty silence hung in the air as the professor took his time looking over Saunskirt's lieutenant. Darren walked over to his mentor and kneeled beside him. The professor may not have been a healer, but the man held more knowledge than most personal libraries. His keen eye was their best hope for bringing Fred fully back. Hethers leaned over Fred's body, resting his ear against the man's chest. "Breath seems a bit shaky, but I don't detect any fluid." Drawing up Fredrick's shirt, he surveyed the various bruises covering his torso. "No swelling around his abdomen. That's a good sign."

Pulling Fred's shirt back down, Hethers moved a hand up to the man's face. Resting the back of his hand against Fred's forehead, he let out a small sigh. "Only slightly feverish. How has his water intake been?" Hethers glanced between Darren and Oriel.

"Minimal, sadly." Darren frowned. "He was able to keep some down for the first time this morning."

The professor pressed his lips together as he continued to survey his patient. "Has he been losing consciousness often?"

"He's only recently come to. Goes in and out a bit now," Oriel offered.

"That's concerning, considering his head wound."

"For all we know, the witch might have used the Elixir on him as well."

Darren's heart flipped in his chest. He hadn't even considered that possibility. Had they beaten Fred for information and then forced that stuff on him when he wouldn't talk?

"I pray they were not that cruel." Hethers paused then snapped his head up, swiveling his attention between each man in the room. "You said *as well*. Don't tell me that they . . . ?"

Darren cast his eyes down, suddenly unable to meet the professor's probing gaze.

"We have lost one man to that darkness." Oriel's words cut against Darren's heart. "By the Father, may Fredrick not be the second."

A soft sniffle caught Darren's ear, drawing his focus to the young girl who stood some distance away. She was still awkwardly clutching some parchments and writing tools. Watching the fretful expression on her face, Darren's shoulders drooped. He stood and made his way over to her. At first, she didn't even register his approach, for her attention was far too consumed with Fredrick's body on the ground.

Darren cleared his throat and extended a hand to her. "Let me take those for you. No need to keep struggling." He smiled gently as she allowed him to take the items. "I'd offer you a seat if we had any." His attempt at humor drew a smile from her lips. "I'm Darren. May I know your name?"

"Sara," she whispered.

"Sara, I'm sorry you have to be in such a scary place." Darren's softened his features as he swallowed around the constriction in his throat.

Sara's lower lip quivered as she took a shaky breath. Her eyes darted over the figures in the room. "Are you . . . you're all . . . from Fitsengea?"

Darren blinked a few times before answering, "All except Oriel, yes."

She pressed her lips together and nodded. Without a word, she walked over to where Fred lay and kneeled beside him. Darren watched, eyebrows stitching together. When the little girl reached out her hands and placed them gently on Fred's side, Darren's pulse quickened. The scene was eerily similar to the boys from X32's refugee camp. He was fighting a losing battle with the hope stirring inside him. Liam had been worse off than Fred was now, hadn't he? So, just maybe . . .

Sara's shoulders slumped and her hands fell to her sides. Pulling into herself, her small frame started trembling. Darren set the writing supplies down before moving cautiously toward her.

"My dear, are you all right?" Hethers asked, his attention drawn to his ward as she sniffled.

Sara shook her head. "I don't understand. Why does the Holy Father pick and choose who He'll save?" Her voice wavered around suppressed sobs.

A weight pulled at Darren's insides, the previous hope now bitterness in the back of his throat.

"Oh, child." Hethers's features melted into sorrowful compassion. "I don't think our friend here is beyond saving." His eyes lingered on Fredrick's face. "I just don't know if he will be able to recover to his full self." He offered Sara a soft smile. "But that doesn't mean the Holy Father has abandoned the lad."

Sara shook her head so that her hair flung about. "What did I do wrong? I must have done something wrong?"

Darren eased down beside her and placed his hands on her shoulders. "Hey, it's okay. Trust the professor. I'm sure he'll get this sorted."

Sara tipped her chin up, tears streaming down her face. "But I saved Miss Iris. He let me fix her. Why can't I do the same for him? Why does he have to stay hurt?"

Darren choked on his own breath. "Miss Iris? Surely you don't mean . . . ?"

Sara sobbed harder and buried her face in Darren's stomach. Arms instinctively wrapping around the child, he swiveled his head over to Hethers. "What did she mean by *saving Miss Iris?*"

"A young lady who hails from our homeland. She had been very ill but experienced a miraculous recovery. Though I hadn't realized this poor child was the source for said healings. There had been rumors . . ."

Darren felt his chest tighten. "You've seen this woman, with your own eyes?"

"Yes?" Hethers tipped his head to the side.

"Reddish-brown hair? Eyes like the petals of the flowers that match her name?" His breath came rapidly.

"Yes—violet-blue, a rare sight, but I—"

"When?"

"When? Darren, my boy—"

"When did you see her last?" Darren leaned over Fredrick's form, eyes burning into his professor.

Sara's weeping halted. "Just a few hours ago," the girl said. "How do you know Miss Iris?" she hiccoughed out around a few errant sobs.

Darren's vision blurred then cleared as tears slipped through the corners. Laughter welled up in his chest and burst from his lungs. Hugging Sara tightly, Darren jumped up and spun her around with a triumphant shout. Sara giggled and squealed as Darren kissed the top of her head.

"Thank you, you beautiful, wonderful child!" Darren set the girl back on her feet.

She looked up at him, her face a mixture of confusion and joy.

"Thank you for saving her." Darren's voice dipped down to almost a whisper.

His eyes bounced between her and his professor. "Will you be able to see Iris again?"

Hethers raised his brows but bobbed his head. "I believe so."

"Pass along a message for me, then, my friend. Let her know we're here, and that one way or another, I'm going to bring her home."

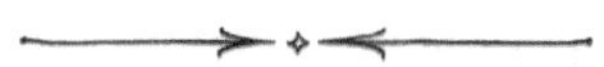

Alive . . . They're alive. Or they might *be, maybe?* Iris drew in a shuddering breath, squeezing her eyes shut for a few counts. Exhaling, she opened her eyes again. Her mind whirred with the same thoughts for the thousandth time. Sara had seen both Jacob and Lori, but almost a week had passed since she'd been separated. Was it wise to let herself hope? Iris shook her head. Hope didn't matter at this point. It wasn't about finding encouragement or strength. It was the fact of bringing them home. Nothing was more important.

A twinge shot through Iris's heart as cold dread spread from the base of her skull. The Holy Father wouldn't keep her from going after them, would He? He was a father first, after all. Her niece and nephew had to take precedence. Unless He cared more for His Yansairen children than her reunion. The cold sensation on her head seeped in deeper, crawling down her neck and through her shoulders. Pulse quickening, Iris cast her eyes around the ceiling of the courtesans' chamber. *You wouldn't. Surely, You wouldn't? Please don't make me abandon them for the sake of these people. Haven't we sacrificed enough?* Sharp tendrils of ice scraped through her chest, making her breath rapid and shallow. Every inhale burned, swirling a building lump of panic, cinching it around her heart. Dizziness rolled through her head and churned in her stomach. The air around her seemed to thicken, pressing in on all sides.

"Pitiable soul, placing your faith in such a vessel. Used and then tossed aside like so many before you."

A jolt careened down Iris's spine, and her head snapped toward the voice. She felt the blood drain from her face as her eyes locked onto a hideous smile—yellow fangs within a cloak of darkness. Black smoke wisped away from its form, dropping to the ground as viscous ink once it strayed too far from its central body. Iris stared at the mouth since the entity had no eyes, a familiar discomfort washing over her, but the terror that *should* have overcome her never came.

"I know you. I've seen you before." Haze coated Iris's thoughts, but the spark of recognition persisted.

"Oh, dear, I had hoped you'd be brighter than this. I do despise wasting my time." The creatures raspy voice rose a few octaves.

Iris blinked and rubbed her eyes. The darkness evaporated, rushing backward and inside an elderly woman. Iris 's head tipped to the side; The woman appeared entirely unfazed. A sharp twist in Iris's gut stabbed through her haze. The Great Mother of Yansair stood before her with the same malicious smile as the entity. *She's bound herself with it.* Iris fought back the revulsion climbing up her throat. Taking a long breath through her nose, Iris braced herself.

"You could make things so much easier on yourself if you desired," the old woman broke the silence.

Eyes narrowing slightly, Iris waited for her to elaborate.

"I once thought your death alone could benefit Yansair, but now I wonder if you can die at all."

Somehow, hearing this woman dissuaded of the benefit of her execution felt more threatening. *I don't know if I can withstand torture, Holy Father.*

A shadow danced across the Great Mother's eyes then receded. "Yes, torture would be effective, wouldn't it? But I'd rather not come to that just yet."

Iris's mouth went dry. *Holy Father, are you there?*

"No, child. I told you—your deity isn't coming."

Was she reading her thoughts, or just her expression? Iris kept quiet, building a mask over her emotions.

"I'll admit, you have made more of an impact on some here than I'd prepared for. Still, it's not enough to secure your freedom."

Several retorts bubbled up inside her. The Great Mother's words created so many contradictions. Iris inhaled deeply through her nose once more, shoving her annoyance down.

"I may be obliged to help you on your way, if you can commit to a minor thing for me." She paused, eyes searching Iris's face, mouth dropping into a serious line. "It seems I spoke rashly earlier. Perhaps you are not a fool after all. What is it that your silence is hoping to get out of me?"

Iris had always been taught to answer and respect her elders, but the sense of danger pulsing off the woman before her overshadowed all etiquette lessons from home. She could still see that creature in her mind's eye. It may not have visibly been in front of her, but she somehow knew it was there. It was the same *knowing* that warned her to neither speak nor back down.

"By the Eye, you blasphemous child!" The Great Mother blurted, throwing her hands into the air. "If we are to strike a deal, you must give me something to work with. Does your freedom mean so little to you? Have you no survival instinct? Or could it be . . ." Her voice trailed off as she slowly lowered her hands to her sides. "You already know. Don't you?"

Strangely, I wish the queen or even the king was here right now. Anything to get this creepy woman out of here.

"Then you realize if you don't cooperate with me, the king will declare the surviving daughters of your home as forfeit. Feed your marquis the information I've prepared, and they will be spared, maybe even returned to you."

Iris's heart thrummed in her ears, a flush growing across her face despite herself. *I can bring them home? Wait, did she say* my *marquis?*

A smile crept across the Great Mother's face. "Your body betrays you, prisoner. Yes, we've discovered your pitiful rescue party. Quite the romantic gesture on your little lover's part. Alas, failure is the only guaranteed outcome when one dares to take on the might of *my* kingdom."

Iris only half heard her taunts. Was Darren here? She *did* mean Darren, right? How could she be sure it wasn't just some random marquis from another nation accidentally mixed up in the middle of this? But that was crazy. What were the odds of *that* sort of coincidence? It had to be him, then. That meant he survived the crash. Maybe the others did too? But now he was their prisoner. She hoped he was okay. Hold on, did this woman call Darren her *lover?*

"So, do we have a deal? Feed the marquis what I tell you, and not only will you leave this place, but I will personally see the children returned to you once we know the message has been properly delivered."

Her wrinkled hand reached into a hidden pocket within the skirt of her dress then pulled out a small rolled-up piece of parchment. She grabbed Iris's hand and slapped the roll into her palm. Iris grasped it while keeping her eyes on the woman.

"Memorize this. Tell that boy these words exactly. Say you got a vision from your deity. If you want him and his friends to go free, if you want those girls back home, you will do this."

Iris bit her tongue and breathed in slowly, keeping her expression neutral.

"I will hear your reply by tonight, not a moment later." Thrusting her chin into the air, the Great Mother spun on her heel in a flourish of flowing fabrics.

As the Great Mother's hand reached for the door, it opened without her touching it, forcing her to take a step to the side. The cowering form of Courtesan Gwen pressed her way inside, halting as her eyes connected with the Great Mother. Gwen's skin tone stripped to a dull ashy color in a moment. Scooping low, Gwen practically leapt to the side so the Great Mother could pass. A shiver trailed down Iris's spine as the heaviness evaporated with the woman's absence.

Closing her eyes, Iris willed her heart to still. But it was no use. Darren was here. She had a way of escape and of saving the girls. *Maybe I should pretend to take the deal and then just tell Darren everything? How would they know? Surely, we could figure out a way around it. Couldn't we?*

The sound of water splashing into a chalice directed Iris's attention to the far table. Gwen took the now-full chalice and set it on a tray beside a heap of fruits and cheeses. Iris watched with raised brows as the courtesan took a few steps toward her, stopped, then moved forward again.

Gwen kept up this strange pattern, though she almost turned away entirely on three occasions. As large as the courtesans' chambers were, it was not a wide enough distance for this to not be obvious and awkward. Laying the tray in Iris's lap, Gwen took a few steps back and waited.

Face twisting in confusion, Iris raised the goblet to her lips, gulping down the pristine water. "Thank you, Gwen. I hadn't realized how much I needed that."

Gwen dipped her head, keeping her gaze on her hands folded in front of her. Iris took to eating the spread before her. Normally, she might have felt uncomfortable having a stranger watch her eat, but Iris's mind was too preoccupied with thoughts of Darren and the others being so near. Were they well? Were they safe? How long had they been Yansair's captives?

What if King Thaylos decided to not let them go after all? Darren may be an outcast, but he was still the king's nephew. She found it hard to believe that King Zaerin would be okay with an enemy nation capturing a relative. Was it possible King Thaylos was unaware of Darren's lineage and that the old woman was scheming on her own?

Iris's eating became mechanical as she pondered things further. How did they discover Darren's title? Did one of the others sell him out? She wouldn't put it past Bryant to try and save his own skin. Heat rose around her ears and flashed down her neck. When had that buffoon of a man ever thought of another before himself? Iris paused, taking a deep breath and releasing it slowly. *That's not fair. You have no idea what happened. Don't accuse him just yet. But still, if Bryant is to blame, I swear!*

"Prisoner, is it true that you serve a powerful deity who responds to your voice?"

Iris's fingers froze above a piece of cheese on her tray. "I suppose, in a way? Though that makes it sound like I can control Him, and trust me, no one can do that. He is not that kind of god."

"The Eye no longer hears my prayers, hasn't for a long time now. Would you beseech your deity on my behalf?"

Iris rested her hands in her lap, fighting to keep a neutral expression. Did she seriously just try to give her cheese and fruit like some sacrificial offering paid at a temple? *Well, at least it's a step up from being called a witch. Sort of. Still, beyond odd.*

"There's this ambassador from Lithos. He has been traveling to Diridos for years now. It's his job to try and forge ties between the Lithos Empire and the Yansairen kingdom. He means well, he really does, but he has never been able to mesh with our court's customs. His awkwardness has placed him in a sour light with the king, and I fear that if he fails once more, the repercussions back in his homeland will be brutal."

"You want me to help fortify Yansair even further? A nation that has painted my home as its enemy?"

Gwen's head snapped up, tears falling from puffy red eyes. "I want you to save a man's life!"

Pressure clenched around Iris's heart. "You love him."

Gwen swiped away her tears. "And he loves me."

"But you're a courtesan?" Iris cocked an eyebrow.

"You assume courtesans aren't capable of real love?"

"Not at all. I'm only concerned that the ambassador might be trying to manipulate you. Your position *is* beneficial to him within the palace, after all."

"You needn't worry about me." Gwen laughed bitterly. "I've been at this long enough to spot the conspirators. Malek has proven himself a hundred times over. In fact"—she smiled—"he would be quite stressed if he knew I was doing this." Her smile dropped. "But what would it matter to you if he was just trying to use me? Why would you worry over a random Yansairen's heart?"

"Just because you're from a country that hates my own doesn't mean I hate you, but you know that already. You were counting on it, even. Why else would you think to come to me at all?"

"Desperation strikes many insane bargains."

Iris smiled softly. Hadn't' she *just* been bargaining with herself on ways to save the others? Yet, was it wise aiding her nation's enemy in gaining more power? Lithos may have only united their many kingdoms a decade ago, but where inner connections weakened them, their natural resources more than made up for it. Dan had declared many times how perfect their steel was. "Saunskirt's favorite import," he'd say.

A sharp scraping raked over her heart as she visualized her brother-in-law bubbling about his passion at the family meal. A lump grew in her throat as she blinked at Gwen Iris drew in a shaky breath against the clawing in her chest.

"What did Malek bring with him this time to boast of Lithos' wonders?" Iris managed at last.

Gwen blinked a few times. "Varying gems and ore samples, I believe."

Not those—those aren't the right access points. The *knowing* stirred within her again.

"What else? Did he travel alone, or with a special escort?"

"Oh no, of course he traveled with a fair-sized company. Do you think the king desires more vassals instead?"

Iris shook her head as a supernatural confidence grew within her. "The beasts of burden that brought them here. To the Lithites, they're commonplace. Malek would see it as almost insulting to mention them."

Gwen's mouth dropped open. "The Wind Stallions?"

Iris grasped a lock of her hair and began to twirl it through her fingers. She pressed her lips together. Wind Stallions, the special horse breed native to the Lithos great desert region, could travel at speeds up to ninety knots and towered a couple heads above most men. They were bred in large litters, which quickly produced large herds. *Perhaps King Thaylos desires to fortify his infantry? I'm just playing guessing games here. I wouldn't have to guess if You would just tell me! Can you not just speak plainly to me what You want, Holy Father?* Iris flicked her eyes to the ceiling with a deepening frown, increasing the speed of her hair twirling.

"You are sure the Wind Stallions are the key?"

She was not, but the Father eluded her. Maybe it had to do with King Thaylos's passion for riding with his father as a child? The image blurred through her thoughts like a foreign memory. Then again, maybe she was simply inventing things to justify her answer. The thoughts felt entirely her own and yet inspired by another world all at once.

"Does he have stallions to spare?"

"I suppose, if he refrained from bringing anything back on this trip, but he might risk the ire of his emperor if he fails to bring back his favored spices." Gwen chewed on the corner of her bottom lip. "But the emperor's anger is already guaranteed if Malek cannot gain an audience with the king anyway. So, perhaps it is worth the risk."

"Have Malek offer King Thaylos the chance to test the steeds, keeping each creature he finds a connection with. His heart should soften toward your love on the ride."

Gwen's eyes glistened. "I will not forget this," she whispered with a smile then spun on her heel to race out of the chamber.

Iris watched Gwen practically bounce around the guards outside the door before it closed with a reverberating thud. Dizziness overwhelmed her, causing her to melt back down onto the daybed. Her emotions leeched out the strength in her limbs. Draping her right arm across her eyes, she released a long, heavy sigh. Freedom, destruction, entire nations hanging in the balance, the chance to see Darren again, to hold Lori in her arms. But it could all crumble to dust. *I truly wasn't built for this. Please, Holy Father just . . . fix it!*

Chapter Twenty

The ancient parchment released small crinkling groans as if protesting its arousal from a deep slumber every time a new stack was shifted. Kamile held her breath each time the more brittle pages came across her path. She swore with just one swift cough, these priceless words would poof away in a cloud of dust. Still, she had to find just the right stack to plant her documents, or it would be too convenient. The professor was cleverer than half the palace gave him credit for. If the Great Mother hadn't kept him under lock and key, he surely would have outed Kamile as a traitor far before Oriel and his Fiesian crew ever stepped foot on the grounds.

A pang of guilt shot through her heart, catching Kamile off guard. She had done well to shut off her emotions so far, so she dare not open that door now. Freezing in place, she repeated quietly to herself the Eye's Eight Tenets of Focus. Shaking off the trembling in her hands Kamile stashed the battle plans in the stack before her. Two days ago, her sister still lived. . . . The knot in her stomach tightened.

"Surrender self, surrender meaning, there is only the Eye." She whispered part of tenet three while turning on her heel to retreat from the records room.

Kamile clenched and unclenched her fists as she walked down the hall. "As a grain of sand along the shore is swept out to sea, so shall the Eye subsume, whether willing or petulant."

Aggravation roiled within her chest. Reiterating the tenets had helped in the past. Why were they so ineffective now? Kamile lifted her eyes from the floor to watch a series of attendants pass by. The hairs on her neck stood on end as she witnessed them practically hugging the opposite wall to avoid her. She ground her teeth and clenched her fists tighter. It was only right that she be ostracized. To them, she was just the relative of the queen's would-be assassin. Despite her best efforts, word still spread. Had she not the covering of the Great Mother, she could only imagine the levels of abuse she'd have to endure. That was if the king didn't choose to execute her after Téleaph to be safe. And yet she wouldn't be in this position at all if the Great Mother hadn't taken advantage of her little sister in the first place.

"Weakness is in feeling. Cast off all attachments and walk in the Eye's wisdom." Why were the tenets always so much easier to say than to follow?

"Kamile! Kamile, wait."

Kamile halted in place as Gwen's voice came bouncing up from behind. Turning to greet her friend, she frowned. "Gwen, what are you thinking?" she hissed once Gwen reached her side.

A flush rested pleasingly across Gwen's cheeks. Her eyes shone with happiness. Even Kamile's curt rebuke could not dim her glow.

"I'm thinking I wanted to talk to my friend." Gwen paused, eyes softening. "I'm not afraid of what others might say. You should not have to face these days alone."

Kamile resumed her walking, noticing the seething glares and hushed whispers as Gwen kept in step beside her. "There is no wisdom nor benefit in linking yourself to a family of traitors."

Gwen turned her head to stare down the others in the hall. Swooping out her hand she linked her arm around Kamile's, locking in around the elbow. The air fled from Kamile's lungs as a gasp from afar scraped across her nerves. She attempted to pull away, but Gwen only clasped tighter.

"I don't care what happened in the past. I don't care what evils may have been associated with you." Gwen kept her face forward as she spoke. "You are my friend. I *know* you. The shadows that chase after you are not who you are."

Heart throbbing, Kamile glimpsed a secluded alcove. Holding her arm around Gwen's, she swung them both inside, out of sight from prying eyes. Anger burned back any tears wishing to fall.

"You know nothing of how deep this runs. And if you don't stop this childish, doe-eyed support, you will go down in flames like all the others."

Gwen gently removed her arm from Kamile. "I know what good looks like, and I know what it looks like when it has been preyed upon. It is no secret how the Great Mother operates, and we on the lower levels know only too well the danger of her innermost circles. Sure, there is power there, but that lust has never once flickered across your eyes in all the years I've known you."

Kamile moved to counter but was stilled by Gwen raising her hand. "You stood with me when no one else would as a silly courtesan fell in love with a noble ambassador. You never tired of my tears nor shamed me for my tirades. You used your sway with the Great Mother to defend the courtesans-in-training from the more wicked tendencies of Mistress Yanira. And I *know* it was you, because things changed only after I confided to you about my childhood in the palace."

Kind as her words were, they fell hollow across Kamile's ears. Gwen had no idea how thick the blood ran from her hands. Warmth pressed beyond the numbness as Kamile realized Gwen had clasped her hands within hers. Her friend raised them up, her eyes shining with sincerity.

"These shadows don't have to win, Kamile. They don't have to overtake you. I've seen that miracles can be real." She paused, eyes glistening. "Malek got his audience with the king, and the king loved him so much he granted him the right to a royal favor!"

Kamile felt a rush in her heart. The tears in Gwen's eyes stirred up her own.

"He asked for the king's blessing to marry me. Kamile, I am betrothed!"

A sob loosed itself from Kamile's throat. "Oh, my dear Gwen!" She flung her arms around the woman and held her tight. "For so long you've dreamed of this. We'd almost given up hope. I am so happy for you!"

They stood in their embrace laughing and crying, years of pent-up heartache pouring out all at once. Kamile marveled at how she felt no bitterness at Gwen's victory. She was far too relieved that there was finally something worth celebrating in her death-stained life. At last, Gwen pulled away from Kamile, holding onto her hands.

"Can't you see what this means, Kamile? There is no fate set in stone. We are not slaves to our circumstances."

Kamile sucked in a breath and stiffened at the naive girl almost twenty years her junior. Gwen squeezed her fingers. "Yours was a miracle, Gwen. A beautiful one. But there is no wisdom in relying on a miracle to free me as well. The Eye has long since turned his gaze from me."

Gwen released Kamile's hand and pressed her lips into a thin line.

Kamile took a step forward. "That does not mean you aren't allowed to embrace your joy."

"It's not that." Gwen's eyes darted to the side as her brow knitted together.

Kamile followed her gaze but saw no one nearby. Turning back to Gwen, she noted her friend's saddened anxious posturing. "No one else is here, Gwen. You needn't worry about palace gossips now. Though I did try to warn you to leave me be earlier."

Gwen's face paled as she gasped. "Oh no. No, I would never be ashamed of you, Kamile. I will always stand by you as my friend. It's just that . . . my miracle was not granted to me by the Eye."

Kamile blinked. "Then how?"

"I . . ." Gwen's hands gripped the sheer, overlaid fabric of her dress, twisting it between her fingers at the sides, "I sought the aid of a heathen god."

Kamile stood silently, uncertain of how to reply.

"Not just any heathen god. I spoke with the prisoner. The witch from Fitsengea. She spoke with her god on my behalf then relayed my instructions. Malek and I will finally be together because of the path she provided."

The weight of Gwen's confession collapsed across Kamile's shoulders. Even as a friend, the risk in telling a close lackey of the Great Mother was monstrous. She had underestimated how deeply Gwen revered their friendship.

"You shouldn't be telling me this."

"No, Kamile, you shouldn't be trapped in the life you are! The deeper sin would be for me to withhold from you a chance for joy."

Kamile's feet pulled a few paces back, and Gwen released a heavy sigh. "At the very least, think on it. I will not burden you with this any further. I will remain your friend, whatever you decide."

Kamile cast her eyes down to the side, battling the rising thrumming of her heart.

"Malek is waiting for me in the courtyard. I'll likely be there till evening if you wish to see me." Gwen started to walk away but paused. "No matter what you choose, do not forget why the ones you lost sacrificed themselves. Even knowing your darkness, they wanted to save you. Don't toss that love aside so frivolously."

Kamile listened as the sound of Gwen's steps faded. The muscles across her neck and shoulders wound so tight that her head began to hurt. What right did Gwen have to taunt her with hope? She was more child than woman compared to Kamile's time here. Hope worked for some, but the Eye had clearly deemed her family line the dumping ground for curses. The very fact that she'd grown up in these lands proved it. Her mother stolen from Sylphaen, her father who left them to die. Her very blood must be an offense to the Eye. Why else would she be standing alone now?

But then, if the Eye hated her so, why did she continue to stand under him? The softest breeze danced around her face, piercing through the heaviness inside. The Great Mother was the Eye's closest follower. Never had she witnessed anything good or pure spring from that woman. And why had it taken her so long to consider these things? Maybe she should speak with the prisoner?

"There you are, girl, losing yourself in thought again."

Breath fled Kamile's lungs hearing the Great Mother behind her.

"Come along, I am kindling a new plan."

Kamile turned and curtsied, falling in step as the Great Mother took off without waiting for a reply. For such an old woman, the Great Mother moved with fluid speed. Some claimed she was in her eighties, but Kamile had suspicions that the Great Mother far surpassed natural ageing boundaries. It would not surprise her if the Eye himself sustained the woman beyond mortal limits. Sweeping down the halls, it wasn't long before they entered the Great Mother's personal study.

"I trust you completed your task in the records room?" The Great Mother said, keeping herself busy by rifling through the items on a shelf.

"Yes, Great Mother."

"Perfect. Then you're free." She pulled out a blank parchment and slapped it into Kamile's hands.

Familiar with the routine, Kamile took the parchment to a desk just large enough for a single occupant and sat down. Opening the drawer on the desk's underside, she procured an inkwell and dip pen.

"Good, now you will write to those heathen upstarts and convince them to try and break out their friends in the dungeons in three nights' time."

Kamile's eyebrows rose despite herself.

"They will be my new scapegoats, so be sure to truly rile them up. Next, you will increase the rumors in the palace and outside of it that these peasants are growing in violence. They have been too tame, and for this to work, I need their blasphemy of the Eye and all Diridos holds dear to be incontestable."

"What is it you are hoping to accuse them of?"

Kamile watched as the Great Mother grew fidgety. The woman's irritation pushed her to take laps around the large ornate space.

"I have no other choice now. I tried, but she took them from me. That woman has made it impossible to return to secure my first plan. She has been seeding doubt, loosening my hold. He has no idea the true threat she possesses!"

Kamile laid her quill down on the tabletop, eyes bent to the parchment but unfocused. The Great Mother's rant sent a chill down her spine. She'd heard her spiral like this before.

"She tries to flaunt her power when she refuses my title. Now she'll learn the mistakes she's made." A crooked smile curved across the Great Mother's lips as she muttered to herself.

A supernatural chill ran through Kamile's fingers and toes. She swallowed and steeled herself against the churning panic.

"Once you've delivered the message, you will take your coin stash set aside for my market days and contact the Viper nomads. They are currently camping on the northern outskirts of Diridos. The Eye's favor has timed these things perfectly."

"And what am I to request of the nomads?"

"They will raid the palace the same night the rebels attempt their rescue of the prisoner and her companions."

"You want all of this accomplished in three days' time? Less, accounting for when the plan is to transpire?"

The Great Mother spun on her heel, eyes burning through Kamile. "That queen will not contaminate my throne a single day longer. She should be grateful for the three days I'm granting her."

Darkness rimmed Kamile's vision. She nodded stiffly as the pressure built inside her chest and her mouth felt fuzzy. Another queen's blood would be on her hands, but the last stain silenced her from warning anyone. This was why the Eye punished her. Because she was a coward. She was too afraid of the freedom death might bring. To survive, the queen had to be sacrificed. Gwen was wrong about her, about everything.

The scurrying of the people to and fro across the palace grounds eerily mimicked the insect trails Tess studied as a child. From her cell in the tower, each person below seemed just as small. Tess raised her fingers, letting the thin sliver of sunlight float around them. Perhaps she should thank Teason for such quality accommodations? Not many had the chance for such a spectacular view, even if the window was only wide enough for half her eye to see out. Still, any chance to ruffle that monster's feathers was one she couldn't pass up. Tess ran a finger along the inner edge of the gap, her nail scratching gently at the stone's grit. If she had the right tools, she could chip away at it. There would be no way to hide her progress, and even if she made her way through, how would she scale down unseen?

Moving away with a heavy sigh, Tess interlaced her fingers and rested her hands on the back of her head. Gazing up at the distant beams, she frowned and turned tight circles within the cramped space. The more she thought on it, the more it seemed that bribery was her only answer. She held no compunction against it. The problem was in obtaining something she could bribe a guard with. Offering her body made no practical sense when, crass a thought as it was, they could just rob her of that if they desired. Best to not plant any thoughts in their heads.

If only she could get a message to her grandfather. He'd easily grease the right palms for her escape. But how wise would it be to involve him when that was exactly who the high minister wanted to be connected to anyway? Thankfully, Grandpap wasn't an easy man to find when deep in his researching season. Tess could always scrounge him up when needed, but she would die before she allowed that snake to coil around him. Tess dropped her hands to her sides. Death might end up being her only true escape.

Maybe she could try faking her death in hopes that she could get out of wherever they tossed her body. Assuming they didn't have their healers verify her death. She should have pursued her herbalist studies more—then she would know how to concoct that sleeping-death decoction that Philestra had mentioned. Doing a slight spin on her heel she reached her bed and plopped down. While raggedy straw mattresses were great for producing knots in every single back muscle, she was grateful for a little padding and even more for the lack of smell. Overall, she was impressed at the upkeep of her prison, nowhere near as disease-ridden as the holes back in Sylphaen.

The image of those vile pits caused Callum's face to spring into her thoughts, making her raise her hand to her neck where the betrothal crystal once lay. Tess sneered, thinking about the way the guard snatched it from her. He deserved the bloody nose, though she wished she could have done more. She huffed a breath through her nose. Tess was one of Sylphaen's best inventors. She should be able to devise an escape. The Grand Senate back home might be able to help, but seeing Fitsengea's most influential person was as corrupt as she suspected, it was doubtful that legal processes would be properly upheld.

Tess leaned back on her cot and closed her eyes. Images of Grayson's pain-contorted face danced in her mind. Popping her lids back open, Tess rolled to her side and curled up into a ball. She didn't want to think on him. For days she had fought back those scenes, but every moment her mind slowed down, he was right there. The hollow echo of footsteps shuffling up the tower spiral granted Tess a welcome distraction. Pushing herself up, she adjusted her hair and clothes to camouflage her distress. Scooting to the edge of the bed, she swung her legs over the side, crossing one over the other. Leaning with one hand braced at her side, she raised her other to study her nails in an unaffected manner.

"Making yourself comfortable, I see." High Minister Teason sneered upon entering her cell.

"Where's your decorum, oh grand minister? Don't you know to never come callin' on a lady unannounced? I have quite a busy schedule today, after all. I just don't know if I have room to fit ya in."

The old man sighed as he moved over to the narrow window and looked out. "The chains you children bind yourselves with."

"Women are fond of shiny jewelry." Tess smiled viciously.

Teason looked back at her, sadness etched into his brow. "If there was any other way to save this land, I would have chosen it gladly. I did not want that boy to have to die."

"Grayson. His name is Grayson. And no one forced your hand. Cold-blooded murderers deserve no sympathy."

"You may not understand now, but you will. Then you will see, painful as it is, sacrifices had to be made. This is all within the Father's will, and we are all merely His servants, whether you recognize that yet or not."

"Ah, so your mother never taught you how to take responsibility for your own actions, I see."

A slow breath hissed out of the minister's mouth.

Tess smiled. "Something bothering you there, sweetie?" she cooed. "Come on now, tell Auntie Tess all about it."

Teason turned slowly, staring at her stone-faced. He took a few calculated steps toward Tess, stopping an arm span away. "This tower to your liking, Ms. Delengando? These accommodations are an act of mercy because *I* convinced the council to not throw a lady amongst the more unfavorable lot in the group holdings."

Tess flattened her tone. "Why, thank you ever so much. You are truly a prince among men."

Teason smirked, making Tess's blood boil.

"I have no intention of executing you."

"Glorious."

"You have a purpose far too great for that, my child."

"I figured."

"Ah, but you haven't. Not truly. If you could grasp this depth, I know I could get you to soften your heart toward me."

Tess's gaze burned through him. "You've got the worst recruiting tactics I've ever seen."

"There are more ways to break a stubborn soul than to threat of death."

"Not many that stick quite as well."

Teason raised a hand, nostrils flaring. Breathing deeply, he lowered his hand once more and rolled his shoulders. "Not very good at allowing someone to finish what they're trying to say, are we?"

Still glaring, Tess smiled. "Oh no, I'm a *wonderful* listener."

The high minister frowned. Tess held his stare with her own combative smile. The contest lasted for almost a full minute.

"Auntie Tess . . ." Teason muttered at last.

Tess's smile slipped.

"You truly did ingratiate yourself with those poor boys, didn't you?"

Teason rested his chin between his thumb and forefinger. Tess held her tongue, careful to not fidget.

"Such a good lot. My heart breaks for all the horrors they've endured. I feel drawn to take a vested interest in their care. Being orphaned as they are now, they'll need someone to look after them. Don't you agree?"

"Feykunt." Tess sneered.

"Now, now, that's not very becoming language for a lady."

Tess leaned forward slowly, applying all the venom she could muster, "*Fey-Kunt.*"

She emphasized every syllable, snapping the ending sound especially.

"I warned you, child. Death isn't the only threat that breaks a stubborn soul." Teason frowned, holding his head high.

The old man turned away and walked over to her cell door. Using a swollen knuckle on his thin index finger, he rapped on the wood a few times.

"I will return tomorrow. By then, perhaps you'll have had more time to collect your thoughts. At the very least, regain a hold of your manners."

The high minister whisked through the door as it opened for him. Once latched shut again, Tess flipped over onto her flimsy straw mattress. Pressing her face into the scratchy fabric, she screeched out every drop of anger.

"I understand fully what you're saying, but what *you* don't seem to understand is I am *also* duty bound."

Kyle peeked open an eye, inspecting the source of the commotion. A couple feet away, one of the healers stood nose to nose with a royal guard. The amount of flack these medicine makers caught every time they attempted to tend to him was almost impressive in its consistency. The guards were right. Treating his wounds was an exercise in futility. His head was bound for the chopping block in the morning anyway. Why waste supplies on him?

"And if you were in that man's place, would you advise the same?"

The woman's shout caused more heads to turn their way. A few other healers took a couple supportive steps toward their teammate. Kyle allowed a small smile to play across his lips. If that guard knew what was best for him, he'd swallow his pride. Never was wise to get on the bad side of someone who would likely be tending to them in the future. A healer may have compunctions against taking a life, but Kyle had seen how wicked their vengeance could get along someone's path to recovery. Now he kind of hoped the soldier *would* keep pressing his luck.

At last, the man stepped aside and let the woman pass. She carried some fresh bandages, and the water boy trailed close behind. Reaching Kyle's bedside, the boy quickly scooped out a fresh portion of water then returned to the other patients. The woman retrieved a small set of scissors and cut off Kyle's last set of bandages.

"Such a shame. You've been healing up quite nicely, Mr. Druthers," the healer said while pulling off the wraps.

"Sorry to waste your efforts," Kyle chuckled.

"It's out of our hands now." She sighed. "On your elbow, please."

Kyle propped himself up, allowing room for the application of new dressings around his torso. "Why do it, then? I'm normally the last to agree with Teason's cronies, but they do have a point. Unless you're thinking you can convert me last minute? Trying to save this wretch's soul from the gallows, are we?"

Kyle flashed A cocky smile, and the woman's cheeks flushed Considering the minimal crinkling around the corners of her eyes and the shine of her deep-brown hair, Kyle gathered she was *maybe* five years his senior. And now he had flustered her, which fueled his mischievous side.

"Oh wait, don't tell me. Are you actually plotting my escape?" Kyle teased.

A metallic clang bounced off the stone floor.

"No, my scissors!" The woman stumbled while trying to retrieve them.

Kyle shut his mouth and furrowed his brow. He watched as the woman's flush spread up to her ears. Her eyes darted from her handiwork to the royal watchmen.

"If you are planning something"—Kyle lowered his voice, keeping his eyes attuned to her face—"don't. You're clearly too scared. They'll catch you."

The healer's eyes met Kyle's for a second before she hunched closer to finish binding up the bandages. Kyle frowned and grabbed onto her hand, forcing her to look at his face. "I said don't. I am not innocent. You'll throw your life away for a man who should die."

"Did you kill the princess?" the woman challenged his glare.

Marriam's face flashed before his mind's eye, robbing him of breath. Kyle swallowed hard and cleared his throat. "Yes."

"Liar," she whispered, studying his eyes.

Kyle broke eye contact, unable to handle the scrutinizing.

"I'm not doing this for *you* anyway," she spoke curtly and stood up straight.

Moving to the wooden cup on the stand next to Kyle's cot, she picked it up and pulled a tiny sachet out of her sleeve. She dumped the contents inside the cup and swirled it around. Turning back to Kyle, she pulled him up into a seated position and put the cup to his lips. "Now drink. All of it."

Kyle obeyed, eyeing her from the side. The slightest floral taste crested his palette but was quickly drowned out by the refreshing coolness of the water. Had he not been looking for it, he likely would have missed the initial flavor altogether.

"You're going to get unbearably warm over the next few hours. Don't worry, you'll sleep through the rest."

Kyle swallowed the last drop and coughed as she pulled the cup away.

"They're going to suspect you," he said.

She smiled at him, the flush in her skin dissipating. "You're going to have plenty more water visits. Make sure to drink every drop every time."

"Why are you doing this? You don't even know me."

"I told you, I'm *not* doing this for you. Now rest."

The healer woman laid Kyle back on his side, gathered up her supplies, then left without looking back.

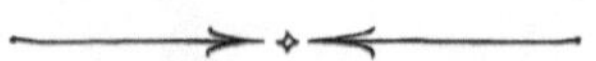

The clink of chisels and thuds of hammers ricocheted through the air as the noonday sun roared down upon anyone foolish enough to remain under its gaze. Leaning against the inner curve of an arched pillar, Queen Aaralee cooled herself under the shaded stone. The central courtyard wafted a refreshing breeze across her face, wicking away small beads of sweat. Aaralee breathed in the fresh air. A few of her personal attendants rested on the benches beneath the overhang propped up by the arch. One saw to mending the hem of Aaralee's favorite pink chiffon gown. Another vigilantly pulled on the rope that raised and lowered a large grass-woven flap from the ceiling, keeping the air from growing stagnant. Typically, the queen and her ladies would relax under a canopy within the courtyard grounds, but they didn't want to risk getting coated in the dirt clouds from the laborers.

Roughly forty craftsmen scurried about the main well near the center, expanding the structure to tap directly into the river water that flowed underneath. Their inventors had recently discovered adapting a new process that used metal tubing to bring water directly to people. King Thaylos decreed it would be tested within palace grounds. They hoped somehow this new process might slow the mass migration to the capital.

If they could find ways to bring water to the people instead of the people having to go to the water, perhaps Diridos might know more peace. Though small-scale for now, if they could get this right, perhaps the scouting parties in the far east could run these systems from any unknown reserves. Praise the Eye Lithos' ambassador had made a deal to start Yansair's own Wind Stallion herd. With the way the rebels attacked the airship factories, they didn't have enough machines to spare. The stallions would not only help increase the search parameters, but if these piping systems *did* work, the stallions would be pivotal in aiding the construction.

Aaralee shifted slightly, keeping her curious gaze upon her people. She desperately hoped this plan would be as their inventors promised. The thought of how many small outlying villages no longer existed thanks to the drought twisted Aaralee's heart into aching knots. She clenched her jaw. The years wasted by the Great Mother shot a prickling across Aaralee's skin. Again and again, she had begged King Thaylos to begin the hunt for hidden water sources. Every time he started to bend her way, the Great Mother would decry heresy and a lack of faith in the Eye. Caroline would spout off how it was their duty to trust the Eye to provide alone, that because of *doubters* the Eye was offended and held back the rains. What Caroline really meant to say was that Aaralee needed to learn her place.

That old woman was the bane of Aaralee's existence. Constantly driving a wedge between her and her king. It felt impossible to pry him away from Caroline's hold. To a point, Aaralee understood. Caroline had been the one constant in King Thaylos's life. She brought him through the death of his father, then the loss of his first wife and child. It was true, the Great Mother held a terrifying power, but Aaralee just couldn't help it: Whenever she looked upon Caroline, all her eyes could see was a scheming old woman.

Aaralee's current tension with the king was all her own making. He had barely looked at her since that day in his study, even taking to sleeping in a different chamber. She supposed she could find some solace in that he hadn't forced *her* to leave. It was a hollow comfort, though.

"Good afternoon, Your Highness. I hope you are faring well today?" the low, sultry tone of Mistress Yanira sang out from behind her.

Aaralee craned her neck to see the keeper of the courtesans walking up the open-aired hall, a young Myrn girl trailing a half step behind. The queen pulled herself away from the pillar to properly greet them. "I am indeed, Mistress Yanira. Tutoring a new assistant, are we?"

The middle-aged woman smiled slightly, keep any chance of wrinkling at a minimum. "Of a sort. This child has been specifically requested by the Great Mother and I—oh, I do beg your pardon." Yanira's eyes flitted off to the side as she stretched out a hand to beckon someone their way.

Aaralee followed her gaze to see one of Caroline's lackeys making her way across the courtyard. The woman's blonde hair was pulled up into a large knot on the top of her head. Her skirts flowed around her like a woman on a mission.

"Kamile," Yanira called.

The woman's head popped up. She halted when she noted Aaralee and the group around her. Aaralee's heart flipped inside her chest, for she recognized the woman immediately. The queen nodded, indicating she was allowed to approach. Aaralee kept her face neutral and her breathing even. Beyond being the close aide to Caroline, this woman had been related to the traitor who attempted to take her life. Each of the queen's attendants stiffened as Kamile approached, one stifled a gasp. Aaralee could feel the repressed smirk from Yanira. The woman was trying to ruffle her feathers. Aaralee refused to give her the satisfaction.

Caroline's lackey approached with downcast eyes and ashen skin. She stopped a few paces away from the group, clearly too uncomfortable to draw any nearer. One of Aaralee's attendants stood from the bench and scooched a little closer to her queen. Noting the defensiveness of her girls helped to settle the thrumming of Aaralee's heart.

"Kamile, is it?" Aaralee addressed the woman.

Kamile dipped her head lower and gave a deep, reverential curtsey.

"It seems the mistress has some business with you?" Aaralee raised an eyebrow.

Kamile kept her head down, but Aaralee still caught the shocked raising of her brows.

"Please, conclude your business, Yanira."

"Yes, Your Majesty."

Yanira curtsied in turn. Not as low as Kamile's, Aaralee noted. The mistress stepped to the side and ushered the young, lanky girl forward. "Go on, Ersmé."

Kamile peeked up her eyes, confusion etched across her features. Ersmé hesitantly stepped through the crowd and joined Kamile at her side.

"The new attendant, per the Great Mother's request."

Kamile's eyes widened as she studied the child. All remaining color drained from the woman's face. Her chest rose and fell quickly. Aaralee feared the woman might pass out. "Are you all right?" she asked.

"Y- yes, Your Majesty," Kamile practically whispered. "It's just that, are you *sure*, Mistress Yanira? She's so young."

The mistress stiffened; a snarl curled across her lips. "And what business of it is yours?"

Kamile dipped her head again. "Forgive me, Mistress Yanira. I spoke out of turn."

Aaralee moved her eyes between the two. Did she see tears in Kamile's eyes? "You may leave my presence," Aaralee commanded gently.

Kamile let out a breath. Curtsying deeply once more, she ushered little Ersmé off with her.

"If it pleases the queen, may I too take my leave to continue with my other duties?" Yanira curtsied lower this time, keeping her head bent waiting for a reply.

"You may leave my presence as well," Aaralee answered.

She watched the keeper of the courtesans depart as uneasiness stirred within her. Though she believed it was happenstance that Yanira and Kamile had converged at her location, Caroline's servant seemed deeply unsettled by the encounter. It couldn't simply be due to Aaralee's presence. Aaralee would not hint at her discomfort so that others might perceive, but she would not be caught unaware as she had been when the prisoner saved her life.

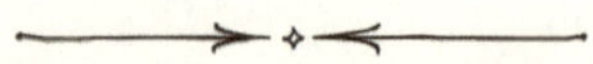

Aaralee's eyelids drooped, blurring the words on the page in a sleepy haze. Relinquishing, she closed her book and set it on the side table. She had spent too long in the heat today. Her energy was all but depleted. Looking around the room, she noticed a soft snoring sound emanating from one of her handmaidens. It appeared she wasn't the only one feeling the drain. The poor girl loosed an extra-loud snort, startling herself awake. Aaralee made eye contact with one of the other handmaidens, and they both fought fiercely to keep their laughter in check. A soft knock on the far door saved them from themselves. An attendant closest to the door stood to receive the caller. Pulling it open, she paused for a second when a young pageboy held out an envelope. Receiving it, the woman returned to the queen's side.

Aaralee raised an eyebrow, studying the wax seal. No indicators of station or family lineage. A second handmaiden procured a letter opener and passed it to her. Cutting open the seal, Aaralee's eyes widened as she read.

The Great Mother plots your death. Trust no one.
Proof will be by the well at next day's sundown.

. . .

"Everything all right, Your Majesty?"

Aaralee folded the paper and smiled softly. "Everything is fine—don't you worry. I do think it is time we all took in some refreshments, how about you?"

"Of course, my queen. Right away."

Aaralee kept a serene smile painted on as she watched the woman go, heart vibrating in her chest. Her dreams had told her this moment would come, but she never wanted to believe it. Now she had to face it alone, for her king would never hear her out, especially not now. The people were either blindly faithful to their Great Mother, or too afraid of her. If she uttered this threat to the guards, valid or not, word would spread without control. She would never be able to have things investigated properly. How could a queen be so utterly powerless within her own palace? Aaralee clenched the letter. She would have to simply take control back.

It was decided—Aaralee would go to the well herself, but not before prepping some things first.

Chapter Twenty-One

Kyle opened his eyes to a strange, red-tinged darkness. The air was moist, a stifling sort of heat that somehow scratched against his skin. The fog coating his thoughts kept his body paralyzed. The world shook around him, smacking him against a solid structure. The impact shook some of the confusion from his mind. Burlap—that's what he was feeling against his skin. His body wasn't paralyzed, just restricted. He was stuffed inside a burial bag. Some other forms pressed in around him, pinning him to the side. The cleansing scent of lavender permeated the fabric, making Kyle's head spin. He was in a death carriage, and he wasn't the only body in here.

Alaster buried all their dead outside the capital walls. They said it helped to cut back on disease. Death carriages were the wooden carts called in to bind up bodies and take them to their final resting grounds. The poor and unwanted were tossed into sacks, while full coffins were reserved for those who could pay for a proper procession. Lavender flowers would be piled on top to combat any smell. Death carriages only ran once a week, so not every corpse was as fresh as the others. Normal soul might have panicked being pressed up against the dead as he was. But after a while, a man can grow desensitized to the morbidity. Kyle was such a man, though he took no pride in it.

Kyle inhaled through his nose, allowing the lavender to engulf his senses. In a twist of irony, the lesser dead-citizens carts were always more lovely to see than the coffin-carrying ones, simply because it took so much more fresh-cut lavender to cover the rot. A small smile worked its way across Kyle's lips as tears burned in his eyes. The lavender came from Marriam. She had used it in the castle for years, and it hadn't taken much of a leap for her to find ways to help the whole capital with it. She had only been twelve when she convinced the council to implement them. This kingdom never deserved Marriam's goodness.

Kyle swallowed hard. Even after death, she still looked out for him. He closed his eyes and continued to focus on the flowers. He could almost feel the sun on his face, her voice lilting through the garden air. Kyle's chest constricted; sweet memories washed away by bitterness. The body lying next to him bounced into his side. The death carriage rocked across some uneven paving stones. He gritted his teeth against the motion, doing his best to allow himself to slide around like a good corpse would. He wondered if the healer's potion was supposed to wear off this early. Hopefully, the gate check wouldn't be that thorough.

"Halt. Present your papers," a voice barked out. The cart rolled to a stop. Kyle took a long, slow breath through his nose then held it. He couldn't risk the motion of his chest rising and falling.

"How many?" the same gruff voice demanded, closer this time.

"Three."

Kyle felt his eyes widen. It was the voice of the woman who'd drugged him. Why did she continue to risk so much for a random criminal? There had to be some greater plot at hand. Kindness was never truly free, at least not when regarding him. Feet shuffled around the wagon's perimeter, making Kyle stiffen and close his eyes.

"Just a bunch of dead vermin. The only beauty attached to them in this world is the flowers to be tossed into the ground with them."

"It's ungentlemanly to speak ill of the dead, sir, especially when they lie before you."

"Right, sure, whatever you say. Pull on through, then. Everything's in order."

"Thank you."

Fire scraped across Kyle's lungs. He just needed to hold out a little longer, at least until he heard the gate close behind them. The heavy creaking of metal chains signified the rotating of the wheel that unlatched the interior locks. A few moments longer, and the carriage lurched forward again. Once more, Kyle praised his foresight in his training. The others had mocked him for building up his ability to hold his breath. A smile crept onto his face at the thought of the original days of the Brethren of Five. But the warm feeling became sour and cruel as Kyle finally took a new breath. Lavender-tainted air filled his lungs. The human heart was such a weak, pathetic tool at times. The ways it could betray a man with a mix of unwanted emotions. It should be clear that hatred was the only noble thing to feel. At least when it came to the hands that ended such a pure and perfect life. That hatred extended to himself, of course. He was the true villain.

Too much time trapped with his thoughts passed before the woman driving the cart spoke up at last. "It's safe now, by the way. No wandering eyes through here. You can come out of that bag now."

Kyle wiggled against the fabric to no avail.

"Did you hear me?"

"I'm trying, okay?" Kyle's muffled growl called out.

The woman sighed. "Just hold on, I'm pulling over."

The horse's hooves muted across the change in terrain as the wagon tipped and rocked over uneven ground. The other bodies in the bed of the carriage smacked into Kyle once more, knocking the wind out of him. Gritting his teeth, Kyle shoved the corpses away. At least the tenderness in his back had finally subsided. He hated to think how bouncing around in the back of a wagon could have hurt, otherwise.

"Sorry about them," the healer called out. "I had to make sure I showed up with someone at the grave site. It would be too obvious if I didn't make an appearance at all."

Kyle opened his mouth to reply but was cut short at the sound of a low, trilling whistle. The cadence was eerily familiar to him. The cart rolled to a stop. Kyle could just barely make out the sound of approaching steps.

"Give him a hand back there, would you? He can't quite make it out of his sack."

"Right," a deep baritone chuckled.

Kyle's body went rigid. He knew that voice. A hand clamped down on the top knot of Kyle's body bag, hoisting him up effortlessly. In the next instant, a knife rent through the rope, allowing the fabric to fall from Kyle's face. Blue-green eyes narrowed at him, the man's frown intensified by the framing of a large drooping mustache, neatly trimmed at the edges of his block-shaped jaw. Ashy black hair fell in chaotic waves against his far-too-broad shoulders. Darren's big brother Devon carried the same foreboding presence as his father. Kyle swallowed back the rising dread.

"Hey there, scar face. Long time no see," Devon growled.

"Devon!" A new feminine voice hissed. "How many times have we said not to call him that?"

Kyle's eyes widened seeing Liesel slapping her brother's arm. Devon merely grunted and shrugged.

"Your mouth's hanging open, Kyle," Liesel noted as Devon turned to speak with the woman at the front of the cart.

Kyle snapped his mouth shut then wiggled himself the rest of the way out of his burlap sack. His eyes narrowed as he juggled his focus between his three supposed rescuers. He watched Devon's hands for a moment. No money appeared to be exchanged.

"What are you after?" Kyle asked.

Liesel blinked and tilted her head. "Paranoid, Kyle? Concerned we're trying to sell you off to a bigger fish?"

Kyle stared back flatly, "Well, are you?"

Liesel rolled her eyes. "Most people would say thank you when being rescued from the gallows."

Kyle painted on an overzealous smile. "Why, thank you, kind madam, indeed. Now, if that's all, then, I'll be on my way."

Kyle grasped the edge of the cart and hefted himself over the side. Feet hitting the ground, his muscles betrayed him, forcing him to grasp onto the cart's side to keep from toppling over. Liesel dove forward to help steady him.

"You've been on bed rest for over a week now. Maybe don't push things so quickly, hmm?" the healer scolded.

Sweat prickled along Kyle's brow. A shuddering grunt escaped through his exhale. He wanted to push Liesel away, but falling flat on his face would have been a greater shame.

"Thought you were on your way." Devon eyed him up and down.

"Stop it," Liesel hissed, "and give me a hand!"

Devon tipped his chin up at the castle healer then strolled over to the pair. The man may have only been a few inches taller than Kyle, but past experience had taught him to never underestimate Devon's strength. In one deft motion, Kyle was swept up and hoisted over Devon's shoulder. He watched the death carriage pull away as their trio walked further into the woods. A few paces later, Devon plopped Kyle into the back of a cramped old traveler's cart. Bolts of fabric and smithy supplies surrounded Kyle. Liesel used one of the wooden wheels as a ladder and hoisted herself up to the front beside Devon, who took the reins. A stout ox waited patiently on his master's command, using the breeching bar of the vehicle as his own personal scratching post.

"Keep your head down till I say otherwise," Devon barked, not bothering to turn around. "And don't go rubbing your filth on that new material, because there are no amounts of miracles that'll save you from Lindsey's wrath."

Kyle thought better of offering up a snide remark, instead allowing himself to sink further down in the bed of the cart. The Turners who lived outside castle grounds weren't the type for setting up elaborate plans of cruelty and revenge. They would have simply let the executioner do his job, had they desired vindication. They *should* have let the executioner do his job. The ways he'd hurt this family for so many years. Kyle peeked up at the back of his rescuer's heads. Their motives weren't wicked, he was sure, but they did have some sort of plan. And somehow, he had become a pivotal part of it.

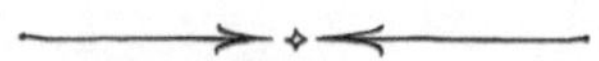

The reddening hues in the sky verified the passing of time for Kyle. The rough terrain jolted and bruised his body to the point of numbness, and the lumbering pace of the ox did little to smooth the ride. Few words were exchanged between the siblings, making each hour tick by even slower. Had Kyle been in better shape, he might have amused himself by torturing Devon. But that was better saved for when he regained his natural swiftness. What unnerved him the most was Liesel's persistent silence. In all his time sneaking in and out of Alaster, he'd never desired to revisit Darren's home, nor his for that matter. He hadn't had to face how their choices had changed some people. Kyle shook his head and refocused his vision on the treetops. No point in thinking on it now; not much he could do about it anyway.

"Home," Devon's voice sighed out in that muscle melting sort of relief.

Kyle's heart flipped, his sudden yearning catching him off guard. He pushed his fingertips against his chest and rubbed the ache away. Within the next few moments, their wagon rolled inside a modest-sized barn. Kyle craned his neck to get a better look. Light flickered off the thick beams from a singular oil lamp awaiting their arrival. The lack of any stone light features struck him as odd. Sure, the outcast royals wouldn't be able to use them as prolifically as the accepted bloodline. But they were still Alastrians at their core. Even the lowest peasant would break down a few pieces to use in multiple ways. But not even Devon's ox wore the typical guiding light.

"Can I get up now?" Kyle groaned.

Devon released a growling sigh. "Yes."

"You need to at least try." Liesel whispered to her brother, almost inaudible to Kyle.

The man took a deep breath and walked over as Kyle pulled himself out of the cart. Devon offered Kyle his large meaty hand. "Come on, scar face. I'll help you inside."

Kyle was tempted to bat his hand away, but considering how wobbly his legs felt, he knew he'd never make it on his own. At least this time Devon granted him the dignity of hobbling at the man's side. It may take twice as long to reach the mid-sized cabin, but his legs probably needed the workout. Kyle looked forward to not having to be so dependent on others again.

"He's back!" a muffled voice shouted from behind the closed front door.

A herd of feet thundered across wooden flooring. Kyle's gut twisted. He had forgotten about Devon's and Lindsey's little army. So much for any hope of recovering in peace. The souring of his disposition didn't have time to settle in before the door flung wide open and four children poured out.

"Daddy!" A girl of seven with brown hair tied in two messy braids broke through the pack and was the first to pounce on her father.

Echoing cries of "daddy" giggled forth as the remaining three piled on, two more girls and one boy. Surprisingly, Devon was able to keep Kyle upright as well as not buckle under the attack. A breath later, the smallest girl gasped.

"Aunt Li Li!"

Allegiances diverted as Liesel became the next recipient of the loving assault. Bounced a few steps side to side between them Liesel had a hard time bracing against their enthusiasm. Devon took the opportunity to shuffle Kyle inside the rest of the way. A simple combined living room and kitchen greeted them. The walls were wood panels, the floor a red-brown oak. The furniture all appeared hand carved with ornate detail. A mirror caught the last rays of the sun from a specialized skylight and flooded the house with warm oranges and reds. Still no stone lights could be seen but a number of lanterns hung about waiting to be lit when evening fell. Devon's wife Lindsey stood next to a large soup cauldron bubbling from its perch over the fire. On her hip, facing away from the flames, sat a chubby baby squirming and squealing as the men approached. Lindsey's wide smile at her husband quickly dropped into a frown and stitched brows on taking in Kyle's shuffling form.

"What happened?" she said.

"All is well. He's just recovering from a previous accident."

Lindsey nodded. "All right, then. Let him rest on Rheese's bed for now."

Kyle remembered Rheese from years back. He was the little Myrn orphan Devon had picked up in his twenties. Though he didn't recall much about Devon's family, he remembered Rheese and his little sister, Cecily, well. Devon found them wandering the alleys of Myrn, starving and afraid. The idea of a single man in his prime taking in a two-year-old and a one-year-old child was ludicrous to him. As far as his fifteen-year-old brain understood at the time, adults found children to be nothing but burdens, something to be rid of as soon as they were able. Unless they could wring some sort of use out of them. It wasn't often that Kyle bumped into Rheese over the years, between their running about and Devon living farther outside of the city. Still, the kid unnerved him with his unblinking stare, like he was studying a man's very soul.

As Devon dropped Kyle onto Rheese's thinning mattress, he wondered if the boy had outgrown his unsettling ways. Instead of lying down, Kyle shifted himself into a seated position with his back and head leaning against the wall. He let his eyes scan the room. Though large, it felt cramped due to the presence of two child-sized bunk beds along with Rheese's standalone. Something stirred under the covers of one of the bottom bunks, causing Kyle's pulse to quicken. Through the darkness, he could make out the shape of another small boy. He was terrible at estimating the smaller ones' ages, but at the very least, Kyle knew the child was well beyond infancy though not fully into boyhood.

He suppressed a groan. If Cecily and Rheese were still both around, then this was a house swarming with children. Eight, in fact. Why did people even bother with such nuisances? It was hard enough to fend for himself. He couldn't imagine having to be responsible for another life.

Kyle's half-brother Malachi came to mind. He hadn't considered Malachi in ages. He might have been expected to watch out for his half-brother, but that meant Kyle had to be reminded of his father every time he looked at him. Still, a part of him wondered if Malachi and Aaron continued to hang around Saunskirt? It wasn't like he'd been given a chance to send them a message. Maybe Devon would help him get his hands on a carrier pigeon? Unlikely.

A pair of dark, angular eyes broke through Kyle's mental fog. Sucking in a breath and stiffening, he kept himself from swinging when his brain registered it was just Lindsey leaning over him.

"Sorry to startle you, Kyle. Just wanted to know if you were hungry?"

In her outstretched hands, she held a wooden bowl almost spilling over with steaming, aromatic stew. Kyle made a grimacing sort of a smile and studied the stew for a moment. Lindsey rolled her eyes and huffed a silky black strand of hair out of her face. She grabbed the spoon, shoveled out a scoop of stew, and took a bite. Swallowing, she stuck the spoon back into the bowl and pushed it into Kyle's hands. "You gotta choose to trust somebody *sometime*, Kyle." Lindsay shook her head and walked away.

Kyle watched her join the rowdy crowd in the living room before looking back at the food in front of him. Trust? Only those looking for an early grave fell into that trap. The scent of well-seasoned beef in a savory garlic-based broth halted all other contemplations. Kyle's mouth watered. Ever since the transport crash, he had been on a strict healer's gruel-only diet. Unable to refrain any longer, Kyle dug the spoon into the bowl and piled a giant bite into his mouth. Warmth spread throughout his body, the heat of the stew soothing aches he didn't know he had. Kyle breathed deep to allow peace to envelop him. The lingering scent of lavender broke through the food's perfume. A weight yanked Kyle's heart down into his stomach, and a chill sliced through his chest. He leaned over and set the bowl on a nearby stool, hunger suddenly eluding him. Kyle tucked himself into a ball and closed his eyes to rest until these Turners decided to inform him of their intentions toward him.

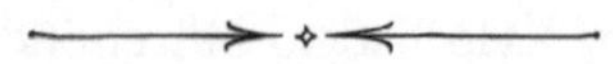

"You want me to *lie?*" Iris blinked up at the queen in disbelief.

"Not *just* lie. You need to be as Caroline instructed. You *have* to make them believe it's true."

Iris turned her head away, clenching her jaw.

"Do you not care for the children of your village?"

Iris winced but held her tongue. She couldn't trust what words might come out.

"I *tried* to fight for you, prisoner. I cannot force my king on these matters." Aaralee tipped up her chin. "You should be grateful that your little rescue party wasn't executed. Or"—she waved her hand to indicate the courtesan chambers—"you could have been tossed back into your cell."

Iris closed her eyes and took in a slow, deep breath. Aaralee whisked to the other side of the daybed to look at Iris face-to-face.

"This is your doing!" Aaralee snapped. "Had you not forced me to speak on your behalf, my king would not have rejected me, leaving you in the hands of Yansair's Great Mother."

Iris popped her eyes back open and stared up at Aaralee. *Holy Father, give me Your words.*

"If I do this," Iris said, "I'm sending the sons, fathers, and brothers of Fitsengea into a trap. Likely to their deaths. If I don't, your husband is going to slaughter the surviving children of Throansburrough and Jaralynx. Is this what Yansairen mercy looks like? *This* is what brings your kingdom pride?"

Aaralee leaned back, eyes blinking rapidly. Iris held her focus on the queen, giving room for the silence to thicken.

"These are not simply lies you ask me to speak," Iris added. "You have placed me in the executioner's role. Either way, I destroy my own people. If you truly support this, then why did you make it so Caroline was unable to meet with me again after her initial proposition? You don't agree with this. You can't tell me you do."

Aaralee pressed her lips into a line, a slight flush rising across her cheeks.

"I know you value life, Your Majesty. Why else would you see to little Sara's protection? Why else risk so much to end the day terrors of your people? You had been dealing with visions long before, so it wasn't simply for your own sake. *That* you were willing to silently bear. And what of your visions? Are all those warnings now to fall on deaf ears because your husband is displeased with you?"

"I do not have the allies in this palace that you think I do," Aaralee cut in.

The queen clenched her jaw, straining the muscles down the sides of her neck. Iris shook her head gently. "You are wrong, Your Highness. Your people love you more than you realize. The king loves you more than you realize. That's why Caroline is so threatened by you."

The queen spun her fingers around each other and began to slowly pace along an invisible path. "If I have the support you claim I do, it is not from anyone with power. At least not the power I need. Love me as he may, my king is still far more loyal to Caroline, and if I were him, I would make the same choice. He has always made that choice." Aaralee's gaze stayed on the floor as she walked.

"You do not give him due credit." Iris sighed.

Aaralee shook her head. "But with *proof*, with proof, he'll have no choice but to listen, to reconsider."

Iris scrunched her brow. "Proof of what?"

Aaralee pulled out a folded piece of paper from a hidden pocket within her dress. Taking a few quick steps, she brandished the letter before Iris. "A way to show Caroline's treasonous intent."

Iris grasped the note. Violent red-hued images assaulted her senses as soon as her fingers grazed the parchment. Fear and foreboding pounded through her heart, her pulse screaming warnings in her ears.

"I go from here to meet with them." The queen paced again, processing her thoughts out loud.

Iris gripped the paper so tight it threatened to tear. *Holy Father, what am I seeing?* No reply. Of course no reply. Even when she had access to the audible voice of the Father, she was still bound up in uncertainties. *Why won't You just make things plain? Is this really what it means to be a Woman of Prophecy? Drifting around with half-understandings and praying I make the right judgment calls to fill in the rest?*

"Prisoner. My letter." Aaralee held her hand out in front of Iris. Iris half jumped, not realizing the queen had stopped in front of her.

"Your Majesty, I don't want to breed needless fear, but I think something awful might be attached to this." Iris passed the note back to the queen.

Aaralee stiffened, tucking the page back into the folds of her pocket. "Tell me, is it common for Fiesian prophets to state the obvious and then claim it as foresight?" The queen sneered down at Iris, conveying the vast gap between their stations with a single curl of her lip. "I am not going into this blindly. You should be grateful that Yansair's queen willingly risks herself to help save you. That is what I mean by Yansair's great mercy."

But you're not doing it for me. You're going to help free yourself from the Great Mother's clutches. Any benefit to me is accidental.

"I don't mean to insult you, Your Majesty. I'm just trying to warn you. There is a lot of death linked to that meeting. Maybe it's best you don't go alone?"

Anger vibrated across Aaralee's countenance. "Or maybe I have fed into your ego too much. Who are you, *prisoner*, to constantly question a queen's actions? Who are you to try and dictate *my* steps? How dare you reach so far above your station. Prophet or not, it is not *my* god you do the bidding of. This is *my* land, *my* kingdom. I will not be ordered about by the likes of you, nor do I have to explain my plans or my actions." Yansair's queen lifted her chin and narrowed her eyes. "Be grateful you still have my pity."

Aaralee turned her back on Iris.

"Your Majesty, wait!" Iris pled as the woman stormed out of the room. "Please, listen. I wasn't trying to insinuate that—I'm just telling you—"

The door slammed shut behind the queen.

Chapter Twenty-Two

The inner courtyard of Diridos' palace sat tucked in by a thick cloak of darkness while the moon partook of its monthly night of rest. A brilliant canvas of stars shone happily in its absence. It had been such a long time since Diridos slumbered so soundly. Not even the stray dogs felt up to piercing the serenity with their howls. Queen Aaralee shifted within the shadows of the unfinished well. Heart still throbbing in her chest, she silently scoffed at the prisoner's last warning. *This* was a place of horrors? The infants of Diridos would find the courtyard more comforting than their own mothers' embraces on a night like tonight.

She had allowed her curiosity and insecurities to coddle the prisoner for too long. She was the queen of a great nation. A queen who possessed great insight and visions long before this heathen prophet darkened their door. She may be at odds with her king right now, but he would never cut her out forever. She had to stop giving into her doubts and recall how great she truly was.

The muscles across Aaralee's shoulders twinged and burned slightly, causing her to roll them to loosen the tension. The queen paused mid-stretch. This great and glorious queen crouched hidden beside a construction project within her own palace. One of Yansair's highest rulers sat in the dirt, hiding alone, in the deep of the night. A cold lead ball thumped down inside her gut. Her hands turned clammy, and beads of sweat pearled across her brow. Had her mother not warned her so many years ago? One day, they would turn on her, and no one would be there to get her out of trouble but herself. Aaralee swallowed the buzzing in her chest. Repressing thoughts of her youth, she unsheathed her dagger from her thigh holster under her skirt. Fingers wrapping around the leather on the grip, a sense of security settled over her.

Soft steps crunched over the dirt path at the far end of the courtyard. Aaralee peered around the side of the well. She cursed the lamplighters for failing their job. She noted to herself to reprimand the staff in the morning. The stars did little to help illuminate the distance, but the sound of the footfalls suggested a smaller frame, which helped to slow the rhythm of Aaralee's heart. She could handle someone closer to her size. Normally, she'd be able to call on the watchman for help, but tonight, the king had called all extras in for a last-minute briefing, some kind of war meeting, leaving a skeleton crew to watch the perimeter. Knowing that even her husband was on the farthest end of the palace grounds recharged her pulse.

The silhouette of a woman emerged in the center of the courtyard. Aaralee strained her eyes and then widened them when she recognized Caroline's closest attendant, Kamile. Clutched in her hands was a leather satchel. The woman clung to it like her life depended on it. Aaralee adjusted her grip on her blade. Of course the traitor's kin would appear! She bit down a curse. Her anger that the prisoner was probably right clouded over her need for self-preservation. Aaralee stood from her hiding place and held her dagger at the ready.

"I should have known." She kept her tone steady. Emotionless.

Kamile jumped back at the queen's appearance. Blood draining from her skin, Kamile fell to her knees and pressed her face into the dirt. Aaralee maintained her defensive posture but raised an eyebrow.

"I am a shame upon this nation, upon my name. A curse to this kingdom. I forfeit my life into your hands, fair queen of Yansair. I have been more than complicit. An active party for treason against the Crown for years."

Aaralee kept her expression neutral as the servant gushed on the ground before her. The queen flicked wary eyes around the courtyard. Could she trust the remorse in the woman's voice? It was easy enough to know the confession was true.

Kamile raised her satchel above her head, voice cracking with emotion. "I have stolen away what I can to prove these years of treachery from my and the Great Mother's hands. For the documents I could not procure, I wrote a lengthy testimony instead."

"Why betray your master now?" Aaralee refused to move forward.

"The Great Mother's scheming has caused the death of my family. Now she brings in another to start the cycle all over again. It *has* to end. The Great Mother will be the death of this kingdom if she continues unchecked."

Studying Kamile's blonde hair, pale skin, and branding on her left arm, Aaralee frowned. "Yansair did not birth you, so how deep could your affection truly be?"

Tipping her face up to meet the queen's gaze, tears cut streams down Kamile's dirt-covered face. "I may have been stolen from my birthplace, but there are people here I have grown to love. More than that, I cannot be responsible for the death of *another* queen."

A rush of cold ran down Aaralee's spine, making her drop her knife hand a little. "What do you mean by another?"

"King Thaylos's lost heir." Kamile took a shaky breath, setting the satchel on the ground before her. "The child was not from him. The Great Mother enticed Queen Linleigh and my brother into an affair. Nekane was put to death for his part, rewritten as the villain." Kamile gestured to the satchel. "I possess the correspondence between them to prove it. The Great Mother fostered the seeds of vengeance in my heart. I already worked in the palace."

Aaralee raised her dagger higher. "You placed the Ash Viper in her chamber?"

"Queen Linleigh's influence over King Thaylos was eclipsing the Great Mother's. Just as yours is now, Your Majesty."

Aaralee studied the woman before her. No weapons as far as she could tell. Her sight lingered on the satchel for a moment before she flicked her blade down to indicate the bag. "Open it."

Kamile nodded, unlatching the buckled straps. The servant kept her movements slow and steady. Aaralee took a small step back as she watched. At last, the woman displayed the bag's contents. Numerous pages were packed tightly within. Kamile moved the pages around to prove nothing was concealed. Closing the satchel again, she leaned forward and placed it on the ground as far away from her as she could.

"There is a reason you didn't call for the guards as soon as I presented myself to you," Kamile said. "You know the Great Mother has labeled you her enemy and I'm the only way you can protect yourself. She speaks for the All Powerful Eye, and not even the royal guards are willing to stand against that. But if I can prove her a charlatan, someone who abuses power for her own gain, then you might survive."

"What does she have planned?" Aaralee asked, at last lowering her blade.

"In three nights, there—"

Boom! An explosive force shook the ground beneath their feet. A fireball rose up, lighting the night sky.

"By the Eye." Aaralee cupped a hand over her gaping mouth.

Shouts and screams rang out from the direction of the blaze. Aaralee's heart shattered to think of her people dying in the flames. Sheathing her dagger, she ran toward the horror.

"Your Majesty, no! Wait!" Kamile jumped toward the queen, clasping her arm.

"How dare you—"

"This is it! This was her plan. She's early—I don't know why. The explosion is a lure."

Aaralee pulled against the woman's grip, still trying to rush to her people's aid. Kamile held tighter.

"Please, Your Majesty! You need to hide!"

Aaralee spun to glare at the servant but halted when she saw the white terror in her eyes.

"We're under attack!" the watchman cried from his post on the wall just a few feet from the courtyard.

Kamile and Aaralee spun in the voice's direction.

"They're breaching the back gate! Sound the al—"

A whistling sound arced through the air, cutting off the watchman's words with a sickening thunk and gurgle.

Kamile squeezed the queen's arm, barely breathing out her whisper, "They're here."

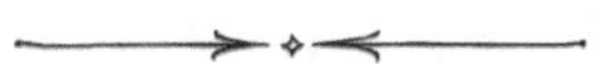

A secondary blast rained down a shower of dirt and dust on Darren's head. He kept his protective stance over Fredrick for a minute more before leaning back. Fred coughed in the clouded air, squinting one eye open at Darren. "Powder," Fred said, grimacing.

"Shh, don't strain yourself." Darren scanned for his wooden cup and frowned. It lay tipped over with the contents soaking into the floor.

"I think he's talking about the armory," Oriel offered.

He stood with his ear against their cell door.

"Lands, you think someone ignited their gunpowder?" Jason gaped from his position on the back wall.

Darren stood and joined Oriel's side. "Can you make anything out?"

Oriel shook his head. "Running, shouting. Nothing clear. Can't tell if it's an accident or an attack."

"Perfect," Darren sighed. "Bringing a new player to the table is the last thing we need right now."

"Sh!" Oriel shot up a hand.

The shouting rose in volume so that even Darren hear it clearly without leaning against the door.

"That's fighting breaking out!" Darren cried.

"Let's pray whoever wins is better for us." Oriel maintained his stance.

Darren gritted his teeth and balled up his fist. The men held their breath, listening to every weapon strike. Then, silence. Oriel exchanged a look with Darren. A rattling on the door made Oriel jump back a few steps. Darren strengthened his stance, and Oriel readied himself beside him. Heavy tumblers clicked open, but the door didn't budge. The shuffling sound of Jason struggling to his feet behind him pricked Darren's ears. Breathing in deeply, Darren gingerly stepped forward.

"Your Grace." Jason hissed his disapproval.

Ignoring the soldier's concern, Darren gripped the metal bar that made up the handle. The cold touch of iron sent a fluttering through his stomach. With a sturdy tug the prison door creaked open. Darren looked over his shoulder at Oriel, who nodded back and joined up behind him. Pulling against the heavy wood, Darren peered out. A mixture of torches and a spattering of stone lights gave the stone hall an unnerving glow. *Empty?* He scanned for any Yansairens.

No cries of protest from the other side encouraged him to open the door further until he was met with resistance. Stepping out into the hall, Darren searched for the obstacle. A body lay on the other side, beside a ring of keys. Oriel stepped out around Darren and squatted next to the still form. Placing his fingers in front of the man's face, Oriel frowned then checked for a pulse.

"He's gone," Oriel sighed.

Noting a red-stained blade still gripped in the fallen soldier's hand, Darren reached over and took it along with the key ring. "I'm going to run ahead and see what's going on."

Oriel's stare bored through him.

"We can't just blindly charge ahead. Not if we're going to carry Bryant and Fred out. Jason can barely hold himself up."

Oriel scratched his beard for a moment before nodding. "You take too long and we'll find our own way out."

Darren's stomach churned, realizing Bryant would likely have to be left behind. "I'll be back."

Clinging to the keys in one hand and keeping his sword at the ready in the other, Darren jogged down the open hall. Reaching a bend in the path, he halted and pressed his body against the wall. His ears reached through the distant sounds, sifting out anything that might be nearby. Peeking around the corner he spied a set of spiraling stairs at the far end of the corridor. Breathing in deeply through his nose and adjusting his grip on the sword, Darren pushed his feet around the corner. He reached the bottom of the stairs in a moment, keeping his steps quick and light. A few trails of sweat worked their way down the center of his back and latched onto the strands of air swirling down from the stairwell.

One of the first things he planned to do when he got out of here was to finally obtain a shirt again. Darren smirked to himself over this trivial and ill-timed desire. *Keeping things light to steady the nerves.* Ascending the steps, he moved with more caution, cursing the spiral design that put him at an immediate disadvantage. Anyone coming from above would easily possess the more defendable position. His best hope was to reach the top unseen.

Time dragged on, despite his speed. Finally, a door came into view. Spying the keyhole, Darren suppressed a groan. The last thing he needed was to have to test out a bunch of keys while a threat could appear at any moment. *Please be unlocked,* Darren pled as he reached for the handle. Before his fingertips could even graze the metal, the door flew open toward him. Darren jumped back just in time, nearly losing his footing on the stairs. A blond-haired man stood in the doorway.

"Elias?" Darren blinked.

"*You?*" Elias practically spat out. "You're already free?"

"Not quite yet." Darren lowered his sword. "Get inside before someone spots you."

"Yeah, that's unlikely," Elias answered but stepped down to comply.

Two more men appeared behind him—faces Darren recognized from the night around the fire.

"Move. We're here to get everyone out," Elias growled.

"Good." Darren ignored Elias's snippiness. "This way."

Without another word, the four of them descended back into the dungeons. While still using caution, Darren had to admit he felt more emboldened returning to the others with a rescue party in tow. When they reached the jail cell, Oriel stood by the door, a small smile spreading across his face. Elias clasped his friend's forearm, and Oriel latched on in kind and gave him a firm shake.

"Looks like the world is falling apart above. Good time for an exit, no?" Elias grinned.

"You did this?" Oriel raised his eyebrows.

Elias shook his head. "Not us, but looks like we're going to benefit from it."

Darren's eyes drifted down to the dead guard on the floor, an uneasiness settling across his shoulders.

"Right, then. This way," Darren instructed the last two men of their procession into the cell.

"Hi, new friends." Jason smiled and waved weakly as he stood leaning against a nearby wall.

"Hey." One half smiled back.

After quickly divvying up responsibilities, two men draped Fredrick across their shoulders while Darren and Oriel took on Bryant's dead weight. Keeping his left arm around Bryant's back and holding onto the man by his trousers, Darren was still able to grip his borrowed sword in his right hand. Elias led the charge, sword at the ready. Bursting through the door at the top of the stairs at last, Darren fought to maintain his focus.

"For the Father!" voices shouted to their right.

A few stray gunshots sounded. Two men with weapons raised above their heads dropped to the ground, but a third pushed onward. The palace guards tossed their firearms to the side and drew out their blades. Were the weapons only worth one use? Darren wondered. Smoke clung to the air in dense plumes, making it hard to breathe or see in the already dark sky. Their main source of light came from an inferno that raged a few yards away.

Fred was right—it had been the armory. Palace attendants ran in all directions. Elias used the chaos to guide them away from the panic. Guards were in shockingly short supply for such a scene. Darren didn't trust that would be the case for long. As he moved as swiftly as possible through a series of open-roofed arches, the layout began to feel familiar.

"We're almost there. Phineah is waiting with the horses just beyond that wall," Elias said.

Eyes lining up with the exterior wall Elias indicated, Darren peered through the murky dark. "How are we getting Fred and Bryant over that?" he huffed.

"Grappling hooks and leverage," one of the men from behind replied. "We prepped for possible injured."

"Fair enough." Darren adjusted his grip on the comatose Bryant.

The lack of confrontation and ease with which they arrived at the wall unsettled Darren.

"Everything going a bit too smoothly to anyone else?" Jason panted as he leaned on the stone.

Elias hissed a breath in through his teeth. "Rule one of good luck— *never* mention having it."

Jason raised his left hand in surrender, pressing his lips together. Darren and Oriel set Bryant down on the ground to catch their breath. Before he could prepare himself, a grappling hook whizzed by overhead. Seconds later, one of their Yansairen helpers was halfway up the wall. Not wasting any time, Darren grabbed Oriel's shoulder and turned the man to look him in the eye. "I'm going back for Iris. Delay as long as you can."

Oriel opened his mouth to reply but closed it again after studying Darren's eyes. He looked at Elias, who nodded in turn.

"Your Grace," Jason protested.

"Sorry, Jason. I don't have time to wait for you."

A pained expression fell across the man's face, but he nodded as well.

"The professor reported Lady Iris last in the courtesans' chambers. It's the separate structure two buildings back behind the armory to the right," Oriel instructed.

Two ropes dropped down as they spoke, with some sort of harness system strapped in between them. Darren clasped Oriel's forearm, who returned the gesture. With time slipping away, Darren spun on his heel and aimed straight for the worst of the chaos.

A small contingent of footsteps slapped across the limestone walkways leading up to the courtyard. The sound rose at a rate that warned Kamile they would not be able to outrun their attackers. Clenching her teeth, she looked to her queen, who had already redrawn her weapon. Kamile searched for a secure hiding place. The darkness of the night seemed to somehow be pushing itself back as she scanned. The well in particular appeared illuminated. Putting a finger to her lips, Kamile signaled the queen's silence. Grabbing Her Majesty by the hand, she pulled her to the well's partially broken opening.

A rope hung down its mouth, stopping just above a narrow wooden bracing ledge placed about one-third of the way down. The builders had been using this construction combination to chip away at the well's interior to make holds for a sturdier platform system. Queen Aaralee turned to Kamile, as if to protest, when the shortened cry of another victim warned them that the Viper nomads had reached the outskirts of the courtyard. Both women instinctively squatted low to the ground, praying the night would help at least partially obscure them.

Kamile wrapped her hands around the heavy rope, its braided strands almost as thick as her forearm. Sitting on the ground, she braced a foot against the sturdier side of the well's outer wall and nodded to the queen. Without delay, Queen Aaralee took hold of the rope and swung silently into the well's mouth. The weight on the rope soon slackened, telling Kamile the queen had reached the narrow ledge. Feet crunched on the dirt path of the courtyard.

Kamile crawled a few feet from the well, hoping to draw the focus to herself. She didn't expect to survive another night, so the least she could do was secure Yansair's queen's survival. Standing, she prepared to run.

"There you are, Kamile," the eerily calm voice of the Great Mother called out, stripping Kamile of all her strength.

Forcing herself to turn around, Kamile faced Yansair's most powerful force. The Great Mother stood a few feet away, shadowed by at least thirty men. In her hand, a large gate key. Each of the men wore long cloaks with cowls obscuring much of their faces. A few held small lanterns that helped illuminate their path. The light from their flames cast a sinister glow so only their mouths could be seen, presenting them as smiling, eyeless monsters. From the grin alone, Kamile recognized Xeres, the leader of the Viper nomads, his abnormally pronounced canines heightening his creature-like aura.

"Great Mother." Kamile curtsied. "Forgive me, did I misreport the times?"

"No, dear." The Great Mother smiled softly, tucking the key away in a concealed skirt pocket. "I changed them."

Xeres used the sword in his hand to silently direct twenty of his men to split off in different directions. The nomadic warriors jogged past Kamile, continuing their search and slaughter. The Great Mother walked forward, closing the gap between her and Kamile. Xeres and his remaining men followed close behind. Kamile knew she should run, but her feet would not obey her. The Great Mother's eyes locked onto her own, and she was powerless to do anything other than stare back at her.

"You have been my assistant for how many years now?" the Great Mother said, standing an arm span away.

"About ten years." Kamile swallowed, fighting back tears.

"Wow, did you hear that, Xeres? Ten years."

The chieftain chuckled, slowly spinning the grip of his sword in his hand.

"You know, my dear Kamile, I don't know if I've ever maintained any other assistants for that long. So many failed me even before the year wore out."

"Yes, Great Mother." Kamile fought the urge to glance over to the well.

She prayed the narrow ledge would hold the queen long enough. One of the chieftain's underlings stepped to the side, drawing Kamile's focus. Watching the man kneel and retrieve her forgotten satchel, Kamile felt her legs tremble, threatening to give out. The Great Mother held out a hand without looking. "I'll take that."

The warrior looked to his chieftain before moving. Xeres nodded, and the man passed the bag off to the Great Mother.

"Tell me, Kamile. If I open this, will I find what I think I'll find?"

Inhale, exhale, she needed to remember to breathe.

"Where is the queen, Kamile?" The Great Mother's eyes grew so dark Kamile swore even the white parts vanished.

"Great Mother, I don't—"

"When you betray someone, stupid child, at least be sure there are no other pages beneath your note."

The Great Mother shook her head and clucked her tongue. She lifted two fingers up to Kamile's face, remnants of charcoal smudged across their tips. "Tell us where you've hidden the queen before Xeres's men find her, and I might be persuaded to let you live."

Kamile glanced over at the weapon in Xeres's hand. He had slunk closer as the conversation lingered. Swallowing back the bile rising in her throat, Kamile studied the Great Mother once more. Her heart battered against her rib cage. Yansair's eternal monster smiled tersely at her, her patience clearly waning. Kamile's lips parted but her tongue refused to move.

"This is taking too long," Xeres growled, taking a step forward.

The Great Mother raised a hand, stopping him in place. "By the Eye, Kamile, I *command* you to tell me."

The firm tone punched the air out of Kamile's lungs. Her head spun and her vision blurred.

"Speak!"

Something snapped inside Kamile's chest, bringing a rush of crisp air back into her lungs. The world solidified and steadiness returned to her legs. Tears rolled down Kamile's cheeks, but a smile rose to meet the drops.

"I renounce the Eye," she whispered.

"What?" The Great Mother's tone fell flat.

Kamile straightened, and a short laugh tumbled from her lips. "I renounce the Eye."

The Great Mother lunged forward, claws snatching her throat. "You insolent—"

Kamile choked out another laugh as the old woman's grip tightened. Her lungs ached, pleading for a new, deep breath. Still, Kamile smiled wider. The Great Mother's nostrils flared as she sneered. She thrust out her free right hand and snatched Xeres's sword from him. In one fluid motion, Caroline ran the blade through Kamile's middle, removed it, and passed it back to the stunned chieftain. The Great Mother released her grip on Kamile's throat, allowing her to collapse to the ground. A smile lay serenely on Kamile's face as her final breath gently eased away.

Chapter Twenty-Three

"Please! You can't leave me in here!" Iris beat her fist against the locked door of the courtesans' chamber.

All courtesans had evacuated by the time the second explosion had sounded. Concerns of a spreading fire had the guard urging them away. Rather than having to attend to a dangerous prisoner such as Iris, the guard opted to lock her inside and allow the Eye to decide her final fate. The smell of the smoke and cries of fear beyond the chamber threw Iris into a frenzied panic. Flashes back to the night of the massacre consumed her. Tears flew from her eyes as her chest grew tighter. *Help me, Holy Father!*

"Please! Not like this!" she screeched between sobs.

She recalled the Holy House. The flames eating at the ceiling. She could taste the smoke. Iris's shoulders shook. Her hands throbbed with each blow against the door. Out. She had to get out! She could hear it now, the steps of that soldier stomping across the wooden floor. She'd hide and then he would die. They would all die. Iris's throat tightened. Air came in tiny streams. She tried to gasp in a deeper breath around her sobs, but it just wouldn't come.

A new terror flooded her thoughts. Had the fire reached her

already? No. No plumes of smoke filled the air. Still, she could not breathe. *Holy Father!* Sweat loosed from nearly every pore on her skin. An awful numbness trailed its way up from her toes to her feet, then to her knees. *Breathe*, Iris screamed in her mind. Why couldn't she breathe? Head spinning, Iris's knees buckled, forcing her to slide against the door and drop to the floor. *I can't. I can't. I can't.* Iris clawed at her throat, begging it to work. Panic mixed with anger as a lesser thought thread attacked her for her weakness. The voice was small but somehow intense, berating her for not holding things together. For not trusting the Father. For believing she was going to die here. *Help me.* Tears blinded her eyes as she sank lower to the floor.

The cold, smooth stone kissed the bare parts of her skin, drawing her closer. Iris rested her cheek on the tiles, an earthy smell enveloping her senses. Her sweat heightened the cool touch of the polished floor, breaking through the numbness and sending a shiver down her spine. The air near the ground somehow felt lighter, even crisp. Breathing came more easily. Her throat no longer felt thick. *You're okay. You're okay. You're okay*, Iris repeated to herself over and over. The rhythm of her heart relaxed with each deep inhale through her nose. The touch of the stone and the smell of the earth brought a sense of stability and assuredness. *You're okay. Holy Father, help me be okay.*

"Please don't . . . don't let me die," Iris rasped between soft, stuttering sobs. "Not like this."

Not like this.

She ground her teeth together, squeezing her eyes shut as another wail burned to escape. Another slow inhale. *Get up, Iris. You have to get up! Lori and Jacob live! They need you.* One more shuddering exhale. *Darren and the others are out there somewhere. What if this is your only chance to free them? Without the evil of Caroline to manipulate them.* Iris swallowed the lump in her throat and rolled herself to her hands and knees with a harrowing yell. Her limbs trembled in that position, and exhaustion taunted her muscles. Sticking out a hand to brace against the door, Iris rose back to her feet.

Crossing her arms over her chest, she held herself as she stood, rubbing her arms in a soothing motion. "Now what?"

Three heavy raps on the other side of the door sounded, making Iris jump.

"Prisoner Iris! If you're by the door, stand back! Malek is going to get you out."

Iris's jaw dropped hearing Gwen's muffled shout from the other side. Shaking her head, Iris collected herself and skittered back.

"Okay, ready!"

Something heavy walloped into the thick wood, making it rattle in the frame. A second later, another hit, this time accompanied by splintering. A third impact, and slivers of timber scattered across the room, making Iris grateful she'd chosen to move far away. A fourth hit, and the wood that housed the lock cracked.

"Next one should get us through," Gwen warned.

A man's battle cry loosed, accompanying an explosion of wooden shards as the door flew inward. A giant barrel-chested man stood in the doorway, every inch of his body stocky thick muscle. His dark tanned skin set off the white of his teeth, and round cheeks partially obscured his eyes as he grinned proudly. Blackish-brown, wavy hair sat in a disheveled topknot on his head. Resting on his shoulder was a terrifyingly large mace with a few straggling pieces of wood embedded on the spikes. Big as the weapon was, it seemed to suit him perfectly.

Iris gaped at the Lithite before her. She had heard stories of their mighty stature but had always assumed they were exaggerations. Now she thought people were underselling them. It was no wonder Wind Stallions were their primary steeds. No other horses could carry them.

"Come, prisoner. We will guide you to your professor and the Throansburrough girl." Gwen beckoned her to follow.

Iris closed her mouth and followed them through the shattered door. "But what of your betrothal? You could jeopardize everything by helping me."

"Just keep your head down and stay behind me. Trust me, no one will ever know you're there." Malek laughed.

Gwen placed Iris between her and her lover. "Queen Aaralee would want this, I'm sure of it. Rue and I overheard enough to gather that much."

Iris gritted her teeth against the weariness in her legs, willing herself to keep the necessary pace down the wide hallways. The vaulted ceilings grabbed hold of the dangers down the way and spat them back in a confusing torrent of echoes. Malek led them down a path splitting off from the more terrifying sounds. Iris fought the urge to look around her protector and gauge the threats that lay beyond. He and Gwen risked everything helping her. The least she could do was keep from antagonizing the situation.

She prayed for Hethers's and Sara's safety. Deep in her gut, she knew this was more wicked than an accidental fire. The shadows within the halls seemed to taunt her with sinister intent. Though unlikely, she hoped the queen heeded her warning. Looking up, Iris spotted a number of unlit torches sitting uselessly between a few stone light features. Why weren't the torches lit? Clouded images of money-changing hands answered her. *So this was planned!* Iris felt her stomach roll as the hairs on her skin rose. Something awful had come for the palace tonight. *Let it be, Iris,* she rebuked herself. *You are about to be free of this place anyway. It's not your concern. Time to care for your people. Once outside these walls, I can go search for Lori. I am sure the Father will guide my way.* She was almost certain Darren would help her too.

"In the name of the Father, where is your queen?" A deep voice growled from somewhere ahead of them.

"I assure you, we don't know."

That was Hethers's voice!

"Hey!" Malek barked.

Iris stepped out from behind him. The professor stood with one arm full of books and scrolls and the other shielding Sara, who cowered against the wall behind him. A man in a hooded cloak pointed his sword toward the old man but turned his head to look at Malek.

"Not a wise choice, whoever you are," Malek rolled his shoulders and moved his mace into an attack position.

Iris held her breath watching the man pause to study Malek. Shaking his head, the man lowered his sword, took a few steps back from Hethers, then turned and ran away. Malek rested his mace back against his shoulder and jogged over to Hethers's side while Iris ran ahead and embraced Sara.

"Are you all right, Professor?" Malek asked, his eyes reminiscent of a distraught puppy's.

"All thanks to you, my good man." Hethers clapped his free hand on the man's arm. "Best timing as ever."

Iris kept a firm grip on Sara. The poor girl clung to her, her entire body rattling. Iris looked between the men with raised eyebrows. "You know each other?"

Malek shrugged. "Of a sort."

Gwen leaned over Iris. "She all right?"

Iris nodded. "Just shaken."

Gwen looked to her betrothed, her face twisting in concern. "You must escort them to the gate. It's clearly too dangerous for them to be on their own."

Malek bristled. "What do you mean by *you*?"

"I must find the captain of the guard. That man was searching for the queen. He must be an assassin."

"You want me to *abandon* you?" Malek's eyes widened. "Never!"

"Professor, you know the palace grounds well enough?" Iris interjected.

"I do."

"Gwen, if Malek is caught with us, imprisonment will be a blessing. Go, warn the guard. We'll be fine." Iris pivoted Sara around and took the girl by the hand.

Gwen's eyes darted between them before she sighed. "You're right. Let's go, my love. We have no time."

Malek grinned and turned his mace over in his hand. "Hunting time."

Before anything else could be said, he took off in the direction of the cloaked man.

"Thank you!" Iris called out after them, watching Gwen keep pace with her beloved.

"This way, my dear, quickly." Hethers walked briskly around Iris and Sara, leading them in the opposite direction. "Bless the Father for bringing us together when He did."

"Miss Iris?" Sara's voice trembled out.

Iris gently squeezed the child's hand. "I'm getting you out of here, Sara. I promise."

Sara nodded, and the three of them raced silently through the darkened halls. Each time they approached a turning point, the professor had them wait along the wall as he surveyed what might be coming next. At some spots, they had to retreat to go down another path as they ran into more of the cloaked men. A knot twisted through Iris's chest each time they spotted them or when they happened upon some soldiers taking them down. A sense of shame pressed around her as if she should be doing something to help. Iris shook her head, erasing the thoughts. She'd be risking Hethers's and Sara's lives, not to mention her chance to search for Jacob and Lori.

The familiarity of fleeing through the night threatened to fling Iris's mind and emotions back into a panicked spiral. Sara's small hand desperately gripping onto hers was the only thing that kept bringing her back from that edge. Iris wondered if she did the same for Sara. For every squeeze Sara gave, Iris returned a reassuring one just in case. *Keep it together so she can make it through this,* Iris commanded herself. *Holy Father, please help me get Sara home!*

As she prayed, the face of Queen Aaralee pressed into her thoughts. *The queen? Why am I—*

Iris's train of thought was again interrupted, this time with an overwhelming sense of dread for the Yansairen ruler. *Not my place, not my task.* Iris frowned, annoyance bubbling up inside. Once more, she squeezed Sara's hand, and the child returned the gesture. What could she possibly do to defend the queen from assassins?

"For the Father, for the professor!" a voice cried out, followed promptly by the sound of gunfire.

Sara stifled a scream. Iris jumped and pulled the girl close to her body. Hethers froze in place, clearly listening for danger. Running feet faded out of earshot.

"For the professor?" Iris whispered, looking at Hethers. "You don't think . . . ?"

Hethers shook his head. "I hope not, but I need to be sure."

Iris nodded. "Quickly, then."

Running to where they believed the shot had come from, the body of one of the cloaked men came into view. Iris kept Sara's face buried in her stomach as she watched for anyone else approaching. Hethers kneeled beside the dead man and rolled him onto his back. He took a deep breath before pulling back the hood. Iris watched the old man's shoulders droop and heard him exhale. Stiffly rising from the floor, he rejoined the ladies.

"That man might have been a nomad," he said. "The ear and nose piercings suggest that, at least."

"You have nomadic followers?" Iris tilted her head.

"Never seen the boy before, and as far as I am aware, none had joined our cause. The nomadic tribes to the east have never cared what Yansair does." Hethers looked back at the body. "But if they have joined up, I hope my students have taught them we are against killing in the Father's name."

Deep furrows of worry etched across the man's forehead. Iris rested a hand on his shoulder. "If things are going wrong, you will set them right again," she said. "But first we have to get out of here."

"Yes, yes." Hethers patted Iris's hand and breathed deeply. "This way should hopefully be clear." He indicated the way with a nod of his head, and they backtracked once more.

Speeding along, fears for the queen's survival assaulted Iris's mind. Suspicion stirred in her gut, birthing a rising anger, but she refused to allow herself to dig deeper on the thought. If she didn't focus on the pressing then she wouldn't be made to act. It was time to take care of her own and no one else. Especially not the literal enemy of her people. She didn't care what the Father wanted. She couldn't keep putting herself in harm's way. She wanted to live. She needed to save her niece and nephew. She wanted to see Darren again. She needed to know he was okay.

"Mr. Hethers, can you direct me to the dungeons?"

"What in the lands for?"

"I have some friends I—"

Hethers halted in his tracks and smacked the back of his head. "Curse this old, deteriorating brain!" Spinning around, he took Iris's free hand. "Forgive me, child. My little Turner, your marquis! Yes, we saw him. Of course we will release him."

"You saw Darren?" Iris gasped.

"Him and some other Fiesians," Sara interjected. "He was very happy to know you were alive. He promised to save you."

"He was okay? And the others? Who else was with him? Any of them hurt? Please tell me they weren't abused."

Hethers held a finger to his mouth and ushered them into a small alcove. A handful of panicked servants ran past, carrying armloads of soaked blankets. They must be circling back to the fire. That, or the flames had spread farther than she'd assumed. *The queen isn't going to make it. Is she? No! Stop it, brain! You want her saved so badly Holy Father, then* You *do something about it.*

"A young lad named Jason, burly man named Bryant, and another man called Fred were all the Fiesians with him," Sara whispered once the servants passed. "There was also a quiet Yansairen guy called Oyell, I think?"

"Oriel," Hethers gently corrected, "and I fear only he and Darren came out physically unscathed." Hethers fixed his eyes on the floor for a minute.

Iris felt her heartbeat quicken. "How badly injured? And what of Kyle and Grayson? You're certain that's all who were in the dungeons?"

Hethers's sad eyes held Iris's for a breath. "Injured enough that

Bryant and Fredrick will need to be carried out. They did not speak of a Grayson or Kyle."

Did that mean . . . Had the guards killed them when they were caught? *No, stop it!* Tears welled up in Iris's eyes as she inhaled a shaky breath. Just because they weren't there didn't mean they were gone forever. She couldn't let go of hope just yet.

A small hand patted the top of Iris's. She looked down to see Sara putting on a brave face. Smiling down at the girl, Iris took another breath and blinked back her tears. Hethers peeked his head out of the alcove then nodded for them to move on. Halfway down the path, a door stood open to a room within that hall. Something dreadful stirred in Iris's chest. She reached out a hand to get Hethers's attention, but before she could speak, a cloaked man strode through the doorway. Iris, Hethers, and Sara froze in place. The man stared at them in silence.

"Run," Hethers whispered hoarsely.

His command seemed to also give flight to the nomad as he sprinted toward them. Iris grabbed the skirt of her dress with one hand and pulled Sara after her with the other. Barreling down the hall, she desperately searched for an escape. Even something to defend them-selves with. Glancing over her shoulder, she was grateful to see Hethers keeping pace with them. At this rate, they might have to surrender themselves to the palace guards for rescue. *Holy Father, help!* The slap-ping of boots against stone doubled in volume behind them. *Don't tell me there's another one!*

Iris willed her feet to move faster, practically dragging Sara now. Pain from her stab wound flared to life, sending a burst of nausea up her throat. Iris clenched her teeth from a threatening wave of dizziness. Gulping down fresh air, she refused to let her body betray her. *Why won't You answer me? Why won't You help?*

A rage-filled shout pierced through her thoughts, followed by the clang of metal striking metal. Iris flung a look back to see their nomadic attacker fending for his life. The world seemed to move in slow motion as her eyes recognized the form of his challenger in the dim light. Iris halted, causing Sara and Hethers to also stop.

"Darren?" she whispered.

Terrifying anger darkened his face. He parried each swing of his enemy's blade, pushing him back with his own forceful strikes. Relentlessly he pursued, teeth bared as if they were fangs. Iris's free hand felt unbearably light. Empty, useless. She yearned to help, but she had nothing, and with the fight raging as it was, stepping in would put Darren in more danger. Her fretting and plotting were cut short as she witnessed Darren use his left hand to grab the man's cloak. Yanking hard, he pulled the man off balance. Darren arced his sword down and struck the man to the ground.

He stood, watching the man on the floor for a minute. Their attacker did not stir again. Darren turned his head toward Iris. His chest rose and fell with heavy breathing and sweat-soaked hair clung to his head and parts of his face. A deep blush took over Iris's face as she registered he wasn't wearing a shirt. The tumbling about of her heart halted seeing a strange expression overtake Darren's face. Her stomach dropped. Was he hurt? Feet moving faster than thought, Iris closed the gap between them. Darren tossed his weapon to the side as she approached. Before she could speak, he wrapped his arms around her and pulled her into a soft hug.

"I made it," his voice croaked, thick with emotion. "I'm bringing you home."

Feeling the slight tremble in his exhale, Iris leaned into Darren and tightened her arms around him. Tears slipped from her eyes. Squeezing them shut as she stood in his embrace, Iris fought for control over herself. She wanted nothing more than to just crumple in Darren's arms. But inside, the warning persisted.

"Save the queen."

The Father's voice was stern this time. More tears fell as Iris held onto Darren. *Please. Don't make me.*

"If you don't, they will all die. Not just the Yansairens."

"My dear girl, I'm sorry, but you must heed Him." The compassion in the professor's voice clawed at Iris's heart.

Darren lifted his head to look at the old man. "Heed who? Professor, what?"

That's a dirty trick, Father. Iris growled inwardly. Taking a deep breath, she peeled herself away from Darren. He stiffened at her shift in demeanor.

"You must go, child."

"I know." Iris closed her eyes and took a step back from Darren.

Darren shot out a hand and grasped her wrist. "Go where?"

Iris laid a hand over the top of his, sad eyes connecting with his worried glare. "To save the queen. The Holy Father commands it."

Darren searched her face for a moment then released his hold. Stooping down, he retrieved his sword. He nodded in determination. "Lead the way."

"No."

The word pierced her heart so that she winced, "No. You must get Mr. Hethers and Sara to safety."

Darren scoffed. "Like hell I'm leaving you!"

"Darren," Iris whispered.

"No, we go together."

Iris could feel the anger and panic surging up within him.

"My boy"—Hethers moved forward, gently resting a hand on Darren's arm—"we cannot delay any further. You have to let her go."

Darren worked his jaw as the muscles tightened along his neck and his nostrils flared. Moisture rose in his eyes as he looked between Iris and his old teacher. Iris's heart ached watching Darren battle through his torment.

"I didn't come all this way just to let you go off and get yourself killed," he said through clenched teeth.

A tear slipped down Iris's cheek as she fought to keep her bottom lip from trembling.

"So promise me, Iris Straton . . ." A tear fell from Darren's eye. "Promise me you'll come back to me alive."

They both knew that wasn't a promise she had the power to make.

"I promise," she choked out.

Darren's eyes lingered on hers for a few torturous heartbeats before he looked to Hethers. "I better not regret this, old friend."

"My hope as well." Hethers sighed then nodded to Iris.

"Mr. Hethers, Darren, promise me you'll search for the children of Throansburrough and Jaralynx. And if you see them before I do, tell my niece and nephew, Lori and Jacob Mainfield, Auntie Iris is coming for them."

"I promise. *Everyone* is coming home." The fire in Darren's eyes stabbed at the longing in her heart.

Iris held Darren's eyes, pleading his forgiveness for leaving. Backing away, she turned to Sara who stood silently crying. Giving her a strong hug, Iris kissed the child on the top of her head before releasing her. *You better bring me back to them*, Iris growled to her Creator.

"Run."

Lifting her skirt once more, Iris flew down the corridor. It was as if a light shone on the path before her, guiding her way. Images of plant life and open skies flew past her mind's eye. She swore she heard rushing water, though there was none to be seen. She sprinted to the right, amazed at how the previous fatigue, pain, and nausea had all left her. A wooden ledge wiggling its way out of a stone wall invaded her thoughts. What in the lands was the Father trying to show her? A stone water well, quite large, silhouetted against the shadows in her mind. A raging river careened between dark, narrow rock. A head smashing into stone. *Was that the queen?* Right turn, left turn, she flew past perplexed palace goers, and yet they didn't try to stop her.

The beginning tinges of daylight pushed back the night's thick curtain. The increased change in lighting encouraged Iris that she was on the right path. Whatever the "right path" was. At last, in the distance, an archway framed an open scene of a manicured lawn and preciously tended flowers. A few bushes and trees marked the start of a dirt path. The closer she drew, the more her view expanded. Cloaked nomads stood scattered across the vegetation. Yansair's Great Mother stood in the middle, a sword in her hand. *What am I doing? I should hide!*

"Keep running."

Was that a body on the ground?

"Faster."

Iris suppressed a growl and pumped her legs harder. In a few breaths, her feet crunched on earthy terrain. The sound swiveled the heads of all in the courtyard in her direction. Panic swirled within, but still she ran. A scream rang out somewhere beyond the central crowd, making them all pivot back in its direction. Their movement opened up Iris's line of sight to see the well from her vision standing before her.

"Jump."

Iris gritted her teeth and burst through the central grouping before they could react. Reaching the broken mouth of the well, she launched herself in feet first. Her stomach felt as if it would fly out of her mouth as nothing but air crested her toes. The yawning mouth of darkness consumed her whole. Iris feared she'd fall forever. The icy shock of water encapsulated her and ripped the air from her lungs. Swim up! The visceral need to breathe tore away all other thoughts. Surprisingly, the well's circumference was wide enough that Iris could easily tread the water. Yet instead of propelling her body upward, she felt herself dragged further down.

Since when did wells have water currents? A warning invaded her panic. *Don't fight it. Follow it.* Praying her lungs would hold, Iris changed tactics and swam with the current. The water carried her down. Pressure built up inside Iris's ears. With a sudden jerk, the water pulled her sharply to the right, popping the pressure in her ears at the same moment. Flying along, Iris's shoulder rammed into jagged rocks, sending starbursts of pain jolting through her body. Bouncing from that wall soon ricocheted her into the next. Her back scraped across more stone teeth. The passage was narrowing. Before she could contemplate the danger, Iris's face collided with a padded surface.

Wait, no, not padded. It was a body! This had to be the queen. Iris reached around and grabbed hold. The form struggled against her grip. Iris wished she could tell the queen she wasn't some beast trying to devour her. The woman had run into some sort of choke point in the underground river, too narrow for a person to fit through. *Kick the wall.* The instruction rang through loudly. Keeping her right arm wrapped around Aaralee's waist, Iris clawed at the stone around her. Scraping her legs up across the narrow passage, she positioned her feet just right for a two-legged kick. Bracing a hand on the rock behind her, Iris launched herself at the wall. The stone buckled slightly on impact. She arched herself back for a second strike, but before she could connect, the water surged forward, yanking Iris and Aaralee along with it.

Out they burst through the rocks, flying through the air into a large cave system. Grabbing her chance, Iris gulped down fresh air as they dropped again with the surging water. The ceiling of the cavern was just high enough that both Aaralee and Iris could keep their heads above the surface. The pitch black of the underground system made it impossible for them to find their bearings. All Iris could think to do was maintain her hold on the queen and ride the current. At least the queen had finally stopped trying to break free of her.

She wasn't sure what good she could do now. She just knew letting go of the queen wasn't an option. Careening through the watery void, both women struggled to keep coming back up for air. A strange purple glow appeared in the distance. The dim light grew in size as they rapidly drew near. On the ceiling, purplish-black crystals clustered in various jagged patches. Iris tried to focus on them, but her vision was obscured by thrashing water. In a blink, they dropped down a foot and swirled to the left. Pulling Aaralee back up with her, they again gasped in their breath. The dark-purple glow increased exponentially as the sharp-cut crystals overtook the rock surfaces.

"No," came the garbled cry of Aaralee, who bobbed in front of Iris.

Struggling to crane her head around the queen, Iris caught sight of a medium-sized cave opening. The light streaming in made the crystals that crowded the entire opening shine an eerie dark purple. They grew in such tight, thin clusters that they practically closed off the cave's mouth. Iris's heart hammered in her ears as she realized the underground river was going to crash them directly into those unforgiving teeth.

Holy Father, help! Iris closed her eyes and braced for the impact. Shooting forward, they crashed into and then through the crystal barricade. Iris could feel the litany of punctures and scrapes scattered across her skin. Though each slice burned in hot, radiating flashes, the crystals somehow only caused surface-level wounding. Launching through the mouth of the cave, the morning sun blinded their eyes, hiding from view the final four-foot drop. Again, Iris's stomach rolled about in brief weightlessness until, with a splash, they were thrown deep into the center of a larger body of water. Queen Aaralee was rent away by the final drop, leaving Iris free to use both hands to help her kick back up to the surface.

Every inch of her body burned and ached. Her mouth felt as though stuffed with cotton, and her vision spun every time she tried to look around. A pulsing pain pounded behind her sinuses. With a determined yelp, she forced her stiffening limbs to pull her over to what she assumed to be a riverbank. Around the spots in her vision, Iris could barely make out Queen Aaralee flopping down on the shore. Swallowing more water than she cared to, Iris kept her face above the surface. Finally, her feet ran across muddy ground. Iris's strength fled from her body, forcing her to drag herself out from the water's edge. Reaching the queen's side, she flopped face-first into the dirt, allowing exhaustion to finally overtake her.

Amber ripples distorted Malachi's reflection, trapping his mind and body in a strange numbing trance. Snoring rumbled across the small circular table, drawing his attention from his mug to the passed-out Aaron. Watching the pool of drool begin to accumulate around the man's face, Malachi shook his head and sighed. All this sitting around wasn't good for them. Aaron had a hard enough time staying sober without the added boredom. Malachi let his eyes scan the tavern. Men of all sizes filled the majority of the tables and stools. Even in a city like Saunskirt, it wasn't normal for a pub to be this packed so early in the morning. Malachi took a sip of his drink, letting his eyes continue to rove over each of the men's faces.

He'd wager the oldest among them was no more than forty. There appeared to be a solid mix of salt-of-the-earth hard workers and back-alley scumbags. Not the sort of company one found readily mixed together, which made for the eerie quiet across the establishment.

Malachi set his drink down and fingered the wrinkled slip of paper in front of him. He and Aaron honestly had no right to be here. They were outsiders sticking their noses into personal affairs. But with no word from Kyle or Bryant for a few weeks now, he needed *something* to occupy his time. Besides, didn't Kyle always tell him their greatest weapon was information?

Ever since arriving in Saunskirt, unrest hung in the background of every conversation. Tensions between locals and Sylphaen visitors in particular were terse at best. Not even the upcoming celebration of the king's birth seemed to lift spirits. It didn't take much for Malachi's keen eye to pinpoint a storm was brewing. Using a gregarious nature as his cover, Malachi soon snagged an invite to a secret meeting. *This* meeting. The paper hadn't given too many details other than the when and where, but the gist of the message seemed to suggest possibly treasonous talk. And if treason was afoot, he could think of at least five different ways to strike rich off such information.

The creak of the tavern door made everyone's heads turn and postures stiffen. Malachi clocked at least a dozen men reaching for some sort of concealed weapon. A trio of Lord Valomeer's soldiers marched in, decked out in their leather training gear—likely to make them seem more connected to the common folk in the room. Then again, these fellows were possibly kin to someone in this very room. Valomeer wasn't typically known for hiring any mercenary or foreign muscle. Malachi was uncertain about the current public opinion on Valomeer's guards, but what *was* obvious was their ability to command all attention.

Two out of the three soldiers moved their way deeper into the crowd, while the third hung back by the door. Reaching the far side of the room, the shorter of the two turned to address the crowd.

"Good men of Saunskirt, it is no accident that you have gathered here this morning," Awkward shifting and glancing about came the reply, "Every man here, no matter his background or current lot in life, is here because of the same deep purpose and passion: a love for his home and the desire to see this kingdom protected at all costs."

A few of the men sat up a little straighter, and others leaned forward slightly. The soldier paused for a breath, gauging the faces around him. "Word has spread recently of an attack against our very own, a senseless and cruel attack. Wiping entire villages off the map, cutting off trade routes. Innocent women and children have been brutalized with their blood crying for justice, and it's fallen on deaf ears. Good, honest Fiesians abandoned! How could we not wonder about the safety of our own?"

Again, he paused, a heaviness seemed to weigh on his shoulders. "I cannot in good conscience proceed any further without offering those of you who are unsure an out. Our solution is not for the faint of heart. In fact, we are about to discuss, to be frank, treason. There is no shame in walking out that door if you do not have the stomach for it."

A few throats cleared as wood creaked under their shifting forms. Yet no one stood. Malachi flicked a glance over to the comatose Aaron, grateful the man's snoring had finally let up.

"Very well. You are all fully aware that you have committed your-selves to a deeply important cause, one that will forever change the future of Fitsengea."

"Enough preamble. Get to the point," a voice barked out some-where in the crowd.

The soldier nodded in the direction of the voice. "The razing of the villages in Throansburrough, Jaralynx, and X32 have been discovered to all be a part of the anti-religious plot from the hedonistic country Sylphaen, to our north. Our allies and trade partners from Yansair have discovered their conspiracy to wipe out any people who believe in any higher power beyond Sylpahen's self-worship of human intellect. They even went as far as to send an assassin to take out our royal High Minister Teason. Praise the Father another man was able to lay down his life to protect our high minister. According to our sources, this is just the beginning, and what is worse—King Zaerin has known of this all along."

The muscles across Malachi's neck and back tightened. Word had spread like wildfire over the assassination attempt in Alaster, but nothing had officially been released concerning the attacker's identity.

"Not only has the king known, but we've recently discovered proof that the king has been doctoring the Sacred Texts to suit his purposes," the taller soldier stepped forward to add.

Audible gasps and slurs sounded through the tavern. Saunskirt may not have been the most religious city within Fitsengea's borders, but they possessed deep pride for their nation's history, the most foundational document of said history being the Sacred Texts. Even Malachi felt a surge of anger rise within him at the notion. But he quickly stuffed it back down, knowing better than to simply take a man at his word. Hard proof was the way men stayed alive.

"It's true," the shorter soldier spoke once more. "He has removed entire sections that cast his family in an ill light. He has also been colluding with Sylphaen to line his own pockets and snatch up their newest inventions."

"It's no wonder he's left those poor villages to rot!" one of the surlier figures in the crowd growled.

Voices echoed his sentiment across the tavern, tangible anger buzzing through the atmosphere. The soldiers held their peace until things died down again.

"Gentlemen, our gracious Lord Valomeer has never been anything but good to us because of his love for the Fiesian people. And as such, he has found himself unable to abide by such a wicked ruler any longer.

"Lord Valomeer's wealth has been our wealth, whereas King Zaerin uses his people's money to care for his lawn before tending to their poverty. Lord Valomeer has recognized the time has come for a new leader over this beautiful kingdom."

"And what, you're wanting us to join you? Even with every able body here paired up with Saunskirt guards, we'd be no match for the king's forces." One of the quieter figures finally spoke up.

A few voices grunted their assent.

"We would not be standing alone. Yansair has committed to be our brothers in the east for this revolution."

Voices erupted at this announcement. Some with overwhelming approval, some indifferent, and others with deep distrust. Concerns and counters began to fly back and forth amongst the gathering. A smile slipped across Malachi's face as he settled in for the long discourse.

Things were about to get *very* interesting.

About the Author

Canadian born but Texas raised, Tiffany Grant completed a master's degree with a split major in history and English from Texas A&M University Texarkana. She is no stranger to living in "different worlds," from her upbringing to her time living in Asia teaching English in Thailand and India. Though Dyslexic she has held a deep passion for reading and writing since she was eight years old. When not writing she balances her time between work and being a beloved aunt to five amazing nieces and nephews.

Sign up for her newsletter to stay up to date on new releases!
https://mailchi.mp/choosethepen.com/home-page

She loves getting to connect with readers! Here's where you can find her online: www.tiffanygrant-choosethepen.com

And find her on these sites:

 facebook.com/choosethepen

 instagram.com/choosethepen

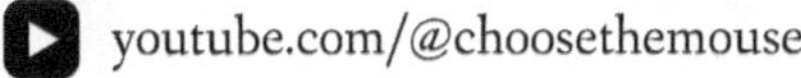 youtube.com/@choosethemouse

WAR
AND
Sacred Tears
RAIN
TIFFANY GRANT